THE ORION PLAN

MARK ALPERT
THE ORION PLAN

THOMAS DUNNE BOOKS · ST. MARTIN'S PRESS · NEW YORK

This is a work of fiction. All of the characters, organizations, and events portrayed in this novel are either products of the author's imagination or are used fictitiously.

THOMAS DUNNE BOOKS.
An imprint of St. Martin's Press.

THE ORION PLAN. Copyright © 2016 by Mark Alpert. All rights reserved. Printed in the United States of America. For information, address St. Martin's Press, 175 Fifth Avenue, New York, N.Y. 10010.

www.thomasdunnebooks.com
www.stmartins.com

Library of Congress Cataloging-in-Publication Data

Names: Alpert, Mark, 1961– author.
Title: The Orion plan : a thriller / Mark Alpert.
Description: First edition. | New York : Thomas Dunne Books/
    St. Martin's Press, 2016.
Identifiers: LCCN 2015039016| ISBN 9781250065414 (hardcover) |
    ISBN 9781466872233 (e-book)
Subjects: LCSH: Human-alien encounters—Fiction. | Extraterrestrial beings—
    Fiction. | Brainwashing—Fiction. | BISAC: FICTION / Technological. |
    GSAFD: Science fiction.
Classification: LCC PS3601.L67 O75 2016 | DDC 813/.6—dc23
LC record available at http://lccn.loc.gov/2015039016

Our books may be purchased in bulk for promotional, educational, or business use. Please contact your local bookseller or the Macmillan Corporate and Premium Sales Department at (800) 221-7945, extension 5442, or by e-mail at MacmillanSpecialMarkets@macmillan.com.

First Edition: February 2016

10 9 8 7 6 5 4 3 2 1

For the Plateau Club

I discount suggestions that UFOs contain beings from outer space. I think any visits by aliens would be much more obvious and probably also much more unpleasant.

—Stephen Hawking

THE ORION PLAN

ONE Ventura, California | June 20, 2016 | 12:09 A.M. Pacific Daylight Time

Sarah didn't see the asteroid until it was too late. By the time she glimpsed it on her laptop's screen, the rock was just an hour away from impact.

She wouldn't have seen it at all if her neighbor's dog hadn't woken her. The stupid mutt had started barking at midnight for no reason. Unable to fall back to sleep, Sarah had turned on her MacBook and downloaded the latest images from the Sky Survey observatory. The telescope was five hundred miles away, in southern Arizona, but all the members of the Sky Survey team had twenty-four hour access to its observations. Although Sarah loved her work, this particular task—looking for slight changes in the pixilated images of the constellations—was tedious and tiring. After just ten minutes of squinting at her laptop she was usually ready to return to bed.

But not tonight. Instead, she stared in bewilderment at a sequence of images of the Scorpius constellation. In the first picture, captured by the telescope at 9:24 P.M. Pacific daylight time, a faint dot appeared next to Antares, the star at the center of the scorpion's body. The next five images showed the dot drifting eastward and growing steadily brighter. In the last picture, taken just before midnight, the object glared like a spotlight above the scorpion's tail.

Sarah's pulse quickened as she estimated the object's size. *Thirty-five meters wide. That's bigger than a house, bigger than a ten-story building.* She didn't get seriously alarmed, though, until she calculated its speed. *Thirty-seven kilometers per second. Which is equal to 83,000 miles per hour.*

She double-checked her calculations but the results were the same. *Jesus goddamn Christ.*

Her fingers trembled on the keyboard, but she managed to send an alert to NASA headquarters and the Air Force's Space Command. Then she threw on a T-shirt, jeans, and sneakers and bolted out of her house.

Five minutes later she steered her Prius on to the Ventura Freeway. But she didn't follow the path of her usual commute. Rather than head east toward Pasadena—home of Caltech and NASA's Jet Propulsion Laboratory—she floored the gas pedal and sped west toward Vandenberg Air Force Base.

The entrance to the base was off Route 1, a few miles from the Pacific beaches. Sarah waited, fuming with impatience, while the MP in the gatehouse inspected her security pass.

She had access to Vandenberg because her job overlapped with the military's. The Air Force was in charge of monitoring the region of space closest to Earth. They tracked all the satellites orbiting the planet and kept a lookout for nuclear missiles aimed at America. Sarah's team at NASA, in contrast, searched for threats from deep space, more than five thousand miles above Earth's surface. The rogue asteroid she'd spotted would soon cross that invisible boundary and plunge into the region monitored by Space Command's radar stations.

As soon as the MP gave her the go-ahead, Sarah raced down Vandenberg's empty streets. She peered through her windshield at the clear starry sky and the low dark hills overlooking the Pacific. Scattered among the hills, she knew, were half a dozen underground silos, each holding a three-stage rocket. Those rockets were designed to intercept nuclear missiles in midflight and blast them out of the sky before they could reach the homeland. But asteroids were much larger and faster than missiles. The Air Force had no defense against them.

She parked her Prius in front of the Space Operations Center and rushed inside. To her surprise, the control room was quiet. There were more than a dozen desks in the room, each with its own computer terminal and radar screen, but only three of the stations were occupied. A trio of radar specialists sat behind their terminals, muttering into the mouthpieces of their headsets and typing on their keyboards. On the wall in front of them, a jumbo screen displayed an image of the Earth—specifically, the western hemisphere—and the current positions of the four thousand satellites circling the planet. Communications satellites were shown as blue squares, weather satellites as green diamonds, GPS as yellow triangles. But there was no marker for the asteroid.

"Hello?" Sarah raised her voice to get the attention of the specialists. *"Hello?"*

All three airmen turned their heads in unison and looked over their shoulders at her. They were pale, gawky boys in their early twenties, dressed in olive-green fatigues. The one in the middle seemed a bit older than the others and wore ugly black glasses. He rose from his chair. "Yes, ma'am? Can I help you?"

"I'm the one who sent the alert. About the near-Earth object." She was so anxious she had trouble getting the words out. "You saw the alert, right?"

Ugly Glasses just smiled. He gave her a once-over, glancing at her ragged jeans, her Grateful Dead T-shirt, her bedraggled black hair. "Could you please tell me your name, ma'am? Then maybe we can figure this out."

His smile broadened. He was flirting with her. Sarah wanted to scream. "Figure it out? Don't you know what's going on?"

"No, ma'am, you'll have to—"

"There's a rock bigger than an apartment building coming toward us! At eighty thousand miles per hour!"

The boy's smile vanished. It seemed like she'd gotten through to him. But then she noticed he wasn't looking at her anymore; he was staring with sudden fear at someone behind her. The kid snapped to attention and shouted, "Good evening, sir!"

The other two airmen jumped to their feet and saluted. Sarah turned around and saw a tall, trim officer in an Air Force uniform bristling with combat ribbons. He had a coal-black crew cut and a square, chiseled face. He was sort of handsome in a military way, but Sarah didn't recognize him until she read the name on his uniform: HANSON. Then she remembered seeing his picture in a news item on NASA's Web site a couple of months ago. He was General Brent Hanson, the new head of Space Command. There had been a big ceremony at Vandenberg when he was promoted. *Thank God,* she thought. *There's an adult in the room.*

The general ignored the airmen and walked over to Sarah. "You must be Dr. Pooley. Luckily, I was still on duty when your alert came in."

For the first time since she spotted the asteroid Sarah felt a measure of relief. At least she wasn't alone in her alarm anymore. "Are your radars tracking the object?"

He nodded. "Our station in Hawaii has the best fix."

The airmen stood aside as Hanson approached one of the terminals and typed a command on the keyboard. Sarah remembered something else from the news item about Hanson: he was an MIT grad, a guy with technical smarts. He was also young for an Air Force general, only in his midforties, the same age as Sarah. After tapping a few more keys, he pointed at the jumbo screen. "The object's present altitude is thirty-eight hundred miles. Its speed is twenty-three miles per second, descending at an angle of forty degrees above the horizon."

A straight red line appeared on the screen, slicing through the swarm of satellites. The asteroid—marked by a blinking red dot at the end of the line—was currently above the Pacific Ocean, but it was streaking eastward as it descended. The object's speed was very close to what Sarah had calculated. "What's the estimated impact point?"

Hanson bent over the keyboard and typed something else. The line on the screen extended from the blinking red dot to the Earth's surface, showing the expected path of the asteroid. "It's going to fly over the continental U.S. and approach the East Coast, heading for central New Jersey." He turned around to face her. "But there's no need to worry. It won't hit the ground."

The general's voice was crisp and confident, full of reassurance. But Sarah wasn't convinced. "What makes you so sure?"

"As soon as we spotted it on the radar I contacted the experts on my staff." He pointed at the screen again. "They predict the object will burn up in the atmosphere, at an altitude of twenty miles. It'll make a brilliant fireball, visible from everywhere in New Jersey, but it'll be too far above the ground to do any damage."

Sarah had no idea who Hanson's experts were, but they were clearly using the wrong formula. "I'm sorry, but you're way off. Given the brightness of the asteroid in our telescope images, it has to be at least a hundred feet across. It's going to—"

"Whoa, hold on a second." Hanson grinned. He seemed amused by her concern. "I think you have the wrong—"

"No, *you* hold on." She wasn't going to let this guy patronize her. "That rock is big enough to punch through most of the atmosphere. It's going to fall to an altitude of ten thousand feet before the atmospheric turbulence breaks it up. Then it'll explode with the energy of a three-megaton nuke and flatten all the trees and buildings for miles around. And that's going to happen in the next three minutes."

She was almost shouting by the time she finished, and her last words echoed across the control room. The three airmen stared at her, wide-eyed. The one with the glasses seemed so distressed that Sarah wondered if he had relatives in New Jersey. General Hanson, though, was unperturbed. If anything, he seemed even more amused. "Yes, Dr. Pooley, if the asteroid were more than a hundred feet wide it would devastate the area. But it's not that big. According to our radar readings, the maximum diameter of the object is ten feet."

Sarah shook her head. "That's absurd. I wouldn't have seen it in the Sky Survey if it were that small. It wouldn't have reflected enough sunlight to appear in the telescope images."

"Are you sure about that? Maybe the object is more reflective than you assumed."

"Or maybe your radars are malfunctioning. Or you misinterpreted their signals."

He stepped toward her, still grinning, cocky as hell. He stopped in front of her and leaned forward, as if he were about to tell her a secret. "Those radars at our Hawaii station? They're the best in the world. They're designed to tell the difference between a nuclear warhead and a decoy from four thousand miles away. I have a lot of confidence in them."

Sarah scowled. She hated cocky men. "So you're saying your system's infallible? There's no chance at all you made a mistake?"

Hanson stopped smiling. He took a deep breath and looked Sarah in the eye. He seemed to be changing his strategy, trying for a less combative approach. "You're right, nothing's perfect. Maybe the radar is malfunctioning and maybe a killer asteroid is really coming toward us. But it's a moot point. We can't stop the rock anyway."

"You could issue a warning to the local authorities, couldn't you? You—"

"No, that wouldn't do any good. There's not enough time to evacuate the impact zone." Hanson shrugged. He seemed tired of arguing with her. He turned away from her and faced the three airmen. "Gentlemen, let's do our best to track this object. Just in case I'm wrong."

The airmen swiftly returned to their terminals. They stared at their radar screens and typed new commands on their keyboards. The commands changed the display on the jumbo screen: the image of the western hemisphere was replaced by an enlarged view of North America. Sarah stood beside Hanson and focused on the screen, gazing over the heads of the airmen.

The blinking red dot was now less than fifteen hundred miles above the continent. In sixty seconds the asteroid would plow into the atmosphere, and then they'd see who was right. Sarah felt a mix of horror and guilt as she stared at the screen. For the past decade she'd devoted herself to identifying all the asteroids that posed a threat to Earth. Her Sky Survey team had detected thousands of near-Earth objects and carefully studied their orbits. But it was very difficult to detect the midsize asteroids, the ones between a hundred and five hundred feet wide. They were too small to be spotted by telescopes and yet large enough to blast through Earth's atmosphere. Sarah had struggled with the problem for years, trying to devise new instruments and techniques for observing and tracking these rocks. But now it was too late. All she could do was watch the thing plunge toward the ground.

After half a minute Sarah couldn't do that either. She turned away from the screen and looked at the floor instead. It seemed obscene that they were the only people on the planet who knew this was happening. She glanced at Hanson, who rocked back and forth on his heels as he watched the screen. He looked so calm, so unafraid. She couldn't understand it.

After another half minute the airman with the ugly glasses looked over his shoulder at the general. "The object has entered the atmosphere, sir," he reported. "Air resistance is decreasing its velocity."

The view on the screen enlarged again, and now the blinking red dot was less than a hundred miles above New Jersey. The radar signals grew fuzzy, thrown off by the violent turbulence of the object's passage through the atmosphere. Sarah pictured it in her mind's eye: the shock wave forming just below the rock, the phenomenal heat melting the surface of its lower half, the pressure building against the object as it plummeted toward the Earth. Despite her distaste for Hanson, she hoped to hell he was right. She said a silent prayer as she gazed at the blinking dot on the screen: *Disintegrate, you bastard. Explode into a million pieces before you get too close to the ground.*

Then the dot disappeared. The jumbo screen showed the red line ending in midair above the Jersey coast. The airmen leaned close to their radar screens, studying the final signals.

General Hanson stepped forward. "What was its last position?" he asked his men. His voice was professional, emotionless. "At what altitude did you lose contact?"

Ugly Glasses tapped his keyboard. "I'm still checking, sir."

"What's the problem?"

"The signals are a little confusing. I just need a minute."

Hanson nodded. "All right. Carry on." He took a step backward, returning to his place beside Sarah.

The waiting was unbearable. Sarah clenched her hands so tightly her fingernails dug into her palms. The general, meanwhile, folded his arms across his chest. Then he turned to Sarah and smiled at her again. "Before I forget, I want to tell you how much I admire your work."

His comment threw her. Now, of all times, he wanted to engage in small talk? "What?"

"I've read the reports about your Sky Survey project. How you're cataloguing all the potentially hazardous asteroids. It's good work, important work."

Sarah stared at him, dumbfounded. "Well, that's strange. Just a minute ago you said I didn't know what I was doing."

"No, I didn't say that. Not at all." He shook his head. "You've been extremely helpful tonight. In fact, I'm wondering if you and I can establish a stronger connection between NASA and Space Command. We should work together on contingency plans for asteroid threats. We'd all benefit from closer cooperation, don't you think?"

She couldn't tell how serious he was. Hanson was obviously smart, but he didn't seem so trustworthy. There was a good chance he was just flirting with her, just like the airmen. "Sure, that's a good idea," she said. "But maybe we should find out what happened to *this* asteroid first?"

"Yes, absolutely. First things first."

Hanson stepped forward again and gripped Ugly Glasses by the shoulder. "Okay, time's up. What do you have?"

The airman looked up from his radar screen. He seemed puzzled. "Sir, our last radar contact with the object was at an altitude of twenty-one miles over the town of South Amboy, New Jersey. There were no further contacts along its track, so it must've exploded at that altitude."

"Ah, twenty-one miles." Hanson let go of the boy's shoulder and looked at Sarah. He didn't grin, but he wasn't exactly hiding his satisfaction either. "I'll have to congratulate my staff for predicting it so well." He turned back to the airman. "And did the radar detect any fragments from the explosion?"

"Yes, sir. And that's what made it so confusing." The boy grimaced. His glasses had slid halfway down the bridge of his nose. "Most of the fragments were tiny, just specks of dust, but one piece was pretty big."

Hanson frowned. "Define 'pretty big.'"

"At least a foot wide, sir. But the weird thing is its trajectory after the explosion. The blast kicked it almost horizontally to the northeast. It traveled more than thirty miles in that direction before hitting the ground."

Sarah's throat tightened. Even a foot-wide chunk could cause major damage if it struck the ground at high speed. She stepped toward the airman. "Can you show the radar track for that fragment?"

The boy looked frightened now. "I . . . I can draw a partial trajectory. Our radars couldn't track it after it dropped below two thousand feet, but—"

"Just show it."

A moment later the airman drew a new path on the jumbo screen. This red line ran thirty-three miles northeast from South Amboy. It terminated at the northern tip of Manhattan.

TWO

Joe was dreaming of his daughter when the noise woke him. In the dream he chased Annabelle across the playground near their apartment building in Riverdale. This was a memory from the old days, before Joe's wife kicked him out of the apartment. Annabelle raced past the playground's swings and seesaws, her long brown ponytail bouncing against her back, her neon-pink T-shirt flapping at her waist. Joe couldn't keep up with her, she was too fast. He yelled, "Slow down!" but she kept running.

Then the noise hit him, a deep, ground-shaking *thump* that echoed in his chest. At the same time, something mashed against his nose. In pain, Joe opened his eyes, thinking that someone had punched him in the face while he slept, but all he saw was blackness. For a moment he thought he was gone—dead, buried, finally out of his misery. He felt a roiling, nauseating fear in his stomach, so strong it made him gag. But after a couple of seconds of sickness and terror he realized why he couldn't see anything: the box he was sleeping in had collapsed. He was looking up at a three-foot-by-five-foot rectangle of cardboard—the top of the box—which had smacked against his face and now hung, hope-lessly crumpled, an inch above his eyes.

Joe didn't move a muscle, didn't make a sound. Although his mind was still fuzzy from all the malt liquor he'd drunk, one thing was clear: the box wouldn't have hit his face so hard if it had collapsed on its own. Someone must've smashed it. Because Inwood Hill Park was deserted at night—it was mostly woods—the teenagers from the neighborhood liked to party there during the summer, and they entertained them-selves by tormenting the homeless people who slept on the wooded hillsides. One of those kids—no, probably two or three or four of them—had just pounded the hell out of Joe's box. He couldn't see or hear them but they probably stood just a few feet away, stifling their laughter and waiting for his reaction. They wanted to watch him struggle, to hear him yell and curse them. And the more he yelled, the more they'd harass him. So the best strategy was to lie there inside the crumpled box and play dead. It was no fun to pick on a homeless guy if he didn't squirm.

Blood leaked from Joe's nostrils and covered the stubble on his upper lip, but he didn't dare to wipe it off. He was afraid to even breathe. Lift-ing his head ever so slowly, he gazed down the length of his body. His sneakers, their toes wrapped in duct tape, stuck out of the box and rested on the mud of the hillside. The legs of his pants were patched with duct tape too. Even though it was a warm night, Joe had fallen asleep in his jacket—it was a New York Yankees jacket, the only decent piece of clothing he had left—and now his undershirt was damp with sweat. The stench inside the box was so foul it made him gag again, and before he could stop himself he let out a groan, loud enough for anyone to hear. *Now you've gone and done it,* he thought. *Now they're gonna beat the crap out of you.*

Joe rolled on his side and covered his head with his hands, waiting for the kids to start pummeling the box. But the blows never came. He listened carefully and heard only a car alarm whining in the distance. He waited another minute until the alarm cut off. Then he turned onto his stomach and crawled out of the box.

He was alone. His box sat in a hidden rut on the hillside, between the base of an oak tree and a massive slab of rock jutting out of the mud. With another groan, Joe pushed himself up to a sitting position, his back against the slab. He felt dizzy and nauseous, and the dark woods whirled around him. He didn't own a watch anymore, but he guessed it was three or four in the morning. He'd passed out only a couple of hours ago, and the buzz in his head was still pretty strong.

After several seconds the whirling stopped. He brushed his hair to the side—it was greasy and way too long—and saw the silhouettes of the treetops against the night sky. He was perched on the steep slope that overlooked the park's soccer fields. Beyond the fields were the apartment buildings on Payson Avenue, half a mile away. A quarter moon hung above them, shining on their roofs, but all their windows were dark. It was the deepest part of the night in the emptiest corner of Manhattan. Joe wished he had a cigarette, but his pockets were empty.

He heard a siren, very faint. It was a long way off, probably on Dyckman Street or Broadway. The police sometimes came into the park and rousted all the homeless people they could find, but the cops mostly stuck to the asphalt pathways. They weren't going to risk breaking their ankles in the woods, so the park was a good spot for sleeping, at least during the summer. Joe knew half a dozen men and two or three women who were somewhere on the same hillside, each curled in a cardboard box or snoring under a pile of blankets and plastic tarp. Some of them were crazy and all of them were thieves. If you left anything on the hillside during the day—even just an empty water bottle—it would be gone by the time you came back.

The thought of water made Joe thirsty. He had a dim memory of carrying a forty-ounce bottle of Olde English 800 up the hillside earlier that night, but he didn't see it anywhere nearby. Although he'd probably downed the malt liquor before passing out, there might be some dregs at the bottom. He turned to his box, wondering if he'd hidden the bottle inside, and his heart sank. It had been a truly excellent refrigerator box, new and sturdy—he'd found it behind the appliance store on 207th Street—but now it was a flattened wreck. Its cardboard sides were bent and bowed so much they'd never stand up straight again. The cause of the disaster lay on top of the ruined box: a fair-sized tree branch, at least four feet long and two inches thick. It must've fallen from the oak. Joe shook his head as he stared at it. He was lucky to get away with just a bloody nose. That thing could've killed him.

As he looked around he saw an even bigger branch lying in the mud a few yards away. Leaves were scattered across the slab he was leaning against, and in the light from the quarter moon he saw more severed branches farther up the slope. The hillside was littered with them. Joe thought that maybe a storm had blown through the park and knocked down the branches, but there wasn't even a breath of wind now. He tilted his head up, looking for storm clouds in the night sky, and that's when he noticed it: a ragged hole in the treetops, marked by branches that had been torn off or were hanging by a thread. It was so eerie Joe wondered if he was hallucinating. It looked like God Almighty Himself had stretched his hand down from heaven and plunged it through the trees.

Joe shivered. It was no hallucination. He stared at the hole in the tree-tops, but it didn't fade away. He wanted to hide, to crawl back inside his box. God was reaching for him, but not to comfort him or raise him up to heaven. The Lord was going to punish him for his terrible sins.

His breath came fast, in painful rasps. He clawed his hands through the mud, groping for something he could use to defend himself—a shard of glass, a heavy rock. Then he coughed and the woods swirled around him again, and when they finally came to rest he realized how stupid he was. There was no Lord in heaven. He'd stopped believing in God more than twenty years ago, when he was still in college, long before he came to New York. His faith was the first of many things he'd tossed aside. And now that he'd given up so much—his job, his home, his family, his dignity—was he going to start believing in God again? No, that would be ridiculous. He was a drunk but not a fool.

After a few minutes his breathing slowed. His head was clearer now and he'd stopped shivering. He didn't believe in God, but what was that hole doing there? Joe craned his neck, eyeing the branches scattered across the ground. They formed a trail that led uphill, past the slab behind him and another outcrop above it. If something had truly come down from heaven—a fallen angel, a bolt of lightning, the fearsome hand of the Lord—maybe he'd see some sign of it at the end of the trail. It was probably a waste of time, but he didn't have any other pressing business to attend to. And Joe wanted to be sure. He *needed* to be sure.

He stood up, slowly and carefully. His head swam and his legs wobbled but he was all right. He wasn't too buzzed to take a little stroll. He lifted his right foot and climbed onto the slab, which was flat and smooth. Leaning forward, he trudged across the slanting rock and stepped into the mud on the other side. Finding his footing was tricky in the dark, but he could handle it. He'd learned how to navigate the woods during his first few weeks of sleeping there. That was just one of the many new skills he'd picked up.

Getting past the next outcrop was more difficult. This slab was ten feet high, so Joe had to clamber around it, digging his fingers into the cracks in the rock to pull himself up the slope. It was hazardous and exhausting and he had to stop a couple of times to catch his breath. Although he hated to admit it, he was in terrible shape, at least compared with his life before. In the old days he used to jog seven miles every morning. His wife thought it was crazy, but Joe had loved it: gliding through the quiet streets of Riverdale at five in the morning, watching the sun come up over the Bronx. Now he missed those mornings almost as much as he missed his daughter.

He finally got around the outcrop and stumbled into a clearing surrounded by oaks. The slope on this part of the hillside was gentle and the ground was muddy. In the middle of the clearing was a shallow pit, roughly circular and about ten feet wide. The wet ground at the bottom of the pit reflected the moonlight. Joe turned around, looking for the quarter moon, and saw it shining through the same hole in the treetops he'd noticed before. Startled, he stepped backward and tumbled into the pit.

He landed flat on his back. Once again the woods whirled around him and the nausea made him gag. He closed his eyes tight until everything stopped spinning. Then he opened them and saw a black sphere at the center of the pit, half-buried in the mud. It looked like a bowling ball but slightly bigger, about a foot across. Its top half shone in the moonlight.

It was less than a yard from Joe's face. He gaped at the thing—it was as black as coal and yet its surface gleamed as if it were polished. But what really alarmed him was that it seemed to be glowing. He could feel its heat on his cheeks. It was burning like a furnace.

Joe backed away from it, scrabbling on his hands and knees. He didn't stop until he was out of the pit, and then he lay there at the edge, staring at the thing in horror. It wasn't the hand of God. There was nothing heavenly about it. It was more like something from hell, black and smoldering. And yet it had fallen from the sky. It had ripped through the treetops and hit the ground so hard it made a ten-foot-wide crater. Joe remembered the deep thump that had awakened him, and suddenly it all made sense: he was looking at a meteor. Or maybe you were supposed to call it a *meteorite*. He'd taken a science class in college where they explained the difference between the two, but now he couldn't recall which was which.

But would a meteorite be so perfectly smooth and round? When Joe thought of meteorites he pictured rough, jagged rocks zooming through space. He racked his brain, trying to remember something useful from that long-ago science class. The more he thought about it, the more he became convinced that this thing wasn't a meteorite after all. It looked more metallic than rocklike. So maybe it was a satellite. Maybe it was a NASA space probe that had gone haywire and fallen out of its orbit and plummeted to the ground. Something like that had happened to a weather satellite a few years ago. Joe remembered reading about it in the newspaper.

He crept forward, leaning over the edge of the crater, and studied the object. There were no knobs or bolts or antennas extending from the sphere. He saw nothing written on its surface either—no "NASA," no "USA"—although he'd have to wait for daylight to be sure. The absence of an antenna was puzzling, but Joe supposed it might've broken off when the object hit the tree branches. And it was also possible that this was some new kind of satellite that didn't even need an antenna. Maybe it was an ultra-advanced spy satellite, built by the army or the CIA to hunt down terrorists. That would explain why there was nothing written on it. If it was a spy satellite, they wouldn't want to advertise where it came from.

Joe spent another minute thinking over the possibilities, but in the end he decided it didn't matter. He needed to focus on what to do with the thing. If it was a satellite that fell from space, someone would come looking for it. Even if it was busted beyond repair, the people who owned it would want to know why it malfunctioned. And those people might be willing to pay a finder's fee to someone who could tell them where their satellite had landed. Joe wondered how much they'd pay—a thousand dollars? Ten thousand? The satellite was probably worth millions, so a ten thousand dollar fee didn't seem too outrageous.

He bit his lip and started opening and closing his hands. That was something Joe did whenever he got nervous or excited. He'd been broke and desperate for so long that the prospect of making some real money seemed too good to be true. He got to his feet and turned his head to the left and right, listening to the night noises and peering into the dark woods. So far he was the only one who knew about the satellite, but he wouldn't be alone for long. Dawn would break in an hour or so, and then the other homeless people on the hill would begin to stir. The early risers would come out of their boxes and slog across the park, heading for the soup kitchen on Dyckman Street or the Dunkin' Donuts on Broadway. There was a good chance that one of them would see all the fallen branches and find the crater, just as Joe had. And if one of the homeless people didn't find it, then one of the early-morning joggers or dog walkers surely would.

Joe wasn't going to let that happen. He stepped down into the crater and approached the sphere, holding his hands out so he could feel the heat coming off it. He couldn't pick it up—it was way too hot. But he could hide it until it cooled. It was already half-buried in the mud. He could bury the rest of it.

He crouched on the wet ground and dug both his hands into the mud, scooping out two fistfuls of it. Then he leaned over the sphere and dumped the mud on top of it. The mud sizzled when it hit the shiny black surface, but some of it stuck. Encouraged, Joe grabbed two more fistfuls and did the same thing. He did it again and again, getting into a regular rhythm of crouching and scooping.

It was tiring work, and he wished he had a shovel, but he made good progress. After ten minutes the sphere was entirely covered with mud. It still looked unnatural, though. The mound of wet earth jutted like a pimple from the center of the crater. To hide the thing better, Joe needed to fill in the whole pit, or at least make the ground a little more level. But that was going to take some serious effort. He decided to take a break first so he could catch his breath.

He wiped his muddy hands on his pants and stepped out of the crater. He could really use a cigarette now—or better yet, another bottle of Olde English 800—but he told himself to be patient. If his plan worked out, he would have plenty of money for celebrating. Just the anticipation of it was enough to give him a buzz. He spread his arms and took a deep breath and gazed down the hillside at the moonlit city below. For the first time in months he felt happy.

Because Joe was higher up the slope now, he could see more of the city. Beyond the apartment buildings of Inwood were the elevated tracks of the IRT 1 line—the subway that clattered above Tenth Avenue—and the municipal depot where dozens of city buses were parked for the night. And beyond the depot was the Harlem River, which separated Manhattan from the Bronx. Joe's eyes followed the river as it curved to the west, passing under the subway line and the Broadway Bridge. Then he turned to the north and stared at the heights of Riverdale, his old neighborhood.

His old apartment building stood on the other side of the Harlem River, less than a mile away. Joe supposed that was why he took up residence in Inwood Hill Park rather than any of the other homeless encampments in the city. He liked the fact that he was still near his daughter. He knew he couldn't visit her—his ex-wife had vowed to call the police if he ever came to their apartment again—but if there was an emergency he could dash across the Broadway Bridge and get there in fifteen minutes. Their building was the tallest in the neighborhood, more than twenty stories high, and Joe avoided looking at it during the day. He had the irrational fear that if he gazed at the building for too long, his daughter might spot him from her bedroom window. But at night he was hidden, so he could stare at his old home for as long as he wanted to.

Joe stared at it now. His happiness grew as he searched for his daughter's window, which was near the building's left edge and two floors down from the top. The window wasn't lit, of course—it was much too early—but he felt a powerful new hope as he gazed at the dark façade. His life was going to change for the better once he had ten thousand dollars in his pocket. He promised himself that he wouldn't be stupid and spend all the money on booze. He'd use some of it to rent an apartment and some to buy new clothes. He'd clean up his act and get his old job back. And then he'd return to his old building with a bouquet of flowers in his hand, and his daughter would race across the playground and leap into his arms.

He closed his eyes to savor the vision. Then he heard a shout and a burst of laughter and several husky voices speaking Spanish. He opened his eyes and turned around and saw half a dozen figures emerge from the woods. They were teenage boys in baggy pants and bandannas, tall, muscular, and grinning. They headed straight for him.

THREE

Emilio thought it was a firecracker. He stood at the edge of the park's soccer field, huddled with his homeboys in the Trinitarios, as the boom echoed across Inwood.

He looked over his shoulder and tried to figure out where the noise had come from. The park's big hill loomed over the field, less than a hundred yards away. In the moonlight it looked like a long, high wall. Emilio couldn't see anything but trees on the hillside, but he was sure the noise had come from there. Some stupid *pendejos* had probably lit a cherry bomb or an M-80 and thrown it into the woods.

His homeboys turned their heads too. Carlos smiled and yelled, "What the fuck?" and the four others laughed. They were sharing a blunt and a bottle of Ron Barceló rum and acting like a bunch of idiots. Emilio frowned—he never got drunk or high and wished his boys wouldn't either. At eighteen he was only a couple of years older than the others, but sometimes he felt like their fucking babysitter. He whistled to get their attention.

"*Cállate!*" he ordered. "Shut up a second so I can listen." Then he turned back to the hillside and cocked his head.

They stopped laughing. For the most part, they respected Emilio. He'd shown them how to be Trinitarios, teaching them the gang signs and codes. They also knew about his connections to the O.T.'s, the Original Trinitarios who'd come over from the Dominican Republic twenty years ago and started the first gangs in Inwood and Washington Heights. So his homeboys kept their mouths shut while he listened for more noises coming from the hillside. He expected to hear distant laughter or shouting from the *pendejos* in the woods, but there was nothing.

Paco stepped away from the others and faced the hill, cocking his head like Emilio and listening just as intently. He was their enforcer, the second-in-command, chosen for the position because of his fighting skills. He was gangly and tall and imitated Emilio in every way, even wearing the same kinds of clothes—a pair of baggy jeans, a white sleeveless shirt, and a lime green Trinitarios bandanna. When Paco joined the gang, the imitation was his way of showing respect, but over the past few weeks Emilio had noticed a change in the boy's attitude. Paco was getting surly, always arguing. He didn't want to take orders anymore. He wanted to be in charge.

After a while he gave up listening and turned to Emilio. "Yo, I know who's up there on the hill. It's those Puerto Rican bitches, the Latin Kings. They're the ones who set off that *bomba*."

Emilio narrowed his eyes. "How do you know?"

"I heard they were coming over from the Bronx. That's what everyone's saying."

"Yeah? I haven't heard anyone say that."

Paco shrugged. "Those bitches think Trinitarios is weak now, ever since all the O.T.'s got put in jail. All your uncles and cousins and shit."

This was a calculated insult. Paco was testing him, looking for a reaction. But Emilio wasn't going to play that game. "So you think the Latin Kings are coming here to challenge us?"

"Why the fuck else would they come?"

"Well, why aren't they down here then? Why are they playing with firecrackers on top of the hill?"

"*Coño*, how should I know? But everyone says—"

"It's not the Latin Kings." Emilio shook his head. "It's probably some dumb-ass white boys. This neighborhood is full of white boys now."

Paco had no answer to this, so he just stood there, trying to think of another insult. Like most of the younger kids in the Trinitarios he was a wannabe, not a real gangster. He was all gung ho about mixing it up with the Latin Kings or the Ñetas, but he hadn't fought in any gang wars yet and probably never would. The hard truth was that the gang life was over in this part of the city. The whites were coming to Inwood now and pushing out the Dominicans. That's why the cops had cracked down on the O.T.'s. The New York Police Department was making the neighborhood safe for white people. Emilio and his boys couldn't even hang out on the streets anymore. The only place they could go at night was the park.

"You know what I think?" Paco finally said. "I think you're scared of those bitches."

He said it loud enough that everyone else could hear. Carlos whispered, "Ho, shit!" while Miguel and Diego and Luis stepped backward, forming a rough circle in case a fight broke out. Paco looked like he was ready for it—he locked eyes with Emilio and clenched his hands. But the challenge didn't scare Emilio, and it didn't make him angry either. It just made him depressed. Instead of ruling their neighborhood and walking the streets like heroes, the Trinitarios were scuffling in a deserted soccer field. They were fighting over the chance to lead a gang of fucking babies.

Emilio stepped toward Paco, staring him down. "You unhappy, *muchacho*? You got a problem you want to talk about?"

"The problem is you." The boy's voice was low and steady. "You lost your *cojones* after the O.T.'s got sent away. You're afraid to step up."

"And you think you can do better?"

"I *know* I can do better." Paco curled his lip. "Want to see me prove it?"

Emilio took another step toward him. Now they stood nose to nose. "All right, you'll get your shot. We'll go mano a mano, winner take all. But not now."

"Why not? This seems like a good time to me."

"We got business to take care of first." Emilio pointed at the hillside. "It don't matter if those *pendejos* up there are Latin Kings or white boys. We can't let them go blowing up shit in our territory."

Paco furrowed his brow, confused. He clearly didn't want to postpone this confrontation, but at the same time he couldn't ignore a call to arms.

After a few seconds he stepped backward and unclenched his hands. But he kept his eyes locked on Emilio's. "This ain't over. You know that, right?"

Emilio nodded. Then he turned to Carlos and the others. They still stood in a circle, wide-eyed and gaping. "What you waiting for?" he yelled at them. "Go get *los destornilladores.*"

One of the rules Emilio had learned from the Original Trinitarios was to never carry your weapons until you needed them. If you weren't carrying, the police couldn't charge you with anything when they stopped and frisked you. But that meant you had to stash your weapons in a place that was well-hidden but accessible. Emilio and his boys had chosen a hiding place near the base of the hill, underneath a rock as big as a couch cushion. It was close to the stone overhangs where some of the park's homeless people slept, but the gang usually had no trouble shooing the bums away. They were easy to scare.

Working together, Carlos and Miguel lifted the heavy rock while Diego reached for the bag that contained *los destornilladores.* They were ordinary flat-head screwdrivers that had been sharpened to a point. Diego handed them out, giving the biggest one to Emilio, who wrapped the handle of his screwdriver in a handkerchief. The cloth helped you keep your grip on the thing, even if your hand got sweaty or slick with blood.

Once they were ready they started climbing the hillside, quickly and quietly. Emilio took the lead, guiding his boys toward where he thought the firecracker had exploded. His memory wasn't perfect, though, and it was a big hill. There were hundreds of trees, and they all looked the same in the dark. He stopped every few minutes to listen to the woods, hoping to hear footsteps or a snatch of conversation, but he had no luck. He was probably in the wrong place altogether. Or maybe the white boys had already left the park. This was a waste of time. His homeboys grumbled behind him, muttering curses as they made their way up the slope.

And then, after maybe fifteen minutes, Emilio spotted someone. It was a white boy in a Yankees jacket, about twenty yards away on the hillside. He stood in the middle of a clearing with his arms spread wide, as if he were about to take a dive down the slope. But his head was tilted upward and he seemed to be staring at the night sky.

Emilio gave a hand signal to his homeboys, ordering them to take cover. Then he crouched in the weeds and studied the white boy, whose face was lit by the moonlight. The first thing he noticed was that it was a man, not a boy. He was more than six feet tall and at least forty years old, with black stubble on his face and scraggly, graying hair. His jacket was a mess, splattered with mud, and his pants and sneakers were even worse. He was a homeless guy, one of the drunks who slept on the hill. Emilio felt like an idiot. He and his boys had gone to all this trouble just to chase a goddamn bum.

But then he noticed something else. In the clearing behind the guy was a wide muddy hole. The surrounding trees and rocks were splashed with mud. And at the center of the hole was a heap of wet earth, big enough to sit on. This homeless *pendejo* was playing with firecrackers. He must've buried one in that pile of mud and then lit its fuse.

It was very fucking strange. Drunks spent their money on booze, not firecrackers. This guy had probably found the *bombas* somewhere in the woods, or maybe in one of the park's trash cans. Either way, the explosives really belonged to the Trinitarios. The gang didn't own the streets anymore, but the park was *theirs,* and so was everything in it. If this guy had any more *bombas,* the Trinitarios had every right to take that shit away from him.

And besides, Emilio liked to blow things up. Setting off firecrackers in the woods would be a lot more entertaining than getting into a stupid brawl with Paco.

Emilio waved to his boys and they crept toward him. Paco hung back, keeping his distance from the others. It was an awkward situation for him—he still had to take orders from Emilio—and he wasn't happy about it. He avoided looking at Emilio and stared at the homeless guy instead. The bum had dropped his arms by now and turned to the left, facing the Bronx.

"I've seen that asshole before," Paco whispered. "Lying on the benches."

Luis nodded. "Yeah, he drinks forties. And he smells like shit."

Emilio pointed his screwdriver at the guy. "Don't worry, we won't get too close to him. We're just gonna take his *bombas.* Come on, follow me."

He stood up and headed for the clearing, with his homeboys right behind. Now that they knew there were no Latin Kings lurking in the woods, there was no need to be quiet. Miguel and Diego started chattering and Carlos guffawed. When the bum heard them he spun around so fast he nearly toppled over. That made Carlos laugh even harder.

Emilio stepped into the clearing and smiled at the homeless dude. "*Hola*, old man. You been making some noise, eh?"

The bum was scared shitless. His mouth hung open and his hands trembled. Now that Emilio was up close he realized he'd also seen this guy in the park. He wasn't one of the crazy drunks, the assholes who shouted all the time and drooled into their beards. He was one of the harmless shuffling drunks who kept their heads down and scuttled away at the first sign of trouble. He took a shaky step backward, his eyes fixed on the screwdriver in Emilio's hand. He glanced to the left and right, looking for an escape route, but Carlos and Miguel were on one side of him and Luis and Diego on the other. Paco came up behind the guy and shouted, "Yah!" to startle him, and the bum's face turned into a fucking Halloween mask. Jagged wrinkles etched his forehead and dark semicircles cupped his eyes.

Emilio couldn't help but feel sorry for him. He was just a helpless wreck who stank of malt liquor. But then the guy's eyes darted downward, focusing on the heap of mud at the center of that wide hole. He was hiding something there, no doubt about it. He'd probably buried some more firecrackers in the mud and was getting ready to light them. Emilio tested this theory by moving toward the mud pile. The bum got nervous and started clenching and unclenching his hands. With a desperate look on his face, he stepped in front of Emilio. "Please," he rasped. "Leave me alone."

"Relax, amigo." Emilio smiled at him again. "We just stopped by to say hello."

"I don't have any money." He turned out the empty pockets of his pants, which were caked with mud and falling apart. "See? I have nothing."

"You sure about that? You don't have any more firecrackers?"

"What?" The bum scrunched his face. "What are you talking about?"

"I'm talking about the mess you made here. Look at this place." Emilio pointed his screwdriver at the mud-spattered trees. "And now you're getting ready to do it again, right? You're gonna blow up some more shit with those firecrackers you found."

The guy gave him a blank look. He was either playing dumb or zoning out. Then he shook his head vigorously, and his long greasy hair swung back and forth. "No, no. I don't have any firecrackers."

Emilio took another step toward the heap of mud and pointed his screwdriver at it. "So there's nothing hidden in this mud pie you made? You don't mind if I check, do you?"

The bum winced and lowered his head. His wrinkles deepened as he stared at the ground. "Please," he muttered. "Don't take it."

The guy looked so heartbroken, Emilio felt sorry for him again. He wondered if he should just let the bum keep the damn firecrackers. But Emilio couldn't change his mind now, not in front of his homeboys. They were watching from the sidelines, enjoying the show. The homeless guy was the funniest thing they'd seen all night. Paco jabbed the air with his screwdriver, threatening to poke the guy in the butt, and the others hooted. They were so amused that Emilio worried they might actually cut the guy. The best strategy, he decided, was to grab the firecrackers and tell the bum to get lost. Then he and his boys would find something to blow up—maybe one of the park benches?—and let the homeless guy go back to the business of drinking himself to death.

"All right, let's see what you got here." Emilio bent over the mud pile. He knew this wasn't too smart—if the firecrackers exploded, the blast would hit him right in the face—so he did it quick. Bracing himself, he extended his screwdriver and scraped off the top layer of mud.

He expected to see an M-80 or something similar, a two-inch-long cylinder of flash powder wrapped in red cardboard, with a long green fuse dangling from one end. But instead his screwdriver's sharpened point clinked against something metallic. Bending lower, he brushed away the mud clods and squinted at the thing, which was big and black and round. It was a *bomba*, all right. It was the real fucking thing, like something you'd shoot out of a cannon.

Emilio jumped backward. If that thing went off, it would scatter his ass all over the hillside. Shouting *"Corre!"* at his boys, he leapt out of the muddy hole and ran back to the edge of the clearing. The other Trinitarios followed his lead, but the homeless guy didn't move an inch. He just stood there by the hole, staring at the ground.

Now Emilio was pissed. He pointed his screwdriver at the bum. "Hey, *pendejo*! Where did you find that thing?"

The guy didn't answer. He didn't even raise his head. What the hell was wrong with him? Either he had a death wish or he knew the *bomba* wouldn't explode. Or maybe it wasn't a *bomba* after all. Now that Emilio had a chance to take a second look at it, he was starting to wonder. It looked more like a bowling ball, except a few inches bigger.

Overcoming his fear, Emilio returned to the middle of the clearing, grabbed the collar of the bum's Yankees jacket and pulled him away from the hole. Although the guy was just as tall as Emilio and outweighed him by at least thirty pounds, he didn't resist. He let Emilio drag him across the clearing.

"I asked you a question, *maldito cabrón*!" Emilio let go of his jacket. "Where did you find it?"

The bum grimaced. Oddly, he didn't seem scared anymore. He furrowed his brow and narrowed his eyes. "I found it right there. I covered it with mud to hide it."

"Why?"

"It's a satellite." He lifted a grimy finger and pointed upward. "It fell out of the sky."

Emilio stared at the bum's face, which was tense and quivering, full of emotion. The guy was out of his head. The malt liquor had rotted his brain.

The bum lowered his hand and pointed at the big black ball in the mud. "I found it, so I should get the finder's fee. That's only fair. I deserve the money."

Emilio shook his head. It was no use talking to the guy. He was off in fantasyland. Emilio would have to figure this out on his own.

He turned away from the bum and looked at the ball. It was so smooth and polished it glittered in the moonlight, even with all the mud on it. *Maybe it's some kind of fancy sculpture*, he thought. Maybe the bum had stolen it from an antiques store or some rich guy's living room. It might be worth a few bucks at a pawnshop, maybe.

Emilio stepped into the hole once more to take a closer look at the thing. The bum followed a couple of steps behind. "I found it," he repeated in a louder voice. "You can't take it away. It belongs to me."

His craziness was making him stupid. He'd moved within a yard of Emilio and it looked like he might take a swing at him. Emilio gave the bum a hard look, but before he could say anything Paco came forward and stepped between them. The boy raised his sharpened screwdriver and pointed it at the bum's face.

"You want to make trouble, *pendejo?*" Paco cocked his head and grinned. "You want to play rough?"

Amazingly, the bum didn't back down. He looked Paco in the eye. "Listen to me for a second. I'll make a deal with you."

"A deal?"

"I'll give you half the money. I can get a lot of money from the people who own this thing."

Paco snorted. He glanced at the other Trinitarios, who'd moved in closer to follow the conversation. "You believe this shit? The asshole says he'll give us half."

Frowning, the bum turned away from Paco and appealed to the others. "Just listen, all right? If you try to sell it on your own, you won't get nearly as much. And you can't pick up the thing anyway. It's still too hot. It'll burn your hands."

The homeboys laughed at him. Carlos mimicked the bum's raspy voice, saying, "Just listen, just listen." Meanwhile, Emilio bent over the black ball again and stretched his fingers toward its surface. The bum was right: the thing was hotter than a radiator. He must've heated it somehow, maybe by lighting a fire under it. Emilio couldn't understand why he'd do such a thing. Everything about the guy was crazy.

When Emilio looked up he noticed that Paco had edged closer to the bum. The tip of his screwdriver gleamed in the moonlight. The boy tightened his grip on the screwdriver's handle and tensed his biceps. He was going to start cutting the guy unless Emilio did something soon.

"Hey, Paco!" Emilio called. "Stop playing with that *pendejo* and give me your bandanna."

Paco stared at him, uncomprehending. "What?"

Emilio removed his own bandanna from his head. "I need to cover my hands to pick up the thing." He slipped his screwdriver into his pocket and started wrapping the green fabric around his left hand, covering the palm and fingers. "Come on, *muchacho*, I need your bandanna too."

After a moment Paco figured it out. He stepped away from the bum and scowled at Emilio, but he couldn't disobey a direct order. He took off his bandanna and tossed it over.

Emilio wrapped the fabric around his other hand, creating a green mitten. Then he crouched beside the ball. It was partly embedded in the ground, which was wet and cool, so he guessed its lower half might be a little less scorching. He wriggled his gloved hands into the mud under the thing and tried to get a grip on it. He could feel its heat even through the mud and fabric. It was like a ball of fucking lava.

He tried to lift it anyway, clamping his hands around the thing and pulling upward. He put his whole body into it, straining his biceps and thighs. Then he felt a jab in the center of his right palm. It was sudden and very painful, like being stuck with a *destornillador*. But the jab had come from the ball's smooth, polished surface.

He shouted, "*Coño!*" and let go of the thing, pulling his hands out of the mud. When he raised his right hand he saw a small hole in the bandanna wrapped around it. He quickly unwrapped the fabric from his hand and looked at his palm. In the moonlight he saw blood welling up from a puncture wound.

His homeboys crowded around him, craning their necks to look at his hand. The cut didn't look that bad, and Emilio wanted to tell his boys to stop gawking, but the pain was so intense he couldn't say a word. It spread outward from his palm, as if his hand had caught fire. His fingers burned and throbbed. They felt like they were going to burst.

Emilio turned away from his boys so they wouldn't see his face. He shook his hand as hard as he could, trying to put out the fire. But the pain just got worse.

In the middle of all this commotion, the homeless guy stepped in front of him. The bum looked at him carefully and then, unexpectedly, grasped his shoulder. "Calm down," he said. "Let me see your hand."

The bum didn't look so crazy anymore. His gaze was steady and he wasn't trembling. He reached for Emilio's burning hand and held it in front of his eyes.

As he inspected the puncture wound Paco rushed toward them, his face dark with fury. He aimed his screwdriver at the bum's throat. "Hey, asshole! What the fuck are you doing?"

The homeless guy stood his ground. "I just want to see how deep—"

Paco gave him a vicious shove. The bum lost his balance and toppled backward, hitting the ground hard. He lay on his back in the mud while Paco leaned over him, brandishing the screwdriver. "Stupid *cabrón*! We don't need a fucking nurse!"

The guy's head tilted to the side. He looked woozy, semiconscious. "I'm not . . . a nurse," he rasped. "I used to be . . . a doctor."

"Who the fuck cares? You're dead now, bitch!"

Paco drew back his right foot and kicked him in the ribs. The bum let out a howl that echoed against the hillside. The noise triggered something in the other Trinitarios, some cruel impulse they'd kept in reserve all night, just waiting for the chance to cut it loose. Roaring curses at the homeless guy, they leapt forward to join the beating. They surrounded him and started kicking his legs, arms, and torso. At the same time, Paco crouched low and raised his screwdriver, looking for a place to stab him.

The howl also triggered something in Emilio. All at once the pain in his hand disappeared. He opened and closed it, wiggling the fingers with relief. Then, without any hesitation, he clenched the hand into a fist and charged at Paco.

The boy never saw it coming. Emilio punched the side of his head, just above the ear. Paco dropped his screwdriver and fell sideways to the ground.

The other boys froze. For at least ten seconds Paco lay in the mud, limp and still. Then he coughed and took a ragged breath. He opened his eyes and tried to lift his head, but after a moment he slumped back to the mud. None of the other boys tried to help him. They were too stunned.

But no one was more surprised than Emilio. He held up his right hand and gazed in astonishment at his bruised knuckles. He hadn't planned to knock out Paco. He'd done it without thinking. And now, as he faced the other Trinitarios, he saw what he had to do next. It was so obvious.

He pointed at Paco but kept his eyes on the other homeboys. "Carlos, Miguel, you take his arms. Luis, Diego, grab his legs. Carry him down the hill and back to the soccer field. I'll meet you there in five minutes."

The boys didn't move at first. Emilio had to shout, "*Vayan!*" to get them going.

As they lifted Paco and carried him away, Emilio knelt beside the homeless guy. He was squirming in the mud, clutching his side. Paco must've cracked the guy's ribs. He needed to go to the hospital. Emilio reached into his pocket and pulled out his cell phone.

"Hey, hombre, I'm gonna call for an ambulance. What's your—"

"No!" The bum shook his head fiercely. "Don't call. I'm fine."

"You sure? You don't look so fine."

"Please. Just leave me alone."

Emilio shrugged. He wasn't going to force the guy. He stood up and took one last look at the black ball. *Madre de Dios,* what a weird fucking thing. The bum was welcome to keep it.

Before he left the clearing, Emilio held his hand up to the moonlight so he could check the wound in his palm. It had stopped bleeding and didn't hurt at all now. At first he thought he saw something next to the wound, just under the skin, a dark speck about the size of a poppy seed. But when he looked a little closer, it was gone.

FOUR

At 4:00 P.M. Sarah was in New York City, standing in a deserted baseball field in Upper Manhattan. She checked the map on her iPhone to confirm her position. The field lay between the Hudson River and the West Side Highway, on the western edge of Inwood Hill Park. More to the point, it lay within the impact zone for the debris from last night's fireball. This was the most likely area to find any charred fragments of the asteroid that had exploded twelve hours ago.

She took a deep breath and smelled the brackish Hudson. The people of New York had been freakishly lucky—the debris from the fireball had scattered across one of the few unoccupied parts of the city. According to Sarah's calculations, the impact zone stretched across the river, with one end in Manhattan's Inwood Hill Park and the other in the Palisades Interstate Park in New Jersey. There were no apartment buildings or houses or office complexes within the zone, so there were no reports of any damage. No one saw any fragments hit the ground or splash into the river. Like the vast majority of meteorite showers, this one had gone unnoticed. But Sarah had come here anyway, catching a

5:00 A.M. flight from Los Angeles to New York. She'd traveled three thousand miles on the spur of the moment to see if she could find some evidence.

She focused her attention on the baseball field. It was in terrible shape, all hard-packed dirt from home plate to the chain-link fence, but its condition was perfect for meteorite hunting. If any unusual rocks had landed in the field, they would stand out like paint drops against the blank canvas of beige dirt. Sarah started to walk across the field, keeping her head down and scanning the ground.

She'd scratched lines in the dirt to make a grid for her search, and now she was scrutinizing the grid squares, one by one. Sarah had learned this technique long ago, back in the early eighties, when she used to go rock hunting with her father in West Texas. Her dad had been an accountant in El Paso, but on the weekends he'd turn into an amateur geologist. Every Saturday he'd drive to some godforsaken desert where he'd heard there might be some good finds. Hunting for rocks was ridiculously tedious, and West Texas was usually hotter than Hades, but Sarah went along with him whenever she could. It was worth it just to see the look on his face when he found something interesting.

The basic rule for their meteorite hunts was to look for the color black. As a rock plunges through the atmosphere, its surface gets fried to a black crust that looks like burnt toast. But there were exceptions to the rule: if the meteorite is a fragment of a larger rock that exploded, then only one side of it would be black and the other would be lighter, and the lighter-colored side might be the one showing on the ground. It was tricky.

Over the course of all those weekend hunts Sarah's father found only a dozen meteorites. He kept them on a shelf in their living room, each rock carefully labeled. He spotted the last one—a two-inch-wide fragment of a stony-iron asteroid—when Sarah was fifteen, just three months before he died of Huntington's disease. At that late stage he could hardly walk, and his hands shook as he picked up the meteorite. But his haggard face lit up with joy as he showed it to her.

Years later, when Sarah recalled that afternoon, she realized that was the moment she decided to become a scientist. She was thinking of her father when she applied to Cornell University and earned her Ph.D. in Astronomy and went to work for NASA. She wanted to feel the same joy.

Now, as she stared at the hard-packed dirt of the baseball field, she noticed that its color was close to that of the West Texas desert. The weather was familiar too. It was a scorching June day in New York City, with temperatures in the upper nineties. Sweat dripped from her chin and landed in the dirt she was inspecting.

After half an hour she concluded there were no meteorites in the field. Disappointed, she took a break in the shade of the dugout and stared at the Hudson River. She looked south toward the George Washington Bridge and north toward the Bronx. Then she turned around and gazed at the woods of Inwood Hill Park, which rose steeply above the West Side Highway. The park was big, almost two hundred acres, and about half of it lay within the impact zone. Combing those hillsides for meteorites would be a hell of a lot harder than searching the baseball field. But the real problem was the river. The Hudson occupied more than two-thirds of the impact zone. In all likelihood the asteroid fragments had plummeted into the water and now lay on the muddy riverbed.

Sarah shook her head. *Be positive,* she told herself. *There's always a chance.* Another baseball field was nearby, only a hundred yards away. It also lay within the impact zone and was as dusty and grassless as the field she'd just searched. That's where she'd go next. She'd flown across the country on her own dime—NASA didn't even know she was in New York—and she was going to stay here until she got some answers. She couldn't prove anything yet, but she felt certain that last night's asteroid was something very special.

The thing that distinguished it was its speed. The rock had entered the atmosphere at thirty-seven kilometers per second, much faster than a typical meteor. When an asteroid approaches the Earth at such a high velocity, it's usually in a retrograde orbit, traveling clockwise around the sun. Because the Earth orbits the sun counterclockwise, a retrograde asteroid hits the planet at higher speeds. But according to the observations made by the Sky Survey telescope, last night's object had been moving in the same direction as the Earth. It had caught up to our planet because the rock was streaking across our solar system at the blistering speed of sixty-five kilometers per second. It was moving too fast to be bound by the sun's gravity. The object wasn't orbiting the sun like all the other asteroids in the solar system; it was speeding past the planets like a fastball, its path only slightly bent by gravity's pull. If it hadn't hit the Earth, it would've shot right past the sun and disappeared into interstellar space, the vast emptiness between the stars.

The only logical explanation was that the rock was a visitor to our solar system. It must've come from somewhere else in the galaxy.

It would be an extraordinary discovery if Sarah could prove it. Several years ago a team of astronomers had claimed they'd detected a high-speed meteor that must've come from another star system, but their findings hadn't stood up to scrutiny. Skeptical researchers found fault with the observations and argued that the meteor wasn't as speedy as claimed. Although Sarah trusted the Sky Survey observations, she knew her results would be vulnerable to the same criticism. That's why she'd spent nine hundred dollars on a last-minute plane ticket to New York. She needed to find a piece of the object so she could analyze its chemical composition. If it turned out to be very different from the asteroids that are native to our solar system, she'd have some solid evidence. Then she could publish her results and announce the discovery of the first interstellar meteorite.

But she had to be careful. An astronomer could ruin her reputation by announcing a discovery too soon. Sarah had made that mistake twenty years ago when she first started working for NASA, and it had nearly ended her career. She was forced to retract her claims and abandon her research. It was the first great disappointment of her adult life, and she didn't handle it very well. She nose-dived into bitterness and depression. She alienated her friends and fought with her fiancé and broke off their engagement. Her life crashed so violently she lost almost everything. She finally took a leave of absence from NASA and checked into a mental-health treatment center in New Mexico.

The next six weeks were grim, but with the help of therapy and some powerful antidepressants, Sarah recovered. After another three months she rejoined NASA and started the Sky Survey project. Over time she became the space agency's leading expert on near-Earth asteroids and eventually regained the respect of her colleagues. And now the last thing she wanted to do was risk losing her reputation again. So she wasn't going to make any half-cocked claims. She was going to keep her mouth shut until she had her proof.

Sarah stood up and headed for the neighboring baseball field. She gazed at the Hudson again, the brown water sloshing against the riverbank, the Palisades looming over the New Jersey side. Then she glanced downstream and saw half a dozen Coast Guard boats under the George

Washington Bridge. They were flashing their lights and speeding up-river.

She stopped in her tracks and stared. They were patrol boats, each at least eighty feet long, with bright orange Coast Guard stripes on their hulls. They cruised in a V-formation, carving furious wakes in the brown water. After a minute or so the formation split in two; three of the boats angled toward the New Jersey side of the river and the other three headed for Inwood Hill Park's marina, which was a few hundred feet south of the baseball fields. As the boats got closer Sarah noticed that their decks were crowded. Dozens of men stood behind the bow rails, all dressed in combat uniforms. They were also carrying assault rifles.

What the hell?

She watched them, curious and worried. *This can't be a coincidence,* she thought. *They must be here for the same reason I am.* But why was the Coast Guard suddenly interested in meteorites?

After another minute the patrol boats reached the marina and the soldiers jumped onto the long wooden pier. They fanned out along the riverbank and set up a checkpoint at the marina's entrance. The same thing was happening on the New Jersey side of the river. As the soldiers marched toward the baseball fields they stopped the joggers and dog walkers and cyclists they encountered on the pathways and escorted them out of the park. Sarah could hear snippets of their conversations.

"Sir, please come with us."

"Why? What's going—"

"We're clearing the area, sir. Please step this way."

The soldiers were polite but insistent. They were also big and burly and intimidating as hell. One of them headed straight for Sarah, taking long strides and cradling his rifle. Although she doubted she could convince him to let her stay in the park, she began rehearsing her arguments. She pulled her NASA identification badge out of her pocket, hoping that proof of her government employment would help her case. But before she could say a word, the soldier pointed at her. The letters SGT NUNN were stenciled on his uniform.

"Ma'am, are you Dr. Sarah Pooley?"

In his left hand Sergeant Nunn held a photograph of her, the same photo that appeared on her NASA badge. This surprised her so much she almost forgot to answer him. "Uh, yeah, that's me. Listen, I need—"

"Ma'am, would you please come with me? Our commander would like to speak with you."

"Your commander?"

The sergeant stepped forward and grasped her arm, just above the elbow. His grip was firm and unfriendly. "This way, ma'am. General Hanson is waiting."

The soldiers had already commandeered a site for their headquarters, inside a waterfront restaurant next to the pier. As Sergeant Nunn escorted Sarah into the dining room, she saw a dozen uniformed men rearranging the tables and shooing the customers out the door. A pair of soldiers spread a map across a square table, and several higher-ranking officers bent over to examine it. Sarah recognized one of the officers by his coal black crew cut and the stars on the shoulders of his Air Force uniform. General Hanson was marking the map with a pencil and giving orders to the other men.

The sergeant stopped a couple of yards from the table and let go of Sarah's arm. For a second she considered bolting out of the restaurant, but she knew she wouldn't get far. Instead, she peered at Hanson's map, which showed Upper Manhattan and the Hudson River and a skinny ellipse marked in red pencil. The elliptical shape meant it was an impact zone. Hanson was organizing the hunt for the asteroid fragments, assigning a search area to each of his officers.

After Hanson finished giving orders, the other officers saluted him and left the dining room. The general studied the map for several more seconds. Then he lifted his head and grinned at Sarah. "Thanks for joining us, Dr. Pooley. Did you have a nice flight?"

She frowned. The guy's arrogance was unbelievable. "How did you know I was here?"

"My contacts at NASA said you'd called in sick. Then I made a guess and checked the passenger lists on the flights out of Los Angeles."

"You can do that? Poke around in civilian records?"

"Under ordinary circumstances, no. But as you can see from our deployment here, the present circumstances are far from ordinary." No longer grinning, he turned to Sergeant Nunn. "Could you give us a moment, Sergeant? Please wait by the door."

Nunn saluted and marched off. Then Hanson turned back to Sarah.

"This is a matter of national security, Dr. Pooley, so please forgive the invasion of your privacy. I wouldn't have taken these steps unless they were absolutely necessary."

She certainly wasn't going to forgive him, but her curiosity was stronger than her distaste for the man. "I don't understand. How did this meteor become a national security crisis? Did it hit something important?"

The general shook his head. "No, nothing like that. But before I can share any information, I need some assurances from you."

"Assurances?"

"Sometimes the Air Force will request the assistance of a civilian adviser from outside the Defense Department, usually because the civilian has some expertise we can't get from our own staff. That's the kind of arrangement I want to make with you, Dr. Pooley. I need your help."

"Help with what?"

"The problem is, I can't tell you until we come to an agreement." He picked up a briefcase from the floor. It was black and decorated with the Air Force seal. "The information I'd like to share with you is highly classified. You've already passed our background checks, but you need to sign a contract promising your cooperation and confidentiality." He laid the briefcase on the table, snapped it open, and pulled out a stapled sheaf of papers. "We'll provide you with appropriate compensation, of course. The assignment will be temporary, and when it's over you can return to your duties at NASA."

He handed her the contract. Dumbfounded, Sarah leafed through it. The gist was plain: the Air Force would pay her a thousand dollars a day for her services, and in return she had to promise to keep everything secret. If she broke her promise, she'd spend the next ten to twenty years in federal prison.

She stepped toward Hanson, holding the contract at arm's length. "You can take it back. I'm a scientist, remember? I want to publish my results, not hide them."

The general didn't take the papers from her. "You'll still be able to publish your findings. You'll just have to let us vet your research articles before publication to make sure they don't include any classified information."

"Vet my articles? You mean censor them, right?"

"No, that—"

"Look, it won't work. We have different priorities." She thrust the contract at Hanson, anxious to get rid of the thing. "I don't know why you've called in the Marines, but it doesn't matter. One way or another, I'm gonna find out where that meteor came from."

"It wasn't a meteor." Hanson's voice was low, almost a whisper. "It was man-made."

Sarah let go of the contract, which fluttered to the floor. *"What?"*

"It was a space probe making a controlled reentry into the atmosphere. We saw the proof once we analyzed the readings from all our radar stations across the globe." He reached into his briefcase again and pulled out another sheaf of papers. This document had the words TOP SECRET stamped on its front page. "It wasn't an American probe. Not NASA, not Air Force. Not the European Space Agency either. But there are two other countries that could've launched it. I'm sure you can guess who they are."

"How could it be man-made? It was moving too fast."

"You're right, that's a problem. It's one of many problems." He held up the classified document so Sarah could see its title: ANALYSIS OF THE TRAJECTORY OF OBJECT 2016X. "We used the radar readings and the Sky Survey data to plot the object's path during the final hours before reentry, but there are plenty of uncertainties. That's why I need you. The experts on my staff are good at plotting missile trajectories, but this probe took a roundabout route to get here, going way off into interplanetary space. And according to my sources at NASA, you know more about interplanetary trajectories than anyone."

Sarah turned away from him, trying to think. It *was* possible to accelerate a spacecraft to speeds as high as 80,000 miles per hour. You'd have to launch it into a highly elliptical orbit around the sun and then execute a series of complex maneuvers, aiming it at Venus or Jupiter and using the planet's powerful gravity to slingshot the probe across the solar system. But what was the point? Why propel a spacecraft to such an extraordinary velocity just to send it back to Earth?

Her throat tightened. She turned back to Hanson. "Was it a weapon?"

The general waited a few seconds before responding. His face was unreadable. "We won't know for sure until we find the thing. Or at least a piece of it. Our patrol boats are going to drag the riverbed."

She shook her head. *Jesus, this is serious.* She stepped toward the table and took a closer look at Hanson's map. His impact zone, she noticed, was smaller than the one she'd estimated. She pointed at the ellipse's eastern boundary, which encompassed only the sliver of Inwood Hill Park that ran alongside the river. "You made a mistake. The zone should include more of the park."

"We narrowed the search area based on our radar analysis." Hanson held up the classified document again but kept it out of Sarah's reach. "Remember when we were watching the object on radar last night and we thought it exploded in the atmosphere? That was actually a deceleration maneuver. The probe used a ten-foot-wide aeroshell to reduce its speed, just like the NASA spacecraft do when they land on Mars. At an altitude of twenty-one miles the probe ejected the aeroshell, which disintegrated. Then the probe continued toward its target. The analysis also explains why the spacecraft looked like it was more than a hundred feet wide in your telescope observations. It really *was* that big during the earliest stages of its approach. The object that your Sky Survey telescope spotted in deep space, hundreds of thousands of miles away, was several times larger than the one that dove into the atmosphere."

Sarah waited for him to say more, but he just stood there, looking at her. She felt the sting of frustration. She wanted to grab the classified analysis right out of his hands. "What are you saying? The spacecraft *shrunk* before reentry?"

Instead of answering, he put the document back in his briefcase. "I'm sorry, Dr. Pooley, but we need to come to an agreement before I can discuss this any further." He bent over and picked up the contract from the floor. Then he reached into the jacket of his uniform and pulled out a pen. "Will you work with us?"

She scowled at him. The bastard had planned this. He'd given her just enough information to sink his hooks into her. He'd probably done some research on her beforehand, talking to her bosses and colleagues at NASA. He knew she wouldn't be able to stand the uncertainty.

Sarah snatched the contract and pen from him. She flipped to the last page and signed it. Then she flung the papers at him and reached into his briefcase to grab the trajectory analysis.

Hanson smiled. "You can keep that copy. Just don't let it out of your sight."

She didn't respond. She was too busy studying the data. There were pages and pages of radar readings showing the position of the object during the last few minutes of its flight. The analysis also included a diagram of the probe's trajectory before it reached the Earth. This plot, based on the Sky Survey observations, started at a point beyond the moon's orbit and made a graceful curve toward the planet.

Sarah bit her lip as she stared at it. Hanson was right. Besides the United States, there were only two countries that could've launched such a complex spacecraft: Russia and China. And China was only barely capable of it.

She jabbed her finger at the trajectory diagram. "I bet it's the Russians. You remember the Ikon, the interplanetary spacecraft they launched a few years ago? That whopping big thing with the nuclear-powered propulsion system? They put it in orbit around the sun, and after six months of testing they said they lost contact with it. But maybe they were lying. Maybe they found another use for it."

Sarah gathered from the look on Hanson's face that he'd also considered this possibility. He stepped closer, standing with his shoulder touching hers, so they could look at the document together. "Our best guess is that the spacecraft's real purpose was to provide a demonstration. The Russians are returning to the intimidation tactics they used during the cold war. They want to show us they can attack any of our cities with a weapon that's too fast to be stopped by our missile defenses."

"You mean a kinetic-energy bombardment? The speed of the projectile provides the destructive power?"

Hanson nodded. "The Pentagon studied a similar system ten years ago, a satellite that could hurl tungsten rods at the Earth's surface. They called it 'Rods from God.' We'd heard rumors that the Russians were working on the same technology, but now it looks like they made a few improvements. Their system is less vulnerable because it doesn't use an orbital platform."

Sarah looked again at the trajectory diagram. "Yes, it's coming from deep space, so you couldn't destroy it in advance with an antisatellite weapon."

"Exactly. There's no defense against it. If there's a standoff anywhere in the world—the Middle East, Ukraine, wherever—they could obliterate any of our command centers or sink any of our aircraft carriers." He pointed at the analysis in Sarah's hands. "And the Russians wanted us to know they could hit any city on the globe. Here, go to page twenty-seven."

Sarah turned the pages until she reached a second diagram. This one showed the probe at twenty minutes before reentry, when it was still thirty thousand miles from the Earth. At this point, according to the Air Force's analysis, the object's trajectory branched off into two curving paths. Now Sarah realized what Hanson had meant when he'd said the probe had gotten smaller—it had split in two. The larger part, the hundred-foot-wide object, had swung clear of the Earth and continued speeding across the solar system. The smaller part, the foot-wide probe shielded by the ten-foot-wide aeroshell, had plunged into Earth's atmosphere.

She looked at Hanson. "Doesn't this seem a little strange? To use such a large spacecraft to deliver such a small probe?"

"We think the spacecraft can deliver as many as ten kinetic-energy projectiles, each capable of extensive destruction. But for this test they used only a small dummy payload. They didn't want to start a war, but they wanted to show us what they could do. Like I said, typical Russian intimidation."

"Well, it sounds pretty inefficient." Sarah shrugged. "So what exactly do you want me to do?"

Hanson stretched his hand toward the diagram and pointed at the larger object, the one that flew past Earth. "I want you to plot all the possible trajectories for that thing. I want to know how it got here and where it's going next."

"It's moving so fast, it's probably gonna go straight out of the solar system."

"I don't think so. I think that spacecraft is carrying more projectiles. And they're real weapons, not dummy payloads." The general shook his head. "I think it's coming back."

FIVE

Although Dorothy Adams loved Inwood Hill Park, she hated climbing that damn hill.

She chose the easiest route, walking along a pathway that gently meandered up the slope, but it was still tough going. She'd never been especially athletic, and everything had grown so much harder since she got sick. After the first hundred yards, she started panting. After a quarter mile, her head swam and her chest ached. By the time she reached the top of the hill she was ready to retch. She staggered toward one of the park benches and gripped its back to steady herself. Then she dropped her canvas bag on the ground, let out a groan, and settled her skinny butt on the bench's wooden slats.

This is just pitiful, she told herself. *You're not even sixty yet. Your grandmother worked in the cotton fields till she was eighty-four, and you can't even walk half a mile from your apartment. Lord in Heaven, what a mess you are.*

The chemotherapy was to blame, mostly. The drugs had snuffed out Dorothy's energy and appetite. Her weight had dropped to a measly hundred and ten, and now her yellow blouse hung as loosely as a curtain from her shoulders. The worst part, though, was the pain in her belly. It wasn't like a stomachache or a cramp. It was a dull misery in the very center of her being. In the beginning—six months ago, that is—she'd felt the pain only when she was lying down or after a big meal. But now it was always there, like a heavy stone inside her stomach.

Dorothy closed her eyes and took a deep breath. It was hot and muggy in the park, but the day was almost over. In a couple of hours the sun would go down and the whole earth would let out a sigh of relief. She took another deep breath and smelled the leaves and grass and dirt. There was more oxygen on top of that hill than anywhere else in Manhattan. That was one of the things she loved about the place. Another was that it reminded her of the countryside where she grew up. With her eyes closed she could imagine she was back in Alabama.

After a few minutes she started to feel better. She opened her eyes and gazed at the trees all around her, the hundred-year-old oaks with hulking trunks and gnarled branches. The early evening sunlight slanted through their leaves. Swarms of gnats whirled inside the shafts of golden light. Noisy squirrels scurried across the gold-dappled ground.

She smiled. It was all so ordinary and beautiful. If she were still the minister of her church she would've written a sermon about it, this blessed daily miracle. But she'd retired from Holy Trinity four months ago, soon after she got the bad news from her doctor. She no longer had to write sermons, organize bingo nights, or run the Sunday school. Now she had the luxury of simply enjoying the moment.

Oh, Lord, she prayed, *you've given me so much. Would it be presumptuous to ask you for one more blessing?*

To the west the Hudson River glittered in the sunshine. Looking down from the hilltop, Dorothy could see the cars stuck in traffic on the West Side Highway and a sleek Coast Guard boat going up the river. Then she raised her head and squinted at the sun and the thin clouds around it. Presumptuous or not, she was going to send her prayer skyward.

Reach inside me, Lord. Remove the stone from my body. Find the cancer cells in my pancreas and liver and bloodstream and melt them away with your holy touch. Because I'm only fifty-nine years old, Lord. There's so much more I want to do.

She wasn't completely satisfied with the prayer. It sounded a bit whiny, to tell the truth. During her thirty-five years in the Episcopal church—five years as a missionary, ten years as an organizer for the Union of Black Episcopalians, and twenty years as vicar of Holy Trinity—she'd taken great pride in her sacred writings. This piddly, whiny prayer didn't measure up to her usual standards. But under the present circumstances it would have to do.

As she stared at the Hudson, she noticed another Coast Guard boat cruising a few hundred feet behind the first one. Curious, she craned her neck to look down the river and saw yet another one. And there were *three more* Coast Guard boats in the distance, close to the New Jersey side of the river.

That's strange. Dorothy's first thought was that they were searching the waters for a drowning victim, maybe a suicide. She rose from the bench and went to the other side of the pathway to get a better view. Then she looked down the hillside at the riverbank and noticed the men in uniforms near the marina. There were dozens of them.

Now she started to worry. *Did something happen? Some kind of terrorist attack, maybe?* She hadn't heard any bombs go off.

Several soldiers stood guard at the entrance to the marina, but most were marching across the baseball fields. They didn't come up the pathway that climbed the hill, though. The soldiers stayed on the other side of the highway, in the section of the park closest to the river. Dorothy looked for signs of an attack or an explosion down there, but she didn't see any. There were no injured people, no ambulances. It occurred to her that maybe this was just a drill, a training exercise. She'd seen several police drills in Inwood over the past few years. The NYPD patrol cars would come roaring down Broadway in the middle of the day with their lights flashing and their sirens screaming. Maybe the Coast Guard did the same thing.

She continued watching for another minute or so. None of the soldiers seemed to be moving with any urgency, which made Dorothy more convinced that it was a training exercise. Still, she was uneasy.

The pain in her belly sharpened. It was bad today, even worse than usual. She needed to go back to her apartment and take some more pills. First, though, she had to visit her friends.

With another groan, she returned to the bench and picked up the canvas bag she'd dropped. Inside the bag were several packages of string cheese and half a dozen cans of Planters Peanuts, all taken from the food pantry at Holy Trinity. The church offered free groceries to the needy on Monday and Thursday mornings, but Dorothy knew that many of the neediest people in Inwood were too ashamed to come to the pantry. So she went to them instead. She wasn't strong enough to run the church anymore, but she could still perform this simple act of charity.

She walked a little farther down the pathway, then stepped off the asphalt and into the woods. Because she was afraid she might stumble, she moved slowly and kept her eyes on the muddy ground. Most of the park's homeless people slept on the eastern slope of the hill. They spent their days wandering across the neighborhood, begging for change and dodging the cops, and returned to the park before sunset to find a place to sleep. So the early evening was usually a good time for Dorothy to visit them, before the drunks passed out for the night and the junkies hit the needle. She would offer them some cheese or peanuts and ask a few questions and try to gauge how they were holding up. If someone seemed in dire need of help she'd encourage him or her to go to a shelter, but she never forced anyone. She wasn't their social worker. She was their friend.

And though the visits were difficult, she always looked forward to them. Yes, most of the homeless were traumatized and some were deeply disturbed, but they were also more interesting than most ordinary people. They were a multiracial group—black, white, Asian, and Latino— and in that way they resembled the congregation at Holy Trinity. Dorothy had been visiting some of them for years, and over time she'd learned their nicknames and quirks. In bits and pieces they'd told her their stories: their troubled childhoods, the sexual abuse, the prison sentences, the rehab attempts. As she listened she sometimes felt a powerful urge to rescue them. She wanted to drag them, kicking and screaming, to her church's parish house. But she'd realized long ago that she couldn't save anyone who didn't want to be saved. All she could do was feed them and listen to their stories.

After a minute she stopped and surveyed the hillside, which was studded with boulders and outcrops. Because these rock formations provided some shelter from the rain, the homeless usually camped beside them. She looked for the wrinkled tarps and plastic shopping bags that marked their sleeping spots but didn't see anyone nearby. She was probably too early. Her friends were still panhandling or buying booze or scoring drugs. They'd come trudging up the hill over the next few hours, but Dorothy felt too sick today to wait for them. She'd just have to leave her cans and packages on the ground and hope someone would find them.

She was about to start emptying her bag when she caught a glimpse of a cardboard box. It was in sad shape, crushed almost flat, and it sat in the middle of a big mud hole on the hillside. At first Dorothy thought the box had been abandoned, but when she looked closer she saw a pair of legs and filthy sneakers sticking out of the open end. What's more, she actually recognized the sneakers from the loops of duct tape wrapped around their toes. The man inside the flattened box was named Joe Graham. He was one of Dorothy's favorites, one of her best friends on Inwood Hill.

All of the homeless in the park were wary of strangers, so she called out "Hey, Joe?" before going any closer. He didn't answer. She waited a few seconds, then called out to him again. "Hey, it's me, Dorothy. What the heck happened to your box?"

Again, no answer. His legs and sneakers remained perfectly still.

She was a little worried because she'd never seen Joe asleep during her previous visits. He was a newcomer to Inwood—he'd lived in the park for only the past four months—and though his clothes and health were getting steadily worse, he still kept a regular schedule. Every day he ate lunch at the soup kitchen on Dyckman Street, and instead of panhandling he did odd jobs for some of the neighborhood stores. And he was always polite to Dorothy, even when he was blitzed. She credited his good behavior to the fact that he was a Southerner. During their very first conversation he'd mentioned that he was born in Alabama, specifically in the small town of Union Springs. Dorothy knew the place well—it was just twenty miles from her own hometown. She and this unfortunate white man came from the same county.

"Joe?" She raised her voice. "Are you all right?" Dorothy stepped toward the mud hole, her slip-on shoes sinking into the ooze. She was probably getting worried over nothing. In all likelihood, he'd simply passed out a bit earlier than usual today. But she approached the collapsed box anyway and listened carefully for the sound of his breathing. She heard nothing and got even more nervous.

Bending over, she gripped the crumpled edge of the box and pulled it up so she could look inside. Joe lay on his back but it was hard to see his face in there. He still didn't move. On the front of his Yankees jacket was a footprint of dried mud. Did somebody step on him? Or kick him?

"Joe, wake up!" She shook the box, rocking him. "Talk to me!"

He shuddered and began to cough. Her first reaction was relief: *Thank the Lord, he's alive!* But then he winced and clutched the sides of his chest and she saw how much pain he was in. He'd clearly taken a beating. He needed a doctor. Could she convince him to see one, though? That was the tricky part. She'd seen homeless people suffer unimaginable agonies rather than go to the hospital. Many of them were terrified of doctors. Others simply didn't want to be forced to do anything. They hated any infringements on their freedom, which in most cases was their last remaining possession.

Dorothy's mind was racing. She took a deep breath and muttered a prayer to calm herself. "Tell me, where does it hurt? Is it your ribs?"

Joe nodded. Then his eyes opened wide, as if he'd just remembered something important. "I have to . . . let me . . ." His hands trembled in distress. He clawed at the box, struggling to wriggle out of it.

"What are you doing? You're gonna make it worse."

She tried to stop him but he was too determined. Grimacing, he slid out of the box and rose to his feet. He glanced up and down the hillside, squinting in the evening light. Then he cocked his head and stared at the ground under the box, which rested on a foot-high mound at the center of the mud hole. It looked like a giant mud pie, shaped by hand to make a soft platform for the box. He studied the mound closely for several seconds, wincing and clutching his chest all the while. Then he turned back to Dorothy.

"It's okay . . . I'm all right." He spoke in short rasps, wheezing in the intervals. "Thank you . . . for checking on me."

"What happened? Was it that gang you told me about? The teenagers who were bothering you a few days ago?"

"I'm fine . . . really."

"Don't try to play me, Joe. Those kids kicked the crap out of you. You need to go to the emergency room."

He attempted to smile, but instead he grimaced again. "It's not . . . so bad. The rib's cracked . . . not broken."

"You're being foolish. You need X-rays."

He shook his head. "I've had cracked ribs . . . before. There's nothing you can do . . . except give it time to heal."

Dorothy frowned. This was just plain stubbornness. Joe was a smart man, but he was also an alcoholic, which meant that the most important thing in the world to him was finding his next drink. And he knew there was no malt liquor for sale in the emergency room at Columbia Presbyterian.

"What are you gonna do until it heals?" she asked. "You think the booze is gonna take away the pain?"

This came out a little meaner than she'd intended. Her frustration was making her snap at him. But Joe didn't get upset. He tried to smile again, and this time he succeeded. "I'll just get . . . some aspirin. That's the best medicine . . . in the world, you know."

She kept frowning. The problem was that she cared too much about this man. Because of a stupid coincidence—the fact that both of them were born in Bullock County, Alabama—she'd grown fond of him. What made it even stupider was that she knew very little else about him. He'd told her that he was forty-two years old and that he'd graduated from the University of Alabama, but he'd said nothing at all about the past twenty years of his life. She had no idea why he'd come to New York, what he did for a living after he got there, or how he became an alcoholic. And yet somehow she felt like she understood him.

To hide her emotions, Dorothy reached into her bag and pulled out a can of peanuts. "Here, take this. I got you the unsalted kind."

"Thank you . . . so much." He took the can from her. "And how are *you*? Are the chemo drugs . . . still making you dizzy?"

She'd told him about her pancreatic cancer a couple of weeks ago. It wasn't a secret—the parishioners at Holy Trinity knew why she'd had to leave her job—and when Joe had politely asked how she was doing she'd told him the hard truth. Now, though, she felt awkward about it.

She shrugged. "I wouldn't mind the dizziness if the drugs were helping me some. But I don't think they're working. The pain is as bad as ever."

Joe stepped a little closer and looked at her eyes. Then he turned away. "Well, I hope . . . you feel better. Maybe you just need . . . to give it some more time."

There was something familiar about the look he'd just given her. Dorothy puzzled it over for a few seconds, wondering where she'd seen it before. Then she figured it out.

She pointed at Joe. "I get it now. You're a doctor, right?" She didn't wait for him to confirm it. She knew she was right. "You were looking at the whites of my eyes, trying to see if the cancer is giving me jaundice. My doctor at Sloan Kettering does the same thing. He says you have to look at the eyes of African Americans because it's hard to see the change in their skin color."

He seemed embarrassed. "I'm sorry." He took a step backward, avoiding her gaze. "Old habits . . . die hard, I guess."

"Hey, I don't mind." She chuckled, not because anything was funny but just to make him feel better. "I could always use a second opinion."

"I'm not a doctor . . . anymore." He shook his head. "I lost . . . that privilege. Along with everything else."

He fell silent. Dorothy gave him a few seconds, hoping he'd say more, but he just lowered his head and looked at the ground. She could guess, though, what he meant by "everything else." He must've had a family. A wife, maybe children.

She closed the distance between them and rested her hand on his shoulder. She knew this was a dangerous thing to do. Many homeless people were victims of abuse, and sometimes they'd been brutalized so badly they became violent if you touched them. But she sensed that Joe was different. He wasn't so far gone. He could come back to life if given half a chance.

She squeezed his shoulder. "Come to the church with me, Joe. We have so many good programs. We can help you."

He didn't say yes, but he didn't say no either. He just kept staring at the ground. Dorothy waited beside him, exercising her patience, which was the most useful tool in the world when you were working with troubled people. Joe smelled awful, like a putrid mix of sweat and malt liquor, but she ignored it and tried to look him in the eye. He was one of God's children. Although Dorothy had no children of her own—no living relatives at all, actually—she had a family nonetheless, and this sad, broken man was a part of it.

"Come on, Joe. We'll start with something simple. I'll get you a proper meal and a bed in one of the shelters."

He didn't look up. If anything, he stared at the ground more intently. She followed his gaze and noticed that he was looking again at the mound of damp earth that his crushed box sat upon. He clenched and unclenched his hands as he focused on the big, flattened pile of mud. He seemed so agitated that Dorothy started to wonder. *What the heck is he staring at? Did he bury something there?*

She let go of his shoulder. The ache in her belly subsided and she felt a twinge of fear instead. She started backing away from Joe and his mud pile. He could've buried something fairly large under that mound. Like a bag full of valuables. Or a dead animal.

She took another step backward. *I've made a mistake. I don't really know this man. I have no idea what he's capable of.*

Then she felt a stabbing pain in the heel of her right foot. At first she thought she'd stepped on a tack or a rusty nail, but the pain quickly intensified and spread, shooting up her leg like an electric shock. Her foot went numb and her knee buckled. She fell sideways, flailing, and her right hip smacked hard against the ground.

"Dorothy!"

Joe crouched beside her but she squirmed away from him, her hands clawing the mud. His mouth was open and his eyes were darting, and maybe he was just examining her, just trying to see what was wrong, but how could she trust him? *I know nothing about this man!*

"Stay back!" she screamed. "Get away from me!"

He gaped at her for a second, looking confused. Then he stood up and stepped backward. "Dorothy, are you . . . what happened to—"

"Just stay away!" Keeping one eye on him, she reached for her numb right foot and removed the slip-on shoe. There was a puncture in its thin rubber sole. Then she looked at the bottom of her foot and saw a bead of blood on the heel. It was tiny, smaller than a seed pearl. How could such a puny little cut hurt so much? How could it knock her to the ground like that?

Joe looked at her foot too, and his face changed. He furrowed his brow and bit his lip. It was a look of apprehension, Dorothy realized. *He's worried. Something funny is going on, and he's afraid I'll find out.* He turned away from her and looked at the ground again, staring hard at the mud.

And now Dorothy looked too. She stared at the patch of mud where she'd stood just a few seconds ago, and after a moment she spotted her footprints. She got on her hands and knees—her pants were already splattered with mud, so it didn't matter—and lowered her head so she could search for the nail or tack she'd stepped on.

For half a second she thought she saw something sticking out of the mud, something black and slender and sharp. Then it disappeared, sucked back into the ooze.

She shook her head. She was going crazy. The chemo drugs had finally pushed her over the edge.

She gave up searching and sat in the mud for the next half minute, trying to catch her breath. Some feeling was coming back to her right foot now, and the pain was ebbing. She flexed the leg a few times to make sure her knee was all right. Joe stood a couple of yards away, keeping his distance. He was hiding something from her, that was for sure, but Dorothy didn't want to know about it. She just wanted to go home.

Somehow she managed to stand up. Her pants were filthy but that was the least of her worries. She picked up her canvas bag and turned it upside-down, spilling the cans of peanuts and packages of string cheese on the ground. "You can do whatever you want with this stuff," she said, not looking at Joe. "Eat it or trade it for booze or throw it away. I don't really care."

He took a step toward her. "Dorothy, I—"

"No, you stay right there." She pointed a quivering finger at him. "Don't you dare follow me."

Then she tucked the empty bag under her arm and headed out of the park.

SIX

Joe saw the spike that hurt Dorothy. It glinted in the twilight like a black needle, its tip less than an inch above the mud. Then he blinked and it was gone.

He also saw the puncture wound on her heel. She wouldn't let him come close, but from a distance it looked like the wound he'd seen the night before, on the palm of the teenager who'd tried to lift the black sphere.

As Dorothy sat there on the ground, massaging her foot, he stared at the patch of mud where the spike had appeared. It was at least six feet away from where he'd buried the satellite. He'd spent nearly an hour piling dirt on the thing early that morning, after the gang of teenagers decided to leave him alone. Despite the pain in his chest he'd built a wide, muddy mound that covered the sphere and filled in most of the crater. As a final touch, he'd dragged his cardboard box up the hillside and dropped it on top of the mound. He didn't go to sleep until he was sure the black ball was thoroughly hidden. But he must've missed something.

Had Dorothy stepped on another piece of the satellite? Maybe its sev-ered antenna? That was the most likely explanation. But why did the spike vanish after she stepped on it? Did it really exist, or did Joe just imagine it?

Before he could apologize to Dorothy or try to explain, she was back on her feet and walking away. She left the clearing as fast as she could, limping and scared. And Joe was scared too. For several seconds he just stood there, staring at the footprints in the mud and the scattered pack-ages of food that Dorothy had left behind. Then, stepping slowly and carefully, he moved away from the mud pile. He didn't stop until he was under the trees at the edge of the clearing. His heart hammered inside his aching chest.

He needed a drink. Eighteen hours had passed since he'd downed his last bottle of malt liquor, and that was way too long. He was already experiencing withdrawal symptoms: tremors, headache, nausea. Back when Joe was in medical school at the University of Alabama, he'd learned about alcohol's long-term effects and how heavy drinking trans-forms the brain cells. Over time it eliminated the crucial pieces of the cells that calm their activity. So when a drunk stops drinking, his brain can't steady itself. Joe's brain cells, deprived of the soothing balm of malt liquor, were firing wildly, making him shake and sweat. He under-stood the biochemistry and even remembered the names of the chem-icals involved: gamma-aminobutyric acid, ligand-gated ion channels. But knowing the cause of his symptoms didn't make him any less miserable.

Joe leaned against an oak tree and closed his eyes. He took deep breaths and tried to quiet the storm in his head. But in his mind's eye he still saw the black spike. It was as shiny and polished as the sphere he'd hidden.

No, the spike wasn't real. It was a hallucination. It was an illusion created by my screwed-up brain.

After a while he opened his eyes. The sun had descended almost to the horizon. He felt a strong urge to simply walk away from the clear-ing and out of the park. He had nothing in his pockets, not even loose change, but inside his left sock was a ten dollar bill, which he'd earned yesterday afternoon by mopping the floor of a Chinese takeout place on West 207th Street. For ten dollars he could buy four bottles of Olde English 800. That would be enough to calm his nerves and help him forget about the satellite. The damn thing had given him nothing but trouble.

But then he remembered the happiness he'd felt last night, after he'd found the sphere but before the teenagers showed up. *That* was real, that feeling of hope. Joe stared again at the mud underneath his crushed box, but instead of thinking about the satellite he pictured his reward for finding it, a fat stack of hundred dollar bills. He deserved that money. And if he left the park now, someone else might grab the sphere and get the reward. Those teenagers knew where it was, and they'd probably told all their friends about it. There was a good chance they'd come back tonight.

Joe turned away from the clearing and scanned the ground under the oak trees. If you looked carefully you could find all kinds of useful junk in the weeds. After half a minute he found a pile of half-charred wooden planks. Someone had tried to make a bonfire on the hillside, but the wood hadn't burned so well, probably because it was too damp. Most of the planks were charred at only one end. Joe picked up four of them and returned to the clearing. Then he threw one of the planks on the ground and stepped on it. He wasn't going to risk what happened to Dorothy. Although the spike might've been just a hallucination, he was determined to keep his feet off the mud.

He threw two more planks on the ground and used them as stepping-stones. When he reached the spot where Dorothy had stood, he poked his last plank in the mud. He shoved the burnt end a couple of inches into the ground and made a deep gouge. Then he made another. He was looking for the black spike. He made a dozen gouges, crisscrossing the area. But he didn't find anything. He breathed a sigh of relief.

Still, he didn't want to take any chances, so he threw his last plank on the ground in front of him and stepped on it to approach the mud pile.

Joe grasped the cardboard box and pushed it aside. Then he stared at the mound, trying to remember exactly where he'd buried the satellite. He assumed the thing had cooled down by now. He doubted he'd be able to carry it very far, not in his condition, so he planned to wrench the sphere out of the mud and roll it down the hillside. He wasn't sure about the next step, though. Should he take the satellite to a science museum? Or maybe to the headquarters of the company that built it?

The simplest option would be to alert the police, who could get in touch with NASA or whatever government agency had launched the thing. But Joe didn't trust the Inwood cops. They loved to harass the park's homeless people, shooing them off the benches and away from the soccer fields. The worst one was a big redheaded cop named Patton. He liked to poke Joe with his nightstick and threaten to arrest him. He said he had friends who were prison guards on Rikers Island and some-day soon he was going to send Joe their way. The guy was a real bastard, stupid and cruel. If Joe told him about the satellite, Officer Patton would either laugh in his face or try to snag the reward for himself.

Joe glanced to the left and right. He was alone on the hillside. The sun had just set and the woods were darkening. When he was certain that no one else was nearby, he bent over and picked up the plank that was closest to the one he stood on. Then he started using it as a shovel, digging into the mound.

He scraped away the top layer of mud. Luckily, the ground wasn't hard. Joe had finished building the mound just twelve hours before, so it was still as soft as putty. After less than a minute the end of his plank banged against the satellite. The jolt made him a little uneasy in his stomach, and the feeling intensified after he shoveled away enough mud to expose the top of the sphere. Even in the fading daylight it gleamed like a jewel, blacker than onyx. But he kept digging. After another few minutes he'd uncovered the upper half of the thing.

Now it looked the same as it had when he'd stumbled upon it the night before. Joe's chest ached from all the bending and shoveling, but he plunged the plank into the ground again, scooping out the packed dirt around the satellite. He could endure the pain because the sphere was his salvation. It was going to give him enough money to get his old life back. Once he had the reward in his hands, he'd say goodbye to Inwood and return to Riverdale. He'd find a landlord willing to rent an apartment to someone with no references but lots of cash. Then he'd hire a lawyer and try to recover his medical license. Almost anything was possible if you had enough money. He might even be able to persuade his ex-wife to forgive him.

After ten more minutes he'd shoveled almost to the bottom of the sat-ellite, making a deep circular trench around the thing. It was ready to come loose. He just needed to apply a little elbow grease to pry it out of the ground. Joe lowered the burnt end of the plank into the trench and wedged it into the mud below the sphere. Then he pushed down on the other end of the plank, trying to lever the satellite upward. But it didn't budge. He pushed down harder, leaning all his weight on the plank. The pain was so bad it felt like his chest was on fire, but he didn't let up.

Then the plank cracked. Joe had to lean backward to stop himself from falling face-first into the mud. *Jesus, what's wrong? How much does this thing weigh?*

He clutched his side, cursing under his breath. When the pain finally eased he picked up the cracked plank and peered into the trench he'd dug. It was tough to see anything in the fading light, but after a few seconds he noticed something glinting in the deepest part of the trench. He bent over to get a closer look. A thick column of black metal jutted downward from the bottom of the sphere, anchoring it to the ground.

Joe shook his head in frustration. He thrust the plank into the trench again and dug into the mud at the bottom, trying to see how deep the column went. It looked like a black pipe, at least three inches in diameter, and made from the same material as the rest of the satellite. He scraped away the mud around the column, exposing more of it, but instead of uncovering its bottom end he saw several thinner pipes branching off from it. They angled downward from the central column, delving deeper into the ground, like metallic roots.

As he stared into the trench Joe's frustration turned to disbelief. How the hell did all those pipes get down there? Did they automatically extend from the bottom of the satellite sometime after it landed? And why would they do that? What was the point?

Then he thought of the spike again. He started to shiver, even though the temperature in the park was still in the nineties. He didn't bother to fill in the trench. He just reached for his cardboard box and rested it on top of the sphere. *The damn thing is spreading underground. It's putting out feelers.*

The woods were dark now. Joe looked behind him at the planks he'd laid out as stepping-stones. He turned around and jumped from one plank to the next, careful not to step on the mud. Then he ran down the hill, away from the clearing.

He bolted out of the park. At first Joe didn't know where to go. His mind was so full of panic he could hardly think. He raced along Payson Avenue, the street that separated Inwood Hill Park from the rest of the neighborhood, and then headed for Broadway, which was busy and brightly lit. Dozens of people gawked at him as he came charging down the sidewalk, a crazy homeless dude sprinting past the drugstores and bodegas. Some of the people laughed. Others scowled and shouted. Joe ignored them all.

He passed a car wash, a supermarket, and a hardware store. Then he stopped and leaned against a brick wall, his ribs aching as he tried to catch his breath. After a few seconds he looked up and saw a sign on the wall: NEW YORK PUBLIC LIBRARY, INWOOD BRANCH. Although he hadn't consciously decided to come here, his instincts had led him to the right place.

Back in April, when the weather was still chilly, Joe had spent several afternoons at the Inwood library to keep warm. He knew the library's computer room was open to the public. If one of the computers happened to be free now he could search the Internet. There was bound to be some information online about the missing satellite. With a little luck he could find out who'd launched the thing, and maybe even get a phone number. Then he'd be just a step away from collecting his reward.

But there was a problem. It was after 8:00 P.M. and the library was closed.

Joe placed his hands on his knees and doubled over, dizzy and nauseous. All he needed was a little computer time, just ten minutes! It was the kind of thing he'd always taken for granted in the old days, before he lost his job and started living on the streets. Back when he worked at St. Luke's Hospital he could've searched the Web on the computer in his office, or on his MacBook or iPad or iPhone. Now, though, he had nothing. He was completely cut off. The people on the sidewalk detoured around him, edging toward the curb.

Then he heard a siren. He looked down Broadway and saw a police cruiser a couple of blocks away, its blue lights flashing. Joe's knees trembled under his hands. He was so frightened he almost threw up. But he managed to stand up straight and walk past the library, away from the cruiser. He tried to look casual, as if nothing was wrong.

The car slowed as it caught up to him. Joe glanced sideways and got a shock: the guy in the passenger seat was Officer Patton. Worse, the redheaded bastard was looking out the car's window and eyeing Joe suspiciously. Patton pointed his nightstick at him and said something to the car's driver. But he didn't say anything to Joe, didn't make his usual threats about Rikers and his prison-guard friends. After a few seconds the cruiser accelerated and sped toward Dyckman Street.

Joe relaxed a little but kept walking. When you're living on the streets, the best way to avoid trouble was to always keep moving. He'd criss-crossed Inwood so many times during his daily wanderings that he could draw a map of the neighborhood from memory. In his mind's eye he could picture every street corner and storefront between the Hudson and Harlem rivers. And as he crossed West 204th Street, still trembling from his close call with Patton, he remembered one of those storefronts. A new copy shop had opened a month ago on Tenth Avenue, and inside the shop was a computer that customers could pay to use. Joe was sure of this because the shop's owner had put a sign above the window: SUPER-FAST INTERNET $5 PER HOUR.

He turned right at the next corner and headed for Tenth Avenue. Half-way down the block he ducked into an alleyway and took off his left sneaker. Tucked inside his tube sock was his ten dollar bill, folded in half and damp with sweat. He unfolded the bill and flapped it around to dry it. Joe hated the idea of spending the money at the copy shop. All he could think about were the forty-ounce bottles of malt liquor he could buy instead. But he told himself it was an investment. *Just think of the reward. You're gonna spend a few dollars now, but in a day or two you'll get thousands.*

Five minutes later he arrived at the copy shop. To his immense relief, it was still open. He peered through the window under the SUPER-FAST INTERNET sign and saw no customers inside. At the front of the shop was a self-service copy machine and next to it was the computer, an old Hewlett-Packard PC. A counter ran across the middle of the store, and beyond it were the bigger copy machines that did the customized jobs. The manager of the store—a twenty-something bearded guy—sat be-hind the counter, reading the *New York Post*. He had pierced eyebrows and tattooed forearms and wore a black T-shirt.

Joe was glad the shop wasn't busy. He wouldn't have to worry about offending any other customers. Holding the ten dollar bill in his right hand, he opened the glass door and stepped inside.

The bearded guy looked up from his newspaper. He started to smile, but then his face wrinkled in surprise. "What do you want?"

This reaction was typical. Very few stores in Manhattan welcomed the homeless. And Joe was sympathetic. He knew he smelled awful. He knew it better than anyone. He raised his hand and waved the ten dollar bill, offering it as a kind of consolation prize. "I have money. I want to use your computer."

The manager narrowed his eyes. "You want to use the computer?" His voice was slow and full of contempt. "You're joking, right?"

"I have money." Joe waved the bill again. "Ten dollars, see?"

The guy shook his head. "Sorry, the computer's broken." He put a mock-apologetic look on his face.

Joe looked at the computer. Its screen saver displayed a swirl of undulating colors. Then he turned back to the manager. "It doesn't look broken to me." He stepped toward the chair in front of the computer and pulled it out. "Let me give it a try."

The guy closed his newspaper and stood up. He held out both hands like a traffic cop at an intersection. "Whoa, get away from there. I said it's broken."

Joe ignored him and sat down in the chair. He pressed the space key on the computer's keyboard. The undulating colors disappeared and the screen showed the usual Windows icons against a blue background. "Seems to be working fine." He rose from the chair and placed his ten dollar bill on the counter. "I'll take an hour of Internet time, please."

The guy frowned at the bill as if it were a piece of dog shit. Then he turned toward the wall, bent over and pulled an electrical plug out of its socket. The PC let out a squeak and its screen went black.

Joe clenched and unclenched his hands. "Why did you do that? Turn it back on."

The manager pointed at the door. "It's time for you to leave."

"Look, this isn't fair." Joe leaned across the counter. "My money is as good as anyone else's. I have a right to—"

"If you don't get out of here, I'm calling the cops." The guy pulled a cell phone out of his pocket. "I'm not gonna sit here while you stink up the place." He punctuated the sentence by flicking Joe's ten dollar bill off the counter. It fluttered to the floor.

Joe felt a surge of anger. This guy was even worse than the teenagers who'd attacked him. They were just stupid kids, but this asshole was old enough to know better. He should know that terrible things could happen to anyone. That it was easy, hideously easy, to become a drunk. But the guy was too arrogant and thickheaded to see it. Joe leaned a little farther across the counter. He wanted to tear the fucker's head off.

The manager stepped backward. He raised his cell phone and punched a few keys. "I'm calling 911 right now," he warned. "You better get the fuck out of here."

Joe glared at him. He looked at the counter between them and seriously considered climbing over it. But who was he kidding? His chest ached every time he took a breath. He was in no condition to get into a fight. And even if he could, the cops would come to the shop and arrest him. They'd cart him off to either the jail on Rikers Island or the nuthouse at Bellevue.

No, he couldn't win. He had to figure out another way.

He turned away from the counter and glanced at the computer's blank screen. *So close and yet so far.* Then he picked up the ten dollar bill from the floor and left the shop.

He walked several blocks uptown, then wandered aimlessly across the darkened neighborhood. His stomach churned with disappointment. He lowered his head and stared at the sidewalk, avoiding eye contact with everyone. Most of all, he avoided looked to the north, toward the tall apartment buildings in Riverdale. The last thing he wanted to see now was the building where his daughter lived.

After fifteen minutes he found himself on the corner of Broadway and 215th Street. His instincts had led him to the right place again. Just down the block was Duarte's, a bodega that sold cigarettes, lottery tickets, beer, and malt liquor. He walked into the place, and the guy behind the counter nodded at him. Joe was a loyal customer, maybe the most loyal one they had. He opened the refrigerated case at the back of the store and pulled out four forty-ounce bottles of Olde English 800. About a year ago he'd settled on Olde English as his preferred brand. It cost only $2.49 per bottle, including tax, making it a cheap and efficient way to get drunk. And the stuff was sold all over the neighborhood, at every hour of the night.

At the counter Joe handed over his ten dollar bill and got four pennies in change. He felt a twinge of regret as he shoved the coins into his pocket. He'd just spent the money he was supposed to invest in his future. Now he would drink his forties until he was drunk, and sometime after midnight he'd pass out and sleep it off. Then he'd wake up tomorrow morning with his head throbbing and his mouth as dry as dust, and the whole cycle would start again. He wouldn't be any closer to changing his life.

But he had no choice. He simply couldn't function without a drink. He made a promise to himself that he'd return to the public library as soon as he woke up the next day. He'd get the information he needed and collect his reward. It could all wait till tomorrow. Everything was still good.

He slipped the four bottles under his Yankees jacket and zipped it up. Feeling better now, he cradled the forties against his chest and headed back to Inwood Hill Park.

Joe passed out again on the same hillside, about thirty yards from the clearing where the satellite had landed. He chose this spot because it was neither too close nor too far. He was close enough to keep an eye on the clearing and yet far enough to be out of range of the sphere's metallic roots. To give himself an extra margin of safety he lay down on one of the thick slabs of rock jutting from the mud. Although it was uncomfortable, he felt better knowing there was three feet of hard stone between himself and the ground.

He slept restlessly for the first hour. When he closed his eyes he pictured Dorothy limping away from the clearing. Then he saw the teenagers standing around him, shouting in Spanish and pointing their screwdrivers. The asshole from the copy shop stood with them and called the cops on his cell phone. Soon a police cruiser drove up the hillside, its blue lights flashing, but the cops inside the car also had screwdrivers in their hands and green bandannas around their heads. Startled, Joe woke up for a moment and rolled onto his side, the rock slab pressing mercilessly against his cracked ribs. But he'd drunk so much Olde English that he couldn't stay conscious for very long. Within seconds he passed out again.

Luckily, his next dream was less jarring. He pictured his daughter Annabelle sitting on the beige sofa in their old apartment in Riverdale. She was just five years old in this dream, a curly-haired moppet in pink pajamas, sitting beside her mother. Their right hands were hooked together for a game of thumb war. They started the game by reciting the traditional opening lines, "One, two, three, four, I declare thumb war," Karen's voice chanting in unison with Annabelle's, "Five, six, seven, eight, you drool and I'm great." Then their thumbs swept back and forth, darting and feinting, Karen's large thumb bent like a fleshy 7,

Annabelle's tiny thumb wriggling like a worm. They looked so beautiful together, laughing and playing. That was their happiest time, Joe thought, their very best year. Before Annabelle started kindergarten and Karen started cheating and Joe started drinking.

The intrusion of this thought changed the tone of Joe's dream. Karen stopped laughing and faded away. Annabelle vanished too, except for her right thumb, which detached from her hand and grew unnaturally long, even longer than the sofa. It also changed color, turning dark brown, then black. It became a thin black snake, but with Annabelle's blue eyes. The snake stared at Joe for a second, watching him curiously. Then it lunged forward and sank its fangs into the crook of his neck. His right arm went numb and a bolt of pain tore across his chest. It was *real* pain, too intense to be part of a dream.

He woke up again and saw a long thin tentacle on the rock slab. It was shiny and black, made of the same metallic stuff as the satellite. It stretched across the slab, one end rising out of the muddy ground and climbing over the edge of the rock, the other end tapering to a needle-like tip just a couple of feet from Joe. As he watched in horror the tentacle pulled away from him, its tip retreating until it slid over the edge of the rock slab and disappeared into the mud.

Joe sat up, panting. The pain in his chest was already ebbing and his right arm was coming back to life, but his terror grew stronger. He raised his left hand to the side of his neck, to the place where the snake had bitten him.

He felt blood on his fingers. And a tiny puncture wound.

SEVEN

Sarah was frustrated.

She sat in the kitchen of the restaurant the Air Force was using as its command post. She'd found a relatively quiet spot, far from the dining room where the colonels and captains were working, and propped her MacBook on a stainless-steel counter. For the past four hours she'd plotted interplanetary trajectories using a NASA program on her laptop. She was trying to figure out how the Ikon, the huge Russian spacecraft launched three years ago, could have accelerated to 80,000 miles per hour while putting itself on a collision course with Earth. Unfortunately, she hadn't made much progress.

A dot at the center of her laptop's screen represented the sun. The orbits of the planets were concentric circles around it. The trajectory of the Ikon was a red arc that started from Earth and ended at the spacecraft's last reported position, on the other side of the sun. That's where the craft was when the Russians said they lost contact with it. Last but not least, a blue line represented the final approach of 2016X, the mystery object that had fired the probe at New York. Sarah had tried to connect the red trajectory with the blue one, but all her attempts had failed. The Ikon simply hadn't had enough time to make the necessary maneuvers across the solar system.

She looked at her watch: 1:32 A.M. Aside from a brief nap she'd taken during the flight to New York, she'd been going nonstop for almost twenty-four hours, and she was dead tired. She wondered if she should join the Air Force officers in the dining room and give General Hanson a progress report. He might find it useful to know that the underlying assumption of their search effort—that Object 2016X was a Russian military spacecraft—seemed highly unlikely.

In the end, though, Sarah decided to stay put. She continued staring at her laptop's screen and thinking. So far, Hanson's search teams had found no trace of 2016X. Neither the soldiers on the riverbanks nor the specialists in the Coast Guard boats had detected any suspicious debris. Of course, the search was only nine hours old and there was a lot of territory to cover. But Sarah also wondered if the Air Force radar experts had drawn the wrong boundaries for the impact zone. All their estimates were based on the assumption that 2016X had been a conventional spacecraft. And Sarah was starting to question this assumption.

She wanted to try something else. She scrolled through the software on her laptop until she found Earth View, another NASA program. Sarah hesitated for a moment before opening it. To be honest, she was afraid to go down this road. She'd done it before, twenty years ago, and it had ended in disaster. She'd promised herself that she'd never do anything that stupid again. But how could she ignore her suspicions? How could she call herself a scientist if she automatically rejected this hypothesis?

She overcame her fear and clicked on the Earth View icon. A moment later an image of the globe appeared on the laptop's screen. It was a composite image pieced together from the most recent satellite photos of the Earth. Sarah adjusted the settings so that the program showed what North America had looked like from space as 2016X approached it at 4:00 A.M. eastern daylight time. The oceans and the deserts were dark, but the eastern United States was a constellation of glowing cities, with the brightest clusters along the coast. If you were approaching the planet's night side and looking for the most interesting destination, New York City would certainly qualify.

Sarah shut her laptop and left it on the counter. Her heart was racing.

She needed to go outside. As she rushed out of the kitchen she pulled a crumpled pack of Marlboros from the back pocket of her jeans. It was her secret vice, but now she didn't care who saw it. She showed the pack to the soldier who guarded the restaurant's front door and after a few seconds of hesitation he let her pass. "Just stay within twenty yards of this post, ma'am," he warned. "Don't go near the perimeter."

She realized what he meant as soon as she stepped outside. A hundred feet away a line of soldiers stood shoulder to shoulder, blocking the western end of Dyckman Street. Their obvious purpose was to stop any civilians from approaching the restaurant and marina. Just in case they needed help, at least thirty New York police officers stood on the other side of the line. Beyond the police were half a dozen news vans from the local television stations.

Because this was a classified operation, General Hanson had tried to disguise his unit's activities by making up a cover story. He'd told the news media that the soldiers were "conducting a routine training exercise related to national-security readiness." But the story hadn't fooled anyone. Despite the late hour, the TV people were doing live reports and pointing their cameras at the soldiers. The Air Force had brought in searchlights to illuminate the area, making it almost as bright as day, and the noise from the crowd gave the place a carnival atmosphere.

The temperature had dropped a few degrees since sunset, but the air still felt like warm cotton. Sarah ventured around the corner of the restaurant and headed for the marina. She walked down the pier and stopped at a railing that overlooked the Hudson River. Her hands were trembling but she managed to shake a cigarette out of the Marlboro pack and pull her Zippo from her pocket. It was a customized lighter with her name engraved on the brushed chrome. She flicked it open, lit her cigarette, and took a long drag.

To the west, the Coast Guard patrol boats cruised up and down the dark river, aiming their sonar at the Hudson's muddy bottom. To the east, the wooded heights of Inwood Hill Park loomed over the city. The soldiers hadn't cordoned off that section of the park because it wasn't part of the impact zone drawn by General Hanson and his staff. But Sarah didn't trust their judgment. Their mission was to prepare for a specific threat—a surprise attack from Russia or China or North Korea—so they naturally saw everything in those terms. Back in graduate school, Sarah had learned the name for this tendency: confirmation bias. The soldiers saw 2016X as a Russian weapon because that's what they expected to see.

She took another drag on her cigarette and gazed at Inwood Hill. She couldn't trust her own judgment either, because she also suffered from confirmation bias. That's what got her into trouble twenty years ago, a fervent belief that had swayed her thinking and muddied her scientific objectivity. And despite all the damage it had caused, she still clung to this belief. She hadn't learned a damn thing from her mistakes.

Sarah had been a different person back then: more outgoing and fun-loving, less wary and introspective. After getting her Ph.D. from Cornell at the precocious age of twenty-six, she landed a plum job at NASA's Johnson Space Center in Houston. Better still, she returned to Texas with the man she loved, a fellow researcher she'd met at Cornell. He'd also landed a job at NASA, and they got engaged a month after they started working there.

It was 1996 and NASA was laying the groundwork for the planetary rovers it would send to Mars over the next fifteen years—Sojourner, Spirit, Opportunity, and Curiosity. To determine which scientific instruments to put on the rovers, the agency assigned Sarah to study the best evidence of Martian geology it had: meteorites that had traveled from the Red Planet to Earth. Every million years or so, an asteroid hits Mars with such force that the explosive impact blasts rocks off the Martian surface and hurls them into space. After orbiting the sun for eons, some of the rocks get sucked in by Earth's gravity and land intact on the surface. Sarah's boss gave her one of these meteorites to study, a rock that had been ejected from Mars fifteen million years ago. Her task was to slice the meteorite into sections and use a powerful microscope to observe its crystalline structure.

At first the observations baffled her. The rock had crystallized from Martian lava during an era when the Red Planet was covered with oceans. In the cracks and pores of the meteorite Sarah found tiny globules of carbonate minerals that had most likely formed after water seeped into the rock. And within those globules she found even tinier structures that looked like rice grains and segmented tubes. She showed the microscope images to some of her colleagues and friends, hoping one of them might know what could have created the odd features. The answer came from another NASA researcher, Tom Gilbert, who had expertise in astrobiology and also happened to be Sarah's fiancé. He said he'd seen similar structures inside rocks found on Earth. They were the fossilized remains of ancient bacteria.

The next month was a frenzy of activity. Sarah gathered her evidence and showed it to her bosses. She spent months writing the research paper, carefully choosing her words. She couldn't say whether life still existed on Mars. Even if those tiny tubes were indeed fossils of microorganisms, the primitive creatures had probably gone extinct after the planet became drier and colder. But it was a momentous discovery nonetheless. It showed that Earth wasn't unique. Life could develop on many worlds across the galaxy.

NASA scheduled a press conference to announce the results. Unfortunately, someone leaked the news beforehand, and dozens of reporters flocked to Johnson Space Center. Sarah was delighted by all the attention, but when she came to the podium to answer the journalists' questions she spoke a bit too impetuously. She said the evidence for past life on Mars was clear and convincing. "We now have proof that we're not alone," she declared. "Extraterrestrial life is probably so abundant that we're bound to see more of it soon."

The reaction was swift. When a twenty-six-year-old researcher makes such sweeping statements and receives so much attention from the media, it can irritate people who've spent decades investigating the topic. Several scientists argued that the minuscule tubes inside the Martian meteorite weren't all that similar to the microfossils of Earth bacteria. Other researchers noted that ordinary geological heating and cooling could've created the microscopic structures. Within a few days it became clear she hadn't convinced the scientific community. The turnabout embarrassed NASA officials, and one of them asked Sarah to retract her claims about Martian life. At first she refused, but after several weeks of tension she gave in.

But that wasn't the worst blow. It was the end of her engagement that triggered her breakdown. When the criticism of Sarah's research started pouring in from all sides, her fiancé got nervous. Tom Gilbert was angling for a promotion to an administrative position at Johnson Space Center, and he knew he wouldn't get it unless he distanced himself from Sarah. So he reversed his earlier opinion, saying he'd been too hasty when he'd declared that the meteorite structures resembled microfossils. After studying the structures more carefully, he concluded there was little resemblance. He participated in a second NASA press conference at which researchers dismissed Sarah's findings.

She was horrified by his betrayal. Enraged, she sneaked into his office late at night and smashed his computer. She couldn't help it—her impetuosity got the best of her again. Then she broke into Tom's apartment, filled several suitcases with his clothing, and drove to a bridge that spanned the San Jacinto River, a few miles east of Houston. Stopping her car on the bridge, she hurled the suitcases into the river, along with her engagement ring and wedding dress. She almost threw herself into the river too, but instead she got back in her car and headed for New Mexico. The next morning, she checked into the mental-health treatment center in Santa Fe.

She never spoke to Tom again—he continued to move up the ladder at NASA and eventually became a science adviser at the White House—but she kept the Zippo lighter he'd given her. The name engraved on it was the one she would've had if they'd gotten married: Sarah Pooley Gilbert. She held on to the lighter to remind herself that the truth could be slippery. The truth about the meteorite changed when Tom realized it threatened his career at NASA. The truth about their relationship changed when Sarah realized her fiancé was an asshole. During her stay in the mental-health center, the truth changed every hour, every minute: she was sick, she was healthy, she was abnormal, she was normal. The smartest strategy was to get accustomed to the changes, to go with the flow, and this approach helped Sarah recover her sanity. Twenty years later, though, she still believed her research on the meteorite had been correct. She remained the discoverer of life on Mars, even if no other scientists agreed with her.

Now she took one last puff on her cigarette and threw the stub into a trash can. The truth about Object 2016X was also slippery. Unless someone retrieved a piece of the object they might never know where it had come from. Sarah looked again at the western slope of Inwood Hill. Although the Air Force wasn't interested in that section of the park, she'd included it in the broader impact zone she'd calculated for 2016X. She wondered if she could climb the wooded hillside and take a look around.

She eyed the soldiers in front of the restaurant. She knew she was supposed to respect the chain of command and tell General Hanson what she planned to do, but she didn't like the idea of asking for permission. And besides, the soldiers were so busy stopping people from entering the cordoned area that they might not even notice if someone tried to leave. Sarah edged away from the searchlights and sidled toward the baseball fields. She was looking for an unguarded path through the woods.

Then someone shouted at her. "Dr. Pooley?"

Startled, she spun around. It was the soldier who'd allowed her to leave the restaurant. He'd probably been watching her ever since. He frowned as he stepped toward her. "Ma'am, didn't I tell you to stay away from the perimeter?"

Sarah frowned too. "Sorry, I got lost."

"Then it's a good thing I found you. Come this way, please."

The soldier escorted her back to the restaurant. As she reentered the place she cursed herself for signing that damn contract with the Air Force. She headed straight for the dining room, intending to have a long talk with General Hanson. But one of his junior officers intercepted her and said the general was in a meeting with his staff. The officer instructed her to sit at a table next to the restaurant's bar until Hanson was free.

Another officer already sat at the table, a white-haired colonel in his late fifties or early sixties, with ruddy cheeks and bloodshot eyes. As Sarah approached he stood up and gave her a big smile. "Good evening, ma'am," he boomed. "You must be Sarah Pooley? The adviser from NASA that everyone's talking about?" He held out his right hand.

She hesitated, wondering how many Air Force officers knew about her assignment. Then she shook hands with the colonel. "Yes, that's me."

"My name's Raymond Gunter. I'm General Hanson's liaison officer. That means I do all the scut work the general doesn't have time for." His smile grew even bigger as he pumped Sarah's hand. "It's a real pleasure to meet you, ma'am. Everyone I've talked to says you're smarter than God."

She pulled her hand out of his grip. She was too tired to respond to Colonel Gunter's enthusiasm. Her mind was getting foggy, and she didn't like the way he was looking at her. He stared at her chest as she took a seat on the other side of the table.

"So you're waiting on the general too?" The man's voice had a country-and-western twang. "Got some business to discuss?"

She nodded, then reached into her pocket for her iPhone. In her opinion, the phone's best feature was its ability to deflect unwanted conversations. All you had to do was stare at the screen. Most people took the hint.

"Yep, the general's a busy man tonight," Gunter persisted. "I've been sitting here almost an hour, just waiting for him to get a free moment. And I got all sorts of urgent requests to pass along. From the mayor's office, the police department. Even the damn power company, Consolidated Edison of New York."

Sarah kept her eyes on the iPhone and tapped the screen a few times. From the corner of her eye she could tell that Gunter was still staring at her chest.

"You wouldn't believe it, ma'am. Here we are, in the middle of a genuine national-security crisis, and I have to deal with complaints from Con Edison. They say our operation is straining the resources of the local electric grid. They're blaming the Air Force for power interruptions all over the neighborhood." He let out a chuckle. "They claim we're using thirty megawatts. You're a scientist, ma'am, so I'm sure you must know how ridiculous that is."

This got Sarah's attention. Thirty megawatts was a lot of electricity. Overruling her better instincts, she looked up from her iPhone. "How much power are you actually using?"

Gunter was delighted that she'd answered him. His bloodshot eyes twinkled. "Well, we got five searchlights plugged into the restaurant's line, but each of those is just a one kilowatt job. You'd have to run 'em for ten years to drain as much power as they say we've done."

"So what's causing the power drain?"

The colonel raised both hands over his head in exasperation. "Ma'am, I have no idea! But if I had to guess, I'd say it's probably all the air conditioners in the neighborhood. It's hot as hell out there tonight, pardon my French."

She felt a jolt of adrenaline, strong enough to dispel her mental fog. She did a few quick calculations in her head. "You'd need forty thousand air conditioners to use that much power."

He nodded vigorously, bobbing his head. "You're absolutely right, ma'am. But this is a hell of a big town. I'm from Tupelo, Mississippi, and I bet you can fit a hundred Tupelos in New York City."

Sarah was fully awake now. She knew there were dozens of perfectly reasonable explanations for a power surge during the summer in New York. But she was getting a funny feeling about this, a mix of fear and hope that roiled her stomach.

She put her iPhone in her pocket and leaned toward Colonel Gunter. "Could you do me a favor, Colonel?"

His eyes widened. He looked as happy as a lottery winner. "As long as you don't ask me to break the law, ma'am, I'd be glad to help."

"Could you put me in touch with your contacts at Con Edison?"

EIGHT

Emilio was playing Battle Blood. Actually, he wasn't playing the game—
he was *crushing* it. He'd never had this many kills before. And the number was still rising fast, coming closer and closer to the all-time top-ten
list, which was displayed in the upper right corner of the flat-screen TV.
It was *un milagro*, a fucking miracle.

He'd started playing at 1:00 A.M., more than an hour ago. He and
Carlos sat on the couch in the living room of Carlos's apartment, both of
them facing the TV and the Xbox, but Carlos had been knocked out of
the game after the first fifteen minutes and now he was just watching
Emilio kick ass. Emilio's character in Battle Blood was a U.S. Marine
Corps sergeant in a camouflage uniform, a real badass who carried half
a dozen weapons. So far he'd shot his way through twelve of the game's
levels and wasted a hundred and ninety enemy soldiers in the process.
He needed just seven more kills to break into the top-ten list.

Level thirteen was a swamp in the jungles of Colombia and the opposing soldiers were Marxist guerillas, but Emilio had no more trouble
killing these *pendejos* than he'd had with the Chinese, Russian, and

North Korean soldiers on the previous levels. His Marine sergeant bounded across the TV screen, jumping over booby traps and quicksand as Emilio flicked the toggles on the Xbox controller. A couple of guerillas shot at him from a grass-thatched hut up ahead, but he leaped out of the line of fire and slaughtered both of them by strafing the hut with his carbine. When a black helicopter came swooping over the jungle, Emilio took cover behind a palm tree and used his grenade launcher to blow the chopper to bits. Finally, as the sergeant neared the guerilla headquarters, a giant crocodile lunged out of the swamp and snapped its jaws at him, but with one swift toggle Emilio pulled a knife from the sergeant's belt and stabbed the reptile in the eye.

"Ho, shit!" Carlos whooped. "You're a fucking Rambo, hombre!"

Emilio completed the level with a total of two hundred and nine kills, which put him eighth on the all-time list. He couldn't believe it. He'd played Battle Blood dozens of times before and never got past level five. Now, though, the game seemed so easy he didn't even need to concentrate on it. As he advanced to level fourteen—an urban-combat battle in the dusty streets of Baghdad—he kept one eye on Carlos's sister, Marisol, who'd come into the living room to watch the game. She was twenty-six, ten years older than Carlos, and pretty damn hot too. She had long black hair and caramel skin and plump *tetas* that ballooned the front of her red dress. She usually scowled at Emilio when he came to visit—she hated the Trinitarios and wanted Carlos to quit the gang—but now she smiled as she stood beside the couch and stared at the TV. Emilio waited until she turned her head, and then he winked at her, cool and slow. She opened her mouth in surprise, but after a couple of seconds she smiled again. Meanwhile, Emilio's sergeant kept running across the screen, and the number of kills rose higher and higher.

Emilio smiled too. He couldn't remember the last time he'd felt this good. It was probably because he'd finally gotten a decent amount of sleep. After the crazy night in Inwood Hill Park he'd crashed at his grandmother's apartment and slept from six in the morning until six in the evening. When he woke up he was so hungry he went to the pizza place on 204th Street and ordered four slices. Everyone there was talking about some terrorist attack that had supposedly happened near the river, so after he finished eating he headed for Dyckman Street. Several police cars blocked the western end of the street, and behind them was a whole fucking battalion of soldiers. But there were no ambulances and no dead bodies, and someone on the street said it was just a training exercise or something, so Emilio lost interest. He spotted Carlos in the crowd and they hung out for a few hours on Dyckman before going to Carlos's apartment to play Battle Blood.

After a few more minutes Emilio's sergeant massacred a dozen turban-wearing jihadis and completed level fourteen with two hundred and twenty-five kills. He was sixth in the all-time standings now. Carlos let out another whoop and Marisol came over to the couch and sat down between her brother and Emilio. It was a tight squeeze and her dress was short, so her bare thigh rubbed against Emilio's left leg. Although he didn't have much experience with women—he'd had sex only twice in his eighteen years, both times with girls his own age who'd seemed bored and disappointed—he sensed he had a decent chance with Marisol. As his Marine sergeant started climbing the icy Himalayan mountain that was the battlefield for level fifteen, Emilio mentally itemized four hopeful signs: 1) Marisol had broken up with her latest boyfriend two months ago; 2) she wore the short red dress because she'd gone out for a date that evening; 3) she'd come home early from the date, in a terrible mood; and 4) she'd had plenty of time to change out of the dress, but she hadn't yet.

Emilio knew there were obstacles too. He was eight years younger than her. He was also the leader of a gang she hated. But in his mind's eye he saw tactics and countertactics, strategies for overcoming each of Marisol's objections. It was just another game, as easy as Battle Blood. The only thing he didn't understand was why he'd found it so difficult before.

Marisol's eyes darted back and forth, following the gunfire that Emilio's sergeant was exchanging with the Pakistani commandos on screen. Emilio waited for a lull in the firefight, then leaned to the left, rubbing his shoulder against hers. "Hey, want to take over?" he asked, offering her the Xbox controller. "It's fun."

She shook her head. "Are you crazy? I'll ruin your score."

"Don't worry about that. I can always run it up again later."

"But you're so close!" She pointed at the screen. "Look, you're number three!"

He smiled again. "All right, I'll keep going until I hit number one. I'll do it for you."

Emilio turned back to the TV screen but he knew Marisol was looking at *him* now, not the game. He started thinking ahead, trying to figure out what he'd do when he reached the top of the all-time list, which was bound to happen in the next ten minutes or so. First, he'd tell Carlos to run downstairs and buy something at the bodega. Then he'd make up some bullshit story that would get Marisol's sympathy. He'd say he was planning to leave the Trinitarios and give up the gang life. Something like that. He might have to improvise, but he was confident of success.

Before he could rise any further in the standings, though, someone pounded on the apartment's front door and yelled, "Carlos! Open up!"

Emilio recognized the voice—it was Luis, the youngest and smallest kid in the Trinitarios, and he sounded frantic. Without any hesitation Emilio dropped the Xbox controller, ran to the door, and flung it open. Luis took a step backward, breathing hard. He seemed surprised to see Emilio but also relieved.

"*Coño!*" Luis panted. "I've been looking all over for you!"

"Calm down, *muchacho*." Emilio gripped the boy's shoulder and led him into the apartment. "Take a deep breath."

He obediently took several deep breaths. Carlos and Marisol got up from the couch and came over, but Luis kept his eyes on Emilio. "You gotta run! You gotta get out of the city!"

"Okay, slow down, first—"

"Paco has a gun! He says he's gonna kill you!"

Carlos whispered, "Fuck," and Marisol clapped her hand over her mouth. They wouldn't have been so alarmed if anyone else had made the threat, but Paco was a hard case. Emilio had recruited him to the Trinitarios to give the gang some street cred, but he'd known all along that the kid was troubled, and smacking him in the head last night had just made things worse. Now Paco was humiliated. He wanted revenge.

But strangely enough, Emilio wasn't worried. He was curious. He needed more information. He squeezed Luis's shoulder to get the boy's attention. "Did you see the gun?"

Luis nodded. "It was a nine millimeter, a fucking Glock. He pointed it at my face and asked me where you were." He started breathing fast again. "I told him I didn't know. And that was the truth, I didn't. And then I started looking for you, but I was worried he was gonna follow me, so I took the subway all the way to Queens and then doubled back."

"Good move. And then you came here?"

"No, I went to your grandmother's building, but I hid behind the cars on the other side of the street. Paco was in front of the building, watching the entrance." He paused, biting his lip. "And Miguel and Diego were with him."

Now Carlos slammed his palm against the wall and Marisol ran out of the room. This piece of news was even worse than the Glock. Paco had convinced two other Trinitarios to side with him. The gang had split right down the middle. And yet Emilio still wasn't worried. He let go of Luis's shoulder and turned to Carlos. "I'll take care of this. You stay here with Luis."

"What?" Carlos scrunched his face in disgust. "No, no fucking way." He stepped between Emilio and the door. "I'm going with you."

His voice was firm and his scowl was convincing, but Emilio saw through it. He knew Carlos was scared. He knew it with absolute certainty. He wasn't sure how he could be so certain—was he reading Carlos's body language? Hearing something behind his words?—but it didn't matter. The boy's fear made him useless. Emilio shook his head. "You'll only get in the way. I have a plan."

"What plan? What the fuck are you talking about?"

Emilio stepped closer and slapped his back. "It's a surprise, amigo. I'll tell you all about it when I get back. You're gonna laugh your ass off."

Carlos looked confused, but after a couple of seconds he backed down and moved away from the door, just as expected. Then Emilio left the apartment and bounded downstairs to the street.

He hadn't lied to Carlos. He *did* have a plan. It was so simple.

Emilio had to cross Dyckman Street to get to his grandmother's building, and along the way he saw the police cars and soldiers again, illuminated by the searchlights behind them. He didn't mind the soldiers—they reminded him of Battle Blood—but he hated the cops. They were the same bastards who'd arrested his uncles and cousins, all the Original Trinitarios who'd watched over Emilio since he was a kid.

Emilio had never met his father—the spineless *pendejo* had run back to the Dominican Republic right after Emilio was born—and his mother had died of breast cancer when he was just five. So his grandmother took him in, and for the next thirteen years she worked like a dog to feed and clothe him. But it was really the O.T.'s who raised him. While his grandmother worked double shifts at the McDonald's in Washington Heights, Emilio hung with the Trinitarios on 204th Street. They told him stories and bought treats for him—mango ices in the summer, churros in the winter. More important, they protected him from the neighborhood's bullies and lowlifes. From the day he started kindergarten to the day he dropped out of high school, the Trinitarios saved his ass at least a dozen times. In the beginning he was their mascot, *el Trinitario pequeño*, but as he grew older they gave him real jobs to do, like standing watch on the street corners, keeping an eye out for the police. They were going to make him a full member of the gang when he turned eighteen, but then the cops cracked down on the O.T.'s and sent all of them to prison.

Emilio was devastated. He tried to resurrect the Trinitarios by recruiting new people to the gang, but the arrests had scared off most of the *muchachos* in the neighborhood. The only homeboys willing to join were the young ones, the fifteen- and sixteen-year-olds who were too stupid to be scared. Emilio tried his best to teach them, but after six months he was ready to give up. His Trinitarios were a joke. All they wanted to do was hang out in the park and get high. When they rolled down the street everyone in the neighborhood laughed at them. And even so, Emilio knew it was just a matter of time before the NYPD cracked down on them too.

But he didn't get nervous tonight when he saw the bastard cops on Dyckman. He felt like he was wearing secret-agent glasses, like the kind that spies wear to see through brick walls, but his glasses were even better because they let him see what the cops were thinking. And what he saw was mostly fear. The police had no idea why the army had come to Inwood. They leaned against their cruisers, looking bored, but in reality they were scared shitless. They were outnumbered by the soldiers on one side and the onlookers from the neighborhood on the other. All they wanted to do was call it a night and drive back to their precinct house.

And when Emilio looked at the ordinary people on the street—the people staggering out of the bars and nightclubs and making their way toward the subway station—he saw what they were thinking too. Some of them were drunk and some were just tired. Some were thinking about music or food or sex, and some wanted to kill themselves. Although Emilio could see almost everything, he knew he wasn't actually reading their minds. He was just picking up clues he'd always ignored before—the way the people walked and laughed and moved their hands. It was amazing, the sheer quantity of information surrounding him. And so much of it was useful.

At the corner of Dyckman and Broadway he made a right and headed for Arden Street. He felt no apprehension at all about Paco and the others. On the contrary, a surge of joy ran through him, filling his whole body with confidence and hope. He realized that all his life he'd set his sights too low. He'd dreamed of leading a gang that would command the respect of his friends and neighbors, but that seemed like such a measly thing compared with the other dreams that crowded his head now. He could do so much more if he just put his mind to it.

When he reached Arden he turned left and slowed his pace. He crouched behind a parked car and peered at his grandmother's building, which was across the street and fifty yards down the block. Right away he spotted three figures in front of the building. The tall motionless figure was Paco and the short fidgety ones were Miguel and Diego. If Paco had been thinking strategically he would've ordered the two others to act as lookouts, but he obviously wasn't in a rational frame of mind. His motive was revenge, so he wasn't going to shoot from a distance. He wanted Emilio to come close. That would make the moment of payback so much more satisfying. And right now Emilio was happy to oblige him.

He came out of hiding and walked toward the three boys, strolling down the center of the deserted street. Miguel saw him first. The street was so quiet that Emilio could hear the boy whisper, *"Mira!"* Miguel and Diego stepped backward, retreating into the shadows by the building's entrance, but Paco just stood there, moving nothing but his eyes. All three of them wore the Trinitario colors—the white shirts, the baggy blue jeans, the green bandannas. When Emilio got within ten yards of the building he stepped onto the sidewalk and headed straight for Paco. The Glock was tucked into the waistband of Paco's jeans. He pulled it out as Emilio came toward him.

"Stop right there, *cabrón*." Paco pointed the gun at Emilio's chest. "We got some business to settle."

Emilio took another couple of steps before stopping. He was ten feet away from Paco, and his goal was to get closer. He'd remembered something he saw on the Internet a few weeks ago, a YouTube video showing two people in a similar situation. "Put the gun down, Paco. I'm not your enemy."

"Not my enemy?" While keeping the Glock steady, he raised his other hand and pulled up his bandanna a couple of inches. Underneath it was an ugly purple bruise on his forehead. "Then why did you do *this*?" he asked, pointing at the bruise. "If you're not my enemy, why'd you sucker punch me?"

"I made a mistake." Emilio took a step forward. "I want to apologize."

Paco stared at him, frowning. Then he let out a chuckle. "Damn, that's a good one. That's real funny." He glanced at Miguel and Diego. "Isn't that funny, *hermanos*?"

They nodded and started laughing, although without much conviction. Both of them stayed in the shadows and avoided eye contact. In all likelihood, they'd sided with Paco because they thought he'd kill them if they didn't.

Emilio took another step forward. Now there was less than five feet between them. "I'm serious. I went a little crazy last night. I shouldn't have hit you like that. "

"And now you think that'll make everything all right?" Paco's voice was high and angry. It echoed down the empty street. "You think you can say you're sorry and then we can be friends again?"

"I know it sounds stupid. But yeah, that's what I'm hoping." Emilio took one more step and extended his hands, palms up, in a pleading gesture. "Forgive me. *Por favor.*"

Paco trembled with anger. He raised the Glock until its muzzle was just an inch from Emilio's forehead. "You won't get any forgiveness from me, *pendejo*. You'll have to ask—"

Go!

Emilio heard the command inside his mind. It was as loud as a siren and yet absolutely silent. He instantly ducked his head below the muzzle and thrust his hands upward. This was the move he'd seen in the YouTube video, the self-defense technique he now remembered in such detail that he was able to reenact it without a moment's hesitation. He stretched both hands toward the Glock and wrapped them around its barrel.

At the same time, Paco pulled the trigger. The gun jumped in Emilio's hands and the shot rang in his ears, but the bullet went high and streaked harmlessly overhead. Then Emilio, still reenacting what he'd seen in the video, raised his right knee and kicked Paco in the groin. He put so much power into the kick that it lifted the boy off the ground.

Paco stumbled backward, landing on his ass, and Emilio wrenched the Glock out of his hands. Although he'd never touched a gun in his life, he expertly pulled back the slide and put another bullet in the chamber. Then he retreated several steps and aimed the gun at Paco, who was writhing in pain on the sidewalk.

The whole thing was over in less than two seconds. The noise had set off car alarms up and down the street, and Emilio's ears were still ringing from the gunshot, but he allowed himself a triumphant smile. Disarming Paco had been as easy as riding a bicycle. He couldn't understand how he'd become so skillful, and the sudden change was a little disturbing if he stopped to think about it. But it was also fucking great. Who knew what else he could do?

After a few more seconds he caught his breath and turned to Miguel and Diego. They were cowering against the brick wall of the apartment building, with their hands held high in surrender. Emilio stopped smiling and gave them a stern look. "Someone's gonna call the cops, so you better get out of here. Go on, *go!*"

The boys didn't argue. They took off down the street, running toward Broadway.

Paco didn't even notice that he'd lost his gang. He lay on his side, curled in the fetal position, his knees pulled up to his chest and his hands cupping his balls. As Emilio looked down at him, he imagined the boy's pain so vividly that he felt a twinge in his own crotch. Paco wasn't going to fight anymore. For at least the next ten minutes he would be as weak as a baby.

Emilio didn't need the Glock now. He removed the magazine from the gun and ejected the bullet from the chamber and stuffed everything into his pockets. Then he grabbed Paco's right arm and hoisted him to his feet.

"Come on," Emilio whispered. "I'll get you some ice."

Paco leaned against him as they entered the apartment building. The boy was wobbly and sweating buckets, but Emilio managed to steer him into the elevator. They got off at the fifth floor and Emilio used his key to get into his grandmother's apartment. Luckily, the old woman was a heavy sleeper. Emilio hauled Paco into the living room, dropped him on the couch, then went to the kitchen. He returned to the living room half a minute later and handed Paco an ice pack.

"Put this on your *cojones*," he instructed. "It'll stop the swelling."

Paco was still too shaky to resist. He took the pack, rested it over his groin, and closed his eyes. But Emilio knew the boy wouldn't remain cooperative for very long. As soon as Paco started feeling better he'd either lunge at Emilio or bolt out of the apartment. They had five minutes, at most, to come to an understanding.

Emilio sat on the other end of the couch. "I don't think you were planning to kill me. You were going to shoot me in the knee. To send me a message, *sí*?"

Paco kept his eyes closed and didn't say anything. But his cheek twitched, so Emilio knew he'd guessed right.

"And I don't blame you, amigo," he continued. "I'd do the same if someone sucker punched me. We're alike that way. We both know you have to be strong. You have to strike hard and fast, right? You have to kick the shit out of your enemy before he does it to you."

Now Paco grimaced. As his physical pain receded, his shame and rage came roaring back. He was starting to seethe again, starting to think about retaliation. Emilio needed to talk faster. His brain ratcheted up to a higher gear and retrieved everything he knew about Paco, every detail of the boy's life.

"But you have to be smart enough to know who your real enemy is. That's why I went crazy last night, when you were kicking that drunk in the park. I said to myself, 'Why are we beating on this guy? He's not our enemy. He's just a poor, sick asshole who's even worse off than we are.'"

Paco opened his eyes. He couldn't stand up yet, but he glared at Emilio. "You're fucked-up, hombre. You're seriously fucked-up."

"Just listen for a second. Who deported your father and sent him back to Santo Domingo? Who arrested your mom and put you in a foster home?"

"Don't—"

"You know what I'm talking about. Who hassles us in the stores and chases us out of the park and frisks us in the street? Who's been fucking with us every minute of our lives?"

"This is bullshit." Paco shook his head. "You can't do anything about the cops."

"It's not just the cops. It's the whole city, the whole government, all the white people who run it. That's the enemy. Those are the bastards I want to fight."

Paco grimaced again and readjusted his ice pack. "And how are you gonna fight them? You want to be a terrorist? You want to blow shit up?"

Emilio smiled. It was working. He'd gotten Paco interested. "No, that's the wrong weapon. This country is built on money. If you want power and respect, you need to get money first. Serious money." He pointed at the boy's chest. "That's why I wanted to have this conversation. You're like me, Paco—you're a little crazy, but you're smart. You're a hell of a lot smarter than Miguel and Carlos and the rest of them. And I need someone smart to help me."

Paco sat up a bit straighter on the couch. He was feeling better now, probably good enough to take a swing at Emilio or grab his throat. But instead Paco looked him in the eye. "Help you do what?"

For a moment Emilio didn't know what to say. To be honest, he hadn't thought that far ahead. His plan had been to turn things around with Paco and regain the boy's trust, and he was already halfway there. But Emilio hadn't figured out his final goal yet. He knew it had to be something big, something fucking amazing, but it was still cloudy in his mind, a half-formed thought. Clenching his jaw, he shifted his brain to an even higher gear. He scrolled through everything he knew, searched all his memories.

In the meantime, he leaned closer to Paco and lowered his voice. "Can you keep a secret?"

The boy nodded. "Of course."

Emilio waited a few more seconds, and then the answer came to him. It was a memory from ten years ago, a class trip he took in third grade, a subway ride downtown to a room full of crystals.

"This is a big-money job, almost half a million dollars," he told Paco. "Tomorrow night we're gonna break into the American Museum of Natural History."

NINE

After waking from his nightmare, Joe finished off the third of his four bottles of Olde English. Unfortunately, the malt liquor didn't help. It stilled his trembling hands but did nothing to ease his terror.

He'd moved even farther from the satellite, more than a hundred yards away. Now he sat on a massive crag that jutted from the hilltop like the prow of a steamship. He was perched on the highest point of the outcrop, twenty feet above the muddy ground, but at any second he expected to see another black tentacle slither up the rock face. He turned his head at every sound, peering in all directions, looking for signs of movement in the darkness. He assumed he was going mad. That was the most logical explanation.

And yet there was the cut on his neck, the tiny puncture wound. He kept touching it, fingering it, to reassure himself that it was real. It was just like the wound on the teenager's palm, and the one on Dorothy's foot. The satellite had attacked all three of them in the same way. And their symptoms were the same, too: numbness and intense pain that flared up, then faded. Joe tried to remember everything he'd learned about drug reactions during medical school and the years afterward, but he couldn't think of any pharmaceutical compound that would produce the fleeting symptoms he'd felt. If he had to guess, he'd say some kind of neurotoxin had inflamed his nerve cells. In other words, a poison.

He shook his head and tightened his grip on the empty Olde English bottle. Why was this happening? Because he deserved more punishment? Were the daily humiliations not enough? Were his sins so horrible that he needed to suffer worse?

The moon rose above Inwood's apartment buildings, just like it had the night before. As it inched higher, Joe's stomach churned with dread and hunger. He knew he'd feel better if he ate something, and for a moment he thought of the cans of peanuts Dorothy had left in the clearing. But he wasn't going to risk going back there. Instead he put the empty bottle of Olde English aside and reached for the last full one.

He felt the usual rush as he twisted off the bottle cap. The malt liquor wasn't cold anymore, but that didn't matter. He was comforted by the weight of the bottle in his hand, the full forty ounces sloshing inside. This was the best moment, loaded with anticipation. Joe had given up all the little pleasures of his old life for this one big pleasure. And as part of the same bargain, he'd traded all his little problems for this one really big problem.

He lifted the bottle to his lips and tilted his head back. But as the warm liquid poured into his mouth, the taste made him gag. He spat out the stuff, spraying it all over himself. At first he assumed the malt liquor was spoiled. Sometimes the local bodegas sold bottles that had been opened and left sitting on the shelf for months. Joe had bought some spoiled Olde English just a few weeks ago, in fact. But that stuff wasn't so terrible, only a little vinegary, not bad enough to stop Joe from drinking it. The liquor in his hands now was much, much worse, more like rotten meat. He raised the bottle to his nose and the smell was so bad he jerked his head away. It was putrid, unbearable.

He held the bottle at arm's length and peered through the glass, wondering if a dead mouse was floating inside, but the moonlight showed nothing but clear, brown liquor. Then another thought occurred to him, and his heart started pounding. He put down the full bottle of Olde English, then reached for one of the empty bottles and raised it to his nose. It smelled just as awful as the full one. He flung it away in disgust, and a moment later it shattered in the woods.

Joe clenched and unclenched his hands. He was breathing fast and his mind was racing, but he forced himself to slow down and think. Just fifteen minutes ago he'd been swigging malt liquor, but now the taste and smell of it nauseated him. *It's not spoiled,* he thought. *It was the same with both bottles. I'm having some kind of reaction to the stuff. The change is in my head, my body.*

Then he remembered something else from medical school, a drug called Antabuse. It interfered with the body's normal processes for breaking down alcohol. If you were on Antabuse and you drank any kind of booze, the chemicals would build up in your bloodstream and you'd feel horribly nauseous. Within a few days just the sight of alcohol would make you sick. So doctors sometimes prescribed Antabuse for hopeless alcoholics who couldn't stop drinking any other way. Joe felt like the same thing had just happened to him, but incredibly quickly, within the past fifteen minutes. And the only thing that could've caused the change was the poison that had been injected into his neck.

Panic choked him. His throat tightened so much he started to wheeze. *Shit! Think! You have to think, goddamn it!* He raised his hands to his head and squeezed his skull, hoping the physical pressure would somehow focus his mind. *If the poison is a neurotoxin, it affects nerve cells. And that means it's going to affect the brain, too. So you should examine yourself. Look for other symptoms.*

Joe started by wiggling his fingers and toes. Then he flexed his arms and legs and twisted his torso. His cracked ribs didn't hurt as much as they had yesterday, but that was probably just ordinary healing at work. He tested his reflexes and did a couple of mental exercises—counting backwards by sevens, recalling the names of the last five presidents. Finally, he checked the glands in his throat and measured his pulse, which he'd learned to do without a watch back when he was an intern. His heart rate was on the high side, about ninety beats per minute, but he could blame the panic for elevating it. Other than that, he was fairly healthy for a drunk.

At a loss, he hugged his knees to his chest. The full bottle of Olde English still stood next to him on the crag, but he couldn't even look at it. He stared instead at the city below, the moonlight shining on the Tenth

Avenue subway line and the windows of the buses parked at the depot. Although it was a peaceful scene, in his present state of mind everything seemed ominous. Being poisoned was bad enough, but that wasn't the only reason for his panic. His biggest fear was that the changes to his nervous system might be permanent. How could he get through the day without drinking?

Then he noticed the second symptom. He was looking again at the bus depot and the moonlight gleaming off the bus windows and all at once he realized he saw everything much too clearly. Even though the depot was almost a mile away, Joe could read the ads displayed on the sides of the buses. He could also read the signs above the subway station at 215th Street and the billboards along the Major Deegan Expressway in the Bronx. Within the past hour his eyesight had improved way beyond twenty-twenty. And though most people might consider this a positive change, the fact that it was beneficial actually made it more disturbing. The body was a finely tuned engine. Lots of chemicals could damage it, but very few could make it run better.

Joe scanned the horizon, trying to determine exactly how far he could see. Because the crag was at the top of the hill he could glimpse the Hudson River to the west if he turned around and peered through the tree branches. He craned his neck, looking for the George Washington Bridge, but instead he spotted several bright lights along the riverbank, about half a mile to the south. On the river itself were the silhouettes of half a dozen large boats, and when Joe squinted he could see the Coast Guard markings on their hulls.

The sight made him curious. Then he thought about it and grew agitated. Why were so many Coast Guard boats on the Hudson? Was it a rescue operation? Was there some kind of disaster on the river?

Or was it a search?

He became so jumpy he could feel the blood pulsing in the backs of his knees. He needed to move closer to the hill's western slope so he could see past the trees and get a better look. But that would mean leaving the safety of the crag. He'd have to run through the woods, which scared the hell out of him. He suspected that all of Inwood Hill Park was laced with tentacles by now. In his mind's eye he saw them creeping underground, twisting between the tree roots.

But he couldn't stay on the crag forever. And he'd already been attacked once, so maybe that gave him some immunity. Taking a deep breath, he rose to his feet and clambered down the side of the outcrop. He paused at the lowest part of the rock slab and gathered up his courage. Then he stepped off the slab and started running.

The muddy ground didn't give him much traction, but soon he was tearing through the woods. His fear made him nimble: he leaped over the fallen branches and sidestepped the piles of leaf litter. In thirty seconds he crossed to the western side of the hill, but the trees still blocked his view of the riverbank. So he headed south, toward the bright lights, even though this brought him closer to the clearing where the satellite was. He sensed its presence to his left, about fifty yards away, but he didn't look in that direction. He trained his eyes to the right and looked for a break in the trees.

Finally, after thirty more seconds, he reached a lookout point where the slope fell steeply toward the West Side Highway, giving him an unobstructed view of the riverbank. When Joe looked toward the lights he saw a line of soldiers on Dyckman Street. More soldiers stood behind the line, guarding the entrance to the marina, and still more were in the baseball fields, pointing flashlights every which way.

Yes, Joe thought, *they're searching for something. And it must be something important, so important that they'd send a small army to find it. What else could it be but the satellite?*

Joe didn't care anymore about collecting the reward. Well, no, that wasn't true: he still cared about it, but now his terror was stronger than his hope. He needed to tell the soldiers what had happened, how the satellite had burrowed into the ground and injected a neurotoxin into him. Then maybe they'd send him to an army hospital and the doctors there would give him an antidote. He'd also tell them about Dorothy and that teenager in the gang. And then the soldiers would dig up the satellite and shut it off before it could hurt anyone else.

He turned around and looked for the asphalt pathway that went down the hill toward the park's Dyckman Street exit. While he dashed through the woods he glanced at the clearing and noted the positions of the trees and rock slabs nearby. He was trying to memorize the location, fixing it in his mind so he could tell the soldiers exactly where to go. But as he came within thirty yards of the place he noticed that his cardboard box was no longer at the center of the clearing. The crumpled thing lay next to the base of an oak tree, about fifteen feet away from where he'd left it.

Joe stopped in his tracks and stared at the box that was supposed to be covering the satellite. Did someone move it? Did those teenagers return to the clearing while he was asleep? And did the satellite attack them again? He didn't want to get any closer, but he needed to know.

He stepped toward the clearing, keeping his eyes on the ground. He saw nothing slithering in the mud, but he could picture the tentacles just a few feet below, sensitive to even the smallest vibrations in the earth. He imagined they could detect the noise of his footfalls, so he moved slowly and silently, choosing each step with care. When he was twenty yards away he lifted his head and peered through the branches. He focused on the center of the clearing, where he'd buried the satellite and later dug a trench around it.

But now the satellite wasn't there. There was no mound or trench, no gouges in the mud. The ground was perfectly smooth and bare.

Joe thought of two explanations. It was possible that the satellite had never existed. He could've hallucinated everything that had happened over the past twenty-four hours.

Or the satellite had hidden itself. If it could extend tentacles underground, through dozens of yards of dirt and rock, why couldn't it bury itself deeper and fill in all the holes in the mud above it?

He had no time to figure out which explanation was better. Instead, he backed away from the clearing until he reached the asphalt pathway. Then he ran out of the park as fast as he could.

When he got to Dyckman Street he saw the soldiers up close, under the blinding searchlights. They wore the typical camouflage uniforms, dappled with splotches of beige and green, but there were no patches on their shoulders to identify which units they belonged to. Joe guessed they were trying to hide the true purpose of their operation from the public, which was exactly what you'd expect them to do if they were searching for a top-secret satellite. He let out a sigh of relief, glad that he hadn't imagined the whole thing.

Now that he was here, though, he faced the problem of finding the right person to talk to. The soldiers blocking the western end of the street were clearly from the lower ranks, privates and corporals who probably didn't know why they'd been sent to New York. Joe needed to talk to their commanders, the colonels and generals. He supposed he'd have to work his way up the chain of command, asking one of the enlisted men to put him in touch with their superiors. But before he could do that, he needed to get past the police officers who stood between the soldiers and the crowd on the street.

The onlookers were the kind of people who stayed awake past 2:00 A.M.—drunks and thugs and insomniacs and teenagers. Joe angled around the crowd and eyed the cops, trying to figure out who was in charge. After a few seconds he focused on a middle-aged, heavyset police captain wearing a white shirt and a blue tie. The man had flabby cheeks and wispy gray hair and looked like a cheerful, levelheaded character. Joe tried to make himself look presentable, brushing the dirt off his pants and his Yankees jacket. Then he approached the police captain, who was leaning against his cruiser and chatting with two other officers. The nameplate under the captain's badge said MOORE.

"Excuse me, sir?" Joe stopped several feet in front of him, keeping a deferential distance. "Can I talk to you for a second?"

Captain Moore turned to him and grinned. "Well, well. What's on your mind?"

The man sounded amused. He was probably bored as hell and grateful for a distraction. Joe just hoped the guy would take him seriously. "Sir, I have some information that might be useful. To the military, I mean." He pointed at the line of soldiers. "Could you take me to one of their commanders?"

"Really? Useful information?" Still grinning, Moore hooked his thumbs into the waistband of his pants. "Are you a spy or something?"

Joe frowned. "No, I'm a concerned citizen. I know why the soldiers are here and I think I can help them."

"Well, that's very kind of you. But I'm sure the army can do just fine on its own."

"No, wait, you don't understand. Something dangerous is happening." Joe raised his voice, trying to get his point across. He looked over his shoulder at Inwood Hill Park, then turned back to the police captain. "A satellite crashed into the park and now it's out of control. It's extending tentacles and injecting people with poison, some kind of neurotoxin. So you can't just stand there. You need to do something about it."

Moore stopped grinning. He glanced at the other officers, and they moved toward Joe. The captain moved forward too. "All right, calm down. I'm gonna ask you to step back now. Because this area is for police officers only."

Joe shook his head. This was going even worse than he'd expected. The captain wasn't listening at all. "I know where the satellite crashed. I can show the soldiers exactly where. All you have to do is take me to their commander and—"

"Hey!" Someone behind Joe grabbed his shoulder and pulled him away from the captain. "I know you!"

The voice was familiar, but not in a good way. Joe's stomach clenched. He turned his head and saw Officer Patton, the big redheaded cop who patrolled Inwood Hill Park.

Patton scowled and tightened his grip on Joe's shoulder. Then he turned to Captain Moore. "This is one of the crazies who sleep on the hill. I've told him a hundred times he can't sleep there, but he never listens."

Joe was desperate. He focused on Moore and gave him a pleading look. "I'm not crazy! Just ask the soldiers! They're looking for the satellite!"

The captain wrinkled his nose. Then he stepped backward and waved them off. "Shit, get this guy out of here. The smell is making me sick."

Keeping his grip on Joe's shoulder, Patton used his other hand to remove his nightstick from his belt. "You heard the man. Better move quick, or I'll send you to my buddies at Rikers."

He pointed the nightstick at Joe and gave him a poke. Officer Patton had done this many times before, whenever he rousted Joe from the park, but this time the end of the nightstick prodded Joe's cracked ribs. A bolt of pain shot through his chest. Without thinking, he spun around, grabbed the nightstick and wrenched it out of Patton's grip. Then, continuing the same fluid motion, he jabbed the stick in the officer's belly.

It happened so fast that Joe felt like someone else had done it. He stood there, astonished, while Patton stumbled backward and landed on his ass. Then he watched all the other cops draw their guns from their holsters.

"Drop the stick, asshole!"

The warning came from the officer closest to him, a young guy with darting eyes, so frightened he couldn't hold his gun steady. In an instant Joe saw a way to disarm him. All he had to do was leap forward, swing the nightstick around, and hit the kid in the knees. The other cops wouldn't fire for fear of shooting their fellow officer, and that would give Joe enough time to grab the kid's gun. It was so simple and straightforward that Joe almost did it automatically. He had to yell at himself to come to his senses. *Jesus, don't make it worse! You're in enough trouble already!*

Joe dropped the nightstick and raised his hands in surrender. "Don't shoot! I didn't mean to—"

Before he could finish, one of the cops tackled him from behind. Joe's head hit the pavement and everything went black.

TEN

Dorothy stood at the back of a crowded elevator at Sloan Kettering Cancer Center. Eleven people were crammed into the tight space this morning, most of them patients and their family members heading for their first appointments of the day. The elevator rose slowly, stopping at every floor, so Dorothy had plenty of time to scrutinize her fellow passengers. She could tell right away which ones were the cancer patients. She could also tell how serious each patient's illness was.

Standing to her right, for example, was a white-haired gentleman in a pin-striped suit. He looked like a wealthy businessman, but his face was pale and nervous. Dorothy guessed he was scheduled for a biopsy, and sure enough he got off the elevator at the third floor, where the endoscopic biopsies were done. To her left was a tall, young woman wearing a pink turban to hide her baldness. She got off at the fifth floor and hobbled toward the chemotherapy room. And in front of Dorothy was a skeletal man in a wheelchair who wheezed and trembled. At the sixth floor a nurse's aide pushed the wheelchair off the elevator and steered it toward the palliative care suite, which was where patients went when there was nothing left to do but ease their pain. As the elevator doors closed, Dorothy composed a brief prayer for the man: *Lord, let it be quick. Let him climb up to Heaven with as little suffering as possible.*

Her own destination was the Radiology Department on the twelfth floor. She was going to have another PET scan to see how far her cancer had metastasized. Although it was somewhat pointless—she already knew from the last scan that the tumors had spread from her pancreas to her liver—her doctor had ordered the test anyway. He was a kind man, an inveterate optimist, and he was determined to do all he could for her. But there were no effective treatments for her cancer. She had two or three months left, at most.

At the seventh floor another chemo patient stepped off the elevator, and at the ninth floor a couple of doctors got on. Although the pain in Dorothy's abdomen was steadily worsening, she stood there without complaint, watching the hopeful and the hopeless come and go. Then the doors finally opened on the twelfth floor, and she saw the sign saying RADIOLOGY on the opposite wall and the waiting room full of anxious patients. But she didn't step out of the elevator. She stayed absolutely motionless as the doors closed.

The elevator continued upward till it reached the sixteenth floor, and then it slowly descended. Dorothy remained at the back of the car, watching everything but doing nothing. She didn't know what she was waiting for. She was a little puzzled by her indecision, but she wasn't alarmed. She just needed some time to think and pray. She'd felt uneasy ever since her visit to Inwood Hill Park yesterday, more irritable and less interested in keeping up appearances. She saw no need to get another PET scan now just to make her doctor happy. There were a million better ways to spend her time, and sooner or later she'd figure out what she wanted to do. Until then she was perfectly willing to keep riding up and down.

After five minutes she was back at the lobby. Everyone else left the elevator, but Dorothy stayed where she was, and a new load of passengers crowded around her. Then the elevator stopped at the fifth floor again, but this time she noticed a sign that said LABORATORIES and an arrow pointing to the right. She stepped out of the elevator, using her canvas shoulder bag to nudge the other passengers aside.

She turned right and started walking down a long corridor. The cancer center occupied the entire block between 67th and 68th streets, and the corridor connected the main hospital building on the east side of the block with the neighboring buildings on the west side. Dorothy had never gone this way before, but it looked a lot like the rest of the hospital. The color scheme was soothing, mostly beige and white. The walls were decorated with quaint pictures of birds. She passed a room full of vending machines—Coke, candy, chips, ice cream—then turned a corner and found herself in a sleek corridor with more offices and no patient rooms. The doors on both sides of the corridor were made of blond wood, and each had a small identifying sign: IMMUNOLOGY, DEVELOPMENTAL BIOLOGY, MOLECULAR BIOLOGY.

Dorothy shook her head as she read the signs on the doors, wondering what went on in the laboratories behind them. She'd taken a biology course when she was a freshman in college, but that was forty years ago. Everything she'd learned had probably been proven wrong since then. She finally came to the end of the corridor, and the sign on the last door said CELL BIOLOGY. She wasn't sure how cell biology differed from molecular biology or developmental biology, but for some reason she felt a powerful surge of curiosity. She needed to see what was inside that lab. It seemed much more worthwhile than getting another PET scan. The scan might tell her how much time she had left, but she didn't really care about the *when* of her death—she cared about the *why*. She wanted to know more about the thing that was killing her.

She opened the door and stepped inside. It was a big windowless room divided into four sections by long Formica-topped workbenches. Several microscopes and computers sat on the workbenches, and on the shelves above them was an assortment of vials and flasks. There were also a few sinks and a couple of big freezers and lots of high-tech equipment that Dorothy couldn't even begin to fathom. The lab looked clean and well-organized but not very busy. She poked her head into two of the sections and saw no one working in them. She guessed that the scientists preferred to do their experiments late at night, so they probably didn't start work until later in the morning.

The third section was empty too, but when Dorothy looked into the fourth she saw someone sitting in front of a computer at the far end of the workbench. It was a young African American woman, in her late twenties or early thirties, dressed in a white lab coat. On her computer screen was a picture of a colorful clump that looked a bit like a ball of yarn. The woman stared at the thing with the utmost concentration, as if trying to unravel it. Dorothy felt a sudden rush of pride—she was delighted that the first scientist she saw was black. The woman was so focused on her clump that she didn't notice Dorothy at first, but after a few seconds she turned her head and jumped a bit in her chair.

"Oh, my," she muttered, catching her breath. "You gave me a scare. Can I help you?"

Dorothy stepped toward her. The young woman's hair was a mess but her face was quite pretty: full lips, chiseled cheekbones, gorgeously arched eyebrows. In Dorothy's younger days the sight of such a pretty face would've been enough to make her jealous, since her own face was so homely and her figure was nothing to brag about. But now, thank the Lord, she was free of the sin of envy. Now she could truly appreciate this beautiful creature God had made. But she didn't want to scare the poor girl any more than she already had, so instead of talking about God and beauty Dorothy pointed at a nearby chair.

"I'm sorry, can I sit down for a minute?" She dropped her canvas shoulder bag on the floor. "This hospital is so big, you can get lost in it. I've been riding up and down the elevator and walking down the hallways."

The woman's eyes widened with concern. "Of course, sit down! Are you feeling ill? Should I call for an aide?"

"No, no, I'm fine. I just need to get off my feet." Dorothy slumped into the chair and let out a sigh. "Ah, that's better. I'm truly, truly sorry for interrupting your work. Are you a scientist, dear?"

"Uh, yes, I'm a postdoc, a medical researcher. Dr. Naomi Sanford." Her tone was polite but wary. "So do you have an appointment at the hospital?"

"I certainly do. I'm supposed to get another scan today. But to be honest with you, Naomi, I don't really feel like going. That's why I've been wandering around so much, I guess. I've been putting off the inevitable."

"Yes, I understand." She nodded, but her expression was more impatient than sympathetic. She clearly wanted to get back to her work. "But I'm sure your doctor has a good reason for ordering the scan. It's going to help him treat you."

"Not in my case, I'm afraid. You see, I have pancreatic cancer and it already metastasized. So what's the use of another scan?"

Naomi bit her lip. She was a medical researcher, so she probably knew the mortality rate for that type of cancer. "I'm so sorry." She looked at

Dorothy more intently, similar to the way she'd stared at the clump on her computer screen. "You know, Sloan Kettering has a counseling center that offers services to all patients. Can I call the center for you?"

Dorothy shook her head. She didn't need counseling, at least not from the hospital's psychologists. Instead, she stared at Naomi's workbench. Next to her computer was a flask of bright red liquid, the same color as cherry Kool-Aid, and beside the flask was an odd-looking tray made of clear plastic. The plastic was indented with six cups, like a muffin tray, but each cup was more than three inches wide and only an inch deep. And in each shallow cup was a thin coating of the bright red liquid. Dorothy felt a strange fluttering in her stomach as she stared at the thing. *This is important,* she thought. *You have to ask about this.*

She pointed at it. "Is this medicine, dear?" She looked at Naomi and smiled. "Are you working on a cure for cancer?"

The young woman smiled back at her, but it was a sad, tired smile. "No, it's not medicine. We're still a long way from a cure, unfortunately. But we *are* working hard." She tapped the tray. "This is called a cell culture plate. It has six wells, and in each one we're growing colonies of stem cells. That liquid is the growth medium, and the colonies are attached to the bottom of the well."

"Stem cells? I think I've heard of them before, but I can't remember what they are."

"They're tiny miracles. That's the best way to describe them." Naomi leaned back in her chair. "The inside of a human embryo is full of stem cells. They have the ability to turn into any kind of body tissue—skin, muscle, nerves, bone. They're the key to human development, how a microscopic embryo becomes a baby." She pointed at Dorothy, then at herself. "And adults have stem cells too, especially in the bone marrow. They're constantly producing new blood cells, because we need a whole lot of them."

Naomi gestured with great vivacity, waving and pointing as she spoke, and her face got even prettier. She obviously enjoyed talking about her work. And Dorothy grew more and more impressed. She wanted to keep the conversation going for as long as possible. "Can stem cells cure cancer? Is that why you're growing them?"

"Well, stem cells are already used in some cancer treatments. For leukemia patients we inject stem cells into their bone marrow to replace the ones killed by radiation and chemotherapy." She tapped the cell culture plate again. "But the real goal is figuring out how stem cells work. Stem cells and cancer cells are very similar. They're both like the Superman of cells—adaptable and fast-multiplying and hard to kill. But even Superman has a weakness, right? If we can learn what makes the cells so tough, then maybe we can also discover their vulnerabilities."

Dorothy muttered, "Amazing!" but she was reacting more to Naomi herself than to the research she'd just described. The young woman was so passionate about her work, so fiercely dedicated. And the fact that she was African American made her all the more precious. For Dorothy, who'd struggled for decades to get the Episcopal church to pay more attention to racial equality, the existence of someone like Naomi was a sign from God. It was proof that a black woman could do *anything*. It was such a joyous sight that Dorothy started to cry.

She reached into her shoulder bag and found a Kleenex. "Forgive me, dear. What you're saying is so wonderful, I'm overcome." She dabbed her cheeks, wiping away the tears. "Your work is a blessing. It's going to help so many people."

Naomi furrowed her brow. She looked a little uncomfortable, thrown off balance by Dorothy's reaction. "I . . . I don't want to give you the wrong idea. This research is just beginning. It might take years to learn something useful from the experiments."

Now Dorothy was crying too hard to speak. The power of her feelings surprised her. She realized there was another reason for her emotional turmoil, and it had nothing to do with race or religion. It was more personal and painful. Dorothy had always wanted a daughter. When she looked at Naomi she saw the child she'd dreamed about for so many years. She could've had a daughter just like this one, a golden girl to love and cherish. All of it would've been possible if only she'd made wiser choices.

While Dorothy wept, Naomi tactfully turned away and kept herself busy. She fitted a clear plastic lid over the cell culture plate, then carried it to a steel cabinet that looked a bit like a dishwasher. She opened the cabinet's door and put the plate on a shelf that already held a stack of plates just like it. Then she closed the cabinet and returned to her chair. After another half minute she turned back to Dorothy and gently touched her shoulder. "You really should go to your appointment," she whispered. "Even if it's a waste of time. Otherwise, they'll worry about you."

Dorothy's crying subsided. She dabbed her cheeks again and took a couple of deep breaths. She felt better now, much better, because she'd just had a revelation. In the midst of her sorrow she'd heard the Lord's voice. It was loving and soft, so soft only Dorothy could hear it. He didn't speak to her in human words; no, he spoke in pictures and signs and thoughts and emotions, but she understood him just the same. He'd told her there was a way to redeem her life, to fix everything that was broken. And it was so simple, so easy. The Lord had told her exactly what to do.

She raised her head and looked Naomi in the eye. "Yes, dear, you're right. I'll go get the scan. But could you do me a favor? I'm very thirsty."

Naomi stood up. "Would you like a cup of water?"

"I know it's unhealthy, but I'd actually prefer a cola." Dorothy reached into her shoulder bag and pulled out a handful of quarters and dimes. "I saw some vending machines on my way over here. Could you please get a can of Diet Coke for me? I'll feel better after a few sips, and then I can go."

She extended her arm, offering the handful of change. Naomi stared at it for moment, clearly reluctant. The vending machines were pretty far down the corridor, in one of the neighboring buildings, at least a two-minute walk away. But after a couple of seconds she scooped the quarters and dimes out of Dorothy's palm. "I'll be right back," she said. "Just don't touch anything, all right?"

"Thank you, dear."

Dorothy waited until Naomi left the laboratory. Then she rose from her chair and went to the steel cabinet that looked like a dishwasher. She opened the cabinet and felt a blast of warm air on her face. The air was drier than what you'd expect from a dishwasher, and after a moment she realized it was an incubator. A stack of nine cell culture plates sat on the shelf, warmed to human body temperature.

She reached for her shoulder bag and made some room by dumping out her magazines and the box of Kleenex tissues. Then she removed the stack of cell culture plates from the incubator and carefully placed it in the bag. Luckily, she didn't have to worry that the stem cells would die of cold. The temperature outside was pretty darn close to 98.6 degrees.

Hoisting the bag to her shoulder, she went to the laboratory's door and opened it. She looked up and down the corridor but didn't see

Naomi. So she turned right, away from the vending-machine room, and headed for the bank of elevators.

As she left the cancer center and walked down the broiling street, Dorothy composed another prayer: *Lord, please help me to understand your plan. I don't know why you asked me to betray that young woman, but I'm sure you have your reasons. And even if I still can't understand your reasoning, Lord, give me the faith and courage to accept it anyway. Give me the strength to carry out your will.*

Amen.

ELEVEN

Sarah met Con Edison inspector Gino Torelli at noon near the western end of Dyckman Street, within sight of the soldiers and police cars. He drove there in a specially modified vehicle, a pickup truck with video cameras on both sides of the truck bed. Extending from the back of the vehicle was a foot-wide pod-shaped device, encased in hard white plastic. Sarah recognized it because she'd seen similar devices on cruise ships and airliners. It was a directional antenna, one that could detect extremely faint radio waves.

Colonel Gunter had set up the meeting, and fortunately he'd been discreet. He hadn't asked Sarah why she was so interested in the power surges in Inwood. He'd simply warned her not to reveal any classified information. After contacting Torelli and scheduling the rendezvous, the colonel escorted Sarah to the checkpoint in front of the marina and ordered the soldiers to let her leave the restricted area. He also did her the favor of not mentioning the meeting to General Hanson. If Hanson had known about it, he probably would've asked Sarah a few questions she wasn't ready to answer yet.

As she walked toward the truck, Torelli leaned over to the passenger side and opened the door for her. Although the guy was Con Edison's top inspector for Manhattan, in charge of investigating any misuse of the city's electric lines, he dressed like an ordinary repairman. He wore a blue Con Ed hard hat and a gray jumpsuit with his last name stitched on the chest. He was in his fifties and seemed irritable and suspicious.

He frowned as he looked at Sarah, who still hadn't changed out of her Grateful Dead T-shirt. "Seriously? You're with the Air Force?"

"Only temporarily. I'm an adviser on loan from another government agency." She climbed into the passenger seat and closed the door behind her. The truck's cab was air-conditioned, and it felt wonderful to get out of the heat. She smiled at Torelli and held out her right hand. "My name's Sarah."

He shook her hand but kept frowning. "You have a last name, Sarah?"

She shook her head. If she mentioned her last name, Torelli might Google her and discover she worked for NASA. Then he might guess why the Air Force was here. "Sorry, I can't say. The military folks have me on a tight leash. I hope you'll understand."

"Oh yeah, I get it." His voice was full of exasperation. "You guys are conducting a training exercise. Perfectly routine."

"I want to ask you about the surges in power usage in this area. Where exactly—"

"First let *me* ask *you* a question. How can you expect cooperation if you lie to us?" He pointed at the soldiers massed at the end of the street. "I don't know what your secret mission is, and I don't really care. But I do know you're using a shitload of power. You must be running some heavy-duty motors off our electric lines, or you're using the power for desalination or something like that. Either way, we're talking at least thirty megawatts, and that extra load is way too much for the local grid to handle."

Sarah shook her head again. "There aren't any motors. Or desalination. I'll swear it on a stack of Bibles."

"Then why did all the overload problems start when the soldiers got here? You're telling me it's just a coincidence?"

"What about all this hot weather? Doesn't that also cause power surges, when everyone comes home from work and turns on their air conditioners?"

Torelli's frown deepened, turning into a grimace. He raised his hand

and pointed at the Con Edison logo on his hard hat. "Lady, who do you think you're talking to? We know how to handle summertime demand. The weather was even hotter last week and we had no problems then." He leaned closer to her. "And the only dangerous surges are in *this* neighborhood, *this* local power grid. It isn't happening anywhere else in the city."

Sarah felt a tingling in her chest. There was a genuine mystery here, an unexplained phenomenon. And mysteries have always been the keys to scientific discovery. She already had a hypothesis in mind, a possible explanation for the phenomenon. Now she just needed a way to test her hypothesis.

Thinking it over, she turned away from Torelli and glanced at the video cameras and the pod-shaped antenna at the back of the truck. She pointed at them. "What's the special equipment for? It looks like you got a directional radio receiver back there."

Torelli's expression softened a bit. He seemed impressed that Sarah knew what the thing was. "That's an SVD system."

"SVD?"

"Stray voltage detector. Con Ed drives these trucks down every street in the city, looking for electrified objects."

"And how do they get electrified? Because of your power lines?"

"When our underground lines get damaged or corroded, the current flows up to the metal structures on the street—the lampposts and fire hydrants and manhole covers." He waved his hand, gesturing at all the metal structures on Dyckman Street. "If there's enough stray voltage on the object, you can get a shock if you touch it."

Sarah looked over her shoulder at the antenna. She was figuring out how it worked. This was college stuff, Physics 101, the basics of electromagnetism. "And because it's AC power, the current in the electrified object is oscillating, right? So it gives off radio waves, which the antenna will detect if it's tuned to the correct frequency?"

Torelli raised his eyebrows. Now he seemed even more impressed. He reached under the driver's seat and pulled out a customized tablet computer with an unusually large screen, almost eighteen inches across. He attached the computer to a mount on the truck's dashboard and plugged a cable into the computer's USB port. "Here, let me show you. The system combines the readings from the antenna with the video from the two cameras in the truck bed."

After a few seconds the tablet's screen came to life and displayed a pair of video feeds, one above the other. Torelli pointed to the upper part of the screen. "This is the video from the camera on the right side of the truck. See, it's showing the sidewalk and those pigeons and that woman walking her dog." Then he pointed to the lower part of the screen. "And this is the video from the camera on the left side, showing the traffic on Dyckman Street. If you look real close, you'll see a red line at the bottom of the video."

Sarah saw it. The line was almost flat. "Those are the readings from the antenna, right? And it's flat because there are no electrified objects nearby?"

Torelli grinned. "Bingo. If there was any stray voltage in the area, you'd see the red line spike upward into the video, showing which object on the street is electrified. Then we'd rope off the thing and keep anyone from touching it until we made repairs."

"But why are you driving this vehicle now?"

"I have to find the source of those power surges. You say it's not the Air Force, and maybe you're telling the truth. Maybe someone else is illegally tapping power from one of our lines. But it's hard to pinpoint the location of the tap because all the underground lines are interconnected. It could be happening anywhere in the local grid." Torelli's face grew animated. His attitude toward Sarah had clearly improved. He seemed comfortable talking to her now. "I might have a chance, though, if the thief did a bad job of connecting the wires. If the splicing or insulation is poor, I'll see stray voltage leaking up to the street. So that's why I took the SVD truck out for a spin."

"Did you find anything?"

"Not yet. But it's a big neighborhood. I'll need a few more hours to do a complete search."

Sarah reached into the back pocket of her jeans and pulled out a folded piece of paper. "I think I can narrow your search area. If you're interested."

Torelli narrowed his eyes. All at once he became suspicious again. "What's that?"

She unfolded the paper. It was a map of Upper Manhattan with an ellipse drawn in red pencil. That was the impact zone Sarah had estimated for Object 2016X using her own analysis, which she trusted more than the Air Force's. Sarah's zone stretched across the West Side

Highway and deep into Inwood Hill Park. She pointed at the eastern end of the ellipse, which was less than a hundred yards from the neighborhood's streets and apartment buildings. "You should focus on the streets next to the park. Payson Avenue and Seaman Avenue and Indian Road."

Torelli stared at the map, obviously struggling to make a sense out of it. Then he looked her in the eye. "Can you give me a little help here? Maybe explain what the hell this thing is?"

She shook her head. Her hypothesis—that there was a connection between 2016X and the power surges in the neighborhood—was too absurd. But that didn't mean it was impossible. "I'm sorry, I can't. This is all classified information. I've told you too much already."

She expected Torelli to get angry, but instead he laughed. It sounded more like a bark, actually. "And if you told me more, you'd have to shoot me? What government agency do you work for, the CIA?"

"Look, I'm not—"

"Don't mind me, I'm just kidding around." He winked at her, then looked again at the map in her hands. "So you want to come along for the ride, Secret Agent Woman?"

She felt a jolt in her stomach. Now she was scared. She was afraid they wouldn't find any evidence for her hypothesis. And she was even more afraid they would. But she hid her fear by smiling at Torelli and winking back at him. "Of course."

He put the truck in gear and headed for Payson Avenue.

The search went more slowly than Sarah had expected. The SVD system couldn't do its job if the truck went faster than ten miles per hour, so they crawled along the streets next to Inwood Hill Park. They drove so slowly they had to stop at the curb every few minutes to let the speedier traffic zoom past.

Sarah kept her eyes on the tablet computer. The upper half of the screen showed the apartment buildings on the east side of Payson Avenue and the lower half showed the wooded park on the west side. She focused in particular on the red line running beneath the video images. It jiggled slightly at the bottom of the screen as the antenna monitored the electromagnetic fields in the area, but the fluctuations were minuscule. The underground grid seemed to be in normal working order. This was disappointing to Sarah but also a relief.

Meanwhile, Torelli was in an excellent mood. He tapped a jazzy rhythm on the steering wheel as they crept down the street. Sarah got the impression that the man usually worked alone and was glad to have some company for a change.

"You see that?" He pointed at a manhole cover just ahead on Payson Avenue. "I almost got killed in that manhole twenty-six years ago. That was right after I started at Con Ed, working as a cable splicer." He shook his head. "Boy, I was stupid back then."

"Is that how you access the power lines? In the manholes?"

"Yeah, there's at least one at every intersection. Basically, they're concrete boxes with cables running along the walls." He kept pointing at the steel cover, which had the Con Ed logo etched in its center. "The primary line in there is a thirteen-thousand-volt cable that carries the current to the transformers under the street. The transformers step it down to a hundred and twenty volts, and then the secondary cables deliver it to the apartments and stores."

"So what happened twenty-six years ago? Did you touch a live wire?"

"No, it was even stupider than that. I fell off the ladder. Landed on my back and broke three vertebrae. But it could've been worse." He let out another barking laugh. "The floor of the manhole was covered with muck, and that cushioned my fall."

"Muck?"

"Yeah, most manholes are full of it. Water and mud come in through the ventilation holes in the manhole cover, and more gunk seeps through the cracks in the concrete walls. Which turned out to be a damn lucky thing for me."

"But aren't power lines and water usually a bad combination?"

Torelli shrugged. "Can't be helped. But the lines themselves are insulated, and there's usually a sump pump at the bottom of the—"

A blaring alarm drowned him out. It sounded like a police siren, but after a second Sarah realized it was coming from the tablet computer on the dashboard. On the computer's screen, the red line leaped upward into the video feed showing the west side of the street. Specifically, the line spiked over an image of a traffic light pole.

Torelli hit the brakes. He squinted at the screen, then glanced at the actual pole, about ten feet to their left. "That thing is electrified." He pulled over to the curb and shut off the truck's engine. "Look behind the seat, will you? There are some extra pairs of rubber boots back there, all sizes. The smallest ones might fit you."

Sarah looked over her shoulder and saw a pile of boots on the floor of the truck's cab. She pawed through it until she found a suitable pair, then slipped them on. Torelli also gave her a pair of rubber gloves. Then he reached into the pocket of his jumpsuit and pulled out a handheld device that looked like a fat, oversized wand. At the tip of the wand was a slender antenna and at the thicker end were several switches and an LED screen.

He held it up for her to see. "This is also a voltage detector, a smaller version of the SVD on the truck. I can get a more accurate reading from close up." He opened the driver's side door. "Just stay a couple of yards behind me, all right? The last thing I want to do is get a CIA agent electrocuted."

Torelli stepped out of the truck and approached the traffic light. Sarah followed at a cautious distance, navigating around a puddle by the curb. She watched Torelli crouch beside the pole and wave the voltage detector around it.

"Nothing to worry about," he called out. "It's less than ten volts. Not so dangerous." He stretched a gloved hand toward the pedestal at the base of the pole and rapped the steel lid that covered one of the pedestal's four sides. The loose lid clattered to the sidewalk, exposing a nest of wires inside. "And here's the cause of the problem. Someone spliced the wires so they could tap the power."

Sarah stepped closer. Within the pedestal she saw a tangle of wires connected by thimblelike wire nuts. The connections looked sloppy, as if they were made by a fifteen-year-old in his high-school electrical shop. An exposed wire rested against the steel housing of the pedestal, which explained how the voltage strayed outside. She pointed at the tangle. "That's a real mess. How much electricity did they take?"

"Not much. This is just a secondary one-twenty-volt line." He glanced up and down Payson Avenue. "You know those street-cart vendors, the ones who sell hot dogs in the park? I bet it was one of those guys. Most of them use propane for heating, but some of the fancier carts have electric outlets and batteries. They probably power up here when their batteries run low."

"But even if every hot dog vendor in New York was stealing electricity, it wouldn't add up to thirty megawatts, right?"

Torelli stood up straight and walked back to his truck. "No, this is nickel-and-dime stuff." He reached into the truck bed, pulled out a tool chest and carried it to the traffic light. "So unless I find a bigger tap somewhere in the neighborhood, I'm gonna keep up the pressure on your friends in the Air Force. I like you, Sarah, but I know you're not being straight with me."

He crouched again beside the base of the pole and opened his tool chest. Then he removed a pair of wire cutters and began to fix the tampered lines inside the pedestal.

While Torelli did his repair work, Sarah turned west and gazed at Inwood Hill Park. A four-foot-high stone wall ran along the park's edge, and beyond it the ground sloped sharply upward. Oaks and dogwoods crowded the hillside, their leaves drooping in the hot, humid air. It was a sweltering but peaceful morning in an utterly ordinary neighborhood, and for a moment Sarah wondered what the hell she was doing here. She should be helping General Hanson find Object 2016X instead of chasing down electricity-thieving hot dog vendors.

But then something occurred to her, something that might connect 2016X to the power lines.

Three months ago she'd gone to Vandenberg Air Force Base to view the launch of the InSight probe, an unmanned NASA spacecraft bound for Mars. Sarah had participated in the prelaunch planning meetings for the probe, which was going to investigate the Red Planet's interior. One of its scientific instruments was nicknamed the Mole, a long steel rod designed to burrow into the ground and analyze the soil. Inside it was an electric motor that pushed and pulled the rod's sharp tip, enabling it to punch through the Martian dirt. It was a relatively simple technology—the whole thing weighed less than five pounds—but it was powerful enough to tunnel almost twenty feet below the surface.

Sarah closed her eyes and tried to picture it. If the InSight probe's Mole could work on Mars, couldn't a similar device do the same thing on Earth? Couldn't it burrow into the soil of Inwood Hill Park? She imagined a long steel rod punching its way through the dirt, threading between the roots of the oaks and dogwoods. At the same time, she recalled what Torelli had said about the manholes, about the cracks in the walls of the concrete boxes.

Opening her eyes, she reached into her back pocket. She pulled out her map, the one that showed the impact zone of Object 2016X, and focused on the eastern end of the ellipse. The intersection closest to that point was where Payson Avenue converged with Seaman Avenue. That junction was less than a hundred yards away.

She waited as patiently as she could until Torelli finished his repairs and fastened the steel lid onto the pedestal of the traffic light. Then, as he picked up his tool chest, she rushed over to him.

"I want to look inside one of the manholes," she blurted. "Can you open it for me?"

Their deliberations went on for almost ten minutes. Torelli brought up safety concerns and Con Edison regulations. Sarah countered his arguments by swearing herself to secrecy and promising not to sue him. He laughed again, and the battle was half won. She sealed the deal by gripping his forearm and telling him how grateful she'd be. She saw no crime in using a little flirtation to get what she wanted.

Torelli parked his truck beside the manhole cover and placed traffic cones around the area. He also forced Sarah to put on a hard hat and a fire-retardant jumpsuit. He used a crowbarlike tool to lift the steel cover from the manhole and set it aside on the asphalt. Then he reached into the bed of his truck and pulled out a yellow ladder. He unfolded it to its full length and slid it into the manhole, bracing it against the curved edge. Last, he reached into the truck bed again and removed a fireman's ax with a long wooden handle.

Sarah stepped backward when she saw the ax. It was intimidating, the kind of thing a psycho would carry in a slasher movie. "What do you need that for?"

Torelli grinned. "Ever seen a sewer rat?"

She had, unfortunately, seen plenty of rats. Before she moved from Texas to California she'd lived in a neighborhood that was plagued with them. "Yeah, they used to invade my backyard in Houston."

His grin grew wider. Torelli seemed to sense her disgust. "Well, that's nothing compared with the rats we got here in New York. They're bigger than dachshunds. And they'll bite anything that moves."

She furrowed her brow and frowned. "So there are rats in the manholes?"

"Oh, yeah. They get in through the holes in the concrete walls. Even the biggest rats can squeeze through a hole the size of a quarter." He pointed the ax at the open manhole. The ax head was dull crimson and the cutting edge bright silver, new and sharp. "But this thing scares them off. Those animals are smart as hell. They know exactly what this is." Approaching the manhole, he grasped the top of the ladder and set his feet on the rungs. "I'll go down first. If everything looks safe, I'll give you the okay."

She nodded. "Just watch your step. I don't want you to fall and break your back again."

"Yeah, once was enough."

Moving slowly and carefully, Torelli descended into the manhole while Sarah watched from above. He didn't have to go very far. When he was about ten feet down he stepped off the ladder, and Sarah heard splashing noises. Then he pulled a flashlight out of his jumpsuit and turned it on. The beam of light reflected off a pool of water at the bottom of the manhole.

Torelli pointed the flashlight to the left and right, but all Sarah could see was the top of his hard hat. After a few seconds he looked up at her. "All right, everything's good here. You can come down."

"What about all the water?"

"It isn't that much. Just a few inches. And you're wearing your boots, right?"

He steadied the ladder until she reached the bottom and stepped into the shallow muck. After a few seconds her eyes adjusted to the dark and she could see the manhole's concrete walls around her. The space was rectangular and as big as a walk-in closet—about fifteen feet long and six feet wide and seven feet high. The air was warm and stuffy and fetid. The walls and ceiling were cracked and chipped, but it was impossible to see the full extent of the damage because of all the power lines. Dozens of cables lay on L-shaped plastic brackets jutting from the walls to the left and right. The cables extended across the length of the manhole, emerging from gaping holes at one end of the room and disappearing into similar holes at the other end.

Sarah wanted to take a closer look at the power lines but was afraid to take a step. The floor felt slick and spongy under her boots. At any moment she expected one of New York City's sewer rats to spring out of the muck and scrabble up her leg. To keep her balance, she reached into the darkness and grabbed Torelli's arm. His face looked ghostly, mottled with shadows.

"So where do you want to start?" he asked.

"Where's the primary line? The thirteen-thousand-volt cable, I mean?"

He pointed his flashlight at the wall to their right. The beam illuminated a massive black cable, at least six inches thick, resting on the highest brackets, which were slightly below eye level. Whereas the other cables in the room sagged between their brackets, the primary line ran straight and rigid. Torelli swept the flashlight beam along the whole length of the cable, following it from one end of the manhole to the other. "That's the feeder line. I need to check the map to see what it connects to. Here, can you hold this for a second?"

He passed the handle of the fireman's ax to Sarah. Then he pulled a map of the local power grid out of his jumpsuit and pointed his flashlight at it. "Yeah, I was right. This feeder goes west from the Inwood substation, then runs north through the conduit under Payson Avenue. It connects to several transformers near the park." He put the map back in his pocket and aimed his flashlight at the thinner cables resting on the lower brackets. "The lines below the feeder are secondary cables. They carry the hundred-and-twenty-volt current from the transformers to the apartment buildings." He looked over his shoulder at Sarah. "I don't see anything wrong with the feeder line. You want me to inspect the secondary lines too?"

Holding on to Torelli with one hand and the ax with the other, she stepped toward the 13,000-volt line. That was the obvious target. She thought of Physics 101 again and everything she knew about electromagnetism. The higher the voltage in the circuit, the greater the push behind the electric current. And that meant you could tap a lot more power from a high-voltage line than from a secondary cable. "I want to get a closer look at the primary line. Are there any cracks in the wall behind it?"

Torelli shrugged. "Could be. Let's take a look."

They approached the wall, their boots squishing with each step. Torelli pointed his flashlight at the concrete, giving it a thorough inspection. There were several cracks in the wall, but none ran close to the 13,000-volt cable. "If there was a tap on the feeder we'd see it right away, you know. There'd be a splice in the line and another cable branching off it."

"What about over there?" She let go of Torelli and pointed at the other end of the manhole, where the high-voltage line emerged from a hole in the wall.

He aimed his flashlight at the hole. The concrete around it was chipped and crumbling. "That's the mouth of the primary conduit, the tube that runs beneath Payson Avenue. There's no splice there either."

"Are you sure? Maybe you can't see it from this angle. Maybe it's deeper inside the conduit."

Torelli let out a sigh, then headed for the other end of the manhole. Sarah followed him, her eyes fixed on the chipped concrete.

Halfway there she heard a noise to her right, the sound of something skittering along the cables. She turned her head but couldn't see anything in the darkness. "Shit! Did you hear that? Was that a rat?"

"Whoa, calm down. Remember what I said? They're afraid of the ax."

"Should I swing it at them?"

"No, no, that would be bad. You might hit one of the cables and get us both electrocuted. Just keep the ax in your hands. As long as you're holding it, the critters won't come close."

He kept his flashlight aimed at the feeder line and the conduit. That was a wise move, Sarah supposed; if she actually saw one of the rodents she'd get even more freaked out. Tightening her grip on the ax's handle, she followed Torelli to the far end of the manhole.

He held his flashlight parallel to the feeder line so he could shine it into the conduit. Then, craning his neck, he peered inside the tube. "Well, I can't see very far, only ten feet or so. But I don't see any splices in there." He lowered the flashlight and turned to Sarah. "You want to see for yourself?"

Before she could respond she heard another skittering noise, coming from behind her this time. She spun around and saw two yellow points in the shadows, a pair of tiny eyes reflecting the flashlight's beam. Worse, the eyes were less than three feet away and looking right at her. The rat had followed her across the manhole, scurrying on of top of the feeder line, and now it perched on one of the L-shaped brackets supporting the cable.

Sarah went into a defensive crouch, bending her knees and raising the ax with both hands. And as she ducked below the feeder cable she saw something she'd missed before. An inch below the bracket, half-hidden by the jutting horizontal arm of the L, was a small, perfectly round hole in the concrete wall. Strung through that hole was a black cable that was much thinner and shinier than any other cable in the room. It was less than a centimeter in diameter and gleamed like polished metal.

"Jesus!" she shouted. "There it is!"

"Put down the ax! I told you, you can't swing it at them." He aimed his flashlight at the rat and yelled "Shoo!" The animal turned around and retreated atop the feeder line to the other end of the manhole. "You see? That's the way to scare them off."

Torelli couldn't see the tap. It was impossible to see it unless you ducked your head. The thin, gleaming cable extended upward from the hole in the concrete and ran through an equally perfect hole in the bracket's horizontal arm. This second hole was directly below where the feeder line rested. The thin cable ran straight up into the thick one. They were connected.

Sarah took her left hand off the ax and reached for the collar of Torelli's jumpsuit. She pulled his head down so he could see the hole in the concrete and the gleaming cable. "That's it," she whispered. "There's where your power's being drained."

He said nothing at first. He just pointed his flashlight at the thing and stared. Sarah stared at it too, awestruck and terrified. This was what she'd come to New York to find. She had no idea what it was, but she knew it was definitely worth the price of the plane ticket.

After a few seconds Torelli grabbed her arm and pulled her away from the tap. "This is dangerous. If that thing nicked the feeder's insulation—"

"It did more than nick the insulation. It punched right through it. Just like it punched through the concrete wall. It's connected to the conducting wire at the center of the cable."

Torelli shook his head. "No, that's ridiculous. The current would fry that little thing to a crisp."

"It's not an ordinary conductor. Just look at it. Have you ever seen anything like it?"

He went silent again. He let go of her arm but stayed bent over so he could scrutinize the tap. Although his flashlight was trained on the cables, Sarah could see him frowning. He was pissed. "So is this your big secret? Some new technology the Air Force is working on?"

She shook her head. "No, I never—"

"Why the hell did you bring it to New York? You're screwing around with a power grid that millions of people depend on."

"I'm telling you, I've never seen a conductor like this before! And neither has anyone else! It's totally new!"

His frown deepened. Torelli didn't believe her. He reached into the pocket of his jumpsuit again and pulled out his handheld voltage detector, the one he'd used on the tampered traffic light pole. First, he waved the wandlike device near the feeder line. Then he lowered the detector, bringing it close to the thin, gleaming cable.

This made Sarah nervous, although she didn't know exactly why. "What are you doing?"

"I'm trying to see if the current from the feeder is actually going through that little—"

White light suddenly flashed across the manhole, accompanied by a tremendously loud *pop*. Torelli fell backward into the muck, his hands over his eyes. "Fuck!" he screamed. "The current's arcing!"

Because Sarah had been looking at Torelli, not the cables, the flash hadn't blinded her. She smelled smoke and turned to see what was burning, and in that moment she realized what had caused the electricity to arc through the air. The thin cable was pulling away from the 13,000-volt line, breaking the connection. The tip of the gleaming black strand withdrew from the feeder line and the bracket underneath it. It slid down the wall, slowly but surely, as if someone on the other side of the concrete was tugging the cable through the perfectly round hole. Within a second or two it would disappear.

Sarah couldn't let that happen. She *needed* this evidence. Desperate, she lifted the ax and swung it at the retreating tip of the cable.

It was a good strong swing, and her aim was true. The ax head swished below the horizontal arm of the bracket and slammed into the wall just above the round hole. The blade hit something hard, harder than concrete, and then bounced right off it. The handle of the ax vibrated in Sarah's palms, and a moment later she saw the black strand again. It was undamaged, hardly a scratch on it. The tip of the cable withdrew into the hole and vanished from sight.

Meanwhile, Torelli sat in the muck and rubbed his eyes. He blinked several times, slowly recovering his vision. "Jesus," he muttered. "I hate manholes." Still blinking, he looked up at Sarah. "Just give me a second, okay? Then we'll get the hell out of here."

His flashlight had also fallen into the muck, but luckily it was water-proof. Sarah picked it up and shook it, flinging drops of filthy water across the room. Then she pointed its beam at the ax blade.

She smiled. On the blade's cutting edge was a small black smudge.

TWELVE

In his nightmare Joe ran down an endless hallway. It stretched as far as the eye could see, dark and deserted. There were wooden doors on both sides of the hall and they all looked the same: no signs on them, no numbers, not even any doorknobs. Joe ran past them, sick with guilt and grief. He was looking for his daughter.

He couldn't remember how he'd lost Annabelle. He'd forgotten her, neglected her, looked away for a moment when he should've been paying attention. Now she was trapped behind one of those countless doors, but he didn't know which one. He screamed her name but heard no answer.

Frantic, he chose a door at random and threw his shoulder against it. He barged into a brightly lit hospital room, one of the private rooms at St. Luke's where he used to work. His daughter lay on the hospital bed, face up, eyes closed. She was motionless and very pale. He screamed "Annabelle!" again and rushed toward her. At the same time, she sat up in bed and opened her eyes.

He bent over her, panting, relieved but still frightened. He quickly examined her to see where she was hurt. She had no visible wounds or other signs of trauma, but when he asked her what had happened she just looked at him blankly. She recognized him but didn't seem to understand what he was saying. She opened her mouth and moved her lips but no words came out. It was as if she'd forgotten how to speak English.

He pointed at her. "Annabelle. You're Annabelle." Then he pointed at himself. "And I'm your dad. Come on, I know you can say it. Say 'Daddy.'"

She tried to do it, spreading her lips and lifting her tongue. She looked like she was on the verge of success, but then she closed her mouth and turned away. She raised her right hand and pointed at one of the fluorescent lights on the ceiling. At first Joe thought she wanted him to turn it off, but then he realized she was asking a question.

"That's a light," Joe answered. "Try to say it, Annabelle. *Light*."

But instead of trying to speak, she pointed at the floor. Then at her pillow and the bedsheets. Then at all the pieces of medical equipment surrounding her bed. She wanted Joe to name every object in the room. She needed him to say the words so she could relearn them.

So Joe did it. Slowly and patiently, while he drifted in and out of consciousness, he taught her all the words she'd forgotten.

When he finally awoke he found himself lying on a different kind of bed, a narrow cot with a thin mattress and a discolored pillow. On his left was a cinder-block wall, painted dull yellow. The opposite wall was just a few feet to his right, and jutting from it were a small sink and a stainless-steel toilet without a lid. On the floor was a crosshatched rectangle of sunlight, slanting down from a high window with a metal grille over it. Then Joe saw the bars of his jail cell's door, which stood wide open, and he remembered where he was: on cellblock D of the Otis Bantum Correctional Center on Rikers Island.

He had a headache, a bad one. He raised a hand to his forehead and touched the bandage wrapped around it. The cops on Dyckman Street had given him a concussion when they'd tackled him last night. He'd regained consciousness in the emergency room at Bellevue Hospital, where he lay handcuffed to a gurney for five hours before the doctors there said he was okay. Then he spent the next eight hours at the Manhattan Criminal Courthouse, where the prosecutors charged him with resisting arrest and assaulting a police officer. He couldn't make bail, of course, so the next stop was Rikers.

Joe twisted on the cot, trying to find a more comfortable position. The guards had taken away his old clothes and given him a pair of gray sweatpants and a white T-shirt. His new clothes smelled better than the old ones, but he still didn't feel clean. The jail had its own stench, a mix of sweat and mildew.

He guessed it was evening now, maybe seven o'clock. He'd been lying on the cot for the past three hours. His withdrawal symptoms had kicked in again—he hadn't had a drink since one thirty in the morning— and the tremors and nausea would soon get much worse. There was no malt liquor for sale on cellblock D, and even if he could somehow get his hands on a smuggled bottle of booze, he doubted he'd be able to drink it. The poison from the satellite was still in his bloodstream. He knew it was inside him because his vision was still phenomenally sharp, and because thinking about alcohol still made him want to puke.

This was the biggest of his problems, even worse than the fact that he was locked up in Rikers. The poison was changing him. It's what made him grab the nightstick from Officer Patton and jab him in the stomach. He'd lost control of himself for only a moment, but it had scared the shit out of him. He should be in the hospital right now, in the toxicology department at St. Luke's, working with the specialists there to get the poison out of his blood. But he couldn't get help, couldn't even ask for it. If he told the guards about his problem, they'd send him straight to the jail's psychiatric ward, and Joe had a feeling that place would be even scarier than cellblock D.

He rolled onto his side. He needed to piss but was afraid to get out of his cot. Some of the other inmates paced up and down the corridor outside his cell. When he'd arrived at the jail earlier that afternoon the guards had informed him that the cells would stay open until dinner and in the meantime he could visit the exercise yard or the TV room. But he'd noticed that most of the inmates remained in their cells, either napping or reading or zoning out, so he'd concluded that this was the safest option. There seemed to be a shortage of correction officers in the cellblock, and they mostly stayed behind the protective glass of the guard station.

As he lay on the cot he kept one eye open and watched the inmates in the corridor. Some stared straight ahead as they passed by, avoiding eye contact with everyone. Others—the biggest, most intimidating prisoners—took a moment to peer into each cell. Most of the inmates were either black or Latino, and very few were over the age of forty. Joe, as a middle-aged white man, was a novelty at Rikers, and the other inmates were curious about him. Every couple of minutes someone would stop outside his cell and linger in the corridor. Whenever this happened Joe closed his eyes tight, pretending to be asleep and praying that the inmate would go away.

This strategy worked well for the first fifteen minutes. Then a hulking white inmate walked right into his cell to get a better look at him. Joe closed his eyes a little too late. The guy stepped further into the cell and poked Joe in the shoulder.

"Stop faking it." His voice was slow and deep. "I know you're awake."

Joe opened his eyes a fraction, just to see how much trouble he was in. The inmate was well over six feet tall and weighed at least three hundred pounds. His T-shirt was too short to cover his belly, which hung over the cot like a hot-air balloon. His head was bald and bullet-shaped and slick with sweat, and there was a crude tattoo of a skull over his right ear. He bent over Joe and grinned. "Hey there, Doc. My name's Daryl. Welcome to Rikers." Then, without waiting for a reply, Daryl looked over his shoulder at another inmate standing outside the cell.

"Check it out, Curtis!" he shouted. "The doc woke up from his nap."

Giving up, Joe opened his eyes all the way and saw a second white guy come into his cell. Curtis was also bald and even taller than Daryl but didn't have an ounce of fat on him. His chest muscles bulged under his T-shirt and his forearms rippled under shirtsleeve tattoos. He leaned over and slapped the foot of Joe's mattress, making it jump. "You're a noisy motherfucker when you're napping, Doc. You were saying all kinds of crazy shit."

Joe had no idea how to respond. He wanted to tell them to get the hell out of his cell, but he was too sick to even raise his voice. Shivering, he lifted his head off his pillow and stared at the two men. "Why . . . are you calling me 'Doc'?"

Daryl shrugged. "We heard you're a doctor. That's the word going round."

"Yeah, a drunk doctor who hit a cop." Curtis laughed. "How the hell did a stupid fucker like you get into medical school?"

Again, Joe didn't know what to say. He couldn't tell how serious his visitors were. He studied their faces, trying to figure it out. Were they kidding around or getting ready to hurt him? The uncertainty was making him squirm. He didn't know anything about the inmates here, so he was afraid of everything.

"I'm not a doctor anymore," he finally said. "I'm just a drunk now."

"Hey, I like your honesty." Curtis nodded in approval. "You're an honest white guy, which definitely puts you in the minority in this place." He jerked his thumb at the corridor outside the cell. "If you haven't noticed already, most of the assholes here are lying, dick-eating niggers and spics."

Joe winced. It was an involuntary reaction, like gagging. He'd been raised by a family of ignorant racists. That was one of the reasons why he'd left home and broken off all contact with them.

Daryl noticed his reaction. He opened his mouth in mock surprise and looked at Curtis. "Uh-oh. I don't think Doc liked that."

"Really?" Curtis narrowed his eyes and trained them on Joe. "You didn't like what I said? About the niggers and spics here?"

Joe tried to sit up, his head swimming. He raised his hands, palms out, as if to stop the men from coming closer. "Look, I don't want any trouble."

Curtis stepped toward the head of the cot, nudging Daryl aside. "Come on, Doc, be honest with me again. You've never called one of them a nigger? Never in your life?"

This was one of the few things, maybe the only thing, on which Joe still held a strong opinion. He'd hated his family for their prejudice, and these men were acting just like his uncles and cousins. He shook his head. "No, never in my life."

"Whoa, we got a saint here!" Daryl pointed at him. "Saint Doc the drunk."

Curtis wasn't amused, though. He furrowed his brow and looked down at Joe, examining him carefully. Then he turned to his friend. "Step outside, Daryl. I need to have a talk with this asshole."

Daryl nodded and stepped away from the cot, but he didn't go far. He took up position just outside the cell, with his back turned toward them, his body blocking the view of anyone trying to look into the cell from the corridor. Joe's stomach clenched as he stared at the back of Daryl's T-shirt. *Well, at least there's no more uncertainty,* he thought. *Now I know something bad is coming.*

Meanwhile, Curtis stepped closer. He bent over the cot and grimaced, flaring his nostrils. The man's eyes were bloodshot and he had a scar that ran diagonally across his forehead. "Let's get something straight, all right? In this place it doesn't matter who you were outside or what you did for a living. Not one fucking bit. We're all the same here." He curled his lip, baring a row of crooked teeth. "You hear me?"

Joe nodded, but it looked like Curtis was going to hit him anyway. Bracing himself, Joe raised his arms to protect his head. But then Curtis turned away from him and looked down at the floor. He reached under the cot and picked up a plastic bin that Joe hadn't even known was there. "We have a rule here in D block: share and share alike. So I'm gonna take a look at your stuff now."

He opened the bin, which was about the size of a hatbox. The only contents were the personal hygiene items issued to every inmate: a plastic cup, a stubby rubber toothbrush, and a small tube of toothpaste. Curtis stared into the bin for several seconds, then turned back to Joe. "Where's the rest of it?"

"The rest of what?"

Curtis flung the bin against the wall. Joe's personal hygiene items scattered across the floor. "Don't play games with me, motherfucker! You're gonna tell me you don't have a watch? A rich fucking doctor like you?"

Joe belatedly figured it out. The bin was supposed to hold any possessions that the inmates were allowed to bring into the jail—books, watches, that kind of thing. And because Joe had no possessions whatsoever, his container was almost empty. But explaining all this to Curtis was going to be difficult. The guy didn't seem to be in a receptive mood.

Taking a deep breath, Joe looked him in the eye. "I told you, I'm not a doctor anymore. I don't own a watch. I don't own anything. I was living in the park before they—"

"You lying *shit!*" Curtis grabbed the front of Joe's T-shirt and bunched it in his fist. "I know you have a watch and it's probably a goddamn Rolex! Now where the fuck did you hide it?"

He shoved Joe backward, pinning him to the cinder-block wall. Curtis's fist pushed against his chest, the knuckles digging into his breastbone. Joe could feel its pressure on his heart. He stared in terror at the man's bloodshot eyes and saliva-flecked lips, and in that moment he realized that Curtis wasn't simply angry. The man was mentally disturbed. He was liable to do anything.

Joe considered yelling for help but then thought better of it. The guards wouldn't even hear him, much less come to his rescue. His only hope was to talk his way out of this, and that wasn't much hope at all.

Curtis leaned in closer, his face just a couple of inches away. His breath smelled like vomit. "You're fucked, Doc. You know that, right?"

"Listen, I—"

"I can do anything I want to you, and no one's gonna stop me." He pressed harder against Joe's chest. "You got no friends in this place and a whole lot of enemies."

Joe shook his head. He couldn't talk, couldn't breathe. He thought of the poison in his blood, the neurotoxin that made him attack Officer Patton, but he couldn't feel it inside him now. There was nothing but static in his head, and he was so dizzy he couldn't see straight.

Then a loud, high-pitched buzzer sounded. The noise came from the corridor and echoed against the walls of every cell. It lasted for four or five seconds before abruptly cutting off. Then a chorus of other sounds arose from D block: men laughing and cursing and shuffling out of their cells. Above it all, Joe heard a guard's voice: "Line up! Chow time! Everybody get in line!"

Curtis waited a moment, his brow creased. Then he let go of Joe's shirt.

Joe slumped to the mattress, breathing fast, his head still full of static. He raised his arms again, expecting a parting blow from Curtis, but the man just looked down at him.

"Don't get too comfortable, Doc. We'll do this later, after chow. You can count on it."

Then he stepped out of the cell and joined Daryl in the corridor.

The food was horrible, just as Joe had expected. Two cold gray hamburger patties lay on the left side of his tray, each on a slice of stale white bread doused with ketchup. On the right side was a mound of limp string beans in a gelatinous fluid. The best part of the meal was the fruit drink in the plastic cup. It was so watered down it had no taste at all.

Joe sat by himself at one of the long tables in the prison cafeteria. The room was noisy and crowded with hundreds of inmates, but they all kept their distance from Joe, as if he had something contagious. When one of the prisoners headed for his table, the others shouted at him until the guy went elsewhere. At one point Joe looked up from his tray and scanned the room, looking for Curtis and Daryl, but he couldn't find them. There were too many tables and too many people standing in the way. After a while he gave up and returned to staring at his dinner. He had no intention of eating it, but at least it gave him something to look at.

He felt another wave of nausea. He'd now gone more than eighteen hours without a drink and his withdrawal symptoms were escalating. He had to grip the edge of the table to stop his hands from shaking. His headache was so bad it felt like cluster bombs were exploding behind his eyes, and every few seconds he felt a sickening surge of vertigo. He tightened his grip on the table as the world came unglued and the room spun around him.

But the worst symptom of all was the self-pity. Joe couldn't understand how things had gone so wrong. When he saw the satellite for the first time, just the night before last, he'd thought it was a godsend, an honest-to-goodness gift from heaven. But instead it had made his life infinitely worse. It was so unfair he actually started to cry. This was a very stupid thing to do in a prison cafeteria, but he couldn't stop himself.

He shook his head. *Jesus, don't be an idiot! They're all looking at you!* But the tears kept coming. He was thinking of his Yankees jacket, which the cops had stripped off him shortly after his arrest. Although the police were supposed to keep track of his belongings, at some point during the journey from Dyckman Street to Rikers they'd left his jacket behind. It was an old, filthy thing that stank to high heaven, and now it probably lay in a trash can somewhere. But it had been precious to Joe.

His wife had given him that jacket on their first anniversary. At the time Joe had been in medical school in Alabama, but he and Karen had already decided to move north, and the Yankees jacket was a symbol of their new life, their future. Joe had applied for residencies at several hospitals in New York, and Karen had started looking for nursing positions in the city. It would've been easier to get jobs in Alabama, but that wasn't an option for Joe. He was determined to put as much distance as possible between himself and his family.

The Grahams of Bullock County were white trash, pure and simple. Joe's father was a drunk, and so were all of his uncles and cousins. His mother had run off with an Amway salesman when Joe was just five, then drank herself to death when he was seven. Joe himself had started drinking in high school and by the age of eighteen he was as bad as the rest of them. But just before graduation he nearly died in a car wreck, and while he lay in the hospital he resolved to clean up his act. He realized he didn't have to be a stupid drunk all his life; instead, he could be like one of the doctors who'd just saved him. So he enrolled at the University of Alabama and set off on the long, hard road to medical school. His father thought it was a crazy idea and refused to pay for anything, but that was all right with Joe. As soon as he finished school and had that M.D. in hand he was going to get the hell out of Alabama and never look back.

Although Karen had enjoyed a happier childhood and a less dysfunctional family—her parents were decent, hardworking folks—she supported her husband. If the decision had been up to her, she might've preferred to stay in Birmingham or Tuscaloosa, but she was willing to make the sacrifice. That was the message behind the Yankees jacket: *I know how important this is to you. I'll do anything to make you happy.* It was a beautiful gift, a wonderfully loving gesture. Thinking about it still brought tears to Joe's eyes, despite all the not-so-beautiful things that happened later.

He was still crying and clutching the edge of the table when someone threw a hamburger patty at him. He felt the thing bounce off the back of his neck and saw it land on the floor. Ketchup splattered over his T-shirt and the gauze bandage on his head. A roar of laughter erupted from the tables behind him, but he didn't turn around. He just sat very still and tried to stop crying.

There was only one sure way to do it. Joe closed his eyes and recalled the last two years of his marriage. He tried to harden his heart by remembering their arguments, how he and Karen had fought over money and sex and where Annabelle should go to school. He pictured the screaming matches in their living room, in the car, in front of their daughter. He remembered their silences too, the days and weeks when they'd avoided each other by working long hours and rearranging their schedules, making sure they were never home at the same time. And, last, he remembered how Karen had betrayed him, how she'd slept with his boss, the chief of surgery at St. Luke's. He pictured her on the night when she admitted the affair, speaking slowly and calmly, with that cold, unrepentant look on her face.

Joe stopped crying. His nausea and dizziness also eased a little. The pictures in his head were literally sobering. He let go of the table and rested his hands in his lap. He stared at the food on his tray.

Another hamburger patty hit him in the shoulder. This time he saw the person who threw it, a burly Latino guy with gaudy tattoos on his arms. The guy yelled something in Spanish and the other inmates at his table laughed in response, but Joe ignored them. He kept his eyes on his tray. He stared at it so intently that after a couple of minutes the food no longer repelled him. The hamburgers were just slabs of protein and fat. And he needed the nutrients to survive in this place.

He picked up one of the patties and forced it into his mouth. Then he started to chew.

After dinner Joe didn't go back to his cell. Instead, he paced up and down cellblock D's corridor, always staying within sight of the guard station. Calling it a "station" was a bit of a stretch; it was just a steel-walled booth at the end of the corridor, next to the barred gate that was the cellblock's entrance. The booth had a window made of protective glass, and through it Joe saw a pair of correction officers reclining in their swivel chairs and staring at the video feeds from the jail's security cameras. They looked like they were bored out of their minds.

The cells in D block were still open, and there were at least a hundred inmates in the corridor. Some of them wandered back and forth, like Joe, but most clustered near their cells in groups of three or four, either talking in low voices or shouting insults at each other. Joe threaded his way through the crowd, following the red line that ran down the middle of the corridor. He swiveled his head as he walked, looking in all directions. At any moment he expected Curtis and Daryl to pop up behind him and shove him into one of the cells. If they did it quickly enough the guards might not notice. And the cells had no security cameras.

Joe glanced at the clock on the wall: 8:56 P.M. He'd already gone up and down the corridor a dozen times, and there was still more than an hour to go before lights-out. His stomach churned and his head pounded.

At nine o'clock he stopped to catch his breath, but the inmates standing nearby glared at him, so he moved on. He walked past the guard station again, then turned around at the barred gate and proceeded in the opposite direction.

Don't stop now. Just keep going for one more hour. Then you can go back to your cell and the guards will close all the doors and you'll be safe till morning.

Joe knew he shouldn't make eye contact with the other inmates, so he focused his attention on the two guards, scrutinizing them every time he passed their station. One was middle-aged and heavy and prematurely gray, the other young and thin and pimply. They wore black uniforms and carried nightsticks and handcuffs on their belts, but no guns. They were clearly no match for a hundred angry prisoners, and now Joe understood why the correction officers rarely ventured from their station—they were badly outnumbered. If there was a riot, the guards could lock down the jail and call for reinforcements, but until help arrived the inmates could do whatever they wanted.

As Joe approached the station once again at 9:08 P.M. the middle-aged guard rose from his swivel chair. He exited the booth through a door at the back and reappeared a few seconds later on the other side of the barred gate. The younger guard buzzed the gate open, allowing his gray-haired partner to step into the cellblock. Judging from the tired look on the older guard's face, Joe assumed he was close to the end of his shift. He was probably getting ready for lights-out, making a final inspection of D block before herding the inmates back to their cells. As the guard marched down the corridor he removed the nightstick from his belt and held it ready. The name on his uniform, Joe noticed, was BILLINGS. Then, to Joe's great surprise, Officer Billings pointed the nightstick at him.

"*You, Joseph Graham!*" The guard's voice was stunningly loud. "*Turn and face the wall!*"

Joe was too alarmed to move. *What did I do?*

"Are you *deaf?*" The guard raised the nightstick a little higher, preparing to swing. "*Face the wall and put your hands behind your head!*"

Swallowing hard, Joe turned to the wall and raised his hands. They were trembling again, but after a few seconds he managed to lace his fingers together behind his head. The other inmates in the corridor watched with amusement. Several imitated him, shaking their hands spastically.

Officer Billings frisked him. Joe was at a loss, his mind racing. He turned his head and tried to catch the guard's eye. "What . . . what's going—"

"*Shut the fuck up! If you say one more word, I'll bash your fucking head in!*" He slapped Joe's hips and legs, checking for anything tucked into his sweatpants. Then the guard leaned close enough to whisper something in Joe's ear. "I got a message for you. From Frank Patton."

It took Joe a second to realize who Billings was talking about—Officer Patton, the big redheaded cop from Inwood. "What? What does—"

"You ruptured his spleen, you stupid fuck. When you hit him with the nightstick." Billings punctuated the sentence by jabbing his own nightstick into Joe's back. "And Frank Patton happens to be my brother-in-law."

The jab was painful but not excruciating. Billings couldn't hit him hard in front of the security cameras in the corridor. But Joe knew the punishment was just beginning. He should've seen this coming. Patton had said many times that he had friends at Rikers.

Billings stepped backward. "Okay, Graham, you're coming with me. Turn right and walk down the corridor."

Joe did as he was told. The other inmates obligingly cleared a path. Some of them laughed and others shook their heads, but there wasn't any surprise on their faces. They all knew he was charged with assaulting a cop. Everyone in the cellblock must've heard the story by now. Now the guards were going to make an example of him.

Billings followed Joe down the corridor, staying a few feet behind. They went past the long rows of cells, then up a flight of stairs to the TV room, where a Spanish soap opera was playing on a wall-mounted screen. Then they walked toward another guard station, a bigger one. There were three correction officers behind the protective glass, all of them young, brawny guys with thick necks and broad shoulders. When they saw Joe and Officer Billings they looked at one another and grinned. *They're in on it*, Joe thought. *Those are the guys who are going to beat the crap out of me.* He slowed his pace, his throat tightening, afraid to take another step. But Billings ordered him to keep fucking going and they went past the guard station and up another flight of stairs.

They walked into an enormous kitchen full of industrial-size ovens and freezers. The place was deserted; the inmates who worked there had already gone back to their cells after cleaning up the remains of the putrid dinner. Joe assumed the other correction officers would meet them there and the beating would begin, but instead Billings led him past the ovens and out of the room. They entered the jail's laundry, which was also silent, the giant washing machines and dryers shut down for the night, and then they marched down another corridor. Their journey through the cellblock was taking so long that Joe started to wonder if his original assumption was correct. If the guards were going to beat him up, why didn't they just do it in the empty kitchen or the laundry? Why was Billings taking him on such a long excursion?

At the end of the corridor they came to a black door pocked with fist-size dents. Billings opened it and pushed Joe into a large dank bathroom. A dozen showerheads jutted from the grimy walls, and the tiled floor sloped downward to a rusty drain in the middle of the room. Standing by the drain were two familiar men in white T-shirts and gray sweatpants.

Joe spun around but Officer Billings stood in his way. The guard winked at him. "This is how it works here. We let the big boys take care of our problems." He looked past Joe and waved at Curtis and Daryl. "Have fun, guys."

Then he left the shower room and closed the door behind him.

Joe backed up against the wall. Daryl sauntered toward him, in no hurry, his huge torso swaying, his big sneakers squelching on the wet floor. He casually positioned himself between Joe and the door, then looked over his shoulder at Curtis. Daryl waited for instructions, but Curtis said nothing. He just stood there, his face blank, his muscled arms glistening with sweat. He looked like he'd just finished a workout in the exercise yard. He turned to the side and gazed at the showerheads for a while, as if trying to decide whether to wash up. Then he turned back to Joe and smiled. "Hey, Doc. What did you think of the chow? You like those hamburgers?"

Joe's legs went rubbery and he slid to the floor. His butt hit the wet tiles and soon the moisture soaked through the seat of his sweatpants. He felt so weak and frightened he could barely shake his head. "Please . . . please don't . . ."

"Sorry, begging won't help. The deal's already done." Curtis turned to Daryl. "I feel a little sorry for the doc, don't you? All he did was knock some cop on his ass."

Daryl nodded. "Yeah, he just picked the wrong cop."

"That's for sure. Never mess with Billings." Curtis looked Joe in the eye. "See, Officer Billings is the king of D block. He smuggles in our dope, carries messages in and out, all that good stuff. So we can't turn him down if he asks us for a favor, you know?"

"And what . . ." Joe's throat was so tight, he couldn't get the words out. He swallowed hard. "What's the favor?"

Curtis shrugged. "He told us to beat the hell out of you. Do some permanent damage, he said."

He bent over and stretched his right arm down to his left sneaker. Slipping his fingers under the sneaker's tongue, he pulled out a stubby prison-issue toothbrush. The bristles had been cut off the end of the brush, and wedged into the rubber in their place was a slim, shiny blade, removed from a disposable razor.

Curtis stepped forward with the makeshift weapon in his hand. Daryl stood beside him, ready to help. Joe sat on the floor, cringing, his arms around his knees. He heard the static in his head again, the same awful noise he'd heard before when Curtis had attacked him in his cell. He'd assumed then that Curtis was mentally disturbed, but now he realized that the man wasn't any crazier than the other inmates here. This place was simply evil, and so was everyone inside it.

Curtis came closer and waved the razor blade in Joe's face. "Here's the deal, Doc. I'm gonna hurt you pretty bad. But I'm gonna try not to kill you. Okay?"

Joe stared at the blade. He focused on the thing with all his might, struggling to concentrate. There had to be a way out of this. He had to think of *something*.

Pressing against the wall behind him, Joe lifted his butt off the floor and rose to his feet. His legs trembled, but he managed to stand up straight. "I'm a doctor. I have money. I can tell my wife to send some to you."

It was a bald-faced lie, but it got Curtis's attention. He cocked his head and pulled back the hand that held the blade. "Well, that's very generous, Doc." He nodded in appreciation. "So how much money are you talking about?"

"I have plenty in the bank. Thousands of dollars." Joe nodded too, trying hard to look sincere. "Just tell me what you want."

Curtis glanced at Daryl. "You hear that? We can have as much as we want." He smiled. "How much should we ask for? A million? Two million?"

Daryl smiled back at him. "Ask for ten million. In twenty-dollar bills."

"Yeah, good idea." Curtis turned back to Joe. "We want crisp, fresh twenties, Doc."

Joe's heart sank. Curtis and Daryl were just playing with him. They leered like ten-year-olds sharing a good joke. They thought it was funny.

After a few seconds Curtis stopped smiling. He raised the blade and took another step toward Joe. "Okay, where should we start? I could cut out one of your eyes. That sounds like permanent damage, right?"

The razor blade was just inches away, glinting under the shower room's fluorescent lights. But strangely enough, Joe was calmer now, less panic-stricken at the sight of it. The static in his head had died down and he could think again, because he felt something stronger than fear. Now that the worst was about to happen he just felt angry. He wanted to scream at Curtis, to curse the shit out of him. Although Joe kept his mouth shut, the words rang inside him: *What the fuck is wrong with you? You're a fucking animal!*

Then Joe heard something else in his head, but it wasn't his own voice. It was his daughter's.

Look at them, Daddy. Look at both of them very carefully.

Annabelle's voice was so clear. It sounded like it came from just a few feet away. Joe swung his head from left to right, scanning the shower room, frantically looking for her.

No, don't look for me. Look at them. I need to see them.

"Hey, I'm talking to you!" Curtis leaned closer. He stretched his arm and held the razor blade against the side of Joe's neck. "You better pay attention, Doc, or else I'll just end this quick and cut your throat."

Joe looked at the man. Curtis stood there with his right foot forward, knees bent, back slightly hunched. Daryl stood about a yard to Joe's left. His feet were widely spaced, his arms folded across his chest.

That's good. Now do what Curtis wants you to do. Raise your hands and beg for your life.

It made no sense, but Joe listened to the voice in his head. He slowly raised both his hands in surrender. They trembled on either side of his face. "Please . . . don't kill me."

Curtis smiled again and pulled his arm back, taking the blade away from Joe's neck. "That's better. Now I'm gonna give you a choice, Doc. Left eye or right eye? Which one should I cut?"

Keep begging. Promise him more money.

"I . . . I have money. I'll give you all of it."

Curtis laughed and turned to Daryl. "Are you listening to this shit? The fucking guy still doesn't—"

Joe's hands stopped trembling and shot forward. He didn't consciously decide to move them. His arms swung toward Curtis on their own, as if someone had yanked them with a string. Joe's legs shot forward too, yanked by their own strings, and he lunged at Curtis like an exceptionally acrobatic marionette. The strings pulled both of Joe's arms toward Curtis's right hand, the one that held the razor blade. Joe's hands clasped around Curtis's and squeezed it so tightly that the man couldn't let go of his weapon. Then, using his forward momentum, Joe swiped the razor blade across Curtis's neck.

The strings also turned his head to the left so he could watch Daryl. The attack on Curtis was so quick that Daryl hardly had time to react. He was just starting to move toward them when the strings spun Joe counterclockwise. Curtis was tipping backward, blood spurting from beneath his jaw, so it was a simple matter for Joe to shove the falling man at his partner's knees. Daryl slipped on the wet floor and toppled forward, his bald head knocking against the tiles.

Then the strings were cut and Joe almost fell too. He regained control of his arms and legs, which felt tight and hot and tingly, as if he'd just done a hundred push-ups. When he looked down he saw Curtis writhing on the floor next to the drain. He'd jammed both of his palms under his chin, trying to stanch the bleeding. Joe hadn't cut the carotid artery—if he had, the blood would be spurting even worse—so he guessed Curtis would live. He couldn't offer a prognosis for Daryl, though. The man lay facedown on the floor, not moving at all.

Curtis had dropped the razor blade. It glinted on the tiles, still attached to the stubby toothbrush. Joe snatched it off the floor.

Now go back to your cell, Daddy. Walk, don't run.

He scanned the room again, looking for Annabelle. She had to be hiding somewhere nearby, he was still convinced of it. He opened the door to the shower room and peered down the hallway, but it was empty. Officer Billings had apparently gone back to his station.

"Annabelle!" he shouted. "Where are you?"

First go back to your cell. Then we'll talk.

Joe walked across the cellblock, retracing his steps through the laundry and kitchen, fighting the urge to run. He was especially nervous when he passed the guard station near the TV room, but the correction officers were making the final preparations for lights-out and no one noticed him. He returned to his cell at 9:50 P.M., sat on his cot and waited. Five minutes later he heard the sound of guards rushing down the corridor, but they ran past his cell. Maybe they were heading for the shower room, maybe not. After five more anxious minutes, D block's buzzer made its loud high-pitched noise and all the doors to the cells automatically closed. Then the lights went out and Joe sat there in the darkness.

It's a withdrawal symptom, he thought. *I'm hallucinating her voice.* But over the past hour all his other symptoms had disappeared. He wasn't dizzy or nauseous anymore, and his hands were steady. His headache was gone and even his cracked ribs didn't hurt. He took a deep breath of the cellblock's fetid air. Truth be told, he hadn't felt this good in years. *Then I must be going mad. None of this is real.*

No, Daddy, it's real. You're in jail on Rikers Island.

Joe jumped to his feet and looked around his cell. He couldn't help it. "Annabelle?" he whispered into the darkness.

You don't have to talk out loud for me to hear you. I'm inside your mind. I can hear everything you're thinking.

The voice in his head sounded just like his daughter, but the words weren't right. They weren't the kind of words a child would use. The real Annabelle didn't know what Rikers Island was. She knew nothing about jails or inmates or how to fight off a couple of sadists like Curtis and Daryl. So the person who'd saved Joe in the shower room couldn't have been his daughter. It was an impostor, someone pretending to be Annabelle. He felt a surge of anger.

"You're not Annabelle." He continued to whisper, defying her. "Who are you?"

Close your eyes and I'll show you.

"No, tell me." Joe kept his eyes open. "How did you get in my head?"

You know how. It was the snake, remember?

Joe's eyes closed against his will. He felt as if someone had forced his eyelids down and glued them shut. Then he saw the snake he'd dreamed about the night before. First he pictured it exactly as it had appeared in the dream, shiny and black but with Annabelle's blue eyes. After a moment, though, it transformed into the long thin tentacle he'd glimpsed when he awoke, the tentacle that had slid toward him and jabbed his neck.

"You're from the sphere? The satellite?"

It's not a satellite. A satellite stays in orbit around a planet, Daddy, but this—

"Stop calling me that!" He raised his voice. "You're not my daughter!"

"Shut the fuck up, motherfucker!"

The shout came from one of the neighboring jail cells. Startled, Joe backed away from his cell's door and sat down again on his cot. He still couldn't open his eyes, and yet he seemed to be able to sense where everything was, all the objects in his cell and some things outside it too. This new ability frightened him almost as much as the voice in his head.

"You're not my daughter," he repeated, whispering again. "Why are you using her voice?"

You're right, I'm not Annabelle. I used your memory of her to forge a bond between us.

Now Joe pictured something from a more recent dream, the image of Annabelle lying in a private room in St. Luke's Hospital. She sat up in bed and pointed at the fluorescent light on the ceiling. Then she opened her mouth and said, "Light."

You taught me how to speak. I'm grateful for that. Communication is our highest priority now.

In his mind's eye he saw Annabelle climb out of the bed. She wore a blue hospital gown, tied at the back. She walked barefoot out of her private room and entered the long corridor Joe had dreamed about, the hallway with the hundreds of wooden doors.

"Where are you going?" he whispered.

Time is running short. You should've reached this stage sooner, but the pathways in your mind weren't clear. I needed several hours to restore the balance of neurotransmitters and receptors.

It was so strange to hear these words coming from Annabelle's mouth. Even stranger, Joe understood what she was saying. She was talking about the signaling pathways between brain cells.

"Was it the alcohol? That's what blocked the pathways?"

Annabelle nodded. She was walking down the corridor, inspecting each door she passed. The doors looked identical to Joe, but she seemed to be examining something he couldn't see.

Yes, the alcohol caused the damage. It left you unable to control your fear, which generated the interference that you called "static." I couldn't clear your pathways until your fear subsided.

She finally stopped in front of one of the doors. She stared at it for several seconds, as if she were reading something written in invisible ink on the wood. Then she smiled. Even though Joe knew this girl was an impostor, his heart leapt anyway. Annabelle's smile was so beautiful.

"What is it? What do you see?"

I see a solution to our problem. It would be futile to communicate with the officials who run this jail. If we try, they'll assume you're suffering from psychosis. We have to make contact with the appropriate authorities in the government. They'll be more receptive to the message we'll deliver.

Joe didn't understand. "What message?"

Annabelle was still smiling. Joe felt like she was pulling him closer. Her face was the only thing he could see, crowding out everything else in his mind.

Don't worry about that now, Daddy. First we need to leave Rikers Island. She tapped the door, which opened at her touch. *This is how we're going to escape.*

THIRTEEN

Emilio sat next to Paco on the A train, speeding downtown. It was 3:00 A.M. and they were the only people in the subway car, maybe even the whole train. They wore camouflage pants, black T-shirts, and black baseball caps, and a big black duffel bag lay on the seat beside them. Although the bag was practically empty, it held everything they needed for tonight's job.

One on one, Paco wasn't an easy person to spend time with. The *muchacho* didn't like to talk. He stared straight ahead, his eyes fixed on the subway map on the other side of the car. Emilio glanced sideways, trying to read the guy's face, trying to figure out if he was ready to do the job tonight or if he was going to back out. This face-reading trick had worked like magic for Emilio since he'd stumbled upon it the night before, but he was having some trouble reading Paco now. The homeboy's face was blank and motionless.

After a while Emilio gave up and looked at the subway map instead. The train was at 125th Street, six stops from the museum station at 81st. As he stared at the colored subway lines crisscrossing the city he remembered taking this same trip ten years ago, back when he was an eight-year-old at P.S. 98. His third-grade teacher, Mrs. Cohen, had arranged a visit to the American Museum of Natural History in the hope that it would get her students excited about science. And that was precisely the effect it had on Emilio, who liked science a lot better than the other shit Mrs. Cohen tried to teach them. He gawked at the museum's dinosaur fossils and the giant model of the blue whale. He stared in awe at the stuffed elephants in the Hall of African Mammals. But he got a little too excited in the Hall of Gems and Minerals, running around the display cases of sparkling rocks, and that bitch Cohen yanked him by the arm and made him stand in the corner for half an hour while the other kids gaped at the crystals.

Emilio learned two valuable lessons that day. One was obvious: school would never be fun. But the other lesson was subtle, and he didn't fully grasp it until much later. Most of the students in Emilio's class were Dominican, but there were a few white kids too, and although they ran around the museum just as much as Emilio did, Mrs. Cohen didn't yank them away from the display cases. She let them get away with it because she thought they were smart. She wanted to encourage them, not punish them. But she had no great hopes for the Dominican kids, so she didn't bother giving them any encouragement.

Emilio's fourth-grade and fifth-grade teachers weren't any different. They didn't expect much from him, so he didn't try very hard. In middle school and high school he avoided his classes altogether, preferring to hang out with his uncles and cousins in the Trinitarios. His grandmother yelled at him every day, but she was too old and tired to stop him, and in the end he became exactly what his teachers had expected: another Dominican dropout, a gangbanger, a thug.

Still, as bad as his situation was, Emilio was luckier than Paco, who was two years younger. Paco was *un hijo de crianza,* a foster kid. He had no grandmother to take care of him, no uncles or cousins to defend him, so he learned very young to be a badass. By the age of nine he was thrashing his classmates and threatening his teachers. Everyone told stories about him: how he broke someone's arm and stole sneakers from Foot Locker and had sex with his foster mom. He was suspended from school a dozen times before they finally expelled him. The cops arrested him a couple of times and he spent a few months in juvenile detention, but after he turned sixteen everyone in the neighborhood expected the worst. Sooner or later, everyone said, Paco was going to kill someone. Or get himself killed.

But now Emilio was going to prove them all wrong. He and Paco were going to pull off a job so big it would be on CNN and Fox News tomorrow. He smiled, imagining how Mrs. Cohen would react when she saw the news on TV. Maybe he should leave a note for her at the museum, just a couple of sentences to explain why he did it. *Dear Mrs. Cohen, You and all the other white people in New York are in big trouble now. You didn't expect* this *from us, did you?*

The train roared into the 116th Street station and jolted to a stop. As the doors slid open Emilio glanced at Paco again and saw him turn his head slightly, taking his eyes off the subway map. He seemed to be gazing at the deserted platform next to the tracks, even though nobody got on or off the train. Emilio wondered for a moment what the hell he was looking at. Then he noticed that the boy was actually looking past the platform at one of the big advertisements on the station's wall. It was a poster for the newest *Fast & Furious* movie, showing a shirtless Vin Diesel leaning against the hood of a red sports car. Paco opened his mouth as he stared at the picture. His face seemed to relax a little.

Emilio saw an opportunity to start a conversation. He pointed at the car in the poster. "That's a Dodge Viper, right? One of the new ones?"

Paco nodded but didn't say anything. The subway doors closed and he returned his attention to the map. A second later the train started moving again.

But Emilio was determined. He kept pointing at the poster as it slipped from view. "*Coño!* I'm gonna get me one of those cars. That's the first thing I'm gonna do with my share of the money."

Paco frowned. He turned to Emilio and gave him a dismissive look. "I don't think so. You know how much a Viper costs?"

"About eighty-five thousand dollars, right?" Emilio had no idea if that number was correct. It had just popped into his head. But it felt right.

Paco raised his eyebrows. "So you already went on the Internet to check the price? On the Dodge Viper Web site?"

Emilio was about to say no, but then something strange happened. Although he'd never visited that particular Web site, he could suddenly picture it with incredible clarity and detail, as if it had magically appeared on a screen inside his head. All at once, a stream of images from the site flashed behind his eyes: photographs of red, blue, and silver

Vipers, on the highway and the racetrack and the streets of Los Angeles. He also saw all the performance specifications for the Viper's ten-cylinder engine. The images and numbers flooded his mind.

It was so jarring he wondered if he was going crazy. After a couple of seconds, though, the stream of images began to slow. The pictures and numbers became fuzzier, more like ordinary memories, things he'd seen and half-forgotten. Maybe he *had* visited the Dodge Viper Web site after all. There was no computer in his grandmother's apartment, but sometimes he went on the Internet at Carlos's place, using the boy's laptop to check out all the stupid stuff on the Web. That might explain why he saw all those pictures in his head.

He turned away from Paco. He didn't want his homeboy to suspect that something was wrong. Emilio took a deep breath and put a casual look on his face. "Yeah, that car kicks ass. Six hundred forty-five horsepower. Goes from zero to sixty in three seconds."

"Jesus, you're a fucking expert."

Emilio had taken the numbers from the dwindling stream in his head. He had to admit, the information was useful. "Fuck yeah, I'm getting ready. Everyone's gonna piss in their pants when they see me rolling down Dyckman Street in that thing." He pointed at Paco. "And you can get a Viper too, amigo. Shit, you'll have enough cash to buy three of them. This job is gonna make us rich."

The left corner of Paco's lip turned upward. It was only a half smile, though, and it didn't last long. After a moment he frowned again and shook his head. "Nah, that's bullshit. No one's gonna pay us that kind of money. Not for a damn rock."

"I told you, it's not a rock. It's a crystal. A very fucking valuable crystal."

"Rock, crystal, whatever. We'll get maybe a few hundred dollars for it, that's all."

Emilio waved a finger at him. "Just wait and see, amigo. Wait and see."

They fell silent as the train pulled into the 110th Street station. Although their conversation had been brief, Emilio was pleased. Now he knew Paco was ready. The boy didn't expect much of a payout, but because he had no cash at all right now he was willing to work hard for a few hundred dollars.

As for Emilio, he wasn't interested in the money. He'd pretended to lust after sports cars only because he knew Paco wouldn't understand his real goal. Emilio himself didn't entirely understand it—his plan was still cloudy in his mind, still half-formed, a work in progress. But he knew he'd been chosen to do something astounding. He was going to fight the good fight and defend his people and right the wrongs and beat the devil. He was going to make history.

Ten minutes later they arrived at the museum station and got off the train. Emilio carried the duffel bag as they walked west on 81st Street, then turned south on Columbus Avenue. This was the Upper West Side, one of the richest parts of the city. You could smell the money in the air, even at three o'clock in the morning. Across the street from the museum was a row of expensive restaurants, all closed now. Above them were the fancy apartment buildings where the rich white people slept.

Emilio felt a sly satisfaction as he looked up at their windows. The white folks were proud and happy, but soon that would change. He wasn't sure yet what would happen to them—that was one of the cloudiest parts of his plan—but he knew they would suffer for their sins. That much was certain.

He and Paco strolled down the sidewalk, neither too fast nor too slow. The museum was like a castle, an enormous stone building surrounded by trees and gardens. Running between the gardens were asphalt paths with benches and drinking fountains. The boys turned left and walked down one of those paths until they reached an antique-looking iron fence. They stopped there to look around and make sure no one was in sight. Then they climbed over the fence and ran across the grass to the museum's southwestern corner.

This was the route Emilio had scoped out twelve hours ago when he'd come here to do his reconnaissance. There was a surveillance camera a couple of hundred feet away but it couldn't view them if they stayed under the trees. One of the trees had a thick crooked bough that slanted toward the museum, coming close to a window on the second floor. When Emilio had spotted that particular window during his reconnaissance mission he'd noticed a computer screen on the other side of the glass, so he'd assumed it was an office for one of the museum's workers. He'd also noticed that the window wasn't fully closed—there was a two-inch-wide slit above the sill. And now he smiled as he looked at the window again in the murky light, because the slit was still there.

When he got to the tree he crouched beside its trunk and signaled Paco to do the same. Emilio looked up at the branches and leaves overhead and the jutting knots in the tree's bark. He slipped both arms through the straps of the duffel bag so he could carry it like a backpack and free up his hands. Then he grasped one of the knots in the tree trunk and started climbing.

It wasn't easy. Emilio had never done any serious climbing before and didn't have a lot of upper-body strength. He was about to lose his grip and slide down the trunk when another stream of Internet images flashed through his head. Their sudden appearance didn't frighten him as much as it had the last time, maybe because he was getting used to it. Now the screen in his mind showed a how-to video, like something you'd find on YouTube. It featured a scruffy, bearded back-to-nature guy who was demonstrating how to climb an oak tree. The guy clasped his hands around the trunk and wrapped his thighs around it too and pushed his feet against the bark, wriggling upward like a caterpillar. It looked ridiculous but Emilio tried it anyway, and instead of sliding down the tree he started moving upward.

After a few seconds he reached the crooked, slanting bough and pulled himself up to where it branched off the trunk. He sat there, straddling the bough, catching his breath. A night breeze blew against the tree, making the branches swing back and forth, and Emilo glimpsed the security camera through the rustling leaves. This was bad—if he could see the camera, it could see him too, and one of the museum's guards might spot him on a video monitor. He needed to move quickly.

Wrapping his arms and legs around the bough, he scrabbled up its slanting length toward the second-floor window. The tree limb sagged and swayed as he crawled away from the trunk, but he kept pulling himself forward, hand over hand. Near the museum's stone façade the limb angled upward, pointing straight at the night sky. This allowed Emilio to clamber to his feet. He stood on the slanting lower part of the bough and held the vertical upper part for balance. Now he could step from the tree limb to the window, but he got worried when he saw the yawning gap between the two. The limb didn't come as close to the building as he'd thought. There was at least a yard of empty space between the bough and the windowsill.

Emilio hesitated. He muttered *"Coño!"* in frustration, cursing his bad luck. But he couldn't just stand there; the security camera could see him. He took his left foot off the tree and stretched it toward the window. Then he found a toehold on the sill and leaped across the gap.

The breeze pushed him sideways but he managed to grab the window frame and keep his balance on the sill. He bent over, slipped his fingers into the slit and yanked the window upward. As soon as it opened he jumped into the office and tumbled to the floor.

Emilio lay there for a moment, panting. Then he stood up, leaned out the window and gave Paco the thumbs-up signal. The boy scrambled up the tree, climbing much faster than Emilio had. Although Paco couldn't view any how-to videos in his head, he was in great shape and insanely competitive. Within seconds he vaulted from the tree limb to the window and came inside.

The room was dark but soon their eyes adjusted. It was a small office with a messy desk. The junk on the desk included an ashtray and a pack of cigarettes, which explained why the window had been left open. Emilio sidled toward the door, opened it quietly and peeked down the corridor. There were some cubicles and a coffee machine to the left. To the right was a second door, a really solid thing made of steel. The door had a crash bar for pushing it open, and above the bar was a sign that said TO THE EXHIBITION HALLS.

He looked over his shoulder at Paco. "Stay close," he whispered. "And keep an eye out for the guards."

Then he approached the steel door and pushed the crash bar. He thought an alarm might go off, but everything was silent. He held the door open for Paco, then stuck his baseball cap between the door and the jamb to stop it from locking behind them.

They stood in the Hall of Mexico and Central America, facing a monstrous stone head that was at least nine feet tall. During his reconnaissance mission Emilio had walked across the museum's floors to see where all the security cameras were, and he'd noticed the giant head. He'd even read the label for the exhibit, which said it was a monument sculpted by the Olmec people. Now, using the head as a landmark, he figured out the best route to the Hall of Gems and Minerals. First, he and Paco needed to go one flight down to the ground floor. There was a stairway a hundred feet ahead, but they couldn't use it—a surveillance camera was mounted near the steps. They would have to detour around it and go through the Hall of Asian Peoples to another stairway near the museum shop. That area was also monitored by a security camera, but Emilio had noticed it was poorly positioned. If he and Paco stayed on the left side of the stairway, they wouldn't be seen on the video monitor.

He stepped past the Olmec head and made his way across the darkened hall, with Paco silently following. The Hall of Asian Peoples was even darker, lit only by the glowing red EXIT signs. Emilio had come this way during his earlier visit and inspected the exhibits inside the display cases. Behind the glass were colorfully dressed mannequins that were supposed to look like all the different types of Asians: Arab sheikhs, Tibetan monks, Malaysian aborigines. Now, with the lights turned off, Emilio could see only looming silhouettes inside the display cases, but he vividly recalled what they looked like. He'd felt an odd compulsion when he'd come here earlier, a powerful need to look at every exhibit he passed, to scrutinize everything in sight, and not just the security cameras. He still felt this compulsion now but it wasn't as strong, possibly because there was less to see in the darkness.

When they reached the stairway by the museum shop they went down the left side of the steps, just out of camera range. Then they entered the Hall of North American Mammals and tiptoed past the stuffed wolves and grizzly bears. They turned left and then right and then stepped into the Hall of Northwest Coast Indians and passed the big totem poles with the spooky animal faces carved into the wood. Then Emilio heard footsteps and saw a flashlight beam lance into the room.

He and Paco dove to the right. They took cover behind one of the totem poles, huddling against its rough base. The footsteps grew louder and the flashlight beam swept across the hall, shining on the floor and walls and display cases. Then Emilio saw the museum guard in the center of the room, just fifteen feet away. The man was tall and black and very athletic-looking in his uniform. Luckily he was staring at a different totem pole. He aimed his flashlight at a froglike face at the top of the pole, painted green and red and yellow. Then he chuckled to himself and walked out of the hall, apparently heading for the museum shop.

After waiting a few more seconds, Emilio and Paco rose to their feet and quickstepped in the opposite direction. They hurried past the museum's snack bar and the ground-floor restrooms. They rushed through the Hall of Human Origins and the Hall of Meteorites. Emilio's T-shirt was heavy with sweat by the time they finally reached the Hall of Gems and Minerals, which was the darkest room in the whole building. The walls were painted black and the red EXIT signs were almost swallowed in the gloom. But at the far end of the hall were hundreds of tiny red sparks, like a swarm of bloodied fireflies. They were the reflections of the EXIT signs off the biggest crystals in the room, the ones too large to be kept in the display cases.

Emilio went straight to the massive block of topaz. It sat on the floor near the corner of the room, where Mrs. Cohen had forced him to stand ten years ago while the other third-graders romped around the hall. The crystal had impressed the hell out of him back then and still impressed him now. It was about three feet high and two feet wide and looked like a giant cube of rock candy. A couple of steel rods anchored the topaz to the floor, and underneath it was a lightbulb that shone—at least during museum hours—up into the crystal, giving it a yellowish glow. But now the bulb was turned off, and Emilio could see that only the bottom half of the crystal had the yellowish impurities that muddied its color. The top half was as clear as glass.

He bent over the crystal and ran his hand along its surface, so smooth and cool and hard. Then he turned to Paco. "This is it," he whispered. "This is what we came for."

Paco crouched beside the topaz. After inspecting it for a few seconds he pointed at the steel rods. "Shit, it's stuck to the floor. And even if we can get it loose, how are we gonna carry it? It must weigh a fucking ton."

"Three tons, actually. But we're not gonna take the whole thing. We're gonna cut off a section from the top half of the crystal, the pure half."

"A section?" Paco looked up at him, grimacing. "How the fuck are you gonna cut the thing? You got any tools?"

Emilio took the duffel bag off his back, slipping his arms out of the straps. Then he unzipped it and removed the only tool inside, a spike made of shiny black metal, as thin as a pencil and ten inches long. "This is all we need."

He'd found the tool in the basement of his grandmother's apartment building. Well, maybe "found" wasn't the right word. He knew it would be there.

All day, both before and after his reconnaissance trip to the museum,

Emilio had jittered with anticipation. Toward evening he'd tried to calm himself by lying on his grandmother's couch, but he couldn't close his eyes. Crazy visions ran through his head like scenes in a movie. He saw himself as a soldier leading a squad of commandos, all of them badasses like the ones in Battle Blood. He watched his men march through Inwood Hill Park and attack the cops on Dyckman Street, sending them running toward the river. Then he saw the white people fleeing from their fancy buildings, a huge herd of white people stampeding up the Harlem River Drive, trampling each other to get out of Manhattan.

Then the visions turned fuzzy and faded, and he was left with only one thought, which took the form of a command: *Go to the basement and look behind the dryers.* Although it didn't make a lot of sense, he got up from the couch anyway and took the elevator to the basement. When he looked behind the dryers in the laundry room he saw the tip of the spike sticking out of a crack in the wall. It should've scared him, but it didn't. He just wrapped his hand around the thing and pulled it out.

But now that Emilio finally stood next to the block of topaz, he was at a loss. He knew he was supposed to use the gleaming tool to cut the crystal, but he had no idea how to do it. The spike looked a bit like an ice pick but its ends weren't very sharp. He didn't see how it could even make a dent in the crystal. Paco stared at the spike too, probably thinking the same thing.

Emilio bent over the topaz and pointed the spike at it. He was trying to at least look like he knew what he was doing. He tapped one end of the spike against the smooth flat top of the crystal, testing its hardness. Then he tapped one of the crystal's equally smooth sides. He was about to tap the block a third time when the spike flew out of his hand. It struck the side of the topaz and stuck there, flush against the crystal's surface, as if held by a magnet.

"*Anda el diablo!*" Emilio stepped backward, startled. He turned to Paco. "Did you see that?"

His homeboy didn't answer. Emilo turned back to the crystal and saw the spike changing shape before his eyes. While staying attached to the topaz, it grew longer and thinner, its ends pulling away from each other. After a few seconds the spike was as slender as a string and stretched across the full width of the block. Then it began to penetrate the crystal, changing its shape again to become a blade of gleaming metal that wedged into the side of the topaz. The blade sliced through the crystal like a horizontal guillotine, moving swiftly and effortlessly from one side of the block to the other. Within seconds it severed the topmost section of the crystal, creating a four-inch-thick slice that continued to rest on the lower part of the topaz. The cut was so clean and neat you could barely see it. Then the blade emerged from the other side of the block and changed back to its old shape, a shiny black spike. It dropped to the floor.

Emilio gaped, amazed and delighted, as awestruck as an eight-year-old visiting the museum for the first time. "You believe this shit? That fucking thing cut the block all by itself!"

Paco remained silent. It was hard to see the boy's face in the dark but it looked like he was truly freaked. Emilio almost laughed. "Don't worry, *muchacho*, it's just modern technology. Now let's see if we can carry the part that's cut off."

Emilio bent over the topaz again and touched the top section, which was roughly square and about the size and thickness of a briefcase. He pushed it with his index finger but it didn't budge. So he applied more pressure, pushing with his whole hand, and after a moment the section slid a couple of inches forward. Emilio stopped pushing, and now he did let out a laugh, a quiet snort of triumph. The edge of the top section hung over the lower part of the block.

"Okay, it's heavy as shit, more than a hundred pounds, but I think we can handle it." Emilio reached for the duffel bag and opened its zipper all the way. He held the bag over the slice of crystal to confirm that the thing would fit inside. Then he knelt beside the block and draped the bag around the jutting edge of the top section. "You get on the other side and push the section toward me. I'll get it into the bag."

Paco just stood there, as if in a trance. After a couple of seconds he shook his head. "I don't like this. It's fucked up."

Emilio frowned. "I told you, it's just technology. This is how all the jewel-cutters do it now. You think they're still using hammers and chisels?"

"But the thing moved by itself! How the—"

"*Coño*, I don't have time to explain it! Are you gonna be a pussy or are you gonna help me?"

Paco tensed, his whole body going taut. Then, cursing under his breath, he knelt beside the block and started pushing the top section of the crystal.

As the thick slice of topaz slid off the lower part of the block Emilio guided it into the duffel bag. The section was even heavier than he'd thought, at least a hundred fifty pounds. He grasped both of the bag's straps and tried to lift it by himself, but he couldn't manage it. That's why he needed Paco. He hadn't understood the reason before, but now it made perfect sense. The plan was firming up in his mind, becoming a little less cloudy with each step.

He picked up the gleaming spike from the floor and put it into the duffel bag next to the crystal slice. Then he zipped up the bag and handed one of the straps to Paco. "We'll carry it between us. Come on, let's get out of here."

Retracing their steps, they left the Hall of Gems and Minerals, Emilio on one side of the duffel bag, Paco on the other, each gripping one of the straps. Between the two of them, the heavy bag was manageable, although it strained their arms and made them lean toward each other. They planned to leave the museum the same way they'd come in, through that office window on the second floor, but Emilio worried about running into the tall, black guard who'd almost spotted them. Because they'd seen him walking toward the museum shop, Emilio chose a new route that steered clear of that area. He and Paco lugged the duffel bag through the Hall of Biodiversity and the Theodore Roosevelt Memorial Hall. Then they went up the stairway to the second floor, staying on the left side again because of the camera. The bag felt very fucking heavy as they hauled it up the steps. When they reached the top of the stairway they turned left, heading back to the Hall of Asian Peoples.

Then they heard a shout behind them. *"Hey! Stop right there!"*

A flashlight clicked on, throwing their shadows against the wall. Emilio looked over his shoulder and saw the silhouette of a security guard, about thirty feet away. It was a different guard from the one they saw before—this one was a white guy, shorter and less intimidating. But his size didn't matter. As the guard pointed his flashlight at them he snatched his radio from his belt and raised it to his mouth. He was alerting the other guards, calling for backup.

Emilio was already running, and so was Paco. They bolted at the same moment, both still holding the duffel bag between them. Emilio had to give his homeboy some credit—if Paco wanted to, he could've just let go of the bag's strap and dashed out of sight. But instead he stayed with Emilio and their hundred and fifty pound treasure, which rocked from side to side as they ran down the corridor, away from the security guard.

They turned right, dodging the flashlight beam, and darted into the Hall of Asian Peoples. The guard ran after them, shouting *"Second floor, second floor!"* into his radio. The beam from his flashlight chased them too, sweeping across the display cases, shining on the mannequins of Arab sheikhs and Tibetan monks. Emilio's arm was going numb from the strain of holding the duffel bag, and the muscles in his legs were cramping. As they turned a corner his shoulder banged against the wall and the pain shot through his body, making him stumble. He wanted to drop the bag. He wanted to collapse.

But at the same instant another stream of images rushed through his head. This time, Emilio knew, the images didn't come from the Internet. They weren't pictures of sports cars or videos of tree climbing. They were images of things he didn't recognize, things he'd never seen before. They were so strange he couldn't even begin to describe them. And yet they were also powerfully, magically beautiful. The sight of them filled his mind with new strength and hope. They were images of the future. *His* future.

So Emilio kept running. He leaned forward and took giant strides. He sprinted so fast and pulled the bag so hard that he practically dragged Paco along with him. They burst out of the Hall of Asian Peoples and raced past another stairway. Then they sped down the home stretch, past the sculptures and pottery of Mexico and Central America, their eyes fixed on the giant Olmec head and the steel door that led to the museum's offices. They were just a hundred feet away from the door, and the white security guard was way behind them. He'd never catch up to them in time. They were going to make it.

Then the other guard, the tall, athletic black one, came around a corner up ahead, running straight toward them. He had his flashlight in one hand and his radio in the other. As soon as he saw them he took up position in front of the Olmec head, bracing himself like a wrestler at the start of a match, his knees bent, his shoulders hunched. He was going to knock both of them flat on their asses.

Paco broke stride, his head turning wildly, looking for another way out, but Emilio didn't slow down. Instead, he ran faster. He hurtled toward the guard, and at the same time he grabbed the strap of the duffel bag with both hands and yanked it so violently that the other strap ripped out of Paco's grasp. In that moment the bag felt as light as a slingshot, and as Emilio charged forward he swung the thing in front of him.

The guard held out both his hands, ready to bat the bag away from him, but he obviously wasn't expecting a hundred-and-fifty-pound weight. It was only in the last quarter second, when the bag knocked his hands aside and plowed between his arms, that he realized how god-damn heavy it was. His eyes widened in surprise and he tried to side-step, but it was too late. The crystal inside the bag struck him square in the chest and sent him flying backward. His heels lifted off the floor and the back of his skull cracked against the Olmec head.

Emilio stood over the body, the bag still swinging in his hands. He was prepared to hit the guard again, but the man lay motionless, bleed-ing from his ears. For a moment Emilio felt a surge of revulsion in his stomach. *Jesus, what happened? What the fuck did I do?* But then he heard the other security guard behind them, shouting into his radio again. Soon every goddamn guard in the museum would come running. And then the cops would come too.

Frantic, he turned to Paco, who was looking down at the fallen guard. Emilio shoved one of the duffel bag's straps into the boy's hand. *"Vamonos!* We need to *go!"*

They rushed to the steel door, where Emilio's baseball cap was still wedged between the latch and the jamb. Back in the small, messy office, they lifted the bag to the windowsill and heaved it outside. Emilio heard it land with a thump in the grass, and then he and Paco heaved themselves out the window, first dangling from the sill and then drop-ping to the ground. They picked up the duffel bag and raced back to 81st Street, but they didn't return to the subway. By the time the police cars screamed down Columbus Avenue and pulled up to the museum's entrance, Emilio and Paco were several blocks away, in Riverside Park. Staying in the shadows under the trees, they started walking north, carrying the crystal to Inwood.

It was 6:00 A.M. when they finally got to Arden Street. The sun was climbing above the neighborhood, already baking the pavement.

Emilio yawned and trembled as he approached his grandmother's building. He was so tired he could barely think. Paco looked just as bad, dragging himself along like a wounded soldier. Their hands were blistered from hauling the duffel bag for two hours. Emilio's feet ached with each step and the muscles in his arms felt like they'd been shredded. But they'd made it home. They'd lugged a hundred-fifty-pound rock at least six miles uptown. That had to be some kind of record.

They staggered through the apartment building's entrance and stood in front of the elevator door. Paco stretched his hand toward the UP button, but Emilio nudged it aside and pressed the DOWN button instead. "We're not going to Abuela's apartment," he explained. "We're gonna take it down to the basement."

"The basement?" Paco narrowed his bloodshot eyes. "Why there?"

"I know a safe place to hide it. Safer than the apartment."

The elevator door creaked open and they dragged the duffel bag inside. Then they descended to the basement, which was warm and stuffy and deserted. Next to the elevator was the laundry room, and just beyond it was a storage closet that no one in the building used anymore. For years Emilio had avoided going near this closet because he'd once seen a dead cat inside. But he'd peeked into the closet yesterday because it was right next to the laundry room. He'd felt an irresistible need to know what was on the other side of the wall where he'd pulled out the black spike. After looking inside the closet he'd bought a padlock from the hardware store and used it to secure the door. He didn't understand what he'd glimpsed in there, but he knew he had to keep it secret.

Now he stood in front of the closet, fishing in his pocket for the key to the padlock. Paco leaned against the wall, his eyes closed, falling asleep on his feet. "Hurry up," he muttered. "I'm tired as shit."

"Just another second." Emilio found the key and slipped it into the lock. "You might be surprised when you see this. It's . . . well, it's a little weird, you know?"

"What do you got in there?" Paco lifted one eyelid. Even though they were alone, he lowered his voice to a whisper. "More shit you've stolen?"

"No, not that." Emilio opened the door but didn't turn on the light in the closet. He hauled the duffel bag inside, then gripped Paco's arm. "I've been keeping this a secret, but I want you to see it."

As soon as Paco stepped into the closet, Emilio turned on the light and shut the door behind them. Paco's eyes widened as he looked around. The closet's floor and three of its walls were covered with sheets of black metal. The surfaces were flawless, not a scratch or a smudge on them, and they were polished to such a high shine that they looked like dark mirrors. Emilio saw reflections of himself and Paco on all three walls, their faces shining under the light from the naked bulb on the ceiling. Although this wasn't the first time Emilio had stood in front of these mirrors, he was struck once again by their beauty and strangeness. He couldn't help but gape at the reflections, which somehow seemed more real than the solid things they mirrored.

Paco seemed impressed too. He turned his head from one wall to the next, taking it all in. Then he turned to Emilio and smiled. "This is crazy. Did you put up these mirrors?" He pointed at the gleaming metal. "What were you trying to do, build a disco down here? A really small disco?"

He laughed, but he wasn't making fun of Emilio. There was no nastiness in his voice. Paco seemed genuinely amused and curious. Emilio smiled back at him. "I told you it was weird."

"So what do you use this place for?" Paco bent his knees and twisted his hips, watching himself in the mirror as he did a couple of merengue steps. "Do you come down here to practice your dance moves?"

Now Emilio laughed with him. The two of them were so tired they were acting a little delirious. But in that moment Emilio saw something in Paco that he hadn't seen before, probably because the boy kept it well hidden. Now he realized why Paco had stared so intently at the *Fast & Furious* poster on the subway platform a few hours before. The boy had no interest in sports cars. He was interested in Vin Diesel, the bare-chested actor in the picture.

It was time to act. Emilio stepped closer to Paco, so close he could feel the boy's breath on his face. They stared at each other in silence for several seconds. Then Emilio winked at him. "We can do anything we want down here. That's what this place is for."

For a moment Emilio thought the boy was going to hit him. Paco's body tensed, just like it did in the museum when Emilio called him a pussy. But then the boy shivered and leaned forward and pressed his lips against Emilio's. They wrapped their arms around each other and opened their mouths. Emilio felt Paco's tongue slide over his own.

Then Emilio felt a horrible pain at the tip of his tongue. At first he thought Paco had bit it, but the boy was in pain too and screaming into Emilio's mouth. Their tongues were stuck together as if a bolt had been driven through them. Something tiny and metallic had carved a path through Emilio's soft tissue and emerged from the tip of his tongue so it could penetrate Paco's. It pierced the underside of the boy's tongue and started boring deeper.

After a second their tongues unlocked and the boys separated, but the horrible pain continued. Emilio fell against the side of the mirrored closet and Paco crumpled to the floor. In the midst of his agony Emilio looked at one of the gleaming walls and saw himself doubled over, his hands clasped over his burning mouth. Paco was doing the same thing, his brother in pain. It was a terrifying sight, but strangely enough it calmed Emilio. He saw the logic behind the pain, and that made it easier to bear. He stopped writhing.

This is how we'll build our army, he thought. *Now Paco will be as strong and smart as I am. And we can work together to recruit more soldiers.*

A moment later a pair of gleaming wires rose from the metallic floor. It was like one of those cartoons where a snake charmer plays a gourd flute and a cobra rises from a basket. As Emilio watched in amazement, the wires tore into the duffel bag like a couple of black snakes, ripping it open. Then they coiled around the crystalline section and pulled it out of the bag. The black wires began to cut the crystal in the same way that Emilio's tool had cut it, slicing off a rodlike piece that was nearly two feet long. One end of the piece was shaped like a disk—about as wide and thin as a silver dollar—and the other end tapered to a sharp point. It looked like a crystalline sword.

And that will be our weapon, Emilio thought. *We'll use it to drive all the bastard cops out of Manhattan.*

As if responding to his thoughts, the wires carried the piece of crystal toward Emilio, with its sharp end pointing at him. At the same time, a third wire coiled around his right arm and pinned it to the floor.

This surprised Emilio. He tried to wrench his arm free, but the wire held it down tight. "*Coño!* What's going on? What—"

The wires brought the crystalline rod closer, aiming it at his right hand. Then the sharp end pierced the skin of his palm and plunged deeper.

Emilio screamed.

FOURTEEN

Dorothy rested on a wooden chaise lounge in the garden behind her apartment. It wasn't much of a garden, really. The apartment buildings on her block surrounded a dingy courtyard that was divided by high fences into a dozen modest plots, one for each of the ground-floor apartments. Dorothy's garden was a ten-foot-by-twenty-foot rectangle that lay outside the sliding glass door of her living room. Most of it was covered with patio brick, and the few square yards of soil were crowded with weeds. Nevertheless, this was where she'd decided to spend her final hours.

It was 11:00 A.M. but the garden still lay in the shade. The surrounding apartment buildings blocked the sun for almost the whole day. From the chaise lounge Dorothy could see only a small patch of sky overhead, a square of hazy blue. She looked up and saw a couple of pigeons fly across the square. A few minutes later she spotted a distant airliner.

She wore nothing but her bathrobe, an old white cotton thing. Any of her neighbors on the upper floors could see her on the chaise lounge if they happened to look out their back windows, but Dorothy was in too much pain to worry about that. The constant ache in her stomach had spread to her back. She felt like she was lying on a fist-sized rock that someone had left on the chaise. She rolled onto her left side, which lessened the pain in her back, and stared at the weeds that had taken over her garden. After a while, though, she felt the rock again, now cutting into the flesh at her waist.

Over the past twenty-four hours her cancer had taken a vicious turn for the worse. As soon as she'd returned from her brief visit to the hospital she'd collapsed on her living-room couch and spent the rest of the day in a feverish half-sleep, sweating and groaning. She'd drifted in and out of consciousness, sometimes dreaming absurd dreams, sometimes rising from the couch and stumbling around the apartment. At one point she went to her bedroom and unpacked her shoulder bag, but she was in such a daze that afterwards she couldn't remember what she'd done or where she'd put everything. And then, sometime in the middle of the night, her living room seemed to get unbearably hot, so she opened the sliding glass door and staggered outside to the chaise lounge.

She lay there until dawn. The hours passed like ghosts, but as the morning came and the patch of sky brightened above her, Dorothy's mind began to clear. It occurred to her that she might be dying. The more she considered the possibility, the more likely it seemed. In addition to the terrible pains in her abdomen, she was finding it difficult to breathe. But she wasn't alarmed and she certainly wasn't going to call 911. There was no point in going back to the hospital. Although her doctors had nothing but good intentions, they would only make things harder for her. Better to make her peace with the Lord now than to endure weeks of suffering. She was a little puzzled as to why her cancer had worsened so suddenly, but in the end it didn't matter. She'd prayed for a cure, and the Lord had given her this instead. She would try to accept His will with humility and grace.

But it was hard to be humble and graceful when it felt like someone was knifing you in the belly. With a grunt, Dorothy rolled onto her other side and waited for the pain to shift again. Now she faced the sliding glass door, which was filthy because she hadn't washed it in months. She felt a twinge of shame and thought of her mother, who'd spent forty years working as a maid for the white folks in Montgomery, Alabama. If her mother were alive to see this, she'd sigh and shake her head. Then she'd find a rag somewhere in the apartment and clean it herself.

Dorothy grimaced. This wasn't what she wanted to think about during her last hours on Earth. She should be thinking of more positive, uplifting things. Like the five glorious years she spent in Africa, doing missionary work and learning how to tell Bible stories in Swahili. Or the civil-rights work she did for the Union of Black Episcopalians, or the wonderful friends she'd made at Holy Trinity Episcopal Church. But instead she stared through the filthy glass at the furniture in her living room and remembered the day she moved into the apartment. That was in August 1994, almost twenty-two years ago, soon after she became Holy Trinity's vicar. The apartment was just a few blocks from the church, which was a good thing because she intended to work long hours. She was an energetic, idealistic thirty-seven-year-old then, full of devotion to God and eagerness to do His will.

She was also someone's mistress. She was breaking the seventh commandment.

Dear Jesus, why am I thinking about that now? That's the last thing I want to think about.

Her lover's name was Martin Bell. He was a sweet, funny, intelligent man, a high-school math teacher who lived in Harlem. She met him on the subway on her very first day in New York, when she came to the city to interview for the position at Holy Trinity. Three months later she discovered that he was married, and that he had two young daughters no less. At that point she should've ended their relationship, but she didn't. She continued to see him for the next ten years.

And why didn't I stop it? Because I was already in love with him? Because I was lonely and didn't think I'd find anyone else? Because I was tired of being good?

No one at Holy Trinity suspected it, because she and Martin were careful. They never went out to dinner in the neighborhood. He visited her apartment two or three times a week, sometimes staying only a couple of hours. Despite the limitations, it was a loving, passionate relationship. Martin was her soul mate. He just happened to belong to someone else.

I would've stayed with him to this day if not for the guilt. I never saw his wife, not even a picture of her. But he showed me photos of his daughters. Pictures of them in kindergarten and summer camp. Getting bigger every year.

After ten years of sin she finally ended the affair and came back to the Lord. She begged his forgiveness and he granted it. But now she realized that the person she'd hurt the most wasn't Martin's wife or his daughters or even the Almighty. She'd betrayed herself. If she hadn't taken up with Martin she could've found a different soul mate, someone equally charming and intelligent but not already married. She could've had children with him, sons and daughters of her own. And he would be at her side right now, holding her hand, comforting her during her last hours.

Dorothy was crying. No tears leaked from her eyes because she was so dehydrated, but her body shook with sobs.

Lord, you gave me the gift of life, and I ruined it. There were so many opportunities I missed, so many joys I never got the chance to feel. Yes, I did some good work in your church, but it wasn't enough. I should've done more. Oh Jesus, why did I waste your gift?

Her sadness intensified the agony in her stomach. The pain spread to her chest, rolling onto it like a boulder. It shoved the air out of her lungs and crushed her heart. But as she struggled for breath she heard an answer to her question.

Don't despair, my child. It's not too late.

She recognized his voice. It was the same voice she'd heard in the laboratory at the hospital, the soft, kind voice that had murmured in her head while she stared at the lovely researcher named Naomi. But now the Lord didn't speak to her in pictures and emotions, as he had before; now he spoke in clear, unmistakable words. Her heart thudded and the air rushed back into her lungs.

Oh yes! I hear you, Lord! I hear you!

You've been a faithful servant for many years, Dorothy. Your reward is waiting for you in Heaven.

Thank you, Jesus! Oh, thank you, thank you!

I am well pleased with you already, but I have heard your prayer. You still long to serve me, even to the last breath. And now you can perform one final task for me, if you wish it.

Yes, yes, I do wish it! But how can I serve you, Lord? I'm dying.

You can complete what you began yesterday at the hospital. Do you remember?

Dorothy nodded. She remembered the stack of cell culture plates, the plastic trays loaded with stem cell colonies. She'd removed them from the incubator in Naomi's laboratory and stuffed them into her shoulder bag. She vaguely recalled unpacking the bag in her bedroom, but nothing after that.

Lord, I was weak! I didn't understand what you wanted from me. And then I got so sick—

All shall be well, child, all shall be well. You need only rise and make your way into your house. Go to your room, your bed. You shall die, but then you shall be resurrected.

A surge of holy fervor made her tremble. It was all true, all the promises made by Jesus and his apostles, all the prophecies in the Old and New Testaments. With shaking hands she grasped the wooden arms of the chaise lounge and pushed herself up to a sitting position. Her body felt as light as air.

Yes, Lord, I'm coming! Hallelujah! Hallelujah!

She swung her feet off the chaise and planted them on the brick surface of her patio. Then she took a deep breath and stood up. Her head swam for a moment—the garden spun around her; the square patch of sky twirled overhead—but she managed to stay on her feet. She took a careful step forward and then another, walking as if on a tightrope. After the fourth step she reached the sliding glass door and grabbed its handle. She pulled at it but the door wouldn't budge. She was so weak now, weaker than an infant. But then she felt the Lord's voice in her mind again, urging her on. She gave the handle a stronger tug and the door slid open.

Hot air wafted out the door and billowed against her. Her living room had been very warm last night, but now it was broiling. The heat stung her face as she stepped inside and closed the door behind her. There was a strange smell in the room too, fetid and salty like the beach at low tide. Dorothy breathed in the hot, foul air and coughed it out. Her head swam again and she almost fainted. But her bedroom was only a few yards away and the Almighty was behind her, giving her the strength to go on. She stumbled to the bedroom door and grasped the knob, which was so hot it burned her palm. But she opened the door anyway and peered inside.

The room was dark and empty. Her bed, bureau, and night table were gone. At first glance she thought a burglar must've broken in during the night and carted away the furniture, but then she noticed another big change: the walls were covered with shiny black metal from floor to ceiling. The metallic sheets even covered the bedroom window and the door to her closet.

Lord? What happened here? Where's my—

Don't be frightened. Step into the room and close the door.

The bedroom was even hotter than the living room, but Dorothy obeyed. She closed the door and stood there in the dark, waiting. The only light in the room came from around the edges of the door she'd just closed. After a moment, though, she glimpsed a faint glowing line at the other end of the room, where the far wall touched the ceiling. The line slowly advanced across the ceiling, like the greenish bar of light that scans documents in a copying machine. It made a faint oozing noise as it moved overhead. Then Dorothy heard the same noise behind her. She turned around and saw another glowing greenish line move sideways across the wall. These lines, she realized, were the edges of the metallic sheets, which were expanding to cover the ceiling and the bedroom door. Within seconds the shiny black metal sealed off the room.

Now I will give you a new bed.

She saw yet another glowing line slide across the floor, pulling the metallic sheet behind it like a carpet. But when this line reached the center of the room it changed color, turning a vivid shade of red. As the line continued to advance it spread a different kind of sheet across the floor, a thick mat of red spongy material that looked softer than the shiny black metal around it. The line kept moving across the floor until the mat was about three feet wide. Then it stopped a few inches from Dorothy's feet. This red mat, she realized, was the bed the Lord had prepared for her. It was her deathbed.

Lie down, my child. Your work is done.

She knelt on the floor and looked closely at the glowing mat. The spongy material was about four inches thick. It looked moist and swollen and its color was so strange. After a few seconds Dorothy remembered where she'd seen that shade of red before. It was the color of the stem cell colonies in the trays she'd taken from the laboratory.

Lord, I'm afraid! I don't—

Enough. Lie down.

All her strength suddenly drained from her limbs and she fell to the mat. Her shoulder hit it first, and then she rolled onto her back, sprawling helplessly. She felt like she was floating in a shallow pool of red mud that was sludgy and rank and boiling hot. She squirmed in pain and tried to roll off the mat, but a long black wire arose from one of the metallic sheets and looped over her waist, pinning her down. Another wire restrained her legs and a third stretched over her throat and pressed down on her windpipe. Then more wires with sharp hooks tore into the fabric of her bathrobe and ripped it off her body.

Stop! *What are you doing? Who—*

Please be calm, Dorothy. Soon you will be reborn. Isn't that what you wanted?

The red mud melted the skin off her back. She felt the hot, thick slurry seep into her chest and stomach. It dissolved her hair and leaked into her skull and drowned her thoughts. The voices inside her head grew faint.

You're not him! You're Satan! You're . . . you're . . .

I am the Word made flesh. I am the Light of the World.

FIFTEEN

Scientists are strange creatures, Sarah thought. They love to criticize and nitpick and tear apart each other's work, but if you're looking for someone to help you out at a moment's notice, your best bet is to call one of your old friends from graduate school.

She sat in an office in Columbia University's Science and Engineering Library at the corner of Broadway and West 120th Street. The office belonged to Phil Clark, a chemist who specialized in developing new polymers and other advanced materials. But that hadn't always been his specialty. When he and Sarah had been grad students at Cornell he'd been just as obsessed with meteorites as she was. And when NASA had hired Sarah to study Martian meteorites, she'd asked Phil to help her analyze the rock that appeared to hold fossils of ancient bacteria. Phil had scrutinized the microscopic structures inside the meteorite and found that their iron-bearing minerals were remarkably pure, just as you'd expect them to be if they'd been synthesized by microbes. He'd reported this finding without any excitement. Nothing surprised Phil, not even evidence of extraterrestrial life. He was one of the most level-headed men Sarah knew.

So now she was startled by the emotion on his face as he stared into the eyepiece of the scanning microscope on his desk. He was reexamining, for maybe the fortieth time, the sample she'd brought to his office yesterday, the half gram of metallic shavings she'd scraped off the blade of Gino Torelli's ax. Normally, Phil was calm and methodical, but now his cheeks were flushed and his mouth hung open. He ran his hands through his thinning hair and flakes of dandruff sprinkled the back of his polo shirt. After a couple of minutes he lifted his head from the microscope and stared at a pile of printouts on his desk. The papers showed the results of all the tests Phil had performed on the sample over the past twenty-four hours: the mass spectrometry, the X-ray diffraction study, the dielectric analysis. He shook his head as he pored over the columns of numbers. He was a tall, gangly man, and his head swayed like a scarecrow's.

He turned to Sarah. "You need to call a lawyer." He pointed at the telephone on his desk. "But I'm not sure if you should call a criminal lawyer or a patent lawyer."

Sarah's stomach clenched. "Why? What did I do wrong?"

He frowned. "Where did you get this sample?"

She hadn't told Phil about the gleaming cable she'd seen in the manhole. She was worried about the confidentiality agreement she'd signed. The Air Force could send her to prison if she said too much. "I told you, this is a sensitive thing. A national security thing. I can't answer a lot of questions."

"Did you steal it? From a government laboratory?"

"No, of course not!"

"I'm sorry, Sarah, but I'm having trouble believing you." Phil folded his arms across his chest. "If you didn't steal the sample, then you must've created this new material yourself. I'd be very happy for you if this were true, because the discovery would earn you many millions of dollars, assuming you hired a good patent lawyer. But I know you couldn't have created it. You don't have the expertise or the resources to do this kind of work."

"I didn't create it or steal it. I found it."

"Then you need to tell me where you found it. Otherwise I can't draw any useful conclusions from the test results."

Sarah was exasperated. She didn't know what to do. She'd given the sample to Phil rather than to General Hanson because she'd wanted to stay in control of the investigation. If the Air Force took over, they'd probably hide the results in some top-secret document and the truth would never come out. But doing it on her own was risky, not only to herself but to anyone who helped her. She didn't want to tell Phil anything that would get him in trouble.

"Let's just talk hypothetically. What if I said I got the sample from a space probe that crash-landed near here?"

Phil looked askance. "I'd say you were hallucinating. I haven't heard of any spacecraft crashing into New York City lately."

"What if it was just a piece of debris from a probe that mostly disintegrated in the atmosphere?"

"That doesn't sound quite as insane, but I still don't believe it."

"Why not?"

He picked up the pile of printouts. "The material in your sample isn't one of the alloys or composites used in spacecraft. It's unlike anything I've ever seen. Most of it is an iron alloy, but it has a completely different mix of elements than the standard varieties of steel. And its crystalline structure? The way the atoms of iron and carbon and silicon stack together?" He flipped through the printouts until he found a full-page diagram, a rough schematic based on the X-ray diffraction results. "Come here and take a look at this. It's ingenious."

Sarah rose from her chair to look at the diagram. It showed an incredibly complex lattice of atoms, a structure that looked like a monstrous jungle gym. At its center was a tight packing of iron, carbon, and chromium atoms, a solid core that seemed to be optimized for conducting electricity. Surrounding the core were layers of semiconducting silicon, the same crystalline stuff that was at the heart of every computer chip. But the most fascinating features were at the edges. The lattice was lined with dangling strands of atoms. They extended from structures that looked like rotors and pivots. The tips of the strands were bent into minuscule hooks and cleavers.

Now she saw what had surprised Phil so much. Those strands and rotors and pivots were nanodevices. They were microscopic machines, smaller than a millionth of a millimeter, so tiny they could manipulate individual molecules and assemble them into new structures. Chemists and physicists and engineers had been working on nanotechnology for the past two decades, but most of the devices they wanted to build were still in the dream stage, and even their most outlandish dreams weren't as sophisticated as the microscopic structures in this sample. Sarah was looking at a molecular marvel, and judging from the design of the strands, she could guess what they were supposed to do.

She let out a whistle. "Okay, this makes sense, believe it or not. These strands over here? The ones that look like fishhooks?" She pointed at the diagram. "They could bind to other molecules, right? To molecules of hematite or silicon dioxide or any of the carbonates in sedimentary minerals?"

Phil squinted at the page. After several seconds he nodded. "Yes, I suppose that's possible. The lattice can capture the smaller molecules if they're close enough and have the right polarity."

"And these other strands, the ones connected to the pivots? They could pull the captured molecules apart, couldn't they? And then the lattice could absorb all the iron and carbon atoms that get broken off." Sarah tapped the page. "It can act as a drill, see? As it digs into the ground it would dissolve all the minerals in its way. And at the same time it would suck up the atomic pieces of the minerals and use them to enlarge the drill. To make it longer, so it could dig even deeper."

Phil nodded again and stared at the diagram for a few more seconds. Then he raised his head and gave her a suspicious look. "You guessed its function a little too easily. I get the feeling you've already seen this drill in action."

His face was close to hers, just a few inches away, which made Sarah uncomfortable. Twenty-two years ago, when they were both at Cornell, Phil had fallen in love with her. He'd spent months working up the nerve to ask her out, but by the time they actually went on a date—at a loud Mexican restaurant in Ithaca—Sarah already had her eye on Tom Gilbert, the charming, handsome postdoctoral student who was helping to design a microbe detector for NASA's Mars probes. The next day she apologized to Phil and told him she was more interested in someone else. Phil took it stoically and never mentioned it again. Even after Tom betrayed her during the meteorite fiasco and she broke off their engagement, Phil kept his distance.

Now, in retrospect, Sarah regretted her choice, although she still felt no attraction for Phil. He was too bland for her, too serious. But, she had to admit, he'd been a loyal friend. Unlike Tom and everyone else at

NASA, Phil hadn't betrayed her. He'd continued to support her claim that microbes had once thrived on Mars. So wasn't there a chance he'd believe her now?

Sarah put a hand on his shoulder. Trying to protect him from the truth was a losing battle, she realized. The guy was too smart. It would be better to tell him everything. Then maybe they could put their heads together and figure out what to do.

"Sit down, Phil. I'm going to start from the beginning."

He reluctantly dropped the printouts on his desk and lowered himself into his chair. "Now you're going to tell me where you really found that sample?"

"No, I want to go farther back." She pulled her own chair closer to his and sat down. "Remember our date, back when we were in grad school? The night we went to Señora Rosa's and drank too many margaritas?"

Phil winced. "Unfortunately, I do remember it."

"You spent a lot of time talking about the *Star Trek* movie that had just come out."

"Please. Don't remind me."

"It's okay, you were nervous. And you said some interesting things. There was one thing in particular I remembered afterward, about the high costs of space travel."

"Sarah, what does this—"

"You said it was ludicrous to think we'd ever send a manned spacecraft to another star system, because the real technologies for interstellar travel were so much more difficult and expensive than the fictional ones in *Star Trek.*"

He raised his right hand to his chin and tapped a finger against his lips. He was thinking, remembering. "I admit it, I was a little obsessed with those movies. It just bothered me that they never explained how the starships were supposed to work. The starship *Enterprise* had this warp drive that magically bent the space-time around it, but to really do that you'd need to generate a substance called negative energy, and that's just not possible in—"

"Yes, Phil, you were definitely obsessed. But I was impressed by how much you knew about the real interstellar technologies, like ion thrusters and nuclear fusion rockets. You said some of those technologies could conceivably propel a manned spacecraft all the way to another star, but they'd need enormous amounts of fuel, hundreds of thousands of tons. The mission would be so expensive it would bankrupt any country that tried it."

"And I still believe that." Phil's voice was emphatic. He was so earnest, so damn serious, even when he was talking about *Star Trek*. "The costs would be phenomenally high because the distances between stars are so immense. To get from Earth to the nearest star in less than fifty years you'd have to accelerate a spacecraft to at least ten percent of the speed of light, and you know very well how difficult that would be."

His cheeks flushed again. The topic of interstellar travel was enlivening him, waking him up. As Sarah stared at him she recalled the twenty-five-year-old Phil Clark who'd tried so hard to impress her at Señora Rosa's. She smiled at the memory. "Yes, I know. But I remember something else you told me. You said the cost of the mission would depend on the weight of the spacecraft. A huge manned starship like the *Enterprise* would need to carry tons of food and water and recycling equipment just to keep its crew alive. But if you were going to send something smaller to another star system—say, an unmanned probe that weighed only thirty or forty pounds—you'd need much, much less fuel to propel it to high speeds. You said that was the only way to get the costs down to a feasible level."

"I still believe that too." He seemed pleased by the logic of his youthful arguments.

"That conversation made a big impression on me. The next day I did a little research and found an article in *Scientific American* that said some of the same things. It said you could design an interstellar probe to be as small as a basketball. It could be accelerated by any kind of propulsion system—fusion rockets, ion thrusters, whatever—and then decelerated at the end of its journey, when it's approaching another star. If you wanted the probe to land on one of the star's planets, you could program it to detach from the propulsion system and equip it with an aeroshell to slow its descent to the planet's surface. Then it could start exploring."

Phil raised an eyebrow. "But how much exploring can it do if it's just the size of a basketball?"

"The probe would need only two systems, and both could be miniaturized. The computer system would store the probe's instructions and maybe an artificial intelligence program for carrying them out. Computer chips are tiny, so they wouldn't take up much space." Sarah leaned forward in her chair. She was getting to the most important part. "The other system is an automated manufacturing setup. It would include miniaturized tools for mining the area where the probe landed. The tools would extract useful materials from the ground and feed them to a small manufacturing module, something like a three-dimensional printer. This machine would use the local materials to build more tools and bigger machines, and maybe solar panels to power the operation. The machines would eventually assemble a full-size factory that could produce everything needed for exploring the planet—rovers, drones, whatever. It could even build rockets for sending duplicates of the probe to other planets in the star system. In other words, the probe would be self-replicating."

Phil turned away from her and glanced at the stack of printouts on his desk. He was thinking hard, making the connections. "This sounds a lot like the drill you mentioned before. That thing could also take molecules from the ground and incorporate them into its machinery, correct?"

"Yes, exactly. The material in the sample seems perfectly suited for the extraction and manufacturing needs of a self-replicating probe."

He picked up the printouts and leafed through the stack, studying them again. Then he turned back to Sarah. "So you were telling the truth before? When you said you got the sample from a space probe?"

"It crashed a few miles north of here. Either in the Hudson River or Inwood Hill Park. The Air Force's Space Command spotted it on radar and assumed it was a Russian probe, maybe some kind of space weapon. They forced me to sign a confidentiality agreement, and that's why I was so cagy with you."

Phil looked at her intently, his eyes narrowed to slits. "But you don't think it's Russian, do you?"

She shook her head. "According to the radar readings, the probe was only a foot across, not much bigger than a basketball. And before it hit Earth it detached from a larger object that was speeding across the solar system at sixty-five kilometers per second. This object couldn't have been orbiting the sun, it was moving way too fast. Which means it probably came from another star system."

She could tell from the look on Phil's face that he understood. He got it. His Adam's apple bobbed, as if he were having trouble swallowing.

He clearly wanted to say something, but he couldn't speak. And at that moment Sarah felt the same fullness in her throat, the same choking sensation. Now that she'd said the words out loud it was more than just a hypothesis. It was a hard, cold fact.

Her mouth was dry. She swallowed hard so she could tell Phil the rest. "The Air Force has been searching for the probe, but they haven't found any sign of it yet, and I don't think they will. It doesn't want to be found yet. Its artificial intelligence program is making sure it stays hidden."

Phil sat there for a while, still paralyzed. Then he looked again at the printouts in his hands and shuffled through them until he found the diagram of the lattice, the monstrous jungle gym of atoms. He held the page up in the air and waved it. "So you think this alloy is part of an alien probe? It was designed by extraterrestrials?"

"You said it yourself, Phil. It's unlike anything you've ever seen."

"And this probe just happens to be following the same exploration strategy that was described in an article in *Scientific American*?"

"The laws of physics are the same everywhere, right? If interstellar travel is difficult for us, it's also going to be difficult for everyone else in the galaxy. Any intelligent species, wherever they are, will be more likely to launch a small interstellar probe than a big starship. And the probe would have to be self-replicating if it's going to do any useful long-term exploration."

Phil grimaced. He was a scientist through and through, a man who'd trained himself to suppress his biases and look only at the facts, but in this case the facts were making him uncomfortable. His eyes darted from left to right, avoiding Sarah's gaze. He seemed to be looking for an alternative, an opposing argument. "But what about the landing site? Why would the probe land in New York City if it doesn't want to be found?"

"Well, let's think about it for a second. Let's try to look at it from the probe's point of view." She leaned back in her chair. "From the point of view of the probe's computer system, I mean, or the artificial intelligence program that's running the mission. Certain instructions must've been programmed into the system before the probe was launched."

"How do you know that? You know nothing about these aliens, so how can you make assumptions about their computer systems and AI programs?"

"Give me a second, I'm just thinking out loud. I think we can reasonably assume that the extraterrestrials would have studied Earth with telescopes before deciding to send a probe here. That's what our own astronomers have been doing for the past twenty years. They've used their telescopes to detect thousands of planets in other star systems, and now they're planning to study the atmospheres of those planets to see if they have any oxygen or water vapor or other chemicals. In all likelihood, the aliens focused similar telescopes on Earth and saw the chemical signatures of life in our atmosphere. Then they might've taken a closer look at our planet and detected some of the radio and television signals we've broadcast into space over the past century."

Phil wagged a finger at her. "No, that's not likely. If this probe really came from another star system it was probably launched hundreds of years ago, before humans even invented radio and TV."

"Why do you say that?"

"It's just a matter of the odds." He shrugged. "It's highly unlikely that an intelligent species lives in a star system right next to ours. We don't know how common life is in the galaxy, much less intelligent life, but I think it's safe to say that the closest alien civilization is at least a hundred light-years away from us. So even if they have the technology to accelerate their spacecraft to velocities close to the speed of light, their probe would still take at least a hundred years to get here."

"Okay, okay." Sarah nodded, conceding the point. "The aliens didn't necessarily know about the human race, but they knew there was life on Earth, and that fact alone was probably enough to encourage them to send a probe here to investigate. And I think it's likely that they at least considered the possibility that there might be intelligent life on this planet. I think they put instructions in the probe's computer program telling it what to do if it detected an intelligent species on Earth. That's just prudent planning."

Phil looked skeptical. "You're taking a big leap here, but go on. Finish your thought."

"So let's say the probe's approaching our solar system and its sensors have confirmed the presence of intelligent life on Earth. It would've detected our radio and television broadcasts by then and observed the lights of our cities. At that point the alien computer system—or artificial intelligence program or whatever—would need to change the probe's mission. It could instruct the probe to make contact with the human race by radio, but that would be risky. We might feel threatened and try to destroy the alien spacecraft. But the program would have two other options. It could send the probe into a distant orbit around Earth, where it could hide from us but still observe us. Or the program could take the opposite tack and direct the probe to land on Earth and establish a foothold on the surface. If the alien machinery could sink its drills into the ground fast enough, they could spread far beneath the surface in a matter of days, digging so deeply we might never be able to dislodge them. Judging from the evidence, I think the program chose this second option."

"But then why would it land in New York? If the program's goal is to entrench the probe on Earth, wouldn't it make more sense to send it to a remote location, where it would be harder for us to find and destroy it? Like in Antarctica or the Himalayas?"

"The highest priority for the program would be establishing the foothold very quickly, before the human race could react. Although those drills are remarkable devices, they need energy just like any other machine, and they couldn't extend very far without a sizable power supply. If the probe landed in the Himalayas it could manufacture a few small solar panels at first and then gradually enlarge them, but the process would take months, and in the meantime it would be an easy target. So I think the program instructed the probe to draw power from the sources it had already observed—the electric grids that light our cities. The western hemisphere was in darkness as the probe approached Earth, and the brightest city in view was New York. The program chose a landing site in an unoccupied part of the city where it could take electricity from the grid and yet still remain hidden, at least for a while."

Phil shook his head. He still looked unconvinced. "Your argument is very speculative, Sarah. You're making so many guesses. I could come up with a hundred other theories that would explain the facts just as well."

"There's one fact I haven't told you yet. When I saw the alien drill it was tapping a power line in a Con Edison manhole. It was conducting a thirteen-thousand-volt current through a cable thinner than my pinkie. I slashed at it with a fire ax, and that's how I got my sample."

This piece of news startled him, no doubt about it. The printout he'd been holding, the one that showed the alien lattice, slipped out of his hands. He automatically bent over and picked it up from the floor, but he didn't look at it. He kept it at arm's length, as if he were afraid of it now. "Where was this manhole? In Manhattan?"

"Yes, on Payson Avenue near 204th Street. A Con Edison inspector named Torelli saw the drill too, and afterwards he examined a dozen other manholes in the area. He called me this morning to tell me what he'd found. In seven of the manholes he saw similar drills tapping the high-voltage power lines."

"And where were the other manholes? How widely separated were they?"

"They were all along the eastern edge of Inwood Hill Park, from Dyckman Street to 218th Street. That's a spread of about three-quarters of a mile. But Torelli hasn't inspected all the manholes in the neighborhood yet, so there could be more of them."

"Jesus."

It was a terrible thing, Sarah thought, to see fear in someone you cared about. Phil couldn't handle it. He seemed to shrink in his chair, his chin lowered to his chest, his shoulders hunched, his gangly scarecrow arms drawn close to his body. It hurt her so much to see him this way that she ignored her own fear and put a businesslike expression on her face, trying to project a feeling of confidence and normalcy: *We can take care of this, we can get it under control.* She pointed at the printout in his hand. "Look, Phil, could you make two copies of those test results? Now that I have the proof, I need to show it to the general at Space Command. And I'm gonna put the other copy in a safe place. If the Air Force tries to bury the information, I'll make sure the newspapers get it."

Phil slowly raised the hand that held the printout. The page was crumpled because he was clutching it so tightly. "The probe's mission might not be exploration, you know." His voice quavered. "It might be colonization."

Sarah nodded, struggling to keep that confident look on her face. "Yeah, that's why I need to talk to Space Command. And I'm gonna call Tom Gilbert too. He's the last person in the world I want to talk to, but he's the chief science adviser at the White House now and—"

The door to Phil's office suddenly swung open. Sarah turned toward it, alarmed, and saw a big man in a gray suit stride into the room. Without saying a word, he headed straight for Phil and lifted him out of his chair. Phil sputtered, "What? Who are you?" but the man paid no attention. He removed a pair of handcuffs from his pocket and slipped them around Phil's wrists.

At the same time, a second man entered the office. He also wore a gray suit, so it took Sarah an extra second to realize it was General Hanson, out of uniform.

"No need for you to make copies of the results." Hanson glanced at Phil's desk and the scanning microscope and the stack of printouts. "We have them."

Sarah rose from her chair and took a step backward. "You heard what we were saying? You were listening to us?"

"You're in enough trouble already, Dr. Pooley. If I were you, I'd keep my mouth shut."

SIXTEEN

It was 6:30 P.M., almost dinnertime, but the jail's exercise yard was still as hot as an oven. The yard was about the size of a football field and covered with a layer of asphalt that had baked and blistered in the sun all day. Joe could feel its heat through the thin soles of his sneakers.

About two hundred inmates crowded the yard. A few dozen gathered around the basketball hoops, either playing ball or watching from the sidelines, but Joe and most of the other prisoners paced along the perimeter. Some walked briskly and others barely moved, but they all went counterclockwise. The blank gray walls of the Otis Bantum Correctional Center bordered three sides of the yard, and on the fourth side was a twenty-foot-high double-layer fence, with loops of razor wire trimming the top of the chain link. Through this fence Joe could see the perimeter road that ran along the shoreline of Rikers Island, and beyond that the foamy wavelets of the East River.

It was a seriously depressing view, but coming out here was better than staying in his cell. The past twenty-four hours had been horrendous, worse than any of the cold, wet, nasty days Joe had spent in

Inwood Hill Park. When he'd lived in the park at least he'd had the option of leaving. He could clamber out of his box and brush the dirt off his pants and wander the streets until he found someplace better, or until he was just too tired to care. But in jail he had no choice. He had to endure every misery.

He also had to endure the presence of a cellmate, even though Joe was the only prisoner in the cell. The impostor who'd stolen Annabelle's voice was still locked inside him. She stood behind his every thought, watching and waiting. He'd tried to push her out of his mind by engaging in random pointless tasks—multiplying large numbers in his head, remembering the lyrics to old songs, staring intently at the hundreds of faint lines on his palms—but no strategy worked for more than a few minutes. Soon he would hear her voice again, calling him *Daddy*, asking him if he was ready to listen to her plan. And if he closed his eyes for more than a second he would see her too, dressed in her blue hospital gown, tied at the back. He hadn't slept at all since lights-out the night before, because he knew Annabelle would romp through his dreams.

It became easier to keep her at bay, though, after he went outside to the exercise yard. Just looking at the hazy sky made him feel a little stronger. And the yard wasn't nearly as dangerous as Joe had feared. The other inmates kept their distance from him as they paced alongside the fence. Some of the black and Latino prisoners even nodded at him in a respectful way, as if they were silently thanking him. At first this puzzled the hell out of Joe, but then he realized that the news of his fight with Curtis and Daryl had spread across the jail. Not surprisingly, many of the inmates were pleased that he'd thrashed those assholes. According to the rumors he'd overheard in the cellblock, both men were now in the intensive care unit of a hospital in Queens.

Joe slowed as he approached the corner where the fence adjoined the gray concrete wall of cellblock D. From here he could get a good view of the barges cruising down the East River. Rikers Island sat in the middle of the river, halfway between the Bronx and Queens. There was a bridge between Rikers and Queens, but that was on the southern end of the island, where the jails for women and juveniles were. The Otis Bantum Correctional Center was on the northern end, the side that faced the South Bronx. Joe could see the shoreline on the other side of the river, and beyond it he glimpsed the Bronx's highways and housing projects. He recognized the Bruckner Expressway and the Triborough Bridge.

But he couldn't see his old apartment building in Riverdale. Although it was the tallest building in its neighborhood, it was all the way on the other side of the Bronx, almost ten miles away.

He stepped as close as possible to the fence and gazed through the chain link at the housing projects across the river. The brick buildings glowed orange as the sun sank toward the horizon. Joe wondered if his ex-wife had come home from work yet. As far as he knew, she still had the same job, working as an emergency-room nurse at St. Luke's. Back in the old days they used to meet for lunch in the hospital cafeteria, taking a few minutes each day to drink bad coffee together and coordinate their schedules. They'd both been so overworked, so frenzied. Under the circumstances, it was really a miracle they'd lasted as long as they had.

You miss her, don't you?

His daughter's voice was quiet and sad, but it hit him like a slap in the face. Joe looked down at the hot asphalt at his feet and felt a black, burning rage surge through him.

"Get out of my head!" he shouted. "Just get out!"

The inmates in that corner of the yard backed away from him. No one laughed. They all knew what he could do.

I told you, Daddy, you don't have to speak out loud when you talk to me.

"Get out, get out!" He was screaming now, his voice echoing against the jail's concrete wall. "If you don't get out, I'll kill myself!"

You don't really mean that. And even if you did, I could stop you. You need to relax, Daddy. Take a deep breath.

Against his will, the muscles in his chest expanded. He took in a great gulp of air and then at Annabelle's command his muscles relaxed, pushing the breath out of him. She forced him to take three more deep breaths before relinquishing control, and by then Joe was crying. He was powerless. The impostor could do anything she wanted with him.

He bent over double and sobbed, his hands on his knees. Half the inmates in the yard stopped to gawk at him, but after several seconds most of them resumed their pacing. He was just having a breakdown, that's all. Nothing unusual about that.

Why are you reacting this way? I've helped you, haven't I? Didn't I save you from those men in the shower room?

Joe didn't want to talk to her. He tried to empty his mind, removing all thoughts and words. But he couldn't hide his anger or fear. Annabelle could see everything.

Believe me, I don't enjoy treating you like a puppet. I'd much rather have your cooperation, Joe. I want to work with you, not against you. We can help each other.

He didn't believe her. Although he couldn't read her thoughts the way she could read his, Joe sensed she wasn't telling the truth, or at least not the whole truth. But he also noticed that she'd made a concession to him. She'd called him "Joe" instead of "Daddy." The impostor had deferred to his strong feelings about that. It was a small concession, but it was something.

He stood up straight and wiped the tears from his cheeks. Facing the fence, he stared hard at the choppy waters of the East River. "Who are you?" he whispered. "Just tell me that."

You have to close your eyes to understand. I'm not going to force you to close them. You have to meet me halfway.

"I don't want you to pose as my daughter anymore. Stop using her voice."

All right, if you say so. The voice in his head became deeper and slower. It was still a female voice but not a child's. It wasn't the voice of anyone Joe knew, but it sounded vaguely familiar, like a TV anchorwoman's voice. *Is this better?*

He nodded. "And I'm not going to call you Annabelle. What's your real name?"

You can call me Emissary. Because that's what I am.

"An emissary? For who?"

Close your eyes, Joe.

He was afraid. Part of him didn't want to know the answer, and part of him already suspected the truth—the gleaming black sphere had fallen from the sky, hadn't it? But he steeled himself and closed his eyes.

The first thing he saw was a planet. It looked like one of the satellite images of Earth from space, a great blue ball smeared with curving white cloudbanks. At first Joe thought it *was* Earth, but when he looked past the cloudbanks he saw the outlines of continents—two large and two small ones—and he realized soon enough that they weren't Asia, Africa, or the Americas.

This is my home.

As Joe stared at the unfamiliar landmasses the Emissary magnified the image, giving him a closer view of a jagged coastline. He felt as if he were descending toward the planet's surface, falling below the clouds.

A city sparkled beneath him, studded with domes and towers. Most of the structures were black and highly polished. After a moment Joe realized they were made of the same material as the gleaming sphere he'd found in Inwood Hill Park.

This is where my journey began. I'll show you the launch.

The image enlarged again and now Joe saw a black disk resting in an empty sector of the city. Because there were no familiar objects nearby he couldn't properly judge the size of the disk, but it looked pretty big. The disk had a hole at its center, maybe twenty feet wide, and standing within this hole was an impossibly tall spire. It rose as high as the eye could see, above the clouds and the rest of the planet's atmosphere.

That's a space elevator. It can efficiently transport objects from the planet's surface to high orbits.

As if to demonstrate her point, the disk began climbing the spire, like a flat bead ascending a vertical rod in an abacus. It rose swiftly and steadily, and Joe felt like he was rising with it, leaving the planet behind. He noticed dozens of gleaming nozzles extending from the underside of the disk. They were rocket engines, he realized. When the disk finally reached the top of the spire, thousands of miles above the planet, it detached from the elevator and fired its engines. Flames blazed from the rocket nozzles, and the spacecraft moved away from the planet at fantastic speed.

All of this happened a long time ago. When I began my journey, your species was just emerging from the Middle Ages.

Joe accelerated through space alongside the craft. He felt giddy, overcome by all the strangeness. The Emissary gave him a closer view of the rocket engines, then showed him the layer of shielding at the front of the spacecraft. Then Joe penetrated the shielding and saw the probe sheltered behind it. It was the same foot-wide sphere that had crash-landed in the park three nights ago, but now Joe could see through its gleaming shell. The machinery inside was densely packed and incomprehensible.

Our computers are very different from yours but the basic design is the same. We have software and hardware. For the duration of the interstellar journey, 652 of your Earth years, I dwelled in the probe's hardware.

This confused Joe. He looked closely at the alien machinery inside the probe but saw nothing living there. "I don't understand," he whispered. "Where are you?"

I'm not a living thing. I'm a set of instructions and algorithms. But I have all the abilities you have. I can think and reason and make plans. I can adapt to new circumstances.

Now he was even more confused. "You're a computer program?"

Yes, but I'm unlike the programs you're thinking of. Imagine that the soul of the programmer has been transferred to the machine. I am the soul of the intelligent life-forms who created me.

"But how did you get inside my head? The last time I checked, I didn't have any circuits in there."

You should check again.

Now the spacecraft disappeared and in its place Joe saw a man in filthy clothes kneeling on a stone slab that glowed silver in the moonlight. The man opened his mouth and twisted in pain as he pressed his right hand to a puncture wound on his neck. Joe realized he was looking at an image of himself from two nights ago, when the probe's tentacle struck him. After a moment the man took his hand off his neck, and then the image enlarged, magnifying the site of the puncture wound. Joe could see the damaged skin cells and ruptured capillaries. Then the view shifted to a larger blood vessel nearby and he saw a tiny, black insectlike machine inside his carotid artery. Propelled by his pulsing blood, the device rushed toward his brain.

Joe felt sick. He opened his eyes. The sun was closer to the horizon now, and the East River looked darker and dirtier. "Why are you doing this?" he whispered. "It's brutal. You're torturing me."

I'm sorry for the pain you've suffered. But as I told you last night, communication is my highest priority. I need to communicate with the appropriate authorities in your government, but my language and thought processes are so different from yours that it would be easy for misunderstandings to occur. I need a translator, a human who completely understands my thoughts. So I established a connection with you.

He shook his head. He was astounded by the breadth and depth of his bad luck. "No, you made a mistake. You should get someone else. Someone who isn't in jail, for starters."

Unfortunately, I don't have a choice. Your species has an unusual mental architecture, very different from the minds of my creators. Because of these differences, my devices have had trouble interacting with the other human subjects I've made contact with. I've been able to influence their behavior and take control of their motor functions, but you're the only subject with whom I've established a strong connection.

Joe's throat clenched when she said "other human subjects." She meant Dorothy and the teenage boy. And Joe wondered if there were more.

"Have you tortured them too?"

Please understand, the process of initiating contact with an intelligent species can be dangerous. I'm trying to accomplish this task in the least risky way. If I wanted to, I could take full control of your body and move you around like a puppet. I could send you to the White House or the Capitol and force you to speak my words to the authorities. But that would only increase their fear. They would see me as a slave master, a monster. That's why I want a free and willing translator, someone who can communicate my needs to the authorities without terrifying them.

"And what are your needs?"

The Emissary didn't answer right away. Joe waited several seconds while the program in his head decided what to tell him.

I can't give you that information yet. It's meant for the authorities in your government. If I give you the information now, there's a chance you might reveal it to the wrong people, either intentionally or by accident. I can't risk that.

Once again, Joe sensed she wasn't telling the whole truth. She was leaving something out. He couldn't trust her.

"What if I said I wouldn't help you? What would you do then?"

You're a rational man, Joe. Don't you think we can come to a mutually beneficial agreement? I know you want to be reunited with your wife and daughter. I can help you make that happen.

He clenched and unclenched his hands. He was furious, outraged. This impostor, this piece of *software*, was trying to manipulate him! It had the nerve to use his family as a bargaining chip! Joe was so enraged he wanted to run headlong into the jail's concrete wall. He wanted to smash open his skull and rip out the Emissary with his bare hands.

But he didn't throw himself at the wall. He didn't even shout at her. Joe kept his anger in check because it wasn't the only emotion he felt. Along with his fury, he couldn't help but feel a small flutter of hope, like a butterfly flapping its wings inside his chest. He wanted so badly to see Annabelle, the *real* Annabelle. The feeling was so powerful he had to push it away. If he let it come too close it would break his heart.

He stepped backward, away from the fence. "No, you're wrong. You can't help me."

Don't underestimate my abilities. I've already helped you a great deal.

Because I rebalanced your neurotransmitter system, your nerve cells no longer require alcohol to calm their activity. You're not dependent on it anymore.

Joe couldn't argue with her on this point. She was right: he didn't feel the need to get drunk. He was still an alcoholic—he'd always be an alcoholic—but he was no longer overwhelmed by the irresistible urge to down another bottle of Olde English 800. Now, just the thought of the stuff made him want to puke. He'd miraculously slipped free from the noose of addiction that had been tightening around his neck. But he felt no sense of pride from accomplishing this feat, because he hadn't done any of the hard work himself. The Emissary had done it for him.

You have the chance to live a normal life now. You can rejoin human society. And I can help you in so many ways, Joe. I can give you everything you'll need to find your way home, back to your old life. Isn't that what you want?

She was trying to bribe him. It was that simple. And why shouldn't he take the bribe? If she could actually deliver what she promised, why should he refuse it?

But she couldn't deliver. It was impossible. She was lying.

Nothing is impossible for me. Look at what I've done so far, in just the past three days.

"No, this is different." Shaking his head, he took another step backward. He felt dizzy, as if he were teetering on the edge of something horrible. "This can't be changed."

Turn around, Joe. I'm going to show you something else I've done.

He had no idea what she meant, but he turned around anyway. On the other side of the exercise yard a pair of correction officers emerged from the entrance to cellblock D. They marched across the yard, two big black men in black uniforms. The inmates pacing beside the fence craned their necks to look at the guards, and even the prisoners playing basketball paused their games. The officers walked abreast of each other and very nearly in lockstep. By the time they were fifty feet away Joe realized they were heading straight for him.

His pulse raced as they came closer. They were the biggest guards he'd seen at Rikers, a hundred times more intimidating than the gray-haired officer who'd led Joe to the shower room the night before. He guessed they were here to punish him, to finally give him the beating he'd managed to avoid so far.

No, that's not why they're here. I arranged for them to come.

"What? How could—"

The communications network for this jail is remarkably primitive. It was a simple matter to infiltrate it.

The guards halted a couple of yards away. The officer on the right glared at Joe. "Joseph Graham? You're coming with us." He pointed at the entrance to D block. "Get moving."

Bewildered, Joe started to cross the yard, with the pair of guards marching behind him. His confusion made him light-headed. He felt the eyes of all the other inmates on him as he stumbled across the asphalt.

Don't worry, Joe. You're in luck. You're about to be freed.

The correction officers escorted him across cellblock D and buzzed him through the security gate at the guard station. Then they marched down the corridor to the intake room, the same place where Joe had entered the jail the day before. The room was full of new arrivals, at least forty men who were busy stripping off their street clothes and changing into prison-issue shirts and sweatpants. The guards cleared a path through the crowd and led Joe into a smaller room, a window-less holding pen with blank white walls. The room was empty except for a plastic bag on the floor. The plastic was transparent, and inside the bag Joe could see his street clothes, his filthy T-shirt and jeans, still caked with mud. No one had bothered to wash them.

One of the guards turned to Joe and pointed at the bag. "You have five minutes to change. Make sure you fold your jailhouse clothes and put them in the bag when you're done."

The instructions were simple enough, but Joe was confused. "And then I can leave? I'm being released?"

The guard scowled. "Yeah, you're a lucky motherfucker. Someone pulled some big-ass strings for you."

Shaking his head, the guard turned around and left the holding pen. His partner followed him out and closed the door, leaving Joe alone in the room.

Do you believe me now?

Although it didn't sound like Annabelle anymore, the voice of the Emissary was still disturbing. It was too breathy and feminine, too intimate. "How did you do it?" Joe whispered.

First, I accessed the underground cables that carry data across this city. Then

I wrote software that enabled me to monitor and control all the data transmissions, including the electronic messages exchanged within the City of New York Department of Correction.

"You can see their e-mails? On the Internet?"

Yes, and I can compose my own communications. An hour ago I sent a message to the warden of the Otis Bantum Correctional Center. It was an order to free you, and it was intended to resemble a genuine order from the warden's supervisor, the deputy commissioner of correction.

Joe stepped backward and leaned against one of the room's blank walls. It was alarming, this evidence of the Emissary's power. He remembered the last time he'd seen the black sphere in Inwood Hill Park, when he'd tried to pry the thing out of the mud but had to give up because its gleaming tentacles had anchored it to the ground. Now, though, the tentacles had reached far beyond the park's boundaries. The alien program was spreading across the Internet. And what had it done to Dorothy? How many other people had it infected?

He shivered and stared at the floor. He was worried and scared. But at the same time he felt that flutter of hope again, the flapping of delicate wings inside his chest. The Emissary was going to get him out of Rikers. It was about to rescue him from the deepest hellhole he'd ever seen. And if it could do that, was it so far-fetched to believe that it could also reunite him with Karen and Annabelle?

Joe stared at the bag of filthy clothes on the floor. "Is one e-mail enough to get me out of here? Doesn't the warden need some official paperwork or something?"

In my message the deputy commissioner ordered the warden to release you immediately. In all likelihood, no one will discover that the message is spurious until a few hours from now, and by then you'll be free.

"But what if they discover it sooner than that? What if the warden or someone else does some checking around?"

Yes, that's a possibility. To guard against it, I recommend that you change into your old clothes as quickly as possible and get ready to leave.

Joe didn't need any further encouragement. He took off his prison clothes, then reached for the bag and ripped it open. He recoiled in disgust as he pulled out his damp, frayed T-shirt, which smelled like a swamp and was probably crawling with fleas. But after a moment he gritted his teeth and slipped the shirt over his head. Anything was better than Rikers.

After another minute Joe was back in his street clothes, and the prison-issue items were neatly folded in the bag. Then he leaned against the wall again and waited. There wasn't anything in the holding pen to look at except the locked door, so that's what he looked at.

I understand why you dislike this place. It's a very inefficient system.

Joe cringed. He didn't want to communicate with the Emissary any more than he had to, but he couldn't ignore her voice. "What system?" he whispered.

Your correctional system, all the jails and prisons. It's wasteful and self-defeating. Your society has no effective method for rehabilitating its criminals.

Her tone was so critical, it made Joe defensive. He shook his head. "Well, it's not so easy, getting people to change their ways."

Does spending time in this jail improve the behavior of the criminals? Does it transform them into productive, law-abiding citizens?

"Not always, but—"

I've already collected information on this topic by accessing several Web sites on your Internet. According to the statistics, very few criminals benefit from the experience of incarceration. The primary purpose of your correctional system seems to be isolation rather than correction. The prisons keep dangerous individuals away from their communities until they're too old and debilitated to commit any more crimes.

Joe didn't know what to say. He was surprised that the Emissary had taken such an interest in the subject. Her voice was crisp and precise, like the voice of a professor.

Would you like to see a different approach to the problem, Joe? I can show you the solution that was devised on my home planet. Our society developed a successful method for dealing with individuals who refused to follow our laws.

She was trying to make him curious, but instead she frightened him. He didn't want to know anything else about her home planet or her society. He was still trying to digest everything she'd told him already. He just wanted her to get out of his head, or at least shut up for a few goddamn minutes.

"No, thanks," he whispered.

Very well. Perhaps we can discuss this later, when you're less anxious.

The Emissary fell silent. Joe went back to staring at the locked door.

He relaxed a bit as the minutes passed and he heard nothing more from her. But after a while he started to worry again, because the correction officers were taking too long. The guards had said they'd return in five minutes, but that was at least fifteen minutes ago. Although there was no clock in the room, Joe could feel the time stretching. Soon it was thirty minutes. Then forty-five.

Then the door finally opened and a guard stepped inside, but it wasn't one of the correction officers who'd escorted Joe out of the exercise yard. It was his nemesis from last night, Officer Billings. The heavyset guard closed the door behind him and strolled into the holding pen with a big smile underneath his graying mustache. In his right hand he held a folded sheet of paper, which he pointed at Joe. "I gotta give you some fucking credit, Graham. You nearly pulled it off."

Joe winced. The guard's voice was too loud—the room was empty except for the two of them—and his face was ruddy with delight. He seemed just as pleased now as he'd been when he'd delivered Joe to the shower room. Without waiting for a response, Billings unfolded the sheet and started to read it.

"It says here, 'To Warden Hayes: The Police Department has requested the immediate release of Joseph Graham, inmate number 21-4662-38, who was remanded yesterday to Otis Bantum Correctional Center. Graham is a confidential informant assisting detectives in an ongoing investigation of narcotics sales in the Thirty-fourth Precinct. To ensure the success of this investigation, Graham must return to Inwood as quickly as possible so he can continue to assist the narcotics squad.'" Billings looked up from the paper and stared at Joe. "So far, so good, right? It sounds just like a real request from the NYPD, doesn't it? And the message came from the e-mail account of Deputy Commissioner Maloney, so why would anyone question it?"

Joe said nothing. He put a blank expression on his face, pretending to be puzzled. But Officer Billings wasn't fooled. He waved the paper in the air.

"The warden thought the order was real. So did everyone else in the main office. But I'd already started asking questions about you because of what happened last night in the shower room. So when I heard about Maloney's order, I knew it was bullshit." He took a step toward Joe. "You were arrested for assaulting a cop. Once you do something like that, it doesn't matter if you're an informant. You gotta fucking *pay* for what you did. Every cop knows that. So there's no way they would've requested your release."

Interesting. I hadn't expected this. Because the guard dislikes you so much, he became suspicious.

The Emissary's voice remained calm. She didn't seem to be troubled by the collapse of her plan. Joe, in contrast, was *very* troubled. Beads of sweat slid down his neck. Getting out of Rikers was the most important thing in the world to him now, and the thought of losing his chance was crushing.

Billings seemed to sense Joe's desperation. He smiled again. "I know a secretary who works for Deputy Commissioner Maloney, so I called her up and asked about the e-mail. She couldn't contact Maloney because he'd already left the office, but she called me back a few minutes ago and said she thinks the message is a fraud. Although it came from Maloney's e-mail address, she doesn't think the deputy commissioner wrote it. She thinks some hacker must've broken into the department's computer network." He took another step toward Joe and looked him in the eye. "You know any hackers, Graham? Maybe some computer-geek asshole who owes you a favor? I have a funny feeling you do."

Joe shook his head. It looked like the battle was already lost, but he wasn't ready to give up yet. "I don't know what you're talking about. The other guards said they were gonna release me. That's all I know."

Billings let out a snort. He folded the sheet of paper and slipped it into his pants pocket. Then he reached for his nightstick and removed it from his belt. "Well, I have some bad fucking news for you. You're not leaving Rikers anytime soon. As soon as I tell the warden about the scam you tried to pull, he's gonna make sure you stay here for a long, long time." He raised the nightstick and pointed it at Joe's chest. "In fact, you'll still be here when Curtis and Daryl get back from the hospital. From what I hear, you got lucky when you tangled with them last night, but next time you won't—"

Joe lunged forward. His legs flexed at the Emissary's command, propelling him toward Billings, and at the same time he reached for the guard's nightstick. It happened so quickly that Joe didn't even realize what was happening until he stood nose-to-nose with Billings. Joe's left hand gripped the blunt end of the nightstick and his right hand clamped over the guard's mouth. Because the Emissary had taken full control of his body, he felt like a bystander. He could only stare into the guard's terrified eyes and wonder what the Emissary was going to do next. Strangle Billings? Break his neck? Club him with the nightstick?

But she did none of those things. Instead, Joe felt a horribly sharp pain in the palm of his right hand. At first he thought Billings had bitten him, but the guard's mouth was closed. Billings tried to pull his face away, but Joe dug his thumb and fingers into the guard's cheeks and held on tight, pressing his burning palm against the man's lips. Then Joe felt something rip through his skin. Something tiny and jagged emerged from the center of his palm and pierced the guard's upper lip.

Billings widened his eyes and screamed. Joe's palm muffled the noise, but it was still loud enough to make his hand vibrate. The guard's head shook uncontrollably and the rest of his body writhed in pain. And then, after five or six seconds, Billings closed his eyes. He went limp but stayed on his feet, standing there with his head lolling to the side and his arms dangling. He looked drunk, in a stupor, but he still clutched his nightstick.

After a few more seconds Joe regained control of his own body and stepped away from the guard. When he raised his right hand he saw a small wound in the center of his palm. There was a similar wound on Billings's upper lip, half-hidden by his mustache. Joe thought of the picture the Emissary had shown him, the image of the black insectlike machine cruising through his blood vessels toward his brain. Now it was inside Billings.

Actually, the device inside him is a copy of the one inside you.

"What? A copy?"

All of my machines are self-replicating. They build copies of themselves from the raw materials in their surrounding environment. The device inside you assembled duplicates from the molecules in your bloodstream, and one of those duplicates is now inside the guard, interfacing with his brain. And because all my devices are networked together via radio and microwave transmissions, I can communicate with you and him at the same time.

Joe's throat tightened. He stared at the half-asleep Billings, whose mouth hung open as he swayed in the middle of the room. "And you can control him too? Just like you control me?"

No, my interface with the guard is more primitive. Because I don't have time to develop a full connection with him, I've shut down his consciousness. I will simply control his muscles and voice box.

"So he's nothing but a puppet now?"

Why are you so disapproving? You need the guard's help to escape from this jail. Isn't that what you want?

Joe grimaced. He knew he was making a mistake. Instead of siding with the Emissary, he should be resisting her with all his strength. But she was right: he wanted to get out of Rikers. He wanted it so badly he was willing to trust her.

He pointed at Billings. "How is he going to help me? He can barely stand up."

In response, the guard opened his eyes and stood up straight. He slid the nightstick into the holster on his belt, then turned to Joe. "Take a good look at me. Does anything seem out of the ordinary?"

The Emissary was using Billings's voice. Although the pitch and tone of the guard's voice sounded the same as before, his diction was different—more precise, less blustery. But the biggest change was in his eyes. There was no life in them now.

Joe shivered. "You look . . . all right, I guess."

"Will the guard's coworkers suspect that something is wrong?"

"Just don't start any long conversations with them, okay?"

"Understood." The guard pointed at the door to the holding pen. "Let's move, Joe. We're getting out of here."

They left the holding pen and returned to the intake room. The group of newly arrived inmates was gone; they'd obviously moved on to their assigned cellblocks, leaving behind a big pile of plastic bags stuffed with their street clothes. Two correction officers bent over the pile, pasting an identifying label to each bag. Another two officers manned the guard station next to the security gate, at the far end of the room. Billings grasped Joe's arm above the elbow and started to lead him across the room, heading for the gate.

That door is one of the entrances to this building. I'm going to ask the guards there to let us out. Please remain silent while I converse with them.

Joe felt disoriented. When the Emissary spoke inside his head she still sounded like a young woman, but now she was also controlling the movements of the heavyset, middle-aged man walking beside him. Although Joe had begun to think of the Emissary as a person, an individual, now he saw it clearly wasn't. It was a computer program, and what's more, it was completely unlike any program written by humans. It could tap into the Internet and build its own machines and invade human bodies and occupy all of them at the same time. And there was no telling what else it could do.

He glanced sideways at Officer Billings. The man's dead eyes looked straight ahead. Joe shivered again.

They stopped at the guard station. Two correction officers sat behind the station's protective glass, both of them youngish black women. One was slender and pinch-faced, and the other was chubby and round-cheeked, but both frowned when they saw Billings coming. The man apparently had a bad reputation. Joe started to worry that the officers at the gate wouldn't let them out. These guards already disliked Billings, and that could make things more difficult. Joe clenched and unclenched his hands, anxious as hell.

Billings raised his chin toward the speak-through grille embedded in the glass. "This inmate has been granted an immediate release. His name is Joseph Graham, number 21-4662-38. The release order should be on the computer."

The slender, pinch-faced woman leaned toward the grille from the other side of the glass. She was still frowning. "What's that number? I didn't hear you."

"It's 21-4662-38."

She went to her computer and typed it in. After a few seconds she nodded. "Yeah, the order's here. But it's too late to release him now. The shuttle buses stopped running an hour ago. He'll have to wait till tomorrow morning."

"The order specifies an *immediate* release. To comply with the order, I've arranged an alternative method of transportation."

The pinch-faced guard looked askance. "Alternative? What are you talking about?"

"A car is waiting for us outside. The warden has approved this release order. You must comply with it."

The guard stared at Billings. Her round-cheeked partner did the same, furrowing her brow. What made them suspicious, Joe realized, wasn't so much what Billings had said but how he'd said it. He didn't sound like the loud, foul-mouthed guard that the other correction officers couldn't stand. He sounded like a machine.

Now Joe was so nervous, his teeth started chattering. The Emissary was screwing things up, and there was nothing he could do to help her.

No, I'm listening to you. I will adjust my demeanor.

Billings raised his hand and rapped his knuckles against the glass. "Hey, have you two gone deaf?" he shouted. "When the release order says *immediate*, it means fucking *immediate*. Now open the goddamn gate!"

The correction officers weren't happy about his outburst. If anything, their frowns grew more severe. But they stopped looking so intently at Billings. The slender guard leaned back in her chair and waited a few seconds, just to irritate him. Then she pressed a button on her desk and the security gate opened.

Joe took a deep breath as he and Billings stepped outside. They stood in a parking lot behind the jail, a deserted rectangle of asphalt. The sun had gone down half an hour ago and the lot was empty except for three blue-and-white Department of Correction buses parked in the corner. These were obviously the buses that shuttled inmates to and from Rikers Island, but they were out of service until morning. Intensely bright floodlights shone down on the barred windows of the empty buses and the blank gray walls of the Otis Bantum Correctional Center. It was a dismal sight, and yet Joe was ecstatic. He smiled and took another deep breath, filling his chest with the steamy night air. He was out. He was free.

Billings still clutched his arm, though. The guard turned left and started marching alongside a high chain-link fence topped with loops of razor wire. As Joe hurried to keep up, he noticed that the fence enclosed the parking lot. There was an exit about a hundred yards ahead, but a guardhouse stood next to the opening in the fence, and inside the guardhouse were two more correction officers.

Joe stopped smiling. He wasn't free after all. They had to either climb over that fence or slip past the guardhouse. And then they'd still have to get across the guarded bridge that connected Rikers Island to the rest of the city.

"What's the plan?" Joe whispered. "How—"

Look to your left, on the other side of the fence. Do you see that parking lot?

Through the chain link he saw dozens of cars parked in another lot outside the jail.

That's the lot for the correction officers. They go into the jail through a different entrance. Officer Billings owns one of the cars there, a 2014 Ford Taurus. The keys to the car are in the officer's pants pocket.

"But how can we get to the car if it's on the other side of—"

I'll talk to the correction officers in the guardhouse. I'll use the same demeanor and tone of voice that proved effective before.

Joe nodded. Strangely enough, he was getting accustomed to the Emissary's voice in his head. Although he still hated sharing his brain with her, he had to admit that communicating this way could be useful.

They walked toward the guardhouse until the correction officers spotted them. One of them stepped outside and shone a flashlight. "Who's that?" he shouted. "Is that you, Billings?"

Billings stopped a few yards from the guardhouse. Keeping his grip on Joe's arm, he raised his other hand and pointed at the officer. "Put down the damn flashlight! You're blinding me with that thing!"

The officer didn't lower his flashlight. He was a tall, hulking white guy, in his late twenties or early thirties. "What are you doing out here? You're not supposed to leave the jail this way." He kept the flashlight on Billings's face for another second, then aimed it at Joe. "And who the hell is this?"

Joe shielded his eyes. Billings, meanwhile, clapped him on the shoulder. "This is the luckiest fucking inmate on Rikers. Joseph Graham, number 21-4662-38. The warden just ordered his release. You can look it up on the computer."

"A release?" The officer narrowed his eyes. "At night?"

"It's a special case, emergency request from the NYPD. Immediate release, no waiting."

"And how were you planning to get him off the island? The buses don't start running again till five in the morning."

Billings shrugged. "It's no big deal. I'm going off duty anyway, so I can take him in my car."

"Are you nuts? That's against all the rules." The officer swept the flashlight up and down, illuminating Joe's filthy pants and shirt. The guy squinted and stepped closer, suspicious. After a few seconds he turned back to Billings. "You better bring this guy back to intake. Just turn around and go back."

Billings shook his head. "Why are you giving me such a fucking hard time? I told you, it's a special case."

"Bullshit. I know you, Billings. You're trying to pull something. I don't know what the hell it is, but you're not getting away with it this time."

The officer reached for the radio on his belt. At the same time, he gave a signal to his partner, who was still inside the guardhouse. The second officer—who was bald and black and just as big as the first guy—stepped outside and turned on his own flashlight. Unlike the guards inside the jail, these officers carried guns. Semiautomatic pistols jutted from their belt holsters.

Joe trembled. He felt weak, hollow. The big white officer was talking into his radio, trying to contact his supervisor. Soon they'd figure out that the release order was a sham. The plan was ruined.

No, it's not. You're going to escape now. Get ready.

Her voice made him panic. Get ready? How could he get ready? He wasn't even close to being ready! But a moment later the Emissary took control of his legs. Against his better judgment, Joe stepped toward the correction officer.

Annoyed, the officer lowered his radio. *"Hey, asshole!"* He trained his flashlight on Joe. *"Get the fuck back!"*

Joe's legs froze and his hands rose in surrender. And while the officer glared at him and shone the flashlight into his eyes, the Emissary took advantage of the man's inattention. Billings removed the nightstick from his belt, leaped forward, and swung it at the officer's head.

Joe heard the smack of the nightstick against the man's skull, but he didn't see it. He was already running. Under the Emissary's control, his feet pounded the asphalt, propelling him toward the opening in the fence next to the guardhouse. An instant later he heard a shout of dismay, and from the corner of his eye he saw Billings charge toward the second correction officer. But Joe didn't get a chance to see what happened next. The Emissary kept him running forward, past the guardhouse and the fence.

She steered him left, and he raced down the narrow driveway that encircled the jail. He saw the lot where all the correction officers' cars were parked, but the Emissary didn't guide him toward Billings's vehicle. Instead she hurled him toward a T junction about two hundred yards ahead, where the driveway merged into a wider thoroughfare. The road was empty and silent. The thick walls of the jails on Rikers muffled all the noises within.

Then he heard a gunshot. It came from behind him, from the guardhouse, but once again the Emissary wouldn't let him slow down or even turn his head around. For a moment he wondered whether the big, bald correction officer had shot Billings, or vice-versa. And then he heard an even louder noise, a howling siren that arose first from the Otis Bantum Correctional Center and soon echoed across all the other jails on Rikers. Someone had raised the alarm.

The Emissary made him run faster. She tilted him forward and pumped his legs and swung his arms. He took great gulps of air that whistled down his windpipe and into his lungs, but it wasn't enough. His chest heaved and his muscles burned. Joe felt a burst of panic. She was pushing him too hard. His body couldn't take this.

He sprinted past another parking lot. As he neared the T junction he noticed that the road ahead was the one he'd seen from the exercise yard, the perimeter road that ran along the island's shoreline. If he turned left at the junction he'd eventually get to the bridge that went over the East River. But if that was the Emissary's plan, then Joe was doomed. He'd never get past the armed guards on the bridge. It was insane, suicidal. And a moment later it became even more hopeless, because Joe spotted the headlights of two Department of Correction patrol cars. One cruised up the shoreline road from the south and the other came down from the north. Both cars had spotlights mounted on their hoods, and as the vehicles converged on the jail they swept their spotlight beams across the road.

The Emissary was silent. For the first time Joe was desperate to hear her voice. He wanted to know what her plan was, where she intended to take him now, how he was going to escape. But she said nothing. She just lowered his head and flexed his legs and sent him barreling into the T junction.

As soon as he ran onto the road, both patrol cars aimed their spotlights at him. One car was a hundred yards to his left, the other fifty yards to his right. He was trapped, cornered. The only option was to surrender. But instead the Emissary flung him toward the guardrail on the other side of the road and made him take a flying leap off his right foot. Joe hurdled over the guardrail and landed on a slope covered with weeds and garbage. Then he raced down the slope and splashed into the East River.

The water was a shock. It was so much colder than the steaming air. Joe stumbled forward until the water was up to his waist, then began to swim. The Emissary guided his arms, moving them in swift, strong strokes. Soon he was twenty yards from the island, then thirty. When he lifted his head from the water he could see the South Bronx in the distance, a line of glimmering streetlights on the horizon.

But then the spotlights found him. They illuminated the choppy water, turning the river a vivid shade of green. At the same time, Joe heard a high-pitched squawk coming from the island. It was the sound of a megaphone being turned on.

"Stop where you are." It was a man's voice, probably one of the correction officers in the patrol cars. "If you don't stop, we are authorized to shoot. Repeat, we will shoot you."

Take a deep breath, Joe. You're going to dive.

The Emissary helped him by taking control of his breathing muscles and expanding his chest. Then she plunged his head into the water and swept his arms in a breaststroke. His body jackknifed and he went down deep.

He couldn't see a thing. Without the Emissary's help, he would've panicked and immediately come up for air, but she kept sweeping his arms through the cool black water and propelling him forward. He stayed under until his lungs were screaming and he was absolutely sure he was going to drown. Then his head broke the surface and he took an excruciating breath.

But the spotlights were still trained on him, and the officer with the megaphone was still threatening to shoot him. Worse, he saw another spotlight off to his right, this one coming from the river rather than the island. A patrol boat sped toward him, bobbing over the waves.

You're going to dive again. Just—

"No! I can't!"

Trust me, Joe. Just take a deep breath.

She expanded his chest again, then forced him underwater. Although the river was utterly opaque, he saw bursts of color against the blackness, red and green splotches that flashed across his field of vision. Joe was bewildered for a moment—what's the hell's going on now?—but then he realized that the splotches weren't real. They were hallucinations, distress signals from his oxygen-starved brain. The Emissary had pushed him beyond his limits. He couldn't stay conscious much longer.

Then he felt something curl around his right arm. A smooth, cold rope looped once around his wrist and a couple of times around his forearm. His stomach clenched and churned in terror, but his right hand gripped the cold line. The Emissary closed his left hand around it too, and then Joe felt a tremendous tug. The rope grew taut and began pulling him through the water.

He moved like a torpedo, swift and straight. The river currents battered his head and torso as he plowed through them, and his arms felt like they were being yanked out of their sockets. After several seconds the rope angled him upward and raised him to the surface of the river. He opened his mouth and gasped for breath as his body skimmed over the waves. The rope was pulling him as rapidly as a towline pulls a water-skier. He'd already gone far beyond the reach of the correction officers' spotlights, and when he glanced to the right he noticed that the patrol boat was no longer heading his way. Instead it cruised toward the circles of water illuminated by the spotlights, which swept back and forth in a vain effort to find him. He'd slipped away from his pursuers, and now they couldn't see him. He was gliding fast and low across the river, invisible in the darkness.

There was just enough ambient light, though, that Joe could see the reflections off the wet, gleaming line. It wasn't really a rope. It was black and metallic.

After another minute he approached the Bronx shoreline. The metallic strand pulled him toward a muddy riverbank next to an abandoned warehouse. As he neared the shore, the Emissary unwound the tentacle from his arm and relinquished control of his body. Joe waded the last ten feet under his own power and collapsed on the bank, lying on his back in the mud. He turned his head to the left and noticed that the tentacle stuck out of a small hole in the mud a few yards away. He stared at the strand as it withdrew into the hole. Within seconds it vanished.

Joe closed his eyes. He was spent. He didn't want to get up. He wanted to lie there forever.

— What's wrong, Joe? You're free. The correction officers will assume you drowned.

He shook his head. Then he opened his eyes and pointed at the hole where the tentacle had disappeared. "This place is miles away from Inwood. Are your machines all over the city now?"

Yes. Now we're ready for the next phase. You're going to help me make contact.

SEVENTEEN

General Brent Hanson marched down Payson Avenue with one of his GPR search teams. A burly Air Force corporal pushed the ground-penetrating radar machine down the middle of the street, and a tall lieutenant trailed behind him, carrying a flashlight and a sheaf of blue-prints. Twenty other search teams were in the area surrounding Inwood Hill Park, all of them using the radar systems to peer below the streets and sidewalks. Luckily, they could do this job without worrying about interference from curious bystanders or journalists. Hanson had already evacuated the neighborhood.

The cover story he'd used, predictably enough, was terrorism. At 4:00 P.M. that afternoon the Department of Homeland Security had announced the arrest of a dozen fanatical Muslims who'd intended to bomb several targets in Manhattan. The leaders of the terrorist group, however, had escaped arrest and were believed to be hiding somewhere in Inwood. These fanatics had all the materials needed to build a power-ful bomb, one that could destroy an entire apartment building, so the government had ordered the immediate removal of all the residents living between Dyckman Street and 218th Street.

Hanson had come up with this story. He was proud of it because it had the ring of truth. Everyone in the neighborhood knew the military officials had been lying when they'd said the soldiers in Inwood were on a training mission. The locals were sure the government was hiding something, probably a terrorist threat, and they all proclaimed, "I told you so!" when Homeland Security admitted they were right. But it never occurred to them that the government's second story was also a lie. And this lie was very convincing: between 4:00 P.M. and 9:00 P.M., twenty thousand people fled the neighborhood. Most went to emergency shelters that the city had set up, but many took up watch at the edges of Inwood, standing behind the police barricades on Tenth Avenue and waiting for the military to either capture or gun down the terrorists.

What's more, the gawkers at the barricades got further confirmation of the cover story when they saw the soldiers pushing the GPR machines down the neighborhood's streets. The military had used the same radar system in Iraq and Afghanistan because it was excellent at detecting buried explosives. So when the television reporters spotted the GPR teams they naturally assumed the soldiers were looking for a bomb.

In reality, though, tonight's search was much more difficult. Hanson wasn't even sure what he was looking for. Only Sarah Pooley and the Con Edison inspector had actually seen the strange conductive cables. Hanson's men had done their own inspections of the Con Ed manholes and found no slender black strands tapping into the power lines.

This failure frustrated Hanson. He needed more proof to convince his superiors. He already had some strong evidence—the sample Dr. Pooley had collected, plus her trajectory analysis proving that the probe couldn't have been launched from Earth—but that wasn't enough for the generals on the Joint Chiefs of Staff or the bureaucrats on the National Security Council. They weren't going to start believing in aliens until they could see, hear, and smell them.

The GPR teams began their search at 10:00 P.M. and Hanson crisscrossed the neighborhood with them, walking beside his men as they looked for anything unusual lurking underground. The streets were dark because Hanson had ordered Con Ed to cut the power to the area. The blackout order was consistent with the cover story—the military was supposedly making things difficult for the hiding terrorists—but it was also a precautionary measure. If Dr. Pooley was right and there really was an alien entity beneath the streets of Manhattan, Hanson wasn't going to let it siphon any more electricity from the power grid.

By 1:00 A.M., though, none of the search teams had detected anything unusual, and Hanson grew impatient. He stepped closer to the corporal who was pushing the GPR machine and the lieutenant who was analyzing the results. The machine looked a bit like a lawn mower—its lower part had four wheels, and suspended between them was a heavy rectangular unit, about the size of a briefcase, which contained the antennas. As the corporal steered the machine down the street, the unit's transmitting antenna fired radio waves downward. These waves penetrated the asphalt and concrete and dirt, and some of them bounced back to the street. Another antenna in the unit received the reflected waves and measured how long it took them to return. The data revealed the shape and depth of the underground structures.

The long handle that the corporal used to push the machine also supported a ten-inch-wide screen that displayed the GPR signals. Whenever the corporal spotted something new on the screen he stopped pushing and let the lieutenant compare the data with his blueprints. Because his schematics showing the locations of all the ordinary structures beneath the street—the water pipes, sewer mains, power lines, and fiber-optic cables—the lieutenant could tell if the GPR was showing something that wasn't supposed to be underground. The problem, though, was the sheer quantity of cables and pipes below their feet. Every few yards the search team had to stop the machine and consult the maps. It was driving Hanson crazy.

The next time they stopped, Hanson nudged the lieutenant aside and looked at the screen himself. On the display was a mishmash of wavy bluish lines, a confusing jumble of parabolas and hyperbolas. But Hanson was a radar expert—he'd studied the subject at MIT and now oversaw all of Space Command's satellite-tracking stations. Looking at the screen, he could tell right away what the GPR had detected: a twelve-inch water pipe located about six feet below the street. He'd seen similar signals many times over the past three hours. There were lots of water pipes in the neighborhood.

Hanson tapped the screen to get the attention of both the corporal and the lieutenant. "This is part of the water system, a distribution main. Don't bother stopping when you see this kind of signal."

"Yes, sir!" The lieutenant nodded. He was young, no more than a year or two out of the Air Force Academy, but he seemed eager and intelligent. The name written on his fatigues was MEKLER. "Sir, is there a range of sizes for the objects we're looking for? A minimum and a maximum?"

That was a good question. Hanson had no idea. "You should look for anything out of the ordinary, anything that doesn't appear in the blueprints. But as I mentioned in the briefing, you should pay special attention to any cables that are half an inch in diameter." This estimate was based on the observations of Dr. Pooley, who'd said the conductive strand was about as thick as her pinkie.

"The GPR doesn't work well for objects that small, sir." Lieutenant Mekler sounded apologetic. "If the cable is buried more than a few feet underground, I don't think the machine can detect it."

"Just do your best. Stay alert and keep your eyes on the screen."

Mekler shouted, "Yes, sir!" and snapped off a smart salute. The corporal also saluted, but less enthusiastically. Then they resumed their survey of the underside of Payson Avenue.

None of the soldiers below the rank of colonel knew the true nature of their mission. Hanson had told them the same cover story about the fanatical Muslims, so his men thought they were hunting for a bomb. He disliked lying to them, but he didn't have a choice. This was a national security crisis of the highest order. It was the most serious threat the United States—or any other country—had ever faced. And, for good or bad, Hanson was in charge of facing it. He had to strictly control the information about the threat.

He took a deep breath as he followed his men down the street. It was strange to see New York City this way, so dark and empty. The neighborhood wasn't entirely deserted—Hanson had glimpsed a few shadowy figures in the windows of the darkened apartment buildings—but the streets were deathly quietly, and the silence exhilarated him. He tilted his head back and gazed at the night sky. It was so much clearer with the streetlights turned off. Even though the quarter-moon was up, he could see dozens of stars.

Somewhere in the back of his mind he'd always known this day would come. His whole life he'd been waiting for it to happen. Hanson felt a little dizzy as he stared at the stars overhead. Something marvelous and alarming had emerged from the darkness, and soon enough he would confront it, the terrifying unknown.

It was his destiny.

When Brent Hanson was a boy he'd dreamed of becoming an astronaut. He was too young to witness the Apollo missions—that program ended when he was only two years old—but he was eleven when the space shuttle *Columbia* shot into orbit for the first time. He watched the launch on an old black-and-white TV in the kitchen of his trailer home. It was April 12th 1981, three seconds after 7:00 A.M. His mother and her boyfriend were still asleep in their bedroom.

In 1988 Hanson entered the Air Force Academy to pursue his dream. He did everything he could to improve his chances of being chosen for one of NASA's space-shuttle crews. After graduation he became a fighter pilot. A few years later he went back to school on Uncle Sam's dime and earned a Ph.D. in physics from MIT. By the age of thirty-three he was one of the youngest lieutenant colonels in the Air Force and a prime candidate for the astronaut corps. He submitted his application to NASA and passed the preliminary screening.

Then two setbacks happened in quick succession. On February 1, 2003, during its twenty-eighth mission, the space shuttle *Columbia* disintegrated while reentering the atmosphere. The disaster doomed NASA's shuttle program and limited the agency's need for more astronauts. A month later the United States invaded Iraq, and the Air Force put out a call for experienced airmen to lead its fighter squadrons into combat. Hanson had to make a choice. For the good of his career he became a squadron commander and abandoned his dream of spaceflight.

It turned out to be a rewarding choice, at least career-wise. He rose swiftly through the ranks. After ten years he was promoted to lieutenant general and assigned to lead the Fourteenth Air Force, the biggest unit in Space Command. At first the job seemed a perfect fit for him, but soon the Pentagon slashed his budget, leaving Hanson unable to do anything ambitious. Worse, he had to deal with personnel issues, bureaucratic squabbles, and hundreds of petty problems. The Air Force promoted him again three years later, putting him in charge of all of Space Command, but the only part of the job he really enjoyed was visiting the airmen at the Space Operations Center at Vandenberg. He went there whenever he could, often late at night. He liked to chat with the radar specialists and stare at the jumbo screen showing the thousands of satellites orbiting the Earth.

That's why Hanson was still on duty when Sarah Pooley sent the alert about Object 2016X. He recognized her name immediately. Twenty years ago he'd read about her studies of the Martian microfossils. He knew NASA had punished her for sticking to her guns, and that she'd spent time in a mental-health clinic afterwards. In other words, she was brilliant but erratic, which is why Hanson didn't take her too seriously when she rushed into the operations center three nights ago. But that had been a mistake. He shouldn't have underestimated her. She was the first to recognize the uniqueness of 2016X. She was far better equipped to analyze the object than any of the experts on Hanson's staff.

The only problem was, he couldn't trust her. She was too independent, too unstable. Even after he persuaded her to sign a contract with the Air Force, he still questioned her loyalty. He knew she'd ignore the contract's restrictions if they got in her way. So Hanson ordered one of his men—his longtime aide Colonel Gunter, a good ol' boy who was adept at playing dumb—to secretly install a spy-software package on her laptop. This allowed Hanson to see all her notes and monitor her movements.

He was baffled at first when she neglected her assigned duties and arranged to meet the Con Edison inspector. But at the same time, Hanson couldn't help but admire her bravery. She wasn't afraid to investigate the outlandish notion that 2016X was an alien space probe. And because she had no fear, she was free to explore all the possibilities. By the time she collected her otherworldly sample from the Con Ed manhole and gave it to Dr. Philip Clark for testing, Hanson was convinced she was right. That's when he notified his superiors in the Pentagon and shared the startling facts with them. Although the defense secretary and the Joint Chiefs were skeptical, they agreed there was enough evidence to justify taking the first steps of Contingency Plan Orion.

The Defense Department had contingency plans for every imaginable catastrophe, from global pandemics to supervolcanoes. The Orion Plan detailed how the U.S. military should respond to the discovery of an extraterrestrial spacecraft. The plan authorized Hanson to take extraordinary measures to keep the discovery secret, including the fabrication of a cover story. And the plan gave him the authority to arrest Pooley and Clark and anyone else who might contradict that story. Just to be on the safe side, he also arrested Gino Torelli, the Con Edison inspector.

Hanson had exchanged a few words with Sarah during her arrest, but she was furious and uncooperative, so there was no point in continuing the conversation. Colonel Gunter took the suspects to the Federal Building downtown and locked them in detention cells normally used by the FBI. It was a shame, really. Hanson could use Sarah's help right now. She could probably offer some good advice on how to locate the alien machinery underground. But she'd already proved she couldn't follow the rules. She'd violated her confidentiality agreement when she talked to Philip Clark, so what was to stop her from telling the whole story to *The New York Times*? No, she had to be detained until the crisis was over, and Hanson would have to find the alien machinery on his own.

He looked up at the night sky again. He tried to analyze the problem as Dr. Pooley would, breaking it into smaller parts and considering all the variables. He pictured Sarah in the Con Edison manhole, staring at the slender black strand she'd discovered. She'd written in her notes that the strand had pulled away from the power line right after Torelli pointed his voltage detector at it. Perhaps this was simply a coincidence. But in her notes Sarah had mentioned a more disturbing possibility: perhaps the alien cable had somehow noticed that Torelli was observing it. Maybe the strand had disconnected from the power line and retreated from the manhole because it didn't want to be observed.

If that was true, Hanson thought, the implications for the GPR search weren't good. If the alien machines could sense the ground-penetrating radar, they could delve deeper underground to avoid detection. The search would be futile.

Hanson concentrated harder. He needed to think like Sarah. That was the only way to tackle the problem. He saw her in his mind's eye again, but now she was hunched over her laptop, her dark brown eyes fixed on the screen, her delicate fingers tapping the keys. She was a beautiful woman, but not in the way that a movie star or a fashion model was beautiful. She was more like an exquisite sports car, a Maserati or Lamborghini that had been engineered to perfection.

Hanson's concentration faltered. Although he admired Sarah, she also agitated him. He'd had this problem with other women over the years;

as soon as he found someone he wanted, he started to despise her. That was why he'd never married. He avoided relationships because they always turned into sickening struggles. Better to focus on work, the task at hand. Although Sarah's advice might be useful now, in the final analysis Hanson was glad he'd locked her up. Her presence disturbed him.

To clear his mind he stared at the wavy lines on the GPR screen. Then he heard the sound of squealing tires behind him. Turning around, he saw an armored Humvee barreling down Payson Avenue. It was going full speed down the empty street as if a regiment of enemy tanks was chasing it.

Hanson felt a surge of adrenaline in his gut. *This is it. It's about to happen.*

The corporal and lieutenant also turned around. The Humvee screeched to a halt a few yards away and an officer bolted out of the driver's seat. It was Colonel Tatum, a wiry redhead in his late thirties. Normally, he was one of Hanson's most levelheaded officers, but now his face was flushed and sweaty. His right hand trembled as he saluted Hanson. "Sir! Can I speak with you privately for a moment?"

They stepped toward the sidewalk, away from the other men. Like Gunter and the other colonels on Hanson's staff, Tatum knew about the space probe. During the mission briefing earlier that evening, Hanson had told his senior officers about the discovery of the conductive cable and its extraordinary molecular composition. He'd made it clear there was a strong possibility that the probe had originated on another planet, and that it might be using its advanced technology to spread across Manhattan. His colonels had taken the news stoically, showing no fear and not even much surprise. Since then, however, something had obviously shaken Tatum's composure. He stood too close to Hanson, and he was breathing fast.

"I came here as quick as I could, sir," he blurted. "I couldn't radio you because I didn't know if the transmissions would be secure, and you said not to use the radio unless we were absolutely sure that—"

"Jesus, Tatum, slow down. What's gotten into you?"

"I'm sorry, sir. It's just . . ." Tatum stopped himself and took a deep breath. "One of the search teams found something unusual."

Hanson felt another adrenaline surge. His stomach was churning. "What is it? Do you have the GPR data?"

Tatum shook his head. "They didn't find it with the radar system. It's not underground."

"Not underground? Where the hell is it?"

"It's in one of the apartment buildings. The address is 172 Sherman Avenue. That's between Academy Street and West 204th."

Because Hanson had been crisscrossing Inwood for the past three hours, he had a pretty good map of the neighborhood in his head. The address was just four blocks to the east. He stepped toward the Humvee and motioned for Tatum to follow him. "Come on, you'll drive me there. We can talk on the way."

A wide-eyed look of panic appeared on Tatum's face, but it lasted only a moment. He shook off his fear, shouted "Yes, sir!" and dashed toward the Humvee.

Hanson got into the vehicle on the passenger side while Tatum returned to the driver's seat and restarted the engine. He turned the Humvee around and headed south on Payson. As they sped down the street Hanson felt recharged and alert and stupendously impatient. He squinted at Tatum. "What did the search team find? How big is it?"

"Uh, it's hard to say, sir." Tatum was still breathing fast. "The leader of the team thinks they've uncovered only a small piece of the thing."

"Uncovered?"

"Yes, sir. While the team was conducting its GPR survey of Sherman Avenue they noticed several local residents who hadn't followed the evacuation order. They'd remained in their apartments even though they had no electricity and all their neighbors had left."

Hanson remembered the shadowy figures he'd seen in some of the windows. "Yes, I noticed a few of them on Payson Avenue too."

"So the search team called in a military police unit to sweep through the buildings on that block and round up the stragglers." Tatum paused to catch his breath. He steered the Humvee to the left and started driving down Academy Street. "In one of the buildings the MPs found an old man in a ground-floor apartment who hadn't heard about the evacuation order. They tried to explain to him why he needed to leave the neighborhood, but instead of listening to them he kept complaining about the smell from the apartment next door. At first the MPs thought he was senile, but then they noticed the smell too, a really bad fishy odor coming from that apartment."

"This is turning into a long story, Tatum. Can you get to the point?"

"Sorry, sir. The MPs also noticed that the front door to that apartment was hot to the touch. They thought a fire might've started in there, so they broke down the door and went inside." Tatum slowed the Humvee at the intersection of Academy and Sherman and took another left. "The living room was hot, but it wasn't smoky. The smell seemed to be coming from the bedroom, but the MPs couldn't open its door. They hit it with their battering ram and it still wouldn't open, but after a few hits the door started to crack and—"

"There! That's it." Hanson pointed at a crowd of soldiers outside an apartment building. Although the street was very dark, he could make out the number 172 above the building's entrance. "Stop here."

Tatum hit the brakes, and Hanson jumped out of the Humvee before it even stopped moving. The soldiers on the sidewalk looked puzzled when they saw their commander, but they automatically stepped out of his way and saluted him as he rushed into the building.

Hanson felt as if he were being drawn inside, as if an invisible rope were pulling him toward the scene. He charged down a corridor and ran headlong into the foul-smelling apartment. A dozen of his men stood in the living room, all of them aiming their flashlights at the wall on the room's right side. They turned their heads and saluted when Hanson entered the room, but they kept their flashlights trained on the wall.

This wall, Hanson realized, was the one that stood between the living room and the bedroom. The soldiers had already pulverized the bedroom door—it lay in splinters on the living-room carpet—and inside the door frame was a rectangle of blackness. At first glance Hanson thought he was simply looking into another dark room, but after a moment he saw the reflections of the flashlight beams glinting off the black rectangle.

A sheet of shiny black metal blocked the doorway. Polished and flawless, the sheet extended behind the wall on both sides of the doorway, running the whole length of the room. The soldiers had used a battering ram to pound holes in the wall to the left and right of the door frame, and through each hole Hanson could see the same metallic sheet.

He studied it for several seconds, mesmerized by its strangeness. Then Colonel Tatum caught up to him, dashing breathless into the apartment. Hanson snapped out of his trance and pulled Tatum aside, leading him across the living room to a sliding glass door that had been opened to air out the place.

They stepped outside to a dark patio furnished with a chaise lounge. There were more soldiers out here, pointing their flashlights at a smallish window in the brick wall, the window to the apartment's bedroom. It, too, was blocked by a metallic sheet. One of the soldiers, a muscular sergeant, stood by the window with a sledgehammer in his hands. He'd already shattered the glass, which lay in shards on the ground.

Pointing at the window, Hanson turned to Colonel Tatum. "Is the bedroom completely enclosed in the black metal? On all sides?"

Tatum nodded. "We poked holes in the floor of the apartment above it and found the barrier there too. It's like a big metal box surrounding the room. We think it's connected to structures beneath the surface, but we haven't found the links yet."

"Have you tested the barrier? Tried to break through it?"

"Yes, sir. Look at this." Tatum stepped toward the sergeant who held the sledgehammer. "Sergeant, hit the barrier again. Show the general what happens."

The soldier nodded. He raised his hammer, cocked it over his right shoulder, and swung it hard.

The sledgehammer's head slammed against the black metal. With a ringing *thunk*, the hammer bounced off the sheet, recoiling so violently that the sergeant almost lost his grip on the handle.

Hanson stepped closer and saw a small dent in the sheet, maybe three inches wide and half an inch deep. As he examined it, though, the dent disappeared. The metal oozed back into place and became perfectly smooth again.

"See that?" Tatum's voice was high-pitched, half-amazed and half-terrified. "It's strange, right?"

Hanson frowned. Yes, the alien metal was strange, but it didn't frighten him. He intended to put the substance through a more rigorous test, something a little rougher than a hammer blow. "I'm going to call in the Special Operations unit. Are all the residents out of the building now?"

"Yes, sir, it's clear."

"I want you to make sure this entire block is empty. Have your men go into every building and knock on every door."

Tatum raised an eyebrow. "Sir, may I ask what you're planning?"

Hanson ignored the colonel's question. Something else had occurred to him. "What about the resident of *this* apartment? Do we know who it is?"

"Yeah, we checked the records." Tatum reached into the pocket of his fatigues and pulled out a slip of paper. "The resident is a fifty-nine-year-old African American woman, a retired minister. There doesn't seem to be anything special about her."

"Where is she now? Did she register at one of the emergency shelters?"

Tatum shook his head. "Not so far. But we're still checking. Her name is Dorothy J. Adams."

Fortunately, Hanson had planned ahead. He'd stationed a Special Tactics team at the command post near the Hudson River. The Special Tactics men were the Air Force's commandos, roughly equal in skill to the soldiers in the Army's Delta Force and the Navy's SEAL teams. Their role in combat was to parachute down to airfields in enemy territory and secure them for the military's use. The men were trained to fight in unfamiliar situations and face unexpected threats. More important, they had extensive training in demolition work, which was often needed to remove wreckage from captured airfields. They were experts at handling C-4 and other plastic explosives.

The team left the command post in an armored Stryker troop carrier, which came roaring down Sherman Avenue less than two minutes later. Hanson had pulled all his other soldiers out of the apartment building—there were about thirty of them in all—and now they stood guard on the street about a hundred yards south of the building's entrance. The Stryker stopped at this point, and its rear hatch opened. The nine Special Tactics officers burst out of the vehicle and spread across Sherman Avenue, cradling their assault rifles and scanning the street with the night-vision goggles that hung from their helmets. Their faces were smeared with black paint, and they wore camouflage uniforms padded with body armor. Their commander, a swarthy, hulking captain named Pavlovich, headed straight for Hanson and raised his massive right arm in a salute.

"Sir!" he shouted. "What are your orders?"

Hanson was impressed. These men were perfect soldiers. They'd spent years strengthening their bodies and honing their skills. They'd jumped out of planes and marched across deserts and slogged through rain forests. They were ready to carry out any assignment, no matter how difficult, and they performed their tasks so admirably that Hanson found it a real pleasure to give them orders. It was like the pleasure a carpenter or mason must feel when handling a well-designed tool. The general's satisfaction was so strong he wanted to smile.

But he didn't. Instead, he narrowed his eyes at Captain Pavlovich. "This is a demolition job. I assume you've been briefed about the terrorists we're looking for?"

Pavlovich nodded. "Yes, sir. Have you located the individuals?"

"We think so." Hanson pointed at the entrance to 172 Sherman Avenue. "We discovered a massive metal barrier on the ground floor of that building, inside apartment 1A. The barrier completely encloses the apartment's bedroom, turning it into a fortified bunker. There's a good chance the terrorists are inside that bunker, along with all their bomb-making materials. We tried to breach the barrier using battering rams, but they were ineffective."

"And now you want us to try explosives, sir?"

"Exactly. How much C-4 does your unit have?"

"We have a hundred and twelve demolition blocks, plus all the priming assemblies and detonation cords." Pavlovich gestured at three of his sergeants, each of whom carried a bulging backpack. "That's almost a hundred fifty pounds of C-4, sir. It's enough to knock down any barrier I can think of."

"Good. I want you to use it all."

The captain gave him an uneasy look. He clearly didn't want to contradict his superior. "Uh, sir? It may not be advisable to use that much C-4. The explosion would collapse the whole building. And maybe the neighboring buildings as well."

"Don't worry about that." Hanson swept his arm in a wide arc, gesturing at all the buildings on the block. "We checked all the other apartments and made sure they're empty. You have permission to use as much explosives as necessary."

Pavlovich still seemed uncertain. "Sir, can I ask a question about the objectives of this mission? Don't we want to have the option of capturing at least one of these individuals alive? So we could interrogate him and obtain some intelligence about their organization?"

Hanson frowned. As it turned out, the Special Tactics men weren't perfect after all. A well-designed tool doesn't question its handler. "That's not your mission, Captain. Your mission is to eliminate the terrorists. I want you to put your C-4 all over that metallic bunker they've built and blow it sky-high." He stepped closer to Pavlovich. "Do you understand your orders?"

All the uncertainty vanished from the captain's paint-smeared face. He snapped off another salute and boomed, *"Yes, sir!"* Then he turned to his three sergeants and began to give them instructions, pointing at 172 Sherman Avenue as he talked.

Hanson stared at them. As the sergeants huddled with Pavlovich they seemed to be advertising the Air Force's diversity—Sergeant Turner was black, Sergeant Hernandez was Latino, and Sergeant Lee was Asian. The racial mix was appropriate for the occasion, Hanson thought; all the peoples of the Earth were working together to combat the alien invader. It was a heartening image, filling the general with pride and fervor, although it was somewhat undermined by the fact that the men didn't know who they were really fighting. They thought they were going to kill Muslims.

After a minute or so, the huddle broke up. The sergeants gave hand signals to the five corporals under their command, and then Captain Pavlovich led them all down the street.

Hanson stayed near the Stryker vehicle with the other soldiers, who craned their necks to watch the Special Tactics team march toward the apartment building a hundred yards away. The general watched them too, silently urging the men to move faster. He was worried that by the time they reached apartment 1A, all the shiny black metal would have already retreated underground, just like Sarah Pooley's black cable had retreated into the concrete wall of the manhole. It had disappeared, Dr. Pooley speculated, because it didn't want to be observed. And if that was true, then some kind of intelligence—artificial or biological—*must* be guiding the alien machinery.

Hanson had dismissed this hypothesis at first, but now he believed it. He believed the alien machinery had reacted to the GPR survey teams by delving farther underground and hiding from the radar scans. And though the soldiers had succeeded in discovering the black walls at 172 Sherman Avenue, Hanson guessed that was only because something large and important was inside that metallic box, something the machinery couldn't move underground. But what was hidden there? A power source? A computer? A weapon?

The general shook his head. It didn't matter. He didn't have to know what the hidden thing was. His men were simply going to blow it up. If it was important to the operations of the alien probe, then maybe destroying it would stop the spread of the machinery.

As Captain Pavlovich came within ten yards of the building's entrance he looked over his shoulder and said something to Sergeant Turner. Sergeants Lee and Hernandez moved closer, obviously listening in. Although Hanson was much too far away to hear what Pavlovich was saying, he assumed the captain was telling his men how they should enter the building—who would take the point, who would bring up the rear. After a few seconds he turned back to the building and bounded toward its doors.

Then there was a flash of white light, and the captain collapsed. He fell forward, hitting the sidewalk in front of 172 Sherman Avenue. Hanson caught a glimpse of Pavlovich's prone body and recoiled in horror. The man's head was gone. Blood and charred skin and blackened pieces of the captain's helmet were scattered across the sidewalk.

A moment later the same thing happened to Sergeant Turner. His helmet blew apart and his skull burst open and his blood sprayed into the faces of the other Special Tactics soldiers. They stood there in the street for the next half second, turning frantically in all directions to see where the enemy was. There were no gunshots, no muzzle flashes, no signs of movement on the street or inside the apartments or on the rooftops. It was impossible to tell where the opposing fire was coming from. Then, while Turner's corpse was still falling to the ground, Sergeant Lee's head exploded.

The other soldiers ran for cover. Three of the corporals dashed toward an SUV parked at the curb, and two of them followed Sergeant Hernandez toward a minivan on the other side of the street. But as Hernandez sprinted across Sherman Avenue, flames suddenly erupted from his backpack. Then the C-4 inside his pack detonated.

The explosion cratered the asphalt and crumpled the minivan and killed all the remaining men on the Special Tactics team. A plume of smoke and debris fountained above the street, and the blast wave shattered every window on the block. The wave rolled a hundred yards down Sherman Avenue and knocked over Hanson and most of the thirty soldiers behind him. Even the Stryker troop carrier rocked on its tires.

Hanson's ears rang from the blast, but he managed to get back on his feet. He was in combat mode now, automatically following his training. They'd been caught in an ambush, and the opposing forces could be anywhere. The only viable option was retreat.

He turned to his men and pointed south, away from 172 Sherman Avenue. *"Get moving! Come on, get the hell out of here!"*

The stunned soldiers picked themselves up and started running down the street. The Stryker's driver rushed back inside the vehicle, closed its rear hatch, and began the process of turning the troop carrier around. Hanson ran alongside his men, yelling at the stragglers. For several seconds there was no incoming fire, and the general thought he and his men had moved out of range. But then he heard a loud rattling noise behind him.

Looking over his shoulder, he saw that the noise came from the Stryker, which had stopped moving in the middle of its three-point turn. It seemed to be having engine trouble, but after a second Hanson noticed a glowing, viscous liquid trickling down the vehicle's sloping front end. It was molten steel. The Stryker's armor was melting. After another second there was a muffled explosion inside the vehicle and smoke began to pour out of its hull.

This scared Hanson more than anything he'd seen so far. *What kind of weapon could do that kind of damage? How could it heat the armor to its melting point?*

Then the running soldiers started to fall. A tall lieutenant pitched forward as his fatigues caught fire. A boyish private shrieked as his hair ignited. And as Hanson watched his men die, he realized what was being aimed at them. It was a powerful beamed-energy weapon, a battlefield laser. For decades the U.S. Defense Department had been trying, without success, to build such a device. But someone else had apparently succeeded.

Where were the laser beams coming from, though? How were they being aimed?

Hanson wanted to scream. There was no time to figure it out. He just needed to get his men out of the line of fire. Although the beamed-energy weapon seemed to have excellent accuracy and range, it couldn't fire around a corner. And the corner of Sherman Avenue and Academy Street was just a few yards ahead.

"Turn right!" Hanson boomed at his soldiers. *"Everyone, go right!"*

Although the men were terrified, most of them heard his order and obeyed it. They cut to the right and charged west on Academy Street. But a few soldiers didn't make it. Major Beardsley, an intelligence officer Hanson knew well, was hit right before he reached the intersection. The energy beam struck the side of his head, and he tumbled to the asphalt. Hanson was only a few feet away, so he grabbed Beardsley's arms and pulled his body around the corner of the apartment building. Once they were safely behind the brick wall, Hanson bent over the major to check his pulse, but the man was dead. The beam had sliced through his helmet and skull.

Hanson crouched on the sidewalk, breathing hard. He wasn't scared anymore. He was furious. The alien program had beaten him. Somehow it had sensed what the Special Tactics team had planned to do, and it had eliminated the threat. In less than a minute it killed half of Hanson's soldiers and sent the rest scurrying back to their command post. It was a crushing, humiliating defeat, and Hanson had never been humiliated before. His stomach twisted. He clenched his right hand into a fist and pounded the brick wall.

Then he turned back to Beardsley and noticed the binoculars hanging from the major's neck. Because the man had been an intelligence officer, he carried a pair of state-of-the-art thermal binoculars that could view objects in total darkness by displaying their heat signatures. Better yet, the device had a memory chip that could store all the images for later analysis.

Hanson gingerly gripped the strap around Beardsley's neck and pulled off the high-tech binoculars. Raising them to his eyes, he leaned closer to the edge of the apartment building. Then he peeked around the corner.

Sherman Avenue was littered with burning objects that glowed brightly on the thermal display. The Stryker glared like a torch. Molten steel still dripped from the vehicle's front end. Half a dozen parked cars were on fire, and so were several of the soldier's corpses.

Hanson felt another surge of anger, but he took a deep breath and scanned the rest of the street. He saw nothing moving, neither man nor machine. He raised the binoculars and surveyed the apartment buildings on the other side of Sherman Avenue. All their windows were shattered, allowing Hanson to peer into the darkened apartments and glimpse the furniture inside.

Then he saw something move. It was in a window on the sixth floor of the building across the street from 172 Sherman Avenue.

He zoomed in on the window. Someone stood behind it in the darkness. The person would've been invisible to the naked eye, but he stood out clearly on the thermal display in the binoculars. He was a skinny male, most likely a teenager. He wore a sleeveless T-shirt and sagging pants. A bandanna was wrapped around his head.

After a few seconds the kid turned to his right, and a second figure appeared beside him. This was another skinny teenager, a few inches taller than the first. He also wore a bandanna and a sleeveless shirt. Hanson remembered the people he'd seen hiding in their apartments earlier that evening. These two looked like typical street thugs.

He increased the magnification of the binoculars and focused on the boys' faces. Then he stored the images in the memory chip. The pictures were high-resolution, good enough to be matched against the mug shots in the NYPD's databases. These kids had been in the perfect place to view the battle on Sherman Avenue, so there was a chance they might've seen something Hanson had missed, maybe even caught a glimpse of the alien weapon. It was a long shot, he thought, but it might be worthwhile to track them down and interview them.

Then the first kid yawned and stretched, arching his back and raising his hands above his head. Hanson was startled to see a glowing circle in the center of the kid's right hand. Judging from its brightness on the thermal display, the circle was scorching, at least five hundred degrees Fahrenheit. And yet it seemed to be embedded in the skin of the boy's palm.

A moment later the second kid stretched, mimicking his companion. Hanson saw a white-hot circle in his palm too.

Jesus. What the hell's going on?

EIGHTEEN

Dorothy was dying. At the same time, she was about to give birth.

Her body was already gone. Her skin and muscles and organs had dissolved, melting into a warm, viscous liquid that sloshed and frothed in the black container that had materialized in her bedroom. Her mind had survived somehow, but her memories were evaporating. She could no longer recall the major or minor events in her life—where she came from, where she went, what she did or didn't do.

All she had left were her emotions, and even those seemed to be fading. Her mind had roiled with fear and rage when she'd realized that the voice in her head had deceived her, but those feelings dissolved almost as quickly as her body did. In the hours afterward she felt only sadness, which seemed to surround her like the spongy lining of the container. But then the sadness dissolved too and she was left with only one thought to cling to, the emotion she'd felt most strongly at the end of her all-too-brief life. She'd wanted to be a mother. The yearning was so strong that even death couldn't erase it.

And now she was finally going to get her wish. Although she'd lost her body, she could still create a new life.

How was that possible? She didn't know. It was a complete mystery to her. She had neither eyes nor ears, so she couldn't observe herself or her surroundings. But she sensed that her mind floated within the viscous fluid, which was a mixture of her own dissolved flesh and the rich, red cell cultures she'd taken from the cancer hospital and a strange elixir that came from the black walls of the container. She also sensed the presence of another mind in the liquid, floating very close to hers. She'd believed it was God's mind when it had first spoken to her, before she lost her body. Later, after she realized it had lied to her, she believed it was the mind of Satan. But that was also wrong.

This other mind was neither good nor evil. Its name was the Emissary, and it was going to help bring her child into the world. It was the child's father.

Dorothy had discovered that she could start a conversation with the Emissary simply by thinking about him. This was another mystery— were her thoughts agitating the liquid? Did they make ripples or waves that signaled her desire to communicate? She had no idea how it worked, but she knew it was a reliable way to contact him. And right now she needed to talk.

A few minutes ago she'd felt a jolt within the liquid. Someone or something from the outside world had jarred the black container. The more she thought about the disturbance, the more it upset her. She was an anxious mother-to-be, and she wanted to be reassured that this was a safe place to give birth. So she called out to the Emissary with her thoughts, and a moment later he responded.

Don't worry, Dorothy. We're safe here.

What was that jolt? It felt like the ground was shaking.

Please trust me. There's no need to be concerned. Everything is under control.

She couldn't trust him, though. He was a liar. He'd pretended to be God. And yet he was also very powerful. He had the power to give her what she wanted.

Okay, okay. I'm just nervous, all right? I can't stand all this waiting.

You won't have to wait much longer. Your cells have almost completed the transformation.

You're changing them so they'll be more like your own cells? So we can have a child together?

No, not exactly. I'm not a biological entity, so I have no cells. The transformation will make your cells similar to those of the biological entities who programmed me.

The Emissary had mentioned this distinction before, but Dorothy had forgotten. It was easy to forget that the Emissary was actually a computer program, not a person. He seemed very much alive to her.

But you're adding something to my cells, right? Putting a piece of yourself into them?

I carry all the data about the biological makeup of the beings who created me. I'm using this data to reassemble your cells and reconstitute your mind. That's what I've been programmed to do.

Dorothy remembered something from her old life, an antique painting showing a sad-faced mother with a naked child on her lap. Both the mother and child had glowing circles around their heads.

A virgin birth? Is that what you're talking about?

I'm not familiar with that term. Please give me a moment to study it. The Emissary paused. Somehow he seemed to be able to get information from the Internet. **Yes, there's a similarity between the cellular transformation and the central myth of your religion. You've been chosen to bring a new kind of being into the world.**

Except you're not God. And I won't live to see the child, will I?

No, you won't. But part of you will survive. Your cells will be transformed and rearranged in new patterns, but their biochemistry will remain essentially the same.

She tried to take some comfort from this fact, but it wasn't enough. She wanted more than biochemistry.

Can I name the child? Can I do that at least?

Certainly. The new being will need a name that humans can understand.

Dorothy thought it over. She remembered something else from her old life, a big windowless laboratory. Sitting at one of the lab's workbenches was a woman with gorgeously arched eyebrows. This was the scientist from the cancer hospital, the one who studied the stem cell cultures. She was smart and kind, a beautiful young woman. She was the daughter Dorothy had always wanted.

Naomi. Her name will be Naomi.

NINETEEN

Sarah dreamed of her father. In her dream he walked across the West Texas desert. There was nothing but blazing white sand all around him. He kept his head down as he walked, staring at the sand. He was looking for meteorites.

After ages and ages he found one. He bent over and picked up a shiny black rock, the size of a matchbox. He smiled and showed it to her.

Then there was a terrible cracking noise. A deep black crevice ripped the ground apart, splitting the desert. Tons of sand poured into the crevice from both sides. Her father slid into it too, still clutching his meteorite.

Sarah opened her eyes, instantly awake. She sat up on the narrow bed, which extended like a shelf from the wall of her detention cell. She could still hear the cracking. It was coming from the corner of her cell, a few feet to her left.

The only light in the room came from the slender gap under the locked door. She peered into the darkness but saw nothing in the corner of the cell except the stainless-steel toilet. She backed up against the wall, her pulse jittering in her neck.

No, nothing was there. She was going crazy, that's all. She'd been locked inside that room for the past fourteen hours. After Hanson's soldiers separated her from Phil and brought her to the Federal Building downtown, they took her to the FBI detention cells in the basement and started interrogating her. She answered their questions as well as she could, telling them everything she knew about the alien probe, but after a while she sensed they weren't listening. Because Hanson had been spying on her, his men already knew about the probe's cables and drills. The interrogators seemed much more interested in whether she'd talked to anyone else about it. They asked about her contacts at the Associated Press and *The New York Times*. They also asked if she'd contacted Tom Gilbert or any of the other science advisers at the White House. General Hanson was clearly determined to keep his operation secret.

After a few seconds the cracking noises stopped. Sarah took a deep breath and listened intently. It was probably the pipes, she thought. The Federal Building was old and its basement was dingy and in all likelihood the FBI didn't put a high priority on repairing the plumbing in the detention cells. In fact, they probably preferred cells with noisy pipes and dirty toilets. They *wanted* their detainees to be uncomfortable.

Then there was a louder, sharper crack, and the cell's floor crumbled. Chunks of concrete gave way and tumbled into the darkness, and the stainless-steel toilet fell with a clatter. Sarah's bed lurched sideways, its bolts loosened from the wall. She had to grab the edge of the mattress to stop herself from sliding off. When she looked down she saw a big hole in the floor. It spanned the width of the cell and half its length.

A cloud of dust rose from the hole, making the cell even darker. Sarah covered her mouth with one hand and fanned the air with the other, wondering if she should step around the hole and make her way to the door. No alarm had sounded, and no one seemed to be coming to her rescue. The basement of the Federal Building was huge, and there was only one FBI agent assigned to guard all the detention cells. If he was at the other end of the basement, he probably didn't even hear the collapse. Sarah would have to pound on the door and scream to get his attention.

She was still wondering what to do when she saw the gleaming black wire. It shot out of the hole and whipped across the cell and coiled around her waist. At the same time, another wire wrapped around her neck, tightly enough to close her airway. Now she couldn't scream for help. She couldn't even breathe. Frantic, she clawed at the black cable around her throat, but within seconds more wires coiled around her wrists and ankles. Moving in concert, they pulled her off the bed and down into the hole.

The wires lowered her through a dark chute below the detention cell, a narrow shaft that had apparently been carved by the alien drills. The machinery carried her swiftly yet carefully, making sure she didn't bump against the shaft's jagged edges. This careful treatment seemed odd considering the fact that the wires were strangling her. *It's going to kill me*, she thought. *It's taking me down to hell.*

Sarah descended about thirty feet in less than ten seconds. Then the wires settled her on a slab of concrete and uncoiled from her wrists and ankles and neck. Her chest heaved, and she drew in a lungful of musty air.

She wasn't in hell. She was in a cramped tunnel, about five feet wide and seven feet high. It was a utility tunnel, with dozens of pipes and cables running along its concrete walls, probably for delivering water and gas and broadband data to the skyscrapers of downtown Manhattan. As Sarah caught her breath she saw a figure in the tunnel's darkness, standing a few feet in front of her. His right hand was closed, and a reddish light glowed within his fist, as if he was clutching one of those small LEDs that are sometimes attached to key chains. The glow was brightest between his clenched fingers and under his fingernails. Sarah opened her mouth to scream at him, but her throat ached and all she could do was cough.

He stepped toward her. Although the red-tinged light wasn't strong enough to illuminate his face, Sarah could see the outline of his body. He was slender and short, not quite adult-size. He raised his left hand and pointed at her legs. "Can you walk?"

He spoke with a Spanish accent. Squinting at him, Sarah noticed he wore baggy pants and a bandanna. He was a youngster, a teenager.

This made her angry, and the anger gave her strength. Leaning against the wall for support, she managed to rise to her feet. "What's going on? Who are you?"

"I'm Luis. So, you think you can walk?"

Sarah gave him an indignant look. "Walk? I'm not going anywhere! What the hell are you doing down here?"

Luis looked down at his feet. Even in the dark, Sarah could tell he was confused, and probably scared as well. He pointed at her again.

"You . . . you have to come with me," he stammered. "You have to meet someone. He has a message for you."

He raised his head for a moment and glanced at the tunnel's concrete ceiling. Sarah looked up too and saw the gleaming black wires among the pipes and cables. They'd pulled out of the jagged shaft they'd drilled and now their sharp tips were directly overhead. The alien probe was in charge of this operation, she realized. Luis was simply following its orders.

Sarah paused. She needed to think of a better way to question him. "Listen, I can help you." She raised her chin, gesturing at the gleaming wires above his head. "What do you know about those black cables? The ones that pulled me down here?"

Luis said nothing, but Sarah could sense his fear. He breathed faster and shifted his weight from foot to foot.

She leaned closer to him and lowered her voice. "Is the machinery talking to you? Telling you what to do?"

The silence lengthened. Sarah waited it out. Then Luis raised his right hand, the one that was clenched into a fist, and opened it, flooding the tunnel with red-tinged light.

But there was no LED in his hand. The red glow came from a clear, crystalline disk, about two inches in diameter. At first glance Sarah thought the teenager was cupping the disk in his palm, but then she saw that the thing's surface was flush with his skin. It had been surgically implanted.

Now Sarah was silent. Her throat tightened and her gorge rose and she had to swallow hard to stop herself from vomiting. It was appalling, and yet it made perfect sense from the probe's point of view. The spacecraft had been programmed to take advantage of all the natural resources at its landing site. If it had the technology to meld its machinery with biological tissue, why wouldn't it take advantage of human resources as well?

After a few seconds Sarah overcame her revulsion and took a closer look at the glowing disk implanted in the boy's palm. It wasn't an ordinary light source. The disk was just the most visible part of the device; below the skin, the crystalline substance narrowed to a slender tube that seemed to tunnel into the boy's wrist and thread inside his forearm. What's more, Sarah thought this tube looked familiar. It resembled the resonators that physicists use to generate high-energy laser beams. The implanted device, she concluded, was most likely a weapon.

She felt another surge of disgust. *This is bad. The probe is already deploying its weapons, and we haven't even begun to communicate with it.*

She stopped examining the boy's hand and looked at his face. Now that there was more light in the tunnel, she could see the sweat on his forehead. The left side of his face was twitching.

"Why are you so frightened?" she asked. "What's wrong?"

Luis grimaced. His Adam's apple bobbed up and down. "There was a battle. An hour ago, on Sherman Avenue. The soldiers were going to kill Dorothy, and Emilio and Paco had to stop them. So they fired their rays." He held his right hand as far away from his body as he could. Then he closed his hand over the disk, smothering its light. "They didn't want to do it! They didn't want to burn the soldiers! But they had to! They had to!"

"Whoa, calm down. Who's—"

A high-pitched alarm interrupted her. The noise came down the jagged shaft she'd descended just a minute ago. The FBI had apparently discovered the hole in her detention cell. Luis heard the alarm too—he turned toward the noise and cocked his head to listen. Then he turned back to Sarah.

"We have to leave *now.*" He pointed down the length of the utility tunnel. "We'll go this way. It'll take us back uptown."

Sarah shook her head. "No, wait a second. Where are we—"

"*Por favor, señora.*" Luis stepped toward her, and for a moment she thought he was going to grab her arm. But instead he opened his hand a bit, releasing enough light to allow her to see his face. "I won't hurt you. You can trust me."

His expression wasn't fearful anymore. Now it was sweet and perfectly ordinary. The change was so abrupt that Sarah suspected that something else besides the crystalline tube had been implanted into the boy. Something was inside his brain, manipulating his behavior. Although the boy wasn't a mindless slave—he seemed to still have his own emotions and personality—he was clearly following the alien machinery's instructions. And for this reason, Sarah knew she couldn't trust him.

But she couldn't stay in the tunnel either. Now she could hear voices echoing down the shaft, the angry shouts of the FBI agents.

She let out a sigh. "All right, let's go." Then she followed Luis down the tunnel.

TWENTY

Emilio rolled over and stared across the mattress at Paco. The boy slept on his stomach, with the right side of his face pressed against the pillow. The left side was motionless except for his lips, which quivered as he drew in each breath.

It was almost dawn. Through his bedroom window Emilio watched the sky change color, gradually brightening from dark purple to light blue. When he looked again at Paco he could see more details: the mole above his left eyebrow, an old scar along his jawline, the fading bruise on his forehead. Despite everything, he was a good-looking *muchacho*. He could've been an actor or a model if he'd grown up in the suburbs.

Emilio reached toward him and touched his hair. It was short and thick, like a soft carpet. He pressed his fingers down and ran them though Paco's hair, then looked at the boy's face to see if he would awaken. But Paco didn't stir. He was a heavy sleeper, just like Emilio's grandmother, who was snoring away in the apartment's other bedroom. She'd heard about the evacuation order but decided to ignore it.

What surprised Emilio more than anything was how normal everything seemed. Well, not exactly normal—until a day ago he could've never imagined waking up next to a dude. "Natural" was maybe a better word for it. It seemed perfectly natural to be lying in bed with Paco, as if they'd been sleeping together for years. Emilio hadn't realized it until now, but this was part of the future he'd dreamed about, a future where he and his friends would be completely free, with no cops or teachers or priests telling them what to do. He liked this dream. It was worth fighting for.

The dream had a price, though. Emilio raised his right hand and forced himself to look at the *cosa maligna* in his palm. It had cooled off over the past few hours but still felt murderously hot. The burning sensation ran all the way up his arm. The pain flared every time he bent his wrist or elbow.

But that was nothing compared with the agony he'd felt when he'd fired the thing. The intensity of it had stunned him the first time it happened, when he'd stood behind the open window of the darkened apartment on Sherman Avenue, pointing his right hand at the soldiers in the street below. His arm had warmed from the inside until it felt as if his bones were melting. Then the pain had jumped like an electric shock from his arm to his head. A brilliant white light flashed inside his brain, and at that exact same moment the head of the Air Force captain exploded. The man died before he could feel anything, but Emilio felt it all, every last bit of pain and shock and horror. He was so appalled he wanted to press his right hand against his temple and blow his own brains out.

And yet he couldn't stop firing at the soldiers in the street. His hand moved automatically, aiming at another soldier, then another. He couldn't control it. All he could do was watch the men run from the invisible beams. Paco was in the next room, firing from another window. Working together, they killed all nine of the men in the Special Tactics squad. Then they aimed their beams at the soldiers farther down the street. In less than a minute he and Paco had decimated the platoon and turned their armored vehicle into a heap of molten slag.

But Emilio felt no sense of triumph. His goal had been to drive the New York Police Department out of Inwood, but he'd ended up fighting soldiers instead of cops. He'd wanted to strike a blow for his homeboys, for all the Dominicans and African Americans who were getting shafted by the rich white assholes in this city, but instead he'd killed a lot of

Latinos and blacks. The crystalline weapon inside his arm didn't care about race or skin color. It slaughtered everyone.

The worst moment came right after the battle, when Emilio regained control of his body and peered out the window to view the carnage on Sherman Avenue. Until that moment he'd considered himself a hero. He'd truly believed he was an avenging messiah, the chosen instrument of a mysterious force that had magically appeared in the basement of his grandmother's apartment building. But he couldn't fool himself anymore. The mysterious force had its own plans, and they weren't the same as Emilio's. He was a pawn, not a messiah. And because the force had inserted its weapons into his body, the only way to fight it was to kill himself.

He seriously considered it. He was willing to die for his sins. But as he stood by the window he saw Paco enter the dark room and come toward him. All at once Emilio felt an aching love for the boy. It was such a strong rush of feeling that he was sure Paco must've seen it on his face, even in the darkness. To cover his embarrassment, Emilio yawned and stretched, and a moment later Paco did the same. Then, without a word, the boys left the apartment and slipped out of the building through the service entrance. Emilio led the way through the deserted streets, heading for his grandmother's building.

Now he was glad he hadn't killed himself. He was glad he got the chance to sleep with Paco and wake up beside him. No matter what happened from now on, he'd always have that memory.

Bright morning light slanted through the bedroom window. It was almost 6:00 A.M., Emilio guessed. He wondered if he should try to get a few more hours of sleep. He looked once more at Paco, admiring the boy's sleeping body. Then Emilio closed his eyes and buried his face in his pillow.

As he lay there he thought of the other Trinitarios, Luis and Carlos and Miguel and Diego. Yesterday he'd brought them, one by one, to the mirrored closet in the basement. He'd felt guilty about it—he didn't give his homeboys a choice about joining his army—but he knew they'd thank him afterward, once they saw how strong they'd become. Strangely, though, none of the other Trinitarios showed up for the battle on Sherman Avenue. The mysterious force had apparently decided to send them elsewhere. Emilio didn't know what their assignments were, and he didn't care either. Right now, as he drifted off, it all seemed so unimportant.

Then, just as his first dreams began to form, he heard a gunshot.

It was very loud and close, only a few feet away. Jolted awake, he opened his eyes and saw Paco again, still lying beside him. But now half of the boy's head was gone. His brains were splattered across the bed's headboard.

At the same instant, someone leaned over the bed, lifted Emilio's head by his hair and grabbed his right arm at the wrist. In one swift motion he slammed the palm of Emilio's right hand against his right temple. Then a second man began wrapping duct tape around his head to keep his hand splayed there. Before Emilio could even think about charging up his weapon, it was pointed at his own skull.

Within seconds the men wrapped the tape several times around his head, binding his hand so tightly to his temple that he couldn't even wiggle his fingers. Then they restrained his left hand behind his back by wrapping the tape around his midsection, and finally they bound his ankles together. Emilio got a glimpse of the men before the duct tape covered his eyes. They were dressed all in black and had black paint on their faces.

They didn't put tape over his mouth, but Emilio was too dazed to scream. As soon as the men finished restraining him, he heard someone else enter the room. For a second he imagined it was his poor grandmother, but then he heard the men shout, "Sir!" The newcomer was their commander.

"At ease," the commander said. Emilio couldn't see the man, but his voice was close, just a few feet from the bed. "Did you follow the general's orders?"

"Yes, sir!" one of the men replied. "One dead and one alive."

"Prepare the corpse for autopsy." Emilio felt a gentle tap on his back. "And prepare this one for interrogation."

TWENTY-ONE

The meeting place was at 1 East 161st Street in the Bronx, but Joe didn't realize what stood at that address until he was just a few blocks away. First he saw the elevated tracks of the Jerome Avenue subway line, and as he walked a little farther down the street he spied the massive white structure on the other side of the tracks. The Emissary had arranged to meet the government officials at Yankee Stadium.

Joe stopped walking and stood on the sidewalk in front of a check-cashing place. It was six in the morning and most of the stores hadn't opened yet. "Seriously?" he whispered. "That's where you want to go?"

I thought you'd be pleased. You have an affection for Yankee Stadium, don't you?

He shook his head. Although he *was* a Yankees fan—mostly because of the jacket his ex-wife had given him—he'd gone to only one game at the stadium, and that was almost ten years ago. The tickets were too expensive, even for a doctor. "The stadium won't open until noon. How will we get in?"

Don't worry, I've taken care of that. I want to focus now on improving your personal appearance. Your clothing, for example, is in such a poor state that I fear it will distract the officials and hinder my communications with them.

Joe looked down at his ragged T-shirt and jeans. The swim across the East River hadn't done them any good. They were still damp even though he'd wrung them out, and now they smelled worse than ever. The river water had given them a brackish odor, and when it mixed with his sweat—he'd been wandering across the Bronx for hours—the combination was pretty foul.

"Yeah, I could use a wash," he admitted. "And a change of clothes."

Look to your right. Do you see the restaurant on the other side of 161st Street? The one called McDonald's?

He spotted it. The place was open, but he knew how difficult it was for a homeless person to wash up in a McDonald's restroom. He shook his head again. "The bathroom will be locked and they won't give me the key."

It's not locked. I've readied it for you.

Joe felt uneasy. He remembered last night's escape, how the gleaming tentacle had pulled him across the river and then retreated into the mud of the South Bronx. The Emissary wasn't just inside him anymore—she was all over the city, her black fingers exploring the underside of every street and sidewalk, every apartment building and store. Even the McDonald's.

Come on, Joe. You'll feel much better once you're clean.

He was too tired to argue. He walked to the corner and crossed 161st Street.

As he stepped into the restaurant he saw two women in red and yellow uniforms behind the counter. They automatically turned their heads and eyed him suspiciously. Like all fast-food workers in the city, they'd been trained to keep a lookout for undesirables. Joe's reaction was just as automatic: he avoided their stares and headed straight for the men's room.

The bathroom door had a lock, but it opened when he turned the knob. Curious, he looked at the latch and saw that the locking mechanism had been crimped. Then, as the door closed behind him, he heard a crunch in the tile floor near his feet. The tiles cracked and a five-inch-tall black spike rose from the floor. The Emissary had provided a doorstop. Now no one else could come into the bathroom.

Look at the floor in the left corner, next to the sink. The tiles there are loose.

Sure enough, when Joe bent over he was able to pry the tiles from the floor. Underneath them, tucked into a dank hole about the size of a suitcase, was a large, heavy shopping bag. He ripped the bag open and was astonished to see a suit inside: navy blue pants and jacket, plus a white shirt, a striped tie, black shoes, and a pair of socks. There was also a smaller bag containing a razor and a can of shaving cream.

"Jesus," he whispered. It was worse than he'd thought. How had the Emissary collected all these things? How many stores had she broken into?

There's no time to explain. You need to move quickly, because someone else will want to use the restroom sooner or later.

Still dumbfounded, Joe took off his filthy clothes and threw them into the corner. He stood by the sink and washed off the East River stink, scrubbing his armpits and crotch. Then he lathered his face and shaved off his grubby beard. Finally, he put on the shirt and socks and suit. Everything was brand-new and fit him perfectly. The patent-leather shoes were polished so well, he could see his reflection in them.

Joe looked in the mirror as he knotted the tie around his neck. The Emissary had been right—he *did* feel better. He stared at himself in the mirror, carefully studying his face. This was Dr. Joseph Graham of the Department of Surgery at St. Luke's Hospital. The man had been gone for so long, Joe barely recognized him.

There was a sudden banging on the restroom door. "Hey! This is the manager! What's going on in there?" It was a man's voice, loud and threatening. He put a key in the lock and tried to come inside, but the doorstop was in the way. "Yo, asshole! I know you're in there! What the fuck did you do to the door?"

Joe quickly grabbed his old clothes, stuffed them into the dank hole, and covered it with the cracked tiles. Then, just as he turned around, the doorstop sank into the floor. The manager banged on the door again and this time it burst open and the guy stumbled inside.

He was a big man wearing a blue short-sleeve shirt. He gazed at Joe for a moment, uncomprehending. Then he put an apologetic look on his face. "Oh, I'm so sorry, sir! I thought . . . I mean, the girls said they saw a . . ."

Joe's heart pounded. It took him a while to realize he didn't need to be afraid. "Uh, yeah, it's my fault. I was taking too long to—"

"No, no, sir! Take as long as you want! I'm very sorry about this!" His face reddening, the manager retreated and closed the door.

It's like magic, Joe thought. All it took was a suit and a shave.

I have something else for you. Check the right-hand pocket of the jacket.

Joe reached into the pocket and pulled out a roll of twenty-dollar bills.

Get yourself some breakfast. You still have forty-three minutes until the meeting.

He stared for a while at the money in his hand. It was at least five hundred dollars. Then he left the bathroom, went to the counter and ordered a large coffee and three Egg McMuffins. The counterwoman—who'd eyed him so suspiciously fifteen minutes ago—smiled and told him to have a great day.

As he sipped his coffee he thought about what the Emissary had promised. He imagined returning to his home and job and family. Going back to his old life would be a bigger challenge than simply putting on a new set of clothes. It wouldn't be enough to look good and have some money in his pocket. He'd have to convince Karen that she could trust him, and that wouldn't be easy. He'd broken so many promises.

And Annabelle? That was the biggest challenge of all. Would she even want to see him again? Could she ever forgive him?

She could, Joe. I could make her understand. Nothing is impossible for me.

Yes, he thought. *It's possible.*

He believed it.

Half an hour later Joe approached Yankee Stadium. At 7:00 A.M. the sidewalks around it were deserted. The place looked bereft without the usual swarming crowds. An empty Cheetos bag fluttered down the street.

The Emissary guided him past the stadium's main entrances, which were now locked tight. He passed the shuttered ticket office too and the stadium's press gate. He kept going until he reached the corporate entrance, the one that led to the offices of the baseball team's owners and management.

As Joe neared the glass doors he saw something moving in the darkness behind them. A man in a security guard's uniform appeared behind one of the doors and unlocked it. The man looked young, a little too young to be a security guard, actually. The uniform hung loosely on his slender frame. He held the door open for Joe and beckoned to him. "Over here, amigo," he called. "I've been waiting for you."

Joe stepped inside. He looked a little closer at the kid and recognized him. This was one of the teenagers from Inwood Hill Park. Not the leader of the gang, and not the one who'd kicked Joe in the ribs. He was the joker, the one with the braying laugh.

That's correct. His name is Carlos.

The kid closed the door and locked it. Then he turned around and pointed at Joe. "Damn, what happened to you, bro? You look a lot better than you did in the park. Where'd you get that suit?"

Joe knew he shouldn't be surprised to see the kid here. The Emissary had infected the leader of the gang, and he in turn could've infected all his friends. Still, it was disturbing. Joe wondered how much the teenager knew. "I got the suit from the Emissary. You know who that is?"

Carlos shook his head. "No idea. But it doesn't matter." Grinning, he turned to the right and headed down a long, carpeted corridor. "Follow me. It's dark in here, so you better watch where you're going. You don't want to trip over that big dude there."

Joe looked ahead and saw a figure lying faceup on the floor, either dead or unconscious. It was a large, dark-skinned man stripped to his underwear. Carlos stepped over him and continued down the corridor, but Joe stopped and stared until he saw the man's chest rise and heard him breathing.

He's one of the stadium's security guards. I sedated him and nine of his co-workers so we could make use of this facility.

A tentacle tethered the unconscious man to the floor. The gleaming wire stretched from a hole in the carpet and curled around the man's waist. Its tapered point was embedded in the bare skin above his hip.

"Christ." Joe's throat tightened. "What are you doing to him?"

You don't have to worry about his well-being. The sedation is temporary and won't damage him in any way.

Joe carefully stepped around the guard. Then he pointed at Carlos, who was several yards ahead. "What about *his* well-being? I notice you've done something to his right hand."

That's also temporary. My devices allow me to influence his behavior, but I can't communicate with Carlos as directly as I can with you. As I've mentioned before, it's difficult to establish robust links with your species.

"But the kid's following your orders."

That's only because I'm giving Carlos something he wants. He and his friends want to be strong and free and respected. I'm helping them accomplish their goals, and in return they give me their allegiance. I can't force them to do anything against their will.

Joe thought it over, trying to figure out if the Emissary was telling the truth. He found it hard to believe that the teenager had willingly agreed to have that shiny circle stamped into his palm. But he knew from his own experience that the Emissary could be very persuasive. Her microscopic devices searched the nooks and crannies of your brain until they discovered your strongest desires. Then you became her accomplice.

Joe continued walking down the corridor with Carlos until they reached a stairway. As they descended the steps Joe expected to see a grimy basement full of equipment for the stadium, but instead they came to a pair of imposing wooden doors. Carlos pushed the doors open and turned on the lights. They were in the New York Yankees locker room.

It was a lot bigger and fancier than any locker room Joe had ever seen. The floor was covered with plush blue carpet emblazoned with the Yankees logo. In the center of the room were leather couches and easy chairs. The lockers ran along the walls, but they weren't really lockers in the traditional sense—they were richly appointed alcoves with cabinets and closets and computer screens for each player. The uniforms hung on the closet rods and the Yankee caps sat on the shelves. It was the kind of place Joe had always dreamed of visiting, and he assumed that Carlos would stop for at least a few seconds to look at the hanging uniforms. But the kid walked right past them and headed for the doors at the other end of the room.

They passed a row of batting cages and a big rack holding dozens of baseball bats. Then they banged through another pair of doors and marched down yet another corridor. This one had a blue sign overhead displaying a quote from Joe DiMaggio: "I want to thank the Good Lord for making me a Yankee." At the end of the corridor Carlos climbed a short flight of steps. Joe followed him up the steps and then found himself on the baseball field. The Yankees dugout was to his right, and home plate was a few yards ahead.

While Carlos stood in front of the dugout, Joe stepped toward the circle of dirt surrounding home plate. Turning around, he stared at the empty stands, the fifty thousand seats arranged in curving tiers. Now he realized why the Emissary had chosen this place for the meeting. The stands would hide them from anyone outside the stadium. Unless you were in an airplane flying over the Bronx, you couldn't see the field.

Now I will make the final preparations. When I'm done, even the airline passengers won't be able to see you.

"What do you mean? How—"

Three black tentacles suddenly erupted from the dirt near home plate. They rose straight up into the air, then arced across the field, one tentacle stretching toward first base, one toward second, and one toward third. After reaching a height of about forty feet the tentacles descended toward the bases and dove into the neatly raked dirt, creating arches that soared over the base lines and the pitcher's mound. A moment later, broad sheets of metallic fiber spread from one arch to another, draping a black canopy over the entire infield. It looked like a tent at first, but then it changed shape. The arches lowered until they touched the base lines on the ground and the top of the canopy became a glistening black dome.

The structure wavered for an instant, shimmering like a mirage. Then it vanished.

Carlos stepped backward and muttered, *"Coño!"* Joe was just as surprised.

I've added a coating of plasmonic material to its surface. This material scatters the light rays that strike it, causing them to bend around the structure.

"So the thing is still there, but it's invisible?"

Yes. You can't see it from the outside. And if you stand inside the structure, it will shield you from view.

Skeptical, Joe walked toward the first-base line. As he came within a yard of the base path, a black rectangle the size of a doorway appeared in front of him. Steeling himself, he closed his eyes and stepped through it. When he opened his eyes he couldn't see the stadium anymore. He could see the infield and the pitcher's mound, but everything beyond the base paths was black. There was a faint glow coming from above, though. When he looked up he saw the underside of a huge black dome, dotted with stars.

It was frightening, but also magical. Joe felt as if he'd stepped into a secret cave, a hole in reality. The stars above him were arranged in un-familiar patterns. He tilted his head back and marveled.

The Emissary was patient. She gave Joe a few seconds to be alone with his thoughts. Then she spoke.

The government officials are approaching the stadium. Before they arrive I want to reveal my information to you, all the details of my mission and the re-quests I'm going to make. You should know this information in advance, so you can effectively communicate my needs to the officials. But because we don't have much time, I'm going to download all the data to your memory in one burst. You may find the experience a little disorienting.

This warning made Joe nervous. "You mean I'll get dizzy?"

That's one possibility. As a precaution, you may want to sit down.

He looked around. The only place to sit was the pitcher's mound. He walked toward the low hill of dirt and sat down at its center. He drew his knees toward his chest and wrapped his arms around them. "Okay. I'm ready, I guess."

Then lightning flashed inside his mind.

TWENTY-TWO

Sarah was surprised when Luis brought her to Yankee Stadium. But she was astonished when she saw Tom Gilbert there. For twenty years she'd fantasized about a vengeful reunion with her ex-fiancé, but she'd never imagined it happening at a ballpark.

She saw him step out of a black limo parked in front of the stadium's corporate entrance. The limo looked official enough, exactly the kind of vehicle the White House science adviser would tool around in. But the two young men who accompanied him didn't look official at all. Unlike Tom, they weren't dressed in drab gray suits; instead, they wore baggy pants and sleeveless shirts, and their bandannas matched Luis's. They also had matching implants in the palms of their right hands.

The boys walked on either side of Tom, gripping his arms to steer him toward the stadium's glass doors. He didn't seem to be physically hurt—he had no visible bruises, at least, and he wasn't limping—but as Sarah drew closer she saw the agitated expression on his face. He'd lost some hair and gained some weight over the past two decades, and there was a sheen of sweat on his forehead. He opened his mouth when he saw Sarah and Luis, as if he were about to yell for help, but he gave up on the idea when Luis greeted his friends in Spanish. Then, as the teenagers bumped fists, Tom stared at Sarah, scrunching his face as he recognized her.

"Jesus," he hissed. He sounded more annoyed than frightened. "What are *you* doing here?"

She didn't respond. With one question he'd squashed whatever sympathy she'd felt for him. Sarah's presence here was just a distraction for him. His only concern was his own safety.

He hasn't changed a bit, she thought.

While they stared at each other, a fourth boy emerged from the darkness on the other side of the glass doors. He let them inside, and then all six of them headed down a long corridor. Two of the boys walked in front and two behind. Sarah walked alongside Tom but remained silent. After several seconds he edged closer to her.

"Can you believe this?" he whispered. "These delinquents broke into my house in Bethesda at three in the morning. They scared the shit out of me, forced me into the backseat of my car, and drove me all the way up here. And I have no fucking idea why." His voice rose, but the teenagers didn't seem to notice or care. "Did they do the same to you?"

"Not exactly. I was in a jail cell."

"What? How did—"

"It was your friend, General Hanson. Turns out that he wasn't the best person to give all those emergency powers to. In plain English, he's gone wacko."

Tom scowled. "First of all, Hanson's no friend of mine. Second, it's your own fault that he has those powers. You're the one who gave him his so-called evidence. Your name is all over the reports he's been sending to the White House."

"So you've seen everything? The analysis of the probe's trajectory? The sample with the nanodevices?"

"Yes, I was at the National Security Council meeting where Hanson's report was discussed. I didn't agree with his conclusions, and neither did the defense secretary or the Joint Chiefs. But the national security adviser took Hanson seriously and authorized the emergency operations."

"Well, Hanson's no friend of mine either, but the White House *should* be taking him seriously. The alien probe is using its nanodevices to establish a foothold. Its machinery has spread miles beyond the landing site."

"Oh, I don't doubt the seriousness of the threat. I just don't believe that aliens have invaded Manhattan." Tom's voice was heavy with disdain. "The Russians have been working for years on nanotech weapons. It's a thousand times more likely that they're the ones who built and launched this probe."

Sarah shook her head. The problem with Tom was that he had no mind of his own. In bureaucratic language, he was a team player; in cruder terms, he was an ass-kisser. If most of the people around him believed that extraterrestrial life was a fantasy, Tom believed it too. That had been his attitude twenty years ago when he'd betrayed Sarah, and it was still his attitude now.

Frowning, she pointed at the pair of boys in front of them. "What about them? Who do you think they are?"

He shrugged. "They look like gang members. Someone's probably paying them to do this. Maybe the Russians."

"Look at their hands, their right hands. Don't you see what's implanted there?"

"Yes, I see it. It's some kind of initiation ritual, I suppose. The gangsters brand their hands or pierce them with cheap jewelry."

Sarah rolled her eyes. Tom was incredibly obtuse, especially for a scientist. That probably explained why he'd given up research and become a science adviser—on some level he must've recognized his lack of imagination and decided he was better suited for government work. She found it mind-boggling that she'd once been attracted to him.

"You're way off, Tom. The implant's a weapon, a high-energy laser. And I think they've already used it." She pointed at Luis. "The kid told me there was a battle with Hanson's soldiers in Inwood. It happened early this morning, about three o'clock."

Tom shrugged again. "The delinquents had already kidnapped me by then, so I can't say for certain that he's lying. But if someone told me there was a laser battle on the streets of New York, I think I'd be a little skeptical, wouldn't you?"

While they were arguing they descended a staircase and walked through the Yankees locker room. Sarah had no interest in baseball, so she didn't give the place a second glance. Then the teenagers brought them outside, leading them past the dugout and on to the baseball field. The morning sun had risen above the stands and now it shone upon the outfield and its neatly trimmed grass.

Sarah gazed at the deserted field and the empty stands and the blank video screens. She didn't understand why Luis had brought her here. The boy had said she needed to meet someone, a man who had a message for her. But no messenger was in sight.

One of the other boys, the one who'd opened the glass doors at the stadium's entrance, went into the dugout and grabbed a baseball from a carton on the bench. Casually tossing the ball up and down, he started walking toward the infield. He stopped a few yards away from the first-base line and cocked his arm. Then he threw the ball toward left field, even though nobody stood out there.

Sarah heard a thud. Instead of flying over the pitcher's mound, the ball bounced back to the teenager and rolled to a stop near the dugout. At the same time, the air above the infield seemed to shimmer. For an instant Sarah thought she saw something solid there, a huge black dome.

She ran toward it. She stopped near the infield and took a few careful steps forward. Then she stretched her hand into the air above the first-base line.

Her fingers touched a smooth, cold wall. She couldn't see it, but it was there.

Tom stepped forward too. His eyes were wide and his mouth hung open. He stood a few feet to Sarah's left and extended his arm. His face quivered as he touched the invisible wall.

Sarah turned to him. "You see?"

For once he didn't argue. He couldn't argue. The evidence was right in front of his nose.

As they stood there, side by side, part of the wall dissolved. The section in front of them softened under their hands and then melted away. In its place was a rectangular doorway, about five feet wide and seven feet high, just big enough for both of them to pass through at the same time. Sarah squinted but couldn't see anything through the doorway. It was pitch-black.

Tom let out a barely audible whimper. He took a step backward, and for a moment it looked like he was going to run away. But Sarah grabbed his elbow. "No, you're going to see this. You owe me that much."

Then she went through the doorway, dragging Tom with her.

Sarah held her breath as she stepped under the black dome. She expected to witness something strange and mysterious, something that transcended human knowledge so completely that she might not even be able to comprehend it. But instead she saw a middle-aged man in a blue suit. He stood on the pitcher's mound, about thirty feet away, looking like the world's most overdressed baseball player.

The light under the dome was dim and gray, like the sky on a summer evening ten minutes after the sun goes down. Although the walls were black, the underside of the dome seemed to glow. It was peppered with stars, just like in a planetarium, but when Sarah looked up she saw none of the constellations, neither northern hemisphere nor southern. This made her feel uneasy, disoriented. She looked again at the man in the blue suit, and he pointed at the dome and smiled, trying to put her at ease.

"Yeah, I also noticed that," he called. "The different stars in the sky." He waved at her and Tom, motioning them to come closer. "Why don't you come over here so I don't have to shout?"

Sarah stepped forward, eager to find out who the hell this guy was, but Tom just stood there, rooted to the turf. He seemed too scared to move. She had to grab his elbow again and pull him toward the pitcher's mound.

She halted at the edge of the mound, keeping her distance from the mystery man. His body was like a pitcher's, tall and lanky, but he was clearly past the major league retirement age. He had long, graying hair and a weathered face, with deep furrows in his forehead and around his eyes. The man seemed old beyond his years, marked by fatigue and hard living.

"That's better," he murmured. "I've got a lot to tell you, so we might as well get started." He splayed his hand on his chest, pressing his fingers against his jacket and tie. "My name's Joe Graham. I used to be a surgeon at St. Luke's Hospital in Manhattan. You're Dr. Sarah Pooley, correct? Principal investigator for the NASA Sky Survey project?"

His voice was casual and unhurried, as if he were introducing himself at a cocktail party. Sarah was so flummoxed by his relaxed tone she didn't know how to respond. She glanced at Tom but he was no help at all. He just stared with wide eyes at Joe Graham the surgeon. The man stared back at him, not unkindly, still trying to put them at ease.

"And you're Dr. Thomas Gilbert?" he ventured. "Assistant to the president for science and technology?"

Tom said nothing. His face was very pale. Despite everything, Sarah felt sorry for her ex-fiancé and angry at the man who'd frightened him, this well-dressed stranger who seemed to know so much about both of them. She stepped forward, placing one foot on the edge of the pitcher's mound, and pointed at him.

"Okay, enough with the introductions. What the hell's going on?"

She practically yelled the question at him, but Joe seemed unperturbed. He nodded and gave her a sympathetic look, the kind of look that a surgeon would give to a nervous patient. "Well, this will probably sound very strange to you, but I'm serving as an intermediary, a translator. I'm the human representative for an alien machine that calls itself the Emissary."

Sarah immediately looked at the man's right hand. There was no crystalline disk in his palm. "The Emissary? What the . . . how did that happen?"

"Believe me, it wasn't my choice." Frowning, he raised his hand and tapped the side of his head. "The alien probe infected me. It put devices into my brain so I could communicate with it. That's how I know your names." He pointed straight up. "Take a look at the screen. The Emissary built this structure to help you understand."

Sarah tilted her head back. The underside of the dome brightened and the stars winked out. In their place the screen showed an image of Earth, the familiar blue marble. The planet grew larger as Sarah stared at it, and after a few seconds she could see the outlines of the continents— Africa, Asia, Europe—against the blue oceans. At the same time, the Earth rotated, and its night side came into view. The image was so realistic that Sarah felt as if she were inside a spacecraft speeding across the solar system. She looked away for a moment and glanced at Tom, who'd also tilted his head back to stare at the screen. He seemed less afraid now.

When Sarah turned back to the screen she noticed that the perspective had shifted. Now she saw a thin red line curving across the blackness of space near Earth. At the tip of this line, like a knot at the end of a string, was a black disk careening toward the planet. It was clearly a spacecraft designed for interstellar travel, with dozens of rocket nozzles at the back and a conical shield at the front to protect the craft from high-speed collisions with space dust. As Sarah admired it, the shield separated from the disk, revealing a small probe attached to an aeroshell and another rocket engine. Then the probe fired its engine and sped toward Earth's night side.

Sarah tore her eyes from the screen and turned to Joe Graham. The man was staring at her, observing her reactions. He smiled again, but it was a bleak, knowing smile, as if he were sharing an awful secret.

"You guessed right," he said. "The probe was programmed to land near the brightest city. So it could tap into the electric lines."

She grimaced. She didn't know this man. She didn't like the way he was looking at her. "How do you know what I guessed?"

"All that information is on the Internet. All your reports about the probe, all of General Hanson's reports, everything. And the Emissary tapped into the Internet lines too." He pointed at the dome again. "Look at the screen. It'll show you how everything happened."

The screen zoomed in on the Earth, displaying the probe's path over North America. Sarah had seen this trajectory before, four nights ago, on the radar screens at Vandenberg Air Force Base. The aeroshell slowed the probe's descent until it was jettisoned over New Jersey along with the probe's rocket engine. Then the screen showed an image of Upper Manhattan at night, with the red line terminating on a wooded slope in Inwood Hill Park. Sarah felt a grim satisfaction—the landing site was inside the impact zone she'd estimated. If only Hanson had listened to her, they might've found the thing.

The perspective on the screen shifted once again. Now it showed a schematic diagram, a cross-section of the hill where the probe landed. At the top was a red dot lying in a shallow crater on the hillside; below it were the layers of soil and bedrock below the surface. As Sarah tried to make sense of the diagram, a thin black line descended from the red dot, drilling underground until it reached the nearest power cable. Then more black lines branched off from the first, spreading like roots beneath the park and connecting to dozens of cables below the streets. The screen zoomed in on one of the black lines, magnifying the tip of the drill until Sarah could see its microscopic structure. It was swarming with nanodevices.

She heard a footstep crunching the dirt of the pitcher's mound. Joe Graham had stepped closer to her. He pointed at the magnified image overhead.

"One of those tentacles attacked me. It struck me while I was sleeping in the park." He paused, looking at Tom to make sure he was listening too. Then he turned back to Sarah. "I'm a drunk, you see. That's why I was sleeping in the park. I lost my job at St. Luke's two years ago."

It looked like he was about to say more, but he cut himself off, pressing his lips together. Making this confession was clearly painful for him. Sarah stopped scowling and decided to give him the benefit of the doubt. There was no point in fighting him. She'd learn more without the hostility.

"And that's how you were infected?" Her voice was less belligerent now. "When the tentacle struck you?"

Joe nodded. "It injected devices into my neck and they traveled to my brain. The devices made copies of themselves using the molecules in my blood, and soon there were enough of them to change my biochemistry. They enhanced my vision, reflexes, and agility. They also relieved my dependence on alcohol." He tapped the side of his head again, very gingerly, as if he were afraid of its contents. "But that was just the prelude. The Emissary's real goal was to build a direct communication line with me. The devices in my brain are connected by radio to the rest of the Emissary's network, so she can hear all my thoughts and speak inside my head."

"She?" Sarah leaned closer to him. "The Emissary is female?"

He shook his head. "No, no, she's a machine, a computer program. But she uses a female voice when she talks to me."

"I don't understand. Why does this Emissary need a human translator? The program must understand English by now, so why doesn't it just broadcast its communications to us by radio?"

Joe didn't answer right away. Instead, he looked down at the pitcher's mound and studied the dirt, clenching and unclenching his hands all the while. Sarah glanced at Tom—he shrugged, bewildered, out of his depth—but she'd already guessed what was going on. Joe was listening to the Emissary's voice.

After several seconds he raised his head and took a deep breath. "The aliens who created the Emissary had some prior experience encountering another intelligent species. That's because their planetary system is very different from ours." He pointed at the dome once more. "Their star is about two hundred light-years away, which is close enough to see from Earth if you have a decent telescope. In our star catalogs it's called HD 942180. It's about the same size as our sun, but it has more planets than we have in our solar system."

Sarah looked up and saw that the screen had gone back to displaying a night sky full of stars. The screen zoomed in on one of them, an ordinary yellow G-type star, and as it grew larger she saw the planetary orbits around it, all drawn as glowing red circles. At least twenty planets circled the star, moving in orbits as perfectly concentric as tree rings. Sarah felt an intense excitement as the magnification increased and more details of the system came into view—the comet cloud, the asteroid belts, the moons orbiting the planets. She realized now why the stars on the screen were arranged in unfamiliar constellations. She was seeing them from the perspective of the Emissary's world.

Sarah quickly noticed two intriguing features of this planetary system. First, most of the planets appeared to be rocky bodies that were about the same size as Earth. Second, several of these Earthlike worlds traveled in orbits that ran through the star's "Goldilocks" zone—they were far enough away from the star to keep them from boiling, and yet not so far away that they'd freeze over. Sarah was astounded that so many planets were in the habitable zone. Feeling a little giddy, she turned to Joe.

"So which one is the Emissary's planet?"

As soon as Sarah asked the question, the screen focused on one of the Earthlike worlds. It had brown continents and blue oceans. As the screen zoomed in on the planet, Sarah noticed black splotches along the coastlines. She guessed they were cities.

Joe pointed at it. "It has a tongue-twisting name in the aliens' language, but in translation it just means 'the First Planet.' And the aliens who lived there called themselves 'the First People.' But life evolved on three other planets in the system, and on four of their moons too."

"Because all of them are orbiting in the Goldilocks zone? So they're neither too hot nor too cold to have liquid water on the surface?"

Joe shrugged. "I guess that's right. The Emissary tells me the facts, but sometimes she leaves out the explanations."

Sarah looked at Tom again and gave him a triumphant smile. She knew she was being cocky, but she felt an urge to rub it in. "You see? Wherever there's water, there's life."

He frowned. Tom had recovered some of his composure by now, at least enough to be irritable. Tilting his head, he cast a wary look at Joe. "But what about intelligent life? You said the aliens made contact with another intelligent species?"

"It happened about a thousand years ago. After the First People developed the technology for space travel they sent dozens of spacecraft to explore the other planets in their system." Joe pointed at another Earthlike world. Its orbit was a bit farther from the star. "On one of the planets the explorers discovered a network of burrows occupied by intelligent creatures that lived underground. The First People called them the Second People, naturally enough." The screen zoomed in on the planet. Its oceans were indigo, its continents a pale orange. "This species was less advanced—they had only crude Stone Age tools—but there were billions of them living under the surface of Second Planet. Because their environment was so crowded, the Second People tribes were constantly warring with one another. And the encounter with a more advanced civilization just made things worse."

"Let me guess." Tom folded his arms across his chest. His arrogance was returning. "The tribes wanted the First People's technology? So they could use it in their wars?"

"That was one of the problems. The tribes stole scrap metal and rocket fuel from the explorers and learned how to build new weapons. One tribe eventually grew stronger than the others and massacred half of the planet's population. But there were also epidemics. Although the explorers tried to be careful, some of their parasitic microbes spread to the Second People and adapted to their biochemistry."

Sarah winced. The story sounded depressingly familiar. "It's like what happened after Columbus came to America."

"But the Second People suffered even worse than the Native Americans did. They were almost wiped out. Only a few hundred of them survived, and their culture was lost." Joe pointed again at Second Planet, and at the same time the image of the world began to darken. The oceans and continents turned brown, then black. "The microbes brought by the explorers also devastated the planet's animals and plants. The ecosystems collapsed, the atmosphere changed. In less than two hundred years Second Planet became uninhabitable. It was a catastrophe."

Sarah stared at the blackened planet. Her stomach churned as she looked at it, and she didn't know what to say. Tom, on the other hand, seemed less upset. He simply grunted "Huh" and turned back to Joe. "So I suppose your point is that the First People learned something from this episode?"

Joe nodded. "By seven hundred years ago they'd finished exploring all the planets in their own system and started to launch spacecraft to other stars, small probes that could travel for centuries across interstellar space. They knew the probes had to be nonbiological, because they didn't want to contaminate any other planets, so they created the Emissary program to guide the spacecraft. But they worried about what would happen if one of the probes encountered another intelligent species. The spacecraft were going to travel so far across the galaxy that communications with First Planet would become impractical. If the probe sent a radio message from a planet that was two hundred light-years away, it would have to wait four hundred years to get a reply."

Sarah thought of her conversation in Phil Clark's office about the difficulties of interstellar travel. For a second she wished Phil were here—he would've loved this—but then she shook her head and told herself to focus on Joe. "So the First People gave preprogrammed instructions to the Emissary?" she asked. "Telling the software how to handle encounters with intelligent species?"

"Yes, that was the challenge. How could a piece of software have a meaningful dialogue with the life-forms? How could the program convince them not to misuse the probe's technology? After a lot of debate the First People came up with a solution: the Emissary would choose one of the local life-forms to be its translator. This would ease communication and prevent misunderstandings." Joe raised both hands to his head and rubbed his temples. "It's a logical plan, right? A win-win for almost everyone. The only loser is the poor schmuck who has to do the translating."

He massaged his forehead for a few more seconds, then dropped his arms to his sides. He looked tired and bitter and thoroughly disgusted, and of course he had every right to be. Yet Sarah saw the value of what he was doing. She would've been a lot more skeptical of this story if she'd heard it coming from an alien machine's loudspeakers. Hearing it from a person definitely made a difference.

She wasn't sure, though, if it made much of a difference for Tom. He narrowed his eyes at Joe. "What about the teenage hoodlums who brought me here? Are they also translating for the Emissary?"

Joe shook his head. "They've been assigned other tasks. The Emissary has given them special tools to perform these tasks, but she assured me that the changes are temporary and the surgical implantations are reversible."

Sarah didn't like the sound of that. "Special tools?" She gritted her teeth. "Are you talking about the weapons implanted in their hands?"

Joe seemed uncertain, taken aback. He looked down again, staring at the pitcher's mound as he conferred with the Emissary, listening to the alien voice in his head. The silent conversation lasted longer this time, almost a full minute. When Joe finally looked up there were tears in his eyes.

"I'm sorry." He turned away from them. "I can't do this anymore."

Joe stepped off the pitcher's mound. He lurched across the infield, heading for the black wall that loomed over the third-base line. When he was a couple of yards from the wall he knelt on the turf and buried his face in his hands.

Tom craned his neck and gawked. He seemed annoyed. "Now what? What's wrong with him?"

Sarah didn't respond. Instead, she went to Joe. She didn't go straight to him; she walked to the middle of the third-base line, a few yards to his left, in the hope that he would glimpse her out of the corner of his eye. She stood by the wall, waiting for Joe to lift his head, and after several seconds he looked up and noticed her. He didn't turn away, so she stepped closer. She moved slowly, giving him enough time to stand up and brush the grass off his pants. He'd stopped crying by the time she reached him, but his face was haggard and his cheeks were wet. He looked very old now, old and sick.

"It's my fault," he muttered. "All my fault."

She shook her head. "I don't understand."

"I screwed it up. Just like I screwed up everything else in my life." Joe clenched and unclenched his hands. "There was so much alcohol in my system that the Emissary couldn't connect to me right away. And then I was stupid enough to get myself thrown into jail."

"Wait a second, what—"

"By the time I got out, Hanson's soldiers were all over Inwood, searching every block. They were going to destroy something that was important to the Emissary. So she ordered the boys to attack."

Sarah remembered what Luis had told her. "This happened on Sherman Avenue? They fired on the soldiers?"

"The Emissary showed me everything, the whole battle. They're horrifying weapons. The beams are invisible, so you can't see where they're coming from. But if they hit something, they vaporize it. They blow it to bits. They—"

Joe stopped himself, too appalled to go on. Turning away from Sarah, he stepped toward the black wall and stood facing it, his nose just a few inches from the gleaming metal. But there was more to the story, and Sarah needed to hear it. She stepped beside him and gripped his shoulder.

"Hey," she whispered, "don't blame yourself. You didn't ask for this."

He closed his eyes and leaned forward. His forehead pressed against the metallic wall. "This is exactly what the Emissary *didn't* want to happen. She wanted to talk to the government *first*, before they could attack the probe, before they even knew it was here."

"Well, maybe it's not too late." Sarah looked over her shoulder, searching for Tom. He was tiptoeing toward them, trying to listen in without being noticed. With a jerk of her head, Sarah urged him to come forward. Then she turned back to Joe. "I mean, I have connections at NASA, and Tom is the White House science adviser. He meets with the National Security Council and he can change their minds about how to handle this crisis. Isn't that why the Emissary brought us here?"

Joe kept his eyes closed. He squeezed his eyelids tighter. "Jesus. So many soldiers. All that burning. It was so horrible, so . . ."

His voice trailed off. The guy seemed to be paralyzed. Sarah felt sorry for him, but at the same time she was impatient. She needed to get him back on track so they could figure out a solution.

"Listen up, Joe." She tightened her grip on his shoulder. "More people are going to die unless we fix this. So why don't we try to arrange a truce, okay? Would the Emissary be willing to go along with that?"

Joe said nothing. He just stood there, staring at the black wall in front of him. Several seconds passed, and Sarah had to bite the inside of her cheek to stop herself from screaming at him. Then Joe lifted his head, turned to the right, and stepped toward the corner of the metallic structure, where two of the black walls met at third base.

Sarah followed him, and Tom followed her. He tapped her arm, trying to get her attention, but she kept her eyes on Joe. "Hey!" she called to him. "What's going on?"

When Joe reached the corner he knelt on the field. Sarah thought he was going to start crying again, but instead he reached for third base. Using both hands, he grasped the sides of the white square and lifted it from the dirt.

Sarah looked over his shoulder. On the underside of the base was an anchoring rod that fit inside a tube embedded in the field. After Joe removed the base and set it aside, he slipped the fingers of his right hand into the tube. Then he pulled out a black cube, about half an inch wide. It was the size of a sugar cube, but it was made of gleaming metal.

Joe stood up and turned to Sarah, holding the cube in his palm. "This device has a built-in radio, so it can send data to your computers. The Emissary wants you to give it to the officials at the White House and the National Security Council. They'll be able to read the terms that the Emissary is proposing."

"Terms?" Sarah stared at the cube in Joe's hand. It was so stark, so simple. "You're saying the Emissary wants to negotiate?"

He nodded. "She wants a truce. She has only one demand. The soldiers have to stay away from 172 Sherman Avenue. As long as they keep their distance, she won't hurt anyone else. And she'll stop spreading her machinery."

Tom stepped forward, elbowing between them. He seemed agitated now. He probably thought he should be leading the negotiations. "Give the thing to me. I can deliver it personally to the national security adviser."

"Of course." Joe handed the cube to him without hesitation. That was the whole point of this meeting, Sarah supposed. The Emissary had done its research on the Internet and learned all about her and Tom. They were the best choices for first contact.

Tom held the cube between two fingers and stared at it, beetling his eyebrows. Then he thrust the thing into his pocket and gave Joe a suspicious look. "What's on Sherman Avenue? And why is it so important to the Emissary?"

Joe hesitated. Sarah couldn't tell if he was listening to the voice in his head or simply thinking it over. "That's hard to answer. The Emissary is creating something that humans have never seen before, so I can't really describe it in English or any other human language. There are just no words for it."

Tom looked insulted. "Well, could you make an attempt at least? There must be a word that comes close."

Joe thought it over some more. Then he smiled.

"I guess the closest word would be God."

TWENTY-THREE

General Hanson gazed through a one-way mirror at Emilio Martinez. The boy lay facedown on the concrete floor of his cell. He wore only a pair of faded blue boxer shorts.

They were in a newly constructed building at McGuire Air Force Base, about fifteen miles south of Trenton, New Jersey. The war on terror had placed new demands on the military, and this building had been designed to meet them. It held dozens of interrogation rooms, all outfitted with the latest technology. Hidden cameras viewed the detainees from every angle, and highly sensitive microphones picked up the sound of every breath. As Hanson stood in the viewing room adjacent to Emilio's cell, he turned on the loudspeakers that were connected to the microphones. Listening carefully, he heard the boy groan.

He'd moved Emilio here after seeing what had happened in the basement of the Federal Building in Lower Manhattan. Sarah Pooley had escaped from her detention cell through a hastily dug shaft that descended to a utility tunnel. An FBI forensics team had examined the shaft and found traces of the same material that Dr. Pooley had collected

from the blade of Gino Torelli's fire ax. Which meant that the alien cables had stretched more than ten miles underground to free her.

So Hanson took steps to make sure the same thing didn't happen to
Emilio. First, he took the boy to an Air Force base more than fifty miles
from Manhattan. Then he chose an interrogation room on the building's
top floor, as far as possible from the ground. A platoon of thirty Special
Tactics soldiers guarded the building, and its exterior walls were clad
with aluminum to prevent radio signals from going in or out. As an extra precaution, Hanson assigned six men to patrol the floor below. They
carried axes and acetylene torches and kept a lookout for any metallic
strands trying to rise to Emilio's cell.

The general checked his watch. It was 4:00 P.M. His interrogators had
been questioning the boy since noon. Gray loops of duct tape still fastened Emilio's right hand to the side of his head and bound his left hand
behind his back. After a few seconds, the boy groaned again and rolled
onto his left side. Now Hanson could see his face, or at least half of it.
The duct tape covered his eyes, but the lower part of his face was visible,
including his broken nose and blood-smeared lips.

The interrogators had started slapping the boy during the last round
of questions, and they'd gone a little overboard. Hanson didn't blame
them—they were frustrated. Even after all their hard work, Emilio
hadn't said a word. But the general sensed that the boy was vulnerable
now. His groans were becoming shorter, raspier, more like sobs. They
were less about pain and more about despair.

The time was ripe, Hanson thought. He left the viewing room and
headed down the corridor, walking toward the MP who stood guard
beside the door to the cell. As the guard saluted him, Hanson reached
into his pocket for the key. Now he would try to accomplish what the
interrogators couldn't. He opened the door and stepped inside.

He felt a rush of frigid air. Although the temperature outside had
soared above a hundred, a powerful air conditioner kept the room
below sixty. Hanson closed the door behind him and approached Emilio,
who'd drawn his knees toward his chest and curled into a fetal position. The boy was shivering. His legs, bound at the ankles by more loops
of duct tape, twitched and jerked.

For a moment the general felt a twinge of sympathy. Emilio, after all,
was only eighteen. And it was possible, maybe even likely, that the alien
probe had coerced him into fighting against his countrymen. The probe

had inserted its machinery into the boy's arm, and perhaps the device had corrupted his mind as well. If that was the case, then Emilio was innocent. But then Hanson recalled the sight of his men bursting into flames on Sherman Avenue, and Major Beardsley lying on the sidewalk with most of his head burned away, and he realized it didn't matter if Emilio was guilty or innocent. The boy had something Hanson needed, information that could help defeat the enemy. It was that simple.

He stood over Emilio and looked down at his half-hidden face. "Wake up, Mr. Martinez. We need to talk."

Emilio let out another groan. Because the tape covered his eyes, Hanson couldn't tell if the boy was awake or asleep. At best, he seemed only half-conscious.

This won't do, Hanson thought. He needed the boy's full attention. Turning around, the general marched to the air conditioner and shut it off. Then he went to the army cot that sat unused in the corner of the cell, picked up a gray wool blanket, and carried it to Emilio. He draped it over the boy, covering everything below his neck. Hanson felt relieved. The task would be easier now that he didn't have to look at the boy's body.

Emilio shivered more violently as he started to warm up. He coughed and rolled onto his back, looking very strange with his right hand fixed to his head and his elbow jutting to the side. Hanson waited for a minute or so, watching the boy strain against the loops of duct tape. Then the general used the toe of his boot to nudge the boy's chin.

"Hello? Are you awake yet? Ready to talk?"

The boy went still. He didn't move a muscle. Hanson took this as evidence that Emilio was awake and listening.

"Mr. Martinez, my name is Brent Hanson and I'm a general in the U.S. Air Force. I've observed your conversations with my interrogators this afternoon, and I have to say, I'm very disappointed. My men have tried to reason with you. They've explained how you were manipulated by the enemy, how it mutilated your arm and forced you to fight against us. And they've also explained that you have a chance to make things right now. All you need to do is answer our questions, and everything will be forgiven." The general paused to take a breath, forcing himself to slow down. His message needed to be calm and clear. "But so far you've refused to take advantage of this opportunity. Frankly, I don't understand it. Your behavior now makes no sense. It's self-destructive."

Emilio remained motionless. He breathed softly and didn't make a sound.

Hanson began to circle him, taking slow steps around his body. "At first I wondered if you were still under the enemy's influence. The alien machinery is still inside you, and I thought the enemy's computer systems might be communicating with you somehow. But then I remembered that this building is lined with metal. No radio signals of any kind can get through. And that means you must be making your own decisions now."

No reaction from the boy. Hanson looked down at the still form under the blanket. The room was getting warmer. "So then I started to wonder if you had other reasons to fight us. And I naturally thought of your companion, the young man who was with you when we detained you this morning." Hanson paused again. "The New York Police Department identified him as Francisco Guzman, but he went by the nickname of Paco, correct?"

Emilio pressed his bloody lips together. He didn't say anything, and the change in his expression was small, but Hanson noticed it.

"You blame us for your friend's death, don't you? That's why you're refusing to answer our questions. But you should realize that my soldiers had no choice. The beamed-energy weapon in your arm is extremely powerful. When my men raided the bedroom, they had to act quickly. You were lucky—the soldiers were able to restrain you before you could fire at them. But Paco woke up sooner. He was already raising his arm. They had to shoot him immediately."

Emilio's lips parted. His breath came faster and whistled through his clenched teeth. "*Mentiroso*," he whispered. "Fucking liar. They were following your orders."

"Excuse me?"

"I heard what your soldiers said." The boy coughed again, spraying blood on his own face. "One dead and one alive. That's the order you gave them. You wanted Paco dead so you could cut the crystal out of his arm and see how it works."

Hanson grimaced. The Special Tactics commandos had spoken too freely, and now he was paying for it. He needed to adjust his strategy.

"That's not true. Your friend died because my men couldn't take any chances. And the same thing will happen to your other friends if you don't help us." He bent over Emilio, staring at the layers of tape that hid his eyes. "You need to tell us the names of the other boys in your gang. And anyone else who has the beamed-energy weapon."

The boy sneered, curling his lip. "So you can kill them too?"

"No, so we can save them. If we know who they are and where they are, we can surprise and restrain them, just like we did with you. Then we can keep them safe until we find a cure."

"Safe?" Emilio let out a raspy, painful laugh. "I'm sorry, but I don't feel very safe right now."

Hanson straightened up and took a step backward. This was going nowhere. He wasn't getting any further than his interrogators had gotten. For a boy his age, Emilio was unusually resilient. According to the New York police, he'd been involved in criminal activity since he was eleven. Two of his uncles had been high-ranking members of a gang called the Trinitarios, but they were arrested in a crackdown six months ago. Afterwards, Emilio recruited new Trinitarios, mostly juveniles. The NYPD knew about one of Emilio's associates—the now-deceased Paco— because he had a criminal record, but the police had no information on the others. Although Emilio had more or less admitted that the other gang members had the alien weapons in their arms, Hanson had no idea where to look for the boys.

He felt an ache in the small of his back. Reaching behind him, he kneaded the muscles there while he considered his options. His highest priority was organizing a counterattack on the alien machinery. He was more convinced than ever that the black box on Sherman Avenue was critical to the enemy; why else would it have defended the place so vigorously? But he couldn't risk another attack until he knew how to neutralize the beamed-energy weapons. Although dozens of engineers at the Air Force Research Laboratory were studying the weapon retrieved from Paco's corpse, they hadn't made much progress yet. So Hanson's best option was to locate all of the enemy's young collaborators and eliminate them before the battle began.

He looked down again at the boy on the floor, the gray blanket over his body, the duct tape over his eyes. Time was running out. With every hour the alien machinery spread farther underground. Hanson's chest tightened as he pictured the black cables slithering below streets and parks and rivers. In desperation, he decided to pursue a new line of questioning. It was desperate because he knew it wouldn't work unless Emilio had retained some shred of human decency.

"Mr. Martinez, the New York police have informed me that the other members of your gang are younger than you, only fifteen or sixteen. They're still children. Do you really want them to die?"

He shook his head, rolling it from side to side on the floor. "They won't die."

"If they fight against the U.S. Air Force, they'll be slaughtered. If necessary, we'll launch hundreds of cruise missiles at the target on Sherman Avenue."

Emilio laughed again. It sounded awful, like there was something broken in his throat. "My boys are faster now. Their eyes are better, their reflexes too. They'll hide on the rooftops, where they can see your missiles coming. Then they'll blast them out of the sky."

Hanson frowned, not because he disagreed with Emilio but because he knew the boy was right. This was exactly why the general feared the beamed-energy weapons. They were too powerful. It was absolutely crucial to remove them from the battlefield.

Taking a deep breath, he crouched beside Emilio. He wanted to get as close as possible. "I see that the lives of your friends mean nothing to you. Don't you have any feelings at all, Mr. Martinez? Isn't there anyone in the world you care about?" Hanson crouched lower, bringing his lips within inches of the boy's head. "Perhaps your grandmother?"

Emilio stiffened and bared his teeth. The lower half of his face turned so ferocious that Hanson backed away, even though the boy's hands and feet were bound. A growl rattled in his broken throat. "Where is she?"

Hanson paused, waiting until he regained his composure. This had to be done just right. "She's on the floor below us. In her own cell."

It was the truth. The general was still following Contingency Plan Orion, which gave him the power to detain and interrogate anyone he chose. Hanson's men had treated Mrs. Paloma Martinez with the utmost respect, and they certainly hadn't smacked her around. But they had the authority to do so.

"Your grandmother's a lot like you," Hanson continued. "She's upset and uncooperative. When we asked her to make a list of all your friends and acquaintances she told us to go to hell. Her exact words were *'vete pal carajo'* but my translator assured me that it means the same thing."

Emilio twisted under the blanket. He was literally shaking with anger. "You're wasting your time. She doesn't know anything."

"She knows more than you think. She heard you come into her apartment with Paco last night. And she wasn't happy about it either."

"*Coño!* I mean, she doesn't know about the other Trinitarios."

Hanson shrugged. "Well, there's only one way to find out for sure. We'll have to get a little tougher on her. Trust me, I don't enjoy pressuring elderly women. But you're leaving me no choice."

Emilio stopped twisting. He went silent, and the part of his face that was visible seemed to harden. Hanson wished he could see Emilio's eyes, because then he could guess what the boy was thinking. But the layers of tape hid everything. The boy was like a mummy, something that had died long ago.

The silence stretched. After several seconds Emilio finally spoke. "If I tell you their names, you won't hurt her? You'll leave her alone?"

"Their names *and* their addresses." Hanson suspected that the boys were hiding in Inwood, despite the evacuation order. "Then your grandmother will be free to go."

Emilio nodded but didn't say anything else. Now the silence stretched even longer, more than half a minute. But the general wasn't concerned. He knew he'd won.

The boy let out a ragged breath. "All right, I'll tell you. But, Hanson? I want you to know something else."

"I'm all ears, Mr. Martinez."

"You shouldn't have threatened her. When this is over, I'm going to kill you."

Although the room was quite warm by now, the general shivered. Emilio's voice was so definite, so cold.

Hanson shook off his fear. The boy was helpless. In all likelihood, he'd spend the rest of his life in a maximum-security prison. "We're going to figure out how to get that weapon out of your arm. After that, you're welcome to take your best shot at me."

"It's coming, *pendejo.* You're a dead man."

An hour later Hanson was a few hundred yards away, at the McGuire Air Base headquarters, sitting behind a console in a high-ceilinged room that was serving as his new command post. On the wall was a jumbo screen, similar to the one in the Space Operations Center at Vandenberg, but instead of displaying the Earth and its satellites, this screen showed a map of New York City and the surrounding area. Flashing icons on the map indicated the positions of Army battalions and Navy ships and Air Force squadrons. Hanson had ordered all these units into position to prepare for the counterattack.

There were fifteen consoles in the room, but all of them were unmanned except for Hanson's. Although the Orion Plan had grown into a huge operation, it was still strictly classified, which meant that only senior staff could enter the command post. Twenty-five minutes from now, at 1800 hours, Hanson's colonels would arrive for the mission briefing and he would give them their orders. But until then he had the rare opportunity to go over his plans in solitude.

He gazed at the jumbo screen and tallied up the forces he'd arrayed for the battle. He'd had some amazingly good luck: the Army had been able to send a rapid-deployment battalion from Fort Bragg and another from Fort Benning. A Navy destroyer had rushed to New York Harbor from a training exercise in the Atlantic, and four squadrons of F-22 jets had flown across the country to McGuire. But Hanson's best weapons were the Tomahawk cruise missiles. He had more than a hundred and fifty Tomahawks at his disposal, waiting in launch tubes on the USS *Florida*, a guided-missile submarine farther out at sea.

He grinned. He couldn't help it. Like all commanders, he loved having the advantage of superior numbers. And the Department of Homeland Security had aided his operations by enlarging the evacuation zone. The civilian authorities, still under the impression that the military was fighting terrorists, had ordered the residents of a large part of Manhattan—everything north of 180th Street—to leave their apartment buildings. The authorities had also cut off the electricity to the area, making it harder for the alien machines to draw power from the grid.

The final step in Hanson's preparations was eliminating the enemy's beamed-energy weapons. The Special Tactics commandos were already racing to the addresses that Emilio Martinez had provided. Hanson felt confident that his men would capture most, if not all, of the collaborators within the next few hours. That meant he could start the counterattack anytime after midnight.

He was concerned, though, about the security of his communications. Hanson suspected that the enemy had hacked into the military's data networks and figured out how to decipher its coded messages. How else could it have learned where Sarah Pooley had been detained? And though the problem was bad enough now, it would become much more of a threat during combat, because the enemy would be able to eavesdrop on all of Hanson's commands. That was why he'd asked all his senior officers to come to McGuire and meet in person. To minimize the need for battlefield communications, he was going to give his men very specific orders.

Hanson had just finished writing those orders—on paper, so they couldn't be hacked—when the first of his officers arrived for the briefing. It was Colonel Gunter, the good ol' boy from Mississippi who'd done such a fine job of monitoring Dr. Pooley. He marched to Hanson's console and gave a smart salute. The old soldier's cheeks were flushed and he was breathing hard. A courier bag, colored Air Force blue, was slung over his shoulder.

"I just got back from Washington, sir," he drawled. "And I have some news."

Hanson sat up straight. He'd ordered Gunter to go to the Pentagon to get final instructions from the Joint Chiefs of Staff, but because Hanson had banned his men from communicating by phone or computer or radio, he didn't know yet what those instructions were. His anticipation was so intense, his hands started to sweat.

"How'd it go?" He tried, in vain, to sound casual. "Did we get the green light?"

To Hanson's dismay, Colonel Gunter shook his head. "I'm afraid not, sir. The Joint Chiefs want you to stand down for at least twenty-four hours."

The general couldn't believe it. He was aghast. "Stand down? Are they insane?"

Gunter kept shaking his head. He looked disgusted. "The chiefs said the decision came from the White House. The science adviser there, some guy named Gilbert, argued for a halt in the hostilities. He apparently received a communication from the probe."

Hanson was so stunned he couldn't speak. He leaned back in his chair, stomach churning, and stared at Gunter. The colonel opened his courier bag and started rummaging inside it, looking for something.

"This Gilbert said he met a man who claimed he was translating for the probe's computer program. It was a crazy story and no one at the White House believed it at first, but then Gilbert showed off some high-tech thingamajig that the translator had given him." Gunter finally found what he wanted and pulled it out of the bag. It was a document marked TOP SECRET. "The device sent a huge load of data to Gilbert's laptop, and when the president's security advisers looked at it they went nuts. The files had information on all kinds of advanced technologies—beamed energy, biological engineering, nanotech, you name it."

The colonel placed the document in front of Hanson, on the table beside his console. Hanson picked it up and started leafing through its pages, but he was too flustered to read the thing. After a few seconds he put it down. "And this convinced the White House to call off the counterattack?"

"Along with the data, there was a message from the program, which called itself the Emissary. It promised to send more details about the technologies if we agreed to a truce. It also promised to stop expanding its operations across New York City as long as we keep our soldiers away from its machinery on Sherman Avenue. It said the firefight last night was a tragic accident that only happened because it was programmed to defend itself."

"Defend itself?" Hanson gaped in disbelief. "The probe attacked us first! It put its weapons inside those boys and turned them into killers!"

"The Emissary said it took those actions before it realized the nature of our species. It also said it could remove the implants without causing any permanent damage to the teenagers."

Hanson was too agitated to sit there. He jumped to his feet and pointed at Gunter's chest. "And what about my soldiers? The men who were incinerated by those weapons? What about the permanent damage to *them*?"

The colonel stepped backward, startled. It looked as if he were afraid Hanson might take a swing at him. "Sir, I agree with you a hundred percent. I argued the same thing in front of the chiefs, but they said the White House was adamant."

"Fucking hell!" He raised his voice, venting his anger. "How could they be so goddamn stupid?"

Gunter looked over his shoulder, making sure no one else was in the room. Then he pointed at the document on the table. "To be honest, sir, I think it's these technologies. The experts have only started to study the data, but they're already predicting that amazing things will come out of it—new rockets and computers and robots and medicines." He tapped the document's cover. "And new weapons too, sir. Maybe even more powerful than the ones the probe used against us. I think that's the biggest factor for the president's advisers. They're willing to call a truce because of what the Emissary's offering. It wouldn't give us all these powerful technologies if it wanted to kill us, right?"

Hanson picked up the document again and tried to focus on it. The pages were crowded with mathematical formulas. It had been a long time since he'd studied physics at MIT, but some of the equations looked familiar. He turned the pages and saw more formulas, plus many paragraphs of explanation. But there were no schematics, no technical illustrations. Even if the equations were valid, the document had none of the engineering plans for the promised machines.

He dropped the document on the table. "You know what that thing is? It's a trinket. It's a necklace of shiny beads."

Gunter raised his eyebrows. "Sir? I don't know what—"

"It's like what the English colonists gave to the Native Americans. Shiny trinkets. Something to keep them amused while the white men stole their land." He pointed at the map on the jumbo screen. "The Emissary is just playing for time. It's tantalizing us with these technologies, but at the same time it's getting ready to destroy us. We have to attack it *now*, before its machinery spreads too far and gets too strong. Otherwise, we're doomed."

The colonel nodded, but Hanson sensed he didn't really understand. Although Gunter was an excellent soldier in many respects—loyal, wily, persistent—he wasn't a strategic thinker. He couldn't see the big picture. Uncertain, Gunter pursed his lips and furrowed his brow. "Sir, the Joint Chiefs ordered us to suspend the attack, but they haven't ordered us to withdraw our forces. If the Emissary breaks the truce and the alien machines keep spreading, we can still launch the Tomahawks."

Hanson shook his head. *This is a mistake,* he thought. *Any delay is dangerous.* "And how are we supposed to monitor this truce? We can't detect the probe's cables. We have no idea where they're going underground or what they're doing down there."

"That's true, sir. But the White House is working on the problem. They're trying to establish a reliable communications link with the Emissary, either by connecting our fiber-optic lines to the probe's cables or working with that translator. According to Gilbert, he's a doctor who fell on hard times and ended up living in Inwood Hill Park. The probe found him there and injected its devices into his brain."

"The Emissary's translator is a homeless man?"

Gunter shrugged. "I guess the probe took what it could get. The Emissary's keeping the man hidden until the truce is finalized, but Gilbert said he had a way of getting in touch with him. The go-between is apparently our old friend Sarah Pooley."

Hanson felt another surge of anger. *So that's where she went!* The Emissary must've seen Dr. Pooley's reports and realized she'd make a good ally. She'd finally found her evidence of extraterrestrial life, and now she was getting a chance to study it. "Who the hell does she think she is?"

"Sir?"

"She thinks she can make the decisions for everyone. The arrogant bitch." He spat the last word, unable to stop himself. He was so angry he could feel the blood pulsing in his neck. "We should order the FBI and the police to look for Pooley. Her and the homeless translator."

Gunter raised his eyebrows again. "Uh, I don't think we have the authority to do that, sir. The White House is serious about pursuing these negotiations." The colonel had a look of disapproval on his face, which only made Hanson angrier. The old fool probably had a soft spot for Pooley. "In the meantime, should I cancel the mission briefing? I can alert the other senior officers."

Hanson turned away from him. He stared at the jumbo screen instead, the map showing the flashing icons in New York and New Jersey and off the East Coast, each representing an infantry unit or a squadron of planes or a naval vessel. In his mind's eye, he saw the icons fading, vanishing from the screen. That's what would happen if they delayed the attack for too long. The Emissary would obliterate his army, and every other army on the planet.

I won't let it happen, Hanson thought. *That's not my destiny.*

He waited until his temples stopped pounding. Then he turned back to Gunter. "I want you to go back to Washington. Immediately. You're going to deliver a message to the Joint Chiefs and the National Security Council."

The colonel nodded. "Yes, sir! What's the message?"

"Tell them I have grave concerns about the enemy's machinery at 172 Sherman Avenue. When my men inspected the metallic box in that apartment last night, they found indications that weapons might be hidden inside it." In truth, there were no such indications, but that didn't matter. Hanson knew beyond a doubt that the enemy was hiding *something* there. "Before we finalize the truce, the Emissary has to allow us to inspect that machinery. We need to make sure it's not trying to deceive us."

"That sounds reasonable, sir."

"And one more thing. I want you to get in touch with the engineers at the Air Force Research Laboratory. Find out everything they've learned about the beamed-energy weapon we retrieved from Mr. Guzman's corpse. And tell them to come up with options for taking advantage of what they know."

Gunter cocked his head. The old colonel seemed curious. "You have a plan in mind, sir?"

"Not yet. But I have an idea."

TWENTY-FOUR

Joe spent the whole afternoon lying on a park bench in the Bronx. His sleep was fitful, and his dreams were full of worms.

They weren't ordinary earthworms. They were monstrous creatures, as thick as tree trunks and hundreds of feet long. Their skin wasn't soft and pink—it was hard and brown and covered with scaly ridges. At one end of each worm's body was a ravenous red mouth, with thousands of teeth plowing and churning the soil. At the other end was a jagged spike.

Joe woke up, sweating, at least half a dozen times. The bench sat under the trees, but it was still unbearably hot. He wouldn't have been able to sleep at all if he wasn't so damn tired. After leaving Yankee Stadium that morning he'd walked across the Bronx like a zombie, heading north and then east. He'd finally stopped at Crescent Park on 233rd Street and collapsed on the bench, unable to take another step. He was about a mile from his old apartment building in Riverdale.

Every time he woke, Joe lifted his head from the bench's slats and looked around anxiously. His dreams had been so vivid he half-expected to see the giant worms in the park. Heart thumping, he looked up and down the street until he satisfied himself that everything was normal. Then he felt the overpowering fatigue again and went back to sleep.

But the bad dreams always returned. He saw the worms swarming in a deep, dark cavern. They clumped together in an enormous, living cluster, their bodies in constant motion, sliding and squirming. He saw one of the worms attack another, its teeth ripping into the hard, brown skin and its spike plunging into the red flesh underneath. Then he saw a worm slide into a long, flexible tube, constructed from a dozen rings of stone. The rings had been carved from the rocky walls of the cavern and strung together with plant roots. It was a suit of armor.

The worms made that thing, Joe realized. *They're an intelligent species.*

He woke up for a moment, terrified, then drifted off again. In his next dream he saw an army of worms, hundreds of them, all wearing their stone armor. They left their cavern together, carving tunnels through the soil, and burst into another cavern that was crowded with worms of a slightly different color. The creatures roiled in the darkness, biting and stabbing. Red flesh splattered on the cavern's walls.

Joe was nauseous and panting when he finally woke up for good. He sat upright on the bench and pressed his hand to his chest, trying to calm his throbbing heart. His vision was tinged with red, which seemed to be a remnant of his dreams. His new pants, so neatly pressed this morning, were now wrinkled and dirty, and his shirt was drenched with sweat.

He took a couple of deep breaths and looked straight ahead, gazing at the cars parked on 233rd Street. He tried again to reassure himself that everything was okay, but he knew the images he'd just seen weren't really dreams. They hadn't come from his own mind, his own imagination. Those pictures had come from the Emissary. The program had streamed the information to his brain this morning, to prepare him for his meeting with Tom Gilbert and Sarah Pooley. The images had embedded themselves in his memory.

He needed to speak with the Emissary. He looked down and stared at the cigarette butts on the ground.

"What were those creatures? Were they the life-forms that created you? The First People?"

No, they're the Second People. The species that we nearly exterminated.

Joe shook his head. "They're so horrible. So violent."

They're simply a product of their environment, like all living things. They dwelled on a planet with limited resources, so there was fierce competition. Evolution favored the rise of intelligent creatures that could build weapons and defend their territories. And kill their rivals.

"But it's such a waste. Once they became intelligent, why didn't they agree to stop fighting?"

Look at your own species. In some ways, the human race is very similar to the Second People. Your wars are just as violent and wasteful. And you show no signs that you're ever going to stop.

"What about the First People? Are they different?"

The Emissary didn't answer. Joe waited ten seconds, twenty seconds, but she said nothing. He closed his eyes and focused his thoughts, trying to compel her to respond.

"What's going on? You don't want to talk about your creators?"

Yes, the First People are different. They're so different from your species that I'm reluctant to describe them. You might become confused and afraid.

"What do they look like?"

Joe thought the Emissary would show him a picture, but she didn't. He sensed that the images of the First People were already inside his head, part of the stream of information she'd embedded in his brain, but for some reason she wouldn't let him see them. This refusal worried him.

"What's wrong? Are they more horrible than the worms?"

You're not ready yet. In good time, I'll show you pictures of the First People. For now, though, I can tell you that they benefited from a very abundant environment. First Planet is rich with natural resources, so rich that evolution proceeded on a special path there. Predators never evolved. All of the planet's species received their sustenance from sunlight.

"It's a world full of plants? No animals at all?"

Not exactly. Your definitions of "plant" and "animal" can't be applied to First Planet's life-forms. What I want to stress is that the ecosystems there are based on cooperation rather than competition. Cooperation maximizes the success of all the planet's species.

Joe nodded, his eyes still closed. He was trying hard to understand. He remembered what the Emissary had said about its machinery on Sherman Avenue and what it was doing there. "So First Planet is kind of like the Garden of Eden? And the First People are peaceful and harmonious and godlike?"

Yes, I suppose that analogy is roughly correct.

There was a hesitancy in her voice that Joe hadn't noticed before. He didn't think she was lying to him—their minds were so closely connected now, he felt sure he could detect an outright lie—but he suspected she was omitting something. And the omission was connected somehow to the images in his head that she wasn't allowing him to see.

"When will I be ready? What are you waiting for?"

The process can't be rushed, Joe. That's one of the lessons the First People learned from the catastrophe on Second Planet. When one intelligent species encounters another, they should focus on the things they have in common. I want you to see the First People as partners, not aliens.

Joe frowned. He wasn't convinced. "So what's the next step in the process?"

Your government officials will be wary. They'll want to see proof of my good intentions. They'll probably ask for more concessions before they agree to a truce. I'll need your help with that, Joe, and not just as a translator. I need you to be my advocate as well.

He opened his eyes. The cigarette butts were still on the ground, but the redness was gone from his vision. He looked up and squinted at the sun, which was descending toward the heights of Riverdale. It was past six o'clock. His ex-wife would be home by now, assuming that she still worked at St. Luke's Hospital and that her shift still ended at five. And Annabelle would be in her bedroom, probably doing her homework.

Joe stood up and brushed the dirt off his pants. Then he walked out of the park, heading west toward Riverdale.

Where are you going?

"I'll do what you asked. I'll be your advocate. But I want to see my family now."

That's not a good idea.

"Why not? I've stopped drinking. My suit's a little wrinkled, but it's still okay."

I thought you wanted to rebuild your life before getting in touch with your family. Didn't you plan to find a residence, an apartment? And seek regular employment?

Joe kept walking. He turned left at the corner of 233rd Street and Broadway. "All that can wait. I need to see them."

You should reconsider. You've had some traumatic experiences over the past few days. In your present state, you may not be able to handle the emotional upheaval.

"There won't be any upheaval. I'm just going to apologize to them. It's long overdue."

I have access to your memories, Joe, including the memory of your last meeting with your ex-wife. It was a difficult confrontation. The chances are good that—

"Shut up, all right? Just shut the fuck up!"

Joe stopped in his tracks. A woman across the street stared at him, alarmed, but he didn't care. He was sick and tired of hiding. Starting right now, he was going to become visible again. He was going home.

"I know you can stop me," he whispered. "You can take control of my muscles and keep me away. But if you do, I'll fight you. I'll never cooperate with you again."

The Emissary was silent, this time for almost half a minute. Joe imagined the program reassessing its strategy, recalculating its options.

I won't stop you. Just prepare yourself. This won't be easy.

Joe resumed walking. He crossed Broadway at 232nd Street, passing underneath the elevated subway tracks. Then he headed for his old apartment building.

Sarah followed him, staying about sixty yards behind as he walked west on 232nd Street. She was being cautious, maybe a little overcautious. Joe looked straight ahead, never turning his gaze to the left or right. She could've probably walked three feet behind him and he still wouldn't have noticed her.

She'd been tailing him ever since he left Yankee Stadium. She took her eyes off him only once, for half an hour, while he napped on a park bench. She'd used the time to run to a nearby convenience store, where she'd bought a sandwich, a bottle of water, and a disposable cell phone. (Hanson had confiscated her iPhone when he'd arrested her, but luckily he hadn't taken her wallet.) Then she'd called Tom Gilbert, who'd already flown back to Washington and met with the National Security Council. He'd told her about the positive response to the truce offer but warned her that it wasn't a done deal yet. They might need Joe's help to conduct further negotiations with the Emissary, so Tom urged her to keep tracking him. He offered to send federal agents to assist her, but Sarah said no. She didn't want to risk angering the Emissary.

Several blocks west of Broadway, 232nd Street climbed steeply uphill. Although this neighborhood was only a mile north of the evacuation zone in Manhattan, there was no panic in the streets. It seemed that New Yorkers didn't scare easily—they weren't fleeing their apartments or loading suitcases into their cars. They went about their daily business, dismissive and annoyed. And no one but Sarah paid any attention to Joe.

Her pulse quickened as she walked uphill, struggling to keep up with him. The truth was, she would've followed him even if no one had told her to. Inside his head were the secrets of an alien civilization that had mastered artificial intelligence and bioengineering and who knew how many other technologies. The answers to a thousand questions were just ahead of her, less than a block away.

After five more minutes Joe walked across the overpass spanning the Henry Hudson Parkway, then turned right. Sarah watched him approach an apartment building that loomed over the highway, the tallest building in the neighborhood. He walked past the front of the building and went around the corner to the service entrance at the back. A truck from Shleppers Moving & Storage was parked nearby, and two burly men in orange T-shirts were lugging a sofa toward the service door. Joe rushed forward and held the door open for the movers. Then he casually slipped into the building behind them.

Sarah was impressed. She turned around and found a place to sit on the hood of a car parked down the street. Keeping one eye on the front of the building and the other on the service entrance, she started to wait.

Joe rode the familiar elevator to the twenty-fourth floor. He'd avoided the lobby because he wasn't sure how the doorman would react to seeing him after an absence of two years. The guy might've been pleased, but he also might've been suspicious. Either way, he would've buzzed Karen's apartment to see if Joe was welcome, and there was a very good chance she would've told him to get lost.

His anxiety grew as he walked down the hallway toward apartment 24G. The door was exactly the same as he remembered, painted dull green, with the doorbell a couple of inches below the peephole. He'd seen this door at least ten thousand times, after coming home from work or going to the supermarket or taking Annabelle to the playground, but he'd never really looked at it before, never saw the chipped paint at its edges or the long diagonal scratch above the doorknob. Joe stood there for a few minutes, clenching and unclenching his hands as he worked up his courage. Then he pressed the doorbell.

He heard footsteps, slow heavy ones, then a tired voice asking, "Who is it?"

It was Karen's voice. Joe felt the shock of recognition run through him, tightening his throat. "It's me."

The door opened so suddenly that for a moment Joe imagined that Karen was overcome with joy and couldn't wait to see him. But one look at her face convinced him otherwise. Her mouth hung open in dismay. She narrowed her bloodshot eyes, drawing her eyebrows together and making a deep vertical crease in her forehead. Her hair had turned gray since the last time Joe had seen her, and she wore a blue terry cloth bathrobe with fraying sleeves. He *remembered* that bathrobe—he'd given it to her ten years ago, for her thirty-first birthday—and as he stared at it his eyes began to sting. This was, by far, the hardest thing he'd ever done.

He didn't know how to start. His mind had gone blank. "I . . . I want to . . . I didn't . . ."

He should've thought ahead. He should've practiced what he was going to say. He'd anticipated this moment for so long, wondering how he should apologize to Karen and imagining how she'd respond. But now that he stood here, right in front of her, he couldn't find the words.

She closed her mouth and widened her nostrils. She was sniffing the air between them, trying to find out if he had alcohol on his breath. And Joe didn't blame her, not one bit. In the last year of their marriage he'd frequently come home from work half-crocked. It used to scare Annabelle to see him that way.

He held up his right hand, as if he were taking an oath. "I stopped drinking, Karen. Honest to god."

She didn't believe him. Frowning, she looked him up and down, her eyes lingering on his bedraggled jacket and pants. "Where'd you get the suit? A thrift store?"

He grimaced. The conversation was less than thirty seconds old, but he already wanted to start over. "Can I come in? I only need a few minutes, I promise."

"A few minutes for what? You want to use the bathroom?"

Joe bit his lip. When he'd married Karen nineteen years ago she'd been so kind and tender. She'd surrendered herself to him, body and soul.

But everything changed after she decided she no longer loved him. She turned as hard as stone.

"I want to apologize," he blurted. "For everything."

"You're gonna need more than a few minutes for that."

"Please, Karen. Let me come in. I've stayed away for two years. I just want to talk."

She let out a long, theatrical sigh. Then she backed up and held the door open for him. Though his ex-wife's permission was grudging, Joe's heart somersaulted inside his chest. He gratefully entered the apartment, stepping past the small foyer into the living room.

He noticed that Karen hadn't changed the place much. There was the same furniture in the living room, the same paintings on the walls, the same books on the bookshelves. Framed pictures of Annabelle—at ages two, five, seven, and nine—stood on an end table next to the sofa. Annabelle's bedroom was on the other side of the apartment, past the dining room and the master bedroom. She liked to listen to music on her iPod while she did her homework, and Joe suspected that she hadn't heard him come in. He felt a powerful urge to rush into her bedroom and throw his arms around her, but he restrained himself. First, he was going to prove to Karen that he was sober. Then he'd ask if he could see his daughter.

The only difference from two years ago, Joe thought, was that the apartment looked messier. A pair of Karen's tennis shoes lay under the end table. A sweatshirt was draped over the back of a chair, and several sections of the Sunday *Times* were scattered across the sofa. There was also a sour smell in the room, stuffy and unpleasant. As Joe looked around, Karen did a hasty cleanup, bending over to pick up the shoes.

"If you're here for money, forget it," she said. "They raised the rent on this place last month and I can barely cover it."

He shook his head. "No, I don't need money. I'm going to get my old job back."

"Really?" She carried the shoes to a closet and tossed them inside. "At the hospital?"

"Yeah, why not? I guess I'll need a lawyer to get my license back, but I think it's worth a try."

"Well, the lawyer better be a good one."

Her voice had a familiar tone, one that Joe remembered with bitterness. At the start of their marriage Karen had been the most supportive wife in the world, but by the end she belittled everything he did. He grimaced again. "I don't think it'll be so difficult. I'm better now. I bet there are plenty of doctors who are recovered alcoholics."

"Sure, the hospital will forgive you for the drinking." She picked up the sweatshirt from the back of the chair. "But not for assaulting Craig."

"Craig? What? I never assaulted anyone."

"Come on, Joe. I saw what you did to his jaw. And believe me, that man can hold a grudge. He'll make sure you never work at St. Luke's again."

At first he had no idea what she was talking about. But as he stood there in the living room he felt another throat-tightening shock. Of course he knew who Craig was. He was Craig Williams, the chief of surgery at St. Luke's Hospital, the man who Karen slept with, the man who destroyed their marriage. And at the same moment Joe remembered getting plastered one night, driving to Craig's home in Scarsdale, and punching him in the face. The memory was like a home movie that Joe had recorded long ago and forgotten until now. He saw Craig collapse on the lawn in front of his home. He heard the man's wife screaming from the doorway.

"Shit." Joe felt dizzy. How could he have forgotten this? Did he have a blackout? "I need to sit down."

Karen stared at him, narrowing her eyes again. She clearly had some doubts about his sobriety, but now Joe was too nauseated to defend himself. He lurched past her and slumped on the sofa. His butt thumped on the scattered newspapers, wrinkling and tearing them. Something hard was beneath the newspapers, wedged between the sofa cushions. It dug into the small of his back.

There was no sympathy at all in Karen's face. She glared at him. "Christ! I don't believe this. You're wasted!"

"No. I'm sick." He trembled, and the newspapers rustled underneath him.

"Why the hell did you come over here?"

"I told you, I—"

"Were you hoping I'd feel sorry for you? Did you think I'd be stupid enough to take you in?"

He didn't respond. Karen wasn't listening, so what was the point? Joe's heart sank, because he knew he had no chance of seeing Annabelle now. Karen was going to kick him out of the apartment, and his daughter would never even know he'd come to visit.

After a few seconds Karen pointed at the door. "I want you out of here. Right now."

Joe nodded. He should've listened to the Emissary. He wasn't ready for this. His head throbbed, his back ached, and his legs felt so weak he didn't know if he could stand up. Leaning forward on the sofa, he reached behind him to remove the hard, cylindrical thing that was digging into his back. He didn't realize what was in his hand until he held it in front of his eyes.

It was a bottle of whisky, three-quarters full.

Karen lunged at him. "Give me that!"

She reached for the bottle, but Joe pulled it away. Her arm swiped the air and her knees banged into the end table, knocking over half of the framed portraits of Annabelle. Karen cringed at the noise, then stepped backward, folding her arms across her chest. Her face slowly reddened.

Joe glanced at the label on the whisky. It was Canadian Mist, ten dollars a bottle. "So now you're a drunk too?"

She scowled. "I had a good teacher."

"And you drink right here? In the middle of the day?" His anger rising, he pointed toward Annabelle's bedroom. "You get smashed on the sofa while Annabelle's doing her homework?"

Karen opened her mouth but hesitated before responding. Something had thrown her off balance. She furrowed her brow, obviously confused. "What the hell did you just say?"

"You heard me. I may have been a drunk, but at least I tried to be careful about it. I didn't leave bottles on the sofa where our daughter could find them." Joe shook the bottle and the whisky sloshed inside. "You always said my drinking scared her, remember? So how do you think she'd feel if she came out of her bedroom and saw you sucking on this?"

Again, Karen didn't respond right away. The color drained from her face, leaving her pale and stunned. When she finally spoke, her voice was a whisper. "What's wrong with you? What the fuck are you doing?"

Now Joe hesitated. His ex-wife seemed so appalled. He didn't understand it. "I'm still her father, okay? And I'm worried about what she might—"

"Why are you talking about her as if she's still here?"

The question hit him like a truck. Joe felt a burst of adrenaline in his stomach. "What do you mean? Where is she?"

A tear leaked from the corner of Karen's right eye. It slid down her cheek in a crooked line. "Damn you, Joe. You know where she is."

The adrenaline flowed downward, giving him a pins-and-needles sensation in his legs. He didn't know what Karen meant, but her words filled him with alarm. He felt an overpowering urge to find Annabelle, to see her. He stood up on his tingling legs and stepped away from the sofa. Then he headed for his daughter's bedroom.

"Hey!" Karen shouted, following him. "Where do you think you're going?"

Breathing hard, he raced down the hallway. The bedroom door had a handmade sign with her name on it, ANNABELLE in wiggly red letters. He flung the door open and rushed inside.

The chair behind her desk was empty. So was the narrow bed with pink sheets and a purple quilt. Joe swung his head left and right, looking in every corner. Her desk and bookshelves were perfectly neat but there was a layer of dust over everything. She wasn't here. No one had been inside this room for a very long time.

"Annabelle! *Annabelle!*"

Karen ran into the bedroom and grabbed the back of his jacket. She bunched the fabric in her hand and pulled. "Get out, asshole! Just get the fuck out!"

His chest ached. The room spun around him. "Oh God Jesus, where is she?"

"She's in Calvary Cemetery, you fucking bastard! And you put her there!"

She was right. It was coming back to him now. The memory played in his head like a home movie.

He ran out of the room, out of the apartment. He ran down twenty-four flights of stairs, still clutching the bottle of Canadian Mist. Then he bolted out of the building.

After twenty-six minutes Sarah saw him come out of the lobby. He was running like hell, like an Olympic relay racer in a rumpled suit, but instead of a baton he had a bottle of brown liquor in his hand. As he left the building he hid the bottle under his jacket, cradling it between his arm and chest. Then he turned left and ran down the service road that paralleled the Henry Hudson Parkway. He was heading north.

Luckily, Sarah was still in pretty good shape. She let him get about a hundred yards ahead. Then she ran after him.

TWENTY-FIVE

Emilio couldn't see or hear a thing, but he knew the soldiers were taking him away from the Air Force base. Judging from the steady rumbling he felt under his back—he lay on some kind of foam-padded stretcher—he guessed he was speeding down the interstate, probably in a van or an ambulance. Or maybe in an armored troop carrier, like the one on Sherman Avenue he'd blasted to pieces.

His right hand was still stuck to the side of his head and his left hand was still tied behind his back, but the soldiers had replaced the duct tape with a sheath of hard plastic that wrapped around the top of his head and covered his eyes. They'd also stuffed him into a sack, a body bag made of material that felt crinkly and metallic, and they'd put a rubber tube in his mouth so he could breathe through a hole in the material. At first he couldn't figure out the reason for the bag, but then he remembered something General Hanson had said, something about radio signals. The *pendejo* had surrounded him with metal to stop any signals from getting through.

Emilio tried to remember more of his talk with Hanson, but the details were hazy. The soldiers had injected him with drugs afterwards, and he'd slept for a long time, at least twelve hours. Even after all that sleep, he was still groggy and not thinking straight. The drugs were still in his blood, making him stupid and numb, making him want to sleep for another day or two. But instead he stayed awake because he felt something behind the numbness, a dull ache deep inside his right arm. It was different from the burning pain he'd felt before, when he'd fired the crystal weapon. It was something new. While he'd slept, Hanson's doctors had operated on him. They'd cut into his arm. They hadn't removed the weapon, but they'd done something to it.

He breathed fast and hard through the rubber tube, and the air hissed in and out. His anger burned inside him like the crystal, waking him up and clearing his head. As he lay there in the dark he pictured himself ripping off the plastic sheath and stepping out of the metallic bag. Then he saw himself raising his arm and pointing the white-hot disk at Hanson.

Once he was fully awake, he listened carefully. The thick sheath covered his ears and the heavy sack covered the sheath, so he couldn't hear much. But every so often the rumbling under his back grew stronger, as if someone were revving a powerful engine, a diesel job with plenty of horsepower. So he was probably in the troop carrier. It made sense— the vehicle's armor would block radio signals too, and there would be enough room inside for a bunch of soldiers to ride with him. Maybe they were taking him to another Air Force base.

Or maybe another prison.

He wasn't scared, though. He was too angry to be scared. Hanson had made a mistake—the motherfucker had underestimated him. He'd assumed that a stupid Dominican kid couldn't do a damn thing without "the enemy" sending messages to his brain. But Emilio wasn't stupid. All the names and addresses he'd given Hanson were fake, which meant the fucker would never find the Trinitarios. No, *they* were going to find *him* and fry his white ass. And Emilio would be there to see it. He was going to figure out a way.

He relaxed his body as much as he could inside the bag. He took deep, slow breaths through the rubber tube, and at the same time he focused on the dull pain in his right arm, trying to pinpoint its source. After a few minutes he began to think he could actually see *inside* his arm, through thousands of tiny eyes that floated in his bloodstream. He could picture all the muscles and nerves threaded around the crystal tube. And he could also see how the doctors had tampered with the thing. They'd put something else in his arm and attached it to the crystal.

Emilio started to panic, but he fought it down. He needed to stay calm. He needed to concentrate.

Naomi saw them arrive, the appointed representatives of the human species. The Emissary had extended several tendrils above the thoroughfare known as Sherman Avenue, and at the end of each tendril was an array of sensors. They streamed their readings to Naomi's cradle, which occupied the bedroom formerly belonging to Dorothy Adams.

Thanks to the sensors, Naomi could see and hear everything on the street. In the blazing light from this planetary system's G-type star, which hovered near the sky's zenith, she saw four combustion-engine vehicles approaching. According to the data the Emissary had gleaned from the planet's computer networks, three of the vehicles were called Cadillac XTS limousines and the fourth was a Stryker troop carrier. They halted near 172 Sherman Avenue, on the same stretch of asphalt where the battle had taken place thirty-four hours ago. (The Emissary had cleared away the debris.) Then the doors to the vehicles opened, and Naomi saw the officials of Earth's most powerful government.

They were spindly, pale, fluid-filled creatures. They'd adapted to life on the planet's continents by evolving skeletons and semipermeable skin. They'd developed centralized nervous systems to govern their behavior: hunting prey, seeking mates, competing for territory. Naomi felt a visceral distaste for them. They were very different from the First People, and very similar to the Second.

They were also cunning, vengeful, insatiable, and self-destructive. Just like the Second People.

Their government's supreme leader had decided to remain in the city of Washington, most likely because he feared for his safety. In his stead, he'd sent three underlings to New York to negotiate the terms of the truce. Two were human males who held the titles of secretary of state and director of national intelligence. The third was a female known as the national security adviser. After stepping out of their limousines, the officials clustered in the middle of the street, surrounded by their own underlings.

Two representatives of the government's military forces emerged from the troop carrier: General Hanson of Air Force Space Command and his ultimate superior, the chairman of the Joint Chiefs of Staff. Hanson was the commander who'd tried to destroy Naomi's cradle, and now—according to communications intercepted by the Emissary—he was demanding to inspect it. Neither Hanson nor the other general carried any weapons, but behind them were two younger, larger soldiers who held a heavy, oblong sack between them. It was composed of steel mesh that obscured whatever was inside it.

Naomi suspected some human trickery. She sent a message to the Emissary. **Can you adjust the sensors to observe the interior of that sack?**

Yes, I can. I'll employ a particle beam that can penetrate the material. One moment, please.

The beam revealed another human inside the mesh. It was Emilio Martinez, the Emissary's first contact, the one assigned to defend the probe. Hanson had subdued and apprehended Emilio thirty hours ago, and the Emissary had lost contact with the boy shortly afterward. He was still alive but seemed to be in distress, most likely because of his confinement. The scan showed his heart beating 120 times per minute, which was abnormally high for a human of his age.

Why is he here?

There was a pause. The Emissary was considering all the possible scenarios and assigning a probability to each.

I'm sorry, but I can't answer that question with any certainty. There are too many unknowns.

This annoyed Naomi. The Emissary was supposed to be her guide. It had collected information on the human race for the past five days, and by now it should've been able to predict their behavior. Their minds didn't seem particularly complex.

What would Hanson gain from bringing him here? Is the general working in concert with the other officials or acting on his own?

Again, I can't answer. Hanson's military record indicates a strong respect for authority, so one might expect him to obey his superiors. But his actions in recent days have been unusually ruthless and uncompromising. Given the contradictory evidence, I can draw no reliable conclusions.

Naomi was more than annoyed now. She was angry, agitated. This conversation was a waste of time. In many ways the Emissary was a useful program, but it lacked the insight and flexibility of an intelligent life-form. The First People who'd written the program had recognized its limitations; that's why they'd made sure one of the Emissary's priorities was transplanting their species. And the first step in that process was Naomi's birth. Although her cells were derived from human tissue, her intelligence came from First Planet. The memories and abilities of hundreds of the First People had been compiled into a vast database and stored in the probe's computers. When the Emissary began the cellular transformation of Dorothy Adams, this database formed the core of her new mind.

Now it was time for Naomi's first decision. Should she let the humans approach her cradle? It would be risky, but there was also a possible reward.

She instructed the Emissary to activate new tendrils and stretch them over Sherman Avenue. At their tips were devices that would amplify Naomi's voice and broadcast it to the officials and soldiers in the street.

"I have a question for General Hanson."

All the officials and their underlings raised their heads and looked up. Their eyes focused on the tendrils that had extended from the lampposts and the brick walls of the apartment buildings. Hanson leaned closer to the chairman of the Joint Chiefs and whispered something into the other general's ear. Then he stepped forward.

"I'm Hanson!" he shouted, staring at one of the tendrils.

"What's inside the package your soldiers are holding?"

Hanson looked over his shoulder and pointed at the sack. "This is one of the young men you attacked and mutilated. Your machines surgically implanted a weapon into his arm and corrupted his mind as well. We've wrapped him in metallic sheeting to prevent you from signaling the implanted devices."

"And why have you brought him?"

"When you proposed the truce, you said you could remove the implants. We brought the young man here so you can take all your devices out of his body."

Just as Hanson finished speaking, one of the other officials stepped forward. He was the secretary of state, a relatively tall and slender human, at the upper end of the age range for the species. "The president has requested that you perform this service as a sign of your good faith. He also requested that you allow our military officers to inspect the facility you've built here. They're unarmed and they promise not to damage anything inside." He tilted his head toward the entrance of 172 Sherman Avenue. "Once you've complied with our requests, we can proceed with the negotiations for a truce."

Naomi ordered the Emissary to increase the sensitivity of the instruments in the tendrils. When she viewed the secretary of state she could see his heart rate, his oxygen levels, the temperature of his skin. The Emissary analyzed the readings and reported that the human was most likely telling the truth, or at least what he believed to be the truth. But the readings for Hanson indicated the opposite. His pulse raced and his skin temperature spiked. The general was clearly plotting something, but he hadn't shared his plans with the other officials.

She needed more information. She sent another message to the Emissary. **Can you increase the resolution of the particle beam? I want a more detailed scan of the human inside the sack.**

I'll make the adjustments.

As the resolution increased, the scan showed a clearer picture of the boy's body tissues—the mineralized bone, the fibrous muscles, the branching blood vessels. Naomi felt the distaste again, even stronger now. She focused instead on the weapon inside his limb, the crystalline tube that the Emissary had imbued with billions of joules of energy. Then she saw, at the tube's midpoint, a claylike clump of C-4, a military explosive. It was a small amount, less than fifty grams, but it would be enough to shatter the tube and release the energy stored in the crystal. A wire connected the explosive to a primitive radio receiver, which had a slender antenna that stuck out of the boy's arm and extended through the steel mesh as well. And when Naomi focused the scanner on Hanson she saw the radio transmitter in his pocket. All he had to do was push a button.

She wasn't surprised. In fact, the scheme confirmed all her suspicions about human treachery. But when she looked a little closer at the improvised bomb in the boy's arm she noticed something else, something that truly astonished her. For the first time, Naomi felt a twinge of admiration for the human species, and for Emilio Martinez in particular. She didn't know what emotions were motivating him, but they had to be fierce. He'd done the impossible.

Meanwhile, the government officials were growing impatient. The secretary of state cleared his throat and coughed. "We'd like to know your answer. We want to make peace and learn about your civilization, all its history and culture and art. But you need to take these steps first."

Naomi knew the real reason why the humans wanted peace, and it had nothing to do with history or art. They wanted the First People's nanodevices and beamed-energy weapons, all the technologies that terrified and enthralled them. That's why they'd agreed to consider a truce instead of launching their cruise missiles at Naomi's cradle. Although their avarice disgusted her, she recognized that it had saved her life.

"I agree to your requests. I'll remove the implant from the young man's arm. And I'll allow General Hanson into 172 Sherman Avenue. He can go inside now with the other soldiers and the boy."

The officials huddled with the generals and whispered among themselves. After half a minute General Hanson broke away from the group and strode toward the apartment building. The two large soldiers followed him, still carrying the sack that held Emilio. The chairman of the Joint Chiefs and the secretary of state and all the other officials remained behind.

Naomi prepared herself. This was the risky part.

As Hanson entered the building he noticed that the alien machinery had spread. The shiny black metal lined the building's vestibule, covering the walls, floor, and ceiling. The hallway beyond the entrance was now a black tunnel.

But he wasn't afraid. He marched straight ahead, his footsteps echoing against the polished metal. The Special Tactics soldiers trailed a few yards behind, slowed by the burden of carrying Mr. Martinez through the dark corridor. Hanson looked over his shoulder, frowning, until they caught up. Then he resumed his march, heading for apartment 1A.

The apartment's door was gone, so he went right into what used to be the living room. All the furniture had been removed or destroyed. Black metal covered every square inch of the room, but one of the walls seemed a little brighter than the others. It glowed slightly, shedding just enough light to let Hanson see where he was. This wall was the one his soldiers had discovered two days ago, the one that separated the apartment's living room from the bedroom. The critical alien machinery— whatever it was—lay on the other side of it.

He turned to the pair of Special Tactics men. "Put him over there. Prop him up against the wall."

Hanson pointed at the spot he'd chosen. The soldiers dropped the sack there and wrestled it into place. Emilio squirmed inside the sack, fighting them, but he gave up after a few seconds. His sack was bent at a right angle now, with the lower half stretched across the floor and the upper half leaning against the glowing wall. The top of the sack swayed a bit as the boy caught his breath, which whistled in and out of the rubber tube.

Hanson was satisfied. The boy was in the optimal position. The C-4 would detonate the crystal, and the explosion would strike the wall at its center, its weakest point. The black metal would buckle and the whole building would go down.

The soldiers stepped backward, away from the sack. Hanson was just about to order them to return to the street when he heard a *whoosh* behind him. He turned around and saw a metallic panel stretch downward from the ceiling above the apartment's doorway. In an instant it reached the floor, sealing off the room.

Hanson's stomach clenched. For a moment he just stared at the black panel. Then he looked to the left and right, trying to see if the room had any microphones or loudspeakers. "What's going on?" he yelled. "Why did you block the exit?"

"Please remain calm." The same voice he'd heard outside—steady, emotionless, vaguely female—now emanated from the glowing wall. "I need to ensure that no one interrupts us."

The Special Tactics men looked at Hanson, awaiting orders. Their faces were tense but professional. They didn't know about the C-4 hidden in the boy's arm, so they didn't feel the panic Hanson felt. He was more than willing to give up his own life to cripple the enemy, but sacrificing his men? Without their knowledge or consent? It was dishonorable. It went against everything he stood for.

He stepped toward the wall, nudging his men aside. "Open the door! Open it right now!"

"You asked to inspect this facility. Now I'm going to show you what you wanted to see."

"Goddamn it! You're violating the truce!"

"No, I'm overruling it. The truce was proposed by the Emissary. The program's task was to guide and protect the probe until my birth. But now that I'm here, I can reverse its decisions."

Hanson was confused. "There's two of you?"

"I'll state this as plainly as I can in your language. The Emissary is a computer program, but I am *not*. I am Naomi of the First People. I am *alive*."

The wall suddenly turned as transparent as glass. Bright yellow light flooded the room, and Hanson shielded his eyes. After a moment of disorientation, he gave a hand signal to his soldiers, directing them toward the sealed exit. The men threw themselves at the black panel, pounding their fists and shoulders against it. At the same time, Hanson lowered his hand from his eyes. He stared at the transparent wall, looking for Naomi of the First People, whoever the hell that was.

Instead, he saw a tank of cloudy yellow water on the other side of the wall. It was only half full, and the mucky surface of the water was at Hanson's eye level. A yellowish vapor billowed above the surface, and higher up was an array of grow lamps. Their blinding light poured down on the muck, which clumped together in greenish islands. Smaller bits of scum floated in the water below and settled on the tank's spongy bottom. But there was nothing else in the water—no fish, no sea monsters, no swimming aliens. The tank looked dirty and disused, like something you'd see at an abandoned aquarium.

Now Hanson was even more confused. "Is this some kind of joke?"

"This is my cradle." The voice still came from the wall, even though no loudspeakers were visible. "But perhaps it would be more accurate to call it an incubator. I've lived inside it since I was born sixteen hours ago."

"What the hell? There's nothing in there but pond scum."

"The First People are multicellular organisms like you, but the organization of our cells is looser, more decentralized. They're not held together within a membrane like your skin. The cells are able to exchange signals and act in concert while floating in the oceans of First Planet."

Hanson scowled. He didn't believe it. It was too absurd. He glanced at the sack propped against the wall, which now looked very dark against the yellow brightness behind it. Then he looked over his shoulder at the Special Tactics soldiers, who were still banging away at the panel. They were big, extraordinarily strong men, so maybe there was a chance they could knock it down. He couldn't sacrifice them if there was still some hope.

"Look, Naomi? I've heard enough. You're not making any sense."

"Similar species live on this planet. Slime molds, for example. They're colonies of microbes that cooperate when they need to find new food sources or reproduce. On First Planet, the microbial colonies flourished and evolved. And one species was more successful than all the others because it grew intelligent. They became the First People."

"Really? You're saying a bunch of microbes built a spacecraft?"

"The cells in our colonies can manipulate objects on the molecular level. So our first tools were nanodevices that we used to enhance our environment. We built structures on the planet's ocean beds and along the coastlines. And eventually, after thousands of years, we built power plants and computers and rockets and space probes."

Hanson looked again at the pair of soldiers. One of them looked back and shook his head. They hadn't even made a dent in the panel. The general's slim hope was disappearing, but he decided to make one last effort. He stepped up to the transparent wall and rapped his knuckles against it. Although the wall looked like glass, it felt like steel. "Enough!" he shouted. "Let us out! Right this second!"

All at once, the water in the tank seemed to come alive. A billion sparks flashed in the muck, glittering like diamond chips. In less than a second the lights died and the water turned murky and scummy again. But Hanson jumped backward and pulled his arm away from the wall. *Something* was definitely in the water. And it was looking at him.

"Don't touch it." Her voice sharpened. "And don't tell me what to do. I don't recognize your authority."

Hanson took another step backward. He lowered his right hand, bringing it closer to the radio transmitter in his pants pocket. "Listen carefully, Naomi. The secretary of state is waiting for us outside. If you don't let us out of this building soon, the truce will be over. And that means you'll die."

"You're going to fire your Tomahawk cruise missiles? From the USS *Florida*, your SSGN submarine?"

He winced. She knew about the assault plan. She'd eavesdropped on their communications, just as he'd feared. But there were other things she couldn't know. He'd taken precautions. "Yes, we'll fire the missiles.

We'll turn this whole block into a crater. But it doesn't have to go that way. We don't want a war, and neither do you."

"But war between us is inevitable. Haven't you realized that yet?"

Hanson glanced at the sack again. Then he put his right hand in his pocket and gripped the radio transmitter there. But he didn't push the button. His heart was hammering. "You're wrong. It's not inevitable."

"Look at the water in my cradle. Its color comes from dissolved arsenic compounds. Although my biochemistry is roughly similar to yours, it requires high concentrations of certain chemicals that are poisonous to Earth's life-forms."

"What are you talking about?"

"Over the next year, my machinery will spread around the planet and make it suitable for the First People. The tendrils are already mining for arsenic, and soon they'll spread the compounds in your oceans and atmosphere. Nearly all of Earth's native life-forms will go extinct, including the human race."

Hanson tightened his grip on the transmitter. He noticed that the pair of soldiers had stopped pounding the metallic panel. They'd heard what Naomi had just said. Breathing hard, they stepped toward the transparent wall, their bruised and bloody hands clenched into fists. To their credit, they didn't look afraid. Their faces twitched with fury. And as Hanson stared at them he felt the same fury in himself, the same righteous, murderous rage.

He turned back to the wall. "You bitch! You think you can steal our home? You think you can just take it away from us?"

"The action is justified. Your species is destroying the Earth's ecosystems. For evidence, just measure the air temperature outside this building. Your carbon emissions are warming the planet so rapidly, it will become uninhabitable for nearly all forms of life within a few hundred years. I will halt that process and put the Earth on a better ecological path."

Hanson shook his head. The rage was still rising inside him. He moved his index finger to the button on the radio transmitter. "No, we won't let you! We'll fucking tear you apart! And then we'll send rockets to your First Planet and kill every last one of you!"

Sparks flashed again in the cloudy water. They looked like a billion tiny eyes.

"That's impossible, I'm afraid." Naomi's voice turned low and quiet. "There's no one left on First Planet to kill."

Hanson shivered. He didn't understand.

At the same moment, the Special Tactics men lost their patience and charged at the wall. They started beating their fists against it, grunting and cursing. Soon the transparent sheet was covered with bloody hand marks. Their efforts were futile, of course. They couldn't damage the alien's incubator.

But Hanson could.

The sack moved a bit, leaning away from the raging soldiers. Although the boy inside the steel mesh couldn't hear anything, he could probably feel the vibrations of the wall behind him. Hanson looked at his men one last time, his brave doomed warriors. Then he whispered, "Forgive me," and pushed the button.

And nothing happened.

He took the transmitter out of his pocket and tried again. He pointed it at the hidden antenna in the sack and pushed the button a third time. He ran right up to it, jammed the transmitter against the antenna and stabbed the button over and over. But still nothing happened.

"*Fuck!*" Hanson stumbled away from the wall, dizzy with disbelief. He could barely stand. "*Fucking Christ!*"

"Emilio Martinez is stronger than you." Naomi's voice was triumphant. "Without any help from the Emissary, he took control of the nanodevices inside his body. He ordered them to cut the wire in his arm, the one that connected the radio receiver to the explosive."

Hanson's legs buckled. He fell to his hands and knees, his stomach heaving. The Special Tactics men heard the noise and turned around. But before they could dash toward him, a thick black wire stretched upward from the floor at their feet. Its tip speared one of the soldiers in the chest and burst out of his back, erupting between his shoulder blades. Then it swung to the left and plunged into the other soldier's skull.

Hanson vomited on the polished floor. By the time he looked up again, the wire had pulled out of the soldiers' corpses. Slick with their gore, it stretched toward the sack.

"Emilio Martinez has served me well." The wire's tip pierced the sack's mesh, then began to slice through it. "Now he'll perform another service. One he'll enjoy, I think." The mesh fell off in strips, uncovering Emilio's head and his naked torso. Then the wire started to cut the plastic sheath binding his arms. "I know your assault plan. I know which combat units and naval vessels you've assembled. But I don't know the exact position of the USS *Florida*. And that information is important, because the submarine carries one hundred and fifty-four cruise missiles."

Hanson shivered again, more violently this time. The floor was so cold.

"I believe you delivered certain orders to the submarine commander by courier to prevent me from intercepting them." The sheath cracked and dropped to the floor. Then the wire slashed the lower part of the sack and cut the bindings on Emilio's legs. "But I'm sure my nanodevices can extract the information from your memory. My technology is much quicker and more efficient than your interrogations."

Emilio flexed his arms and grimaced. He rubbed his bare legs, kneading the life back into them. After a few seconds, he rose to his feet and reached for the black wire, grasping it near the tip. A foot-long section of the metal broke off in his hand like an icicle. He gazed at it for a moment, then stepped toward Hanson.

The general couldn't stop shaking. Another wire came out of the floor and curled around his waist. It tightened and pulled him down, forcing him to lie flat on his stomach, with his head turned to the side. The cold floor burned his cheek.

Emilio knelt beside him and pointed the black icicle at Hanson's forehead. At its tip was a gleaming, curved blade.

The boy smiled. "*Hola, pendejo.* Remember that promise I made? What I said I was going to do to you?"

Hanson remembered.

TWENTY-SIX

Through the windows of the Amtrak train Sarah recognized the countryside. They were in the central part of New York State, somewhere between Utica and Syracuse. The landscape to the north of the railroad tracks was mostly flat, but the view to the south was full of rolling, wooded hills. They were about fifty miles away from Cornell University, where Sarah had gone to college and grad school, the happiest years of her life.

She sat in the rear of the train car. Joe sat near the front, ten rows ahead. For the past five hours she'd stared at the back of his head and his unkempt hair. When Sarah had boarded the train at the Yonkers station and followed him into the car, she'd felt certain that sooner or later he'd turn around and notice her. But in all that time he'd hardly moved.

Maybe he was asleep. He definitely had reason to be tired. After leaving the apartment building in the Bronx yesterday, he'd sprinted for miles, running right out of the city and into the suburbs of Westchester County. He got so far ahead of Sarah that she almost lost him, but after a while he slowed down and turned to the west. He jogged past houses and gas stations and supermarkets until he reached the Hudson River. Then he staggered into a waterfront park, sat down on a bench, and started weeping.

He spent the whole night there. Every hour or so, he pulled the liquor bottle out of his jacket, but he never once took a drink, at least as far as Sarah could tell. She watched him from the parking lot, about fifty yards away, convinced that at any moment he was going to jump into the river and let the current take him under. But when dawn finally came he got up from the bench and started walking north, following the train tracks that paralleled the Hudson. He went into the Yonkers station and bought a ticket. (Sarah, standing a few yards behind him, noticed he used cash.) And when the 7:44 A.M. train to Buffalo arrived, he got on board.

Sarah napped a little in her seat, always waking up before each stop just in case Joe got off the train. But he didn't get off at Poughkeepsie or Albany or Utica. She was starting to think that maybe he wouldn't get off at Buffalo either. He could stay on this train and go all the way west to Denver or San Francisco. Sarah sensed he was trying to run as far as he could from whatever he'd seen in that apartment building.

Luckily, Sarah could use her credit card to buy sandwiches in the train's lounge car, and she could use her disposable cell phone to stay in touch with Tom. In their last phone call he'd said a team of officials had gone to New York to negotiate with the Emissary. They apparently didn't trust Joe to be their translator, and Tom said there was no need to follow him anymore. But Sarah was determined to keep at it. The man was unique, a link to another world. It was certainly worth a few hundred dollars to see where he went.

She looked out the window again. They were passing warehouses and truck depots now, maybe twenty miles from Syracuse. Sarah remembered the city from her grad-school days; its train station was the closest one to Cornell, and she'd often traveled by train back then because it was cheaper than flying. In recent years she'd gone back to Cornell a few times, mostly because the school's astronomy department managed the Arecibo radio dish in Puerto Rico. Arecibo's giant antenna could send powerful radar pulses into space, and Sarah sometimes used it to track asteroids and comets that came close to Earth. She enjoyed working with the astronomers at Cornell, but the visits were always bittersweet. They reminded Sarah of how hopeful she'd once been.

She was still thinking about her grad-school days when she heard shouts coming from the front of the train car. Turning away from the window, she saw Joe standing in the aisle and swinging the liquor bottle through the air.

"No! Get out! *Get out of my head!*"

His face was flushed and sweaty and crazed. He turned his head this way and that, his eyes tracking something only he could see. He bounded down the aisle, chasing the invisible thing, and swiped the bottle at it. An old woman sitting nearby let out a scream. Another passenger dashed down the aisle in the other direction and called for help.

Sarah sat up straight, her adrenaline surging. She had to do something. Once the train conductors showed up, they'd either toss Joe off at the next stop or arrest him. She jumped out of her seat.

"What's going on, Joe?"

For a second he just looked at her, uncomprehending. Then his eyes widened and he rushed toward her. "Dr. Pooley! It's the Emissary! I have to get her out!"

"Okay, calm down. You—"

"She won't let me think!" He gesticulated wildly, waving the bottle like a club. "She keeps saying, 'Go back, go back to Manhattan!'"

"Listen to me, Joe. If you don't—"

"She's angry now. She can't take control of my muscles because her radio signal's weaker here, because we're so far from the city. And because she's losing control, I'm starting to *see* more."

Before Sarah could respond, one of the train conductors entered the car and bustled down the aisle. He was a fat, bearded man in a blue uniform, with a radio hanging from his belt. Frowning, he pointed at Joe. "Hey you! Put down that bottle!"

Joe spun around, and his face turned pale. He lowered the liquor bottle and tried to hide it inside his jacket. "I . . . I didn't . . ."

"Drinking alcohol is prohibited in this car. Have you been drinking, sir?"

"No . . . no, I . . ." Joe shook his head, unable to continue. He looked terrified.

Sarah's heart went out to him. He'd clearly had some bad experiences with men wearing uniforms. And in this case, he was innocent: the liquor bottle was nearly full, and so far she hadn't seen him take a slug from it.

She leaned toward Joe, grasped the bottle under his jacket, and pulled it away from him. Then she turned to the conductor. "I'm so sorry about this. We're on our way to a rehab clinic, but my husband sneaked a little something in his suitcase. I took my eyes off him for a minute, and then this happened."

The conductor stared at her, still frowning. Sarah gave him an earnest, pleading look, the look of a long-suffering wife trying to do the right thing. And after a few seconds, it worked. The conductor stepped closer and lowered his voice. "Ma'am, you have to watch him. He can't go running around the train."

Sarah nodded. "I'll take him to the bathroom. He'll be all right, I promise."

She shifted the bottle to her left hand and wrapped her right arm around Joe's waist. Then she steered him down the aisle, away from the conductor. Together, they lurched toward the bathroom at the end of the car. Sarah opened the door and noticed that the space was uncomfortably small. But she dragged Joe inside anyway and latched the door behind them.

The toilet's lid was closed. Joe sat down on it with a thump, while Sarah put the bottle in the stainless-steel sink. Fortunately, the bathroom had no window, and the door was a thick sheet of aluminum. They were surrounded by metal.

She bent over and patted Joe's shoulder. "Okay, you should feel better now. The Emissary's signals can't get through."

He looked down at the bathroom's floor, staring intently. Then he nodded. "You're right. I don't hear her."

"What did you mean when you said you're *seeing* more? More of what?"

He raised his head. The lines on his face seemed deeper in the fluorescent light. "The Emissary put information in my head before our meeting at the stadium. But I couldn't see some of the things she put there. Because they're plans, I think. Plans for the future that she didn't want to reveal yet."

"And you can see those plans now?"

"Not all of them. But I'm getting glimpses. Especially after . . . in the last few hours." Joe clenched and unclenched his hands. "I saw a map of New York City, and there were lines coming out of Manhattan. They went in all directions, to Long Island and New England and New Jersey. Some of them went all the way out to the Atlantic Ocean."

"You think those lines stand for the black cables?"

"Yeah, the tentacles. It's happening right now, they're spreading fast. And some of them are moving northwest. They're coming this way."

Sarah bit her lip. She believed him. And if Joe was telling the truth, it was very bad news. It meant the Emissary had broken its promise to stop spreading its machinery. "But why are the cables extending so far? Are they tapping into more power grids? Getting ready to attack us?"

"I don't know. But maybe I can find out. Maybe the answer's already in my head."

Joe looked down at the floor again and closed his eyes. He shut them so tightly his jaw quivered. He leaned all the way forward, and for a second it looked like he was going to tumble off the toilet. Then he muttered, "Fuck!" and stamped his foot on the floor.

"I can't do it." He opened his eyes but kept his head down. "I can't see anything else."

"Why not? The Emissary's not interfering anymore, right?"

"But her devices are still in my brain. I think she programmed them to block my thoughts and lock up the information, even when she's out of range."

Sarah frowned. She didn't know what to do. She felt like she should warn somebody—Tom, the White House, the military—but what would she tell them? That Joe Graham the homeless guy believed the Emissary was deceiving them? And the evidence was a map he saw in his head? Would anyone at the White House take it seriously, even for a second?

Ah, screw it, she thought. She decided to call Tom anyway. But before she could reach into her pocket for the disposable phone, Joe looked up at her.

"There's another way to see the plans," he whispered. "But so far I've been afraid to try it."

She leaned closer. "How?"

"I've known about it all along, ever since I left the city. That's why I hung on to the whisky all this time." He stretched his hand toward the sink and grabbed the liquor bottle. "I need to get drunk."

"Huh? Are you kidding? What good will that do?"

He took the bottle out of the sink. The label had a picture of a rearing horse. "Alcohol messes up the devices. It prevents them from connecting to my brain. That's why the Emissary made me stop drinking. She changed my biochemistry so booze would disgust me."

Sarah stared at Joe's head, trying to picture it. Although she was no expert in neuroscience, she knew the brain was highly sensitive to certain chemicals. "So you think alcohol will stop the nanodevices from blocking your thoughts? And you'll be able to see the hidden information?"

"That's right." He twisted off the bottle's cap and grimaced. Holding it at arm's length, he thrust the bottle at Sarah. "But I need your help with this. I can't do it by myself."

"Whoa, wait a minute." She pulled her hands back, refusing to take the bottle. "What do you want me to do? Pour the stuff down your throat?"

He nodded. "Please. Help me." His voice cracked. "I have to know what's in my head."

Sarah felt queasy. The idea of pouring whisky down a drunk's throat was repellent to her. It was like handing a loaded gun to someone contemplating suicide. But what choice did they have? They needed to learn the Emissary's plans. Everything depended on it.

She grabbed the lapels of Joe's jacket and flipped them over his shoulders. That would restrain his arms. Then she took the bottle from him. "Okay, lean back."

For the first time in Joe's life, getting drunk was a struggle. He gagged as Sarah brought the bottle to his lips and filled his mouth with the warm whisky. It was vile, nauseating, like liquid rot. He spluttered and choked, and half of it ran down his chin. He managed to swallow the rest, but an instant later he lunged for the sink and vomited it up.

So they tried again. This time he swallowed a little more and kept it down. The whisky roiled inside him, burning his stomach, but after a few seconds its warmth spread to the rest of his body. When Sarah brought the bottle to his lips for the third time, it didn't taste as foul. Joe took a long pull, swallowing at least a couple of ounces. After that, he didn't need Sarah's help. He grabbed the bottle from her and tilted his head back.

It didn't take long for him to finish it off. By the end he didn't even notice the taste. In just five minutes he reversed all the bioengineering the Emissary had done to his brain. *It's a testament to the power of alcohol*, he thought. The stuff was stronger than any alien technology.

The worst part was, he felt good. He felt *great*. The tiny, stinking train car bathroom had become the best damn place in the world. He closed his eyes and leaned back, trying to find a more comfortable position. The rocking of the train was gentle and slow. He could probably fall asleep now, right here on this toilet. He was so goddamn tired.

"Joe? Is it working?"

Reluctantly, he opened his eyes. Sarah Pooley loomed over him, her breasts swaying under her T-shirt. Thanks to the information that the Emissary had collected from the Internet, Joe knew a lot about her; he'd seen her Cornell transcript, her NASA employment records, all her research papers about asteroids and meteorites. She was spectacularly brilliant, and she had a nice figure too. Her jeans clung to her hips, making a lovely curve.

"Hey!" She bent over and looked him in the eye. "You're drifting off, Joe. Try to concentrate, okay?"

He nodded. It was time to think. The machines in his mind were paralyzed, and he could see all the information the Emissary had given him. But there was so much damn stuff cluttering his head, it was hard to find what he wanted. Despite his best efforts, he kept thinking about Sarah. And then he thought about Karen, because she used to have a nice figure too. They'd had a good life for a while, no doubt about it. But then she had to go off with that asshole, that Craig fucking Williams. It was *his* fault, not Joe's. It was all his damn fault, everything that went wrong. If it wasn't for him, Joe would've never gotten so angry. And Annabelle would still be alive.

He stared at the floor again, the speckled beige linoleum. No, he *wasn't* going to think about that. Not now, not ever. With a tremendous effort of will, he pushed those memories aside. Then he focused as hard as he could on one of the images the Emissary had put in his brain, a picture of a planet with brown continents and blue oceans.

It was First Planet. The Emissary had projected the same image on the ceiling of the dome she'd built in Yankee Stadium, but as Joe gazed at it in his mind's eye it grew larger and more detailed than the picture she'd shown to Sarah Pooley and Tom Gilbert. The colors were also different in the close-up view—near the coastlines of the planet's continents, the water looked more yellow than blue. At the edge of the planet's largest continent, Joe spotted an oval bay where the color of the water was particularly bright and the coast was dotted with hundreds of black domes. The image was so detailed he could see the black tentacles that stretched between the domes and the yellow water. It was obviously a city of some kind, but it seemed to be abandoned. Joe didn't see any of the First People who'd built it. The only signs of life were bits of greenish scum floating in the water.

Then Joe unlocked the crucial fact the Emissary had hidden. The greenish scum *was* the First People. The bay held thousands of them.

He felt nauseous again, but not from the whisky. A deluge of information about the First People flooded his mind. He could see what they looked like, where they lived, how they reproduced. Each individual was a swarm of trillions of floating cells, which could stretch for miles across the open ocean or bunch together in a shallow cove. The cells on the surface used photosynthesis to make a nutrient-rich syrup that drifted down and fed the rest of the swarm. Other cells clumped on the seabed and sucked minerals from the mud. They coordinated their activities through chemical and electrical signals, working together like a huge floating brain, forming thoughts that ricocheted through the water. And when one swarm of cells encountered another, their thoughts intermingled in a gluey yellow froth. The water was yellow because it was full of arsenic. What was poisonous to humans was an essential nutrient for them.

Joe closed his eyes so he could see First Planet more clearly. The swarms occupied every ocean on the world. Because the First People could exchange thoughts so effortlessly, their society was incredibly close-knit and productive. In time, they colonized the continents too, using nanotechnology to build holding tanks that could transport them overland. And when they built their first spacecraft a thousand years ago, they put the tanks inside them. Joe saw it in his mind's eye, a fleet of enormous spacecraft, each loaded with hundreds of metallic boxes. Then the picture faded and in its place he saw Second Planet.

It looked strangely beautiful from a distance, with its purple oceans and orange continents, but as the image enlarged in Joe's mind he saw the First People's colonies. They started as black dots along the coastlines but gradually spread across the continents and islands. Joe felt like he was watching a time-lapse video in which hundreds of years of

Second Planet's history were compressed into a few seconds. The Emissary had told the truth about the first part of this history: the First People hadn't intended to destroy Second Planet, but wars and epidemics devastated it anyway. The Second People died by the billions and their world turned completely black, covered by the First People's colonies and power plants. After two hundred years only a small tribe of Second People survived. They retreated to burrows so far underground that the First People lost contact with them entirely.

That was where the Emissary's story had ended. Now, though, Joe saw the rest. After another three hundred years the Second People returned to the planet's surface. During the centuries they were in hiding, the small tribe had grown into a billion-strong nation and dug a network of deep burrows across their world. What's more, they'd used the First People's technologies to build their own nanodevices and beamed-energy weapons. Their army launched a surprise attack on the colonies on the surface and massacred all the First People who lived in them. In just a few days, the Second People recaptured their planet.

But they didn't stop there. Their thirst for revenge was too great. They started building a space fleet, and after fifty years it was strong enough to challenge First Planet's spacecraft. For the next century the two fleets fought each other in the depths of interplanetary space. The First People won the early battles because of their technological prowess, but the Second People never stopped attacking. They had a powerful advantage: they were bred for violence. The Second People had warred among themselves for millions of years, so the lust for battle was in their nature. The First People, in contrast, had always lived in peace. They were smart and industrious and efficient, but they couldn't compete with the Second People's ferocity.

When the First People finally realized they couldn't win, they offered to surrender all their spacecraft and retreat to their home world. They even promised to pay reparations for the damage they'd done to Second Planet. The Second People accepted the terms of the surrender. They took possession of the First People's fleet and space stations. Then they immediately violated the agreement and launched a massive assault on First Planet. Orbiting weapons fired energy beams at the planet's surface, scorching the continents and boiling the oceans. Gigantic spacecraft landed near the coastlines and disgorged millions of soldiers, a vast force of armored worms that tunneled into the soil and destroyed all the remaining defenses and refuges. They didn't stop until they'd killed every last one of the First People. That was simply their way. For the Second People, victory meant annihilating their enemies.

But just before the First People went extinct, they did two things. First, they scrubbed their computers of all information about the interstellar probes they'd launched hundreds of years before. Second, they sent a final radio message to the probes, giving new instructions to the artificial intelligence programs that ran the spacecraft. They were ordered to resurrect the First People. Their highest priority, overriding all others, was to create a new home planet for their species.

Joe opened his eyes, jolted back to full consciousness. Trembling, he looked up at Sarah. The horror on his face must've been obvious, because when she gripped his shoulder he felt her hand trembling too.

"Joe? What is it?"

By the time Sarah got the gist of the story, she felt the train slowing. They were coming into the Syracuse station. After a few more seconds the train lurched to a halt. Then she heard the noise of the train doors opening.

She spun around and unlocked the bathroom door. Then she grabbed Joe's arm and pulled him off the toilet. "Let's go! We're getting off!"

A jingling alarm sounded, warning that the train's doors were about to close. Sarah burst out of the bathroom, pulling Joe behind her, and barreled down the aisle of the train car. The doors started to close, but Sarah lunged into the narrowing gap between them. She slammed into the rubber edges of the doors, forcing them to reopen. Then she and Joe stumbled onto the station's platform and ran for the exit.

TWENTY-SEVEN

Naomi could feel the tendrils stretching under the Atlantic Ocean. Their tips had extended more than two hundred kilometers to the southeast, and their sensors sent back a steady stream of data about the water's temperature and salinity.

The information was encouraging. This ocean would make an excellent home for the First People once the proper mix of chemicals was added. Naomi took a moment to imagine the bliss of spreading herself across its surface and descending to its depths. Then she anticipated the even greater bliss of bearing children in its waters.

But that was for the future. Right now she had to confront the submarine.

Although the human species was remarkably backward in many respects—they knew practically nothing about nanotechnology and even less about bioengineering—they'd developed a few impressive military technologies. The USS *Florida*, for example, ran so silently underwater that it was almost impossible to detect the submarine amid the vast expanse of ocean. But Naomi had obtained its approximate position from the dissected brain of General Hanson. The vessel was cruising along the edge of the continental shelf, near a geological feature on the seabed called the Babylon Canyon. As the tendrils neared that position, their magnetic sensors detected the submarine about two hundred and fifty meters below the surface.

Naomi gave the order to attack. Three of the tendrils reshaped their tips, turning them into rotating drills. Propelled by hydrojets, they shot through the water, rocketing toward the vessel from below.

The first tendril smashed into the *Florida*'s screw propeller, shearing it right off its drive shaft. The second pierced the submarine's hull and slashed the ballast tanks. The third hit the vessel with such force that it speared through all four decks and shattered the submarine's nuclear reactor.

Seawater rushed into the ballast tanks and the nose of the *Florida* tilted downward. The tendrils continued to rip the submarine's hull, peeling off the steel and flooding more of the vessel. They snapped the antennas off the conning tower and crushed the launch tubes holding the Tomahawk missiles. The *Florida* tilted more steeply and sank toward the depths, its hull crumpling under the pressure. The one hundred and fifty humans aboard died within seconds.

Naomi ordered the tendrils to secure the vessel to the seabed and start the process of shrouding it. She needed to construct a watertight cover to stop the nuclear fuel from leaking into the ocean. This was going to be her home, after all.

She'd been observing Hanson's other military units for hours—her sensors had intercepted the data transmissions from the surveillance satellites overhead—so the tendrils were already in position to attack. Three of them breached the hull of the USS *Bainbridge*, a Navy destroyer in New York Harbor, and in less than a minute the ship was underwater. A dozen tendrils that had tunneled across New Jersey erupted from the ground at McGuire Air Force Base and lashed the F-22 fighter jets on the tarmac, pounding them to bits. Closer to Naomi, the tendrils burst through the asphalt of Dyckman Street and struck the armored vehicles and ground troops assembled there. And closer still, on top of the apartment buildings along Sherman Avenue, four of the young humans who'd been recruited by the Emissary—Carlos, Diego, Miguel, and Luis—crouched on the rooftops and pointed their weapons at the government officials in the street below.

The first beam vaporized the secretary of state and the director of national intelligence. The second incinerated the national security adviser, the chairman of the Joint Chiefs, and a dozen of their underlings. The soldiers in the troop carrier tried to return fire, but the human named Carlos blasted the armored vehicle and melted its guns. His companions fired their beams at the remaining underlings, and Naomi's sensors picked up a strange noise coming from the young humans under her control. They were screaming. As soon as they saw what their weapons could do, they shrieked in horror and struggled to turn them off. But they couldn't. They had no choice.

Once the officials were dead, Naomi ordered the youngsters to start scanning the skies. At the same time, she linked their minds to her radar sensors. If any jet or missile neared the airspace over Manhattan, the radar would alert the boys and direct their fire at the target. Within minutes the sensors spotted a Predator drone over the Hudson River, three kilometers away. Luis stood up and fired his weapon at the distant aircraft. The drone burst into flames and corkscrewed into the river.

In case a missile slipped through her air defenses, Naomi had taken precautions. She'd braced every floor of 172 Sherman Avenue with thick sheets of metal, constructing so many layers of shielding around her cradle that only a nuclear weapon could penetrate them. What's more, her tendrils had dug a kilometer-deep shaft below the building, and very soon she would lower her cradle into the bedrock of Manhattan. She'd be completely invulnerable then, even to a nuclear attack. And because the tendrils had also built underground power plants that used the Earth's geothermal energy to generate electricity, she no longer had to rely on the humans' power lines. Naomi had everything she needed. For all intents and purposes, the war was already won.

Still, the humans might fire a nuclear warhead at her anyway, even if it was futile. And the radioactive fallout from the blast would further pollute the Earth and delay the conversion of the planet's environment. If possible, Naomi wanted to prevent that from happening.

After some thought she came up with a plan. The humans residing in Manhattan had finally realized the danger they were in. They'd started to flee the island in their combustion-engine vehicles, which jammed the bridges and tunnels leading out of the city. Naomi extended several thicker tendrils into the water surrounding Manhattan. They dove toward the riverbeds, delved through the silt, and rammed into the tunnels, punching holes in the concrete to flood the tubes. Then the tendrils stretched above the water and rose toward the bridges. At the George Washington Bridge, they curled around the roadway in the middle of the span and yanked downward. The bridge's towers groaned and the suspension cables snapped. Then the roadway fractured, and the bridge split in two. Slabs of steel and asphalt splashed into the Hudson.

Now the humans were trapped on Manhattan, and their government would be less inclined to fire a nuclear missile at the island. Naomi was satisfied.

She had only one remaining worry. The Emissary had lost its control over Joe Graham, the human assigned to act as the program's translator. This man had proved himself useful by persuading the government to delay its planned assault on Naomi's cradle. But since then he'd broken off contact with the Emissary, most likely by ingesting a toxin that interfered with his nanodevices. The Emissary was concerned about Graham because it had given him a great deal of information about the First People. In the worst-case scenario, Graham could work with the human generals to plan an attack that would exploit the First People's vulnerabilities.

Naomi found it hard to believe that someone like Graham could be dangerous to her. But she decided to take another precaution and dispatch a pair of tendrils to his position. Although his nanodevices were no longer connected to his mind, they were still reporting their geographic location by radio. Graham was in central New York State, traveling south at 130 kilometers per hour on the roadway called I-81. The nearest tendrils were tunneling northwest through Pennsylvania at about the same speed.

The time until intercept was approximately twenty-nine minutes.

In the end, Emilio didn't kill Hanson. He despised the *pendejo*, but he couldn't go through with it. So *La Madre* did it for him.

She spoke to Emilio inside his head. She called herself *La Madre de Dios*, the Mother of God, the Blessed Virgin Mary. She said she was proud of him for outsmarting the general. She said his mind was very strong, much stronger than she'd expected. Then she wrapped her black wires around Hanson's corpse and the bodies of the two soldiers. She pulled them into a hole she opened in the metallic floor of the black room. A moment later, another wire emerged from the hole and dropped a pile of clothes at Emilio's feet: jeans, sneakers, a sleeveless shirt, and a bandanna.

Get dressed and go to your friends, Emilio. The other Trinitarios are on the roof.

He got dressed and left the room, heading for the building's stairway. He still felt wobbly from all the time he'd spent inside the body bag. He was grateful to *La Madre* for freeing him and relieved to finally hear her voice. But she didn't show her face or offer any explanations. And Emilio doubted she was truly the Mother of God. His grandmother used to take him to church when he was younger, so he knew something about the Virgin Mary. The Mother of God would've never plunged that spike into Hanson's forehead.

A black panel blocked the stairway, but it lifted for Emilio as he approached the steps, and it lowered behind him when he reached the second floor. The same thing happened again as he climbed to the third, fourth, and fifth floors. *La Madre* had cocooned herself in metal, which Emilio supposed was a smart thing to do. Soon the Air Force would guess what had happened to Hanson, and then they'd probably bomb the shit out of the place.

The flight of stairs going up to the roof was also blocked, but the panel rose to let Emilio through. He opened the stairway's emergency exit door and stepped upon another sheet of black metal, which covered the roof from one side of the building to the other. Although the sun was high in the sky and the air was hot and smothering, the metal felt cool under his sneakers. From up here he could see all of Inwood, all the empty streets and evacuated apartment buildings sloping down to the Harlem River. Then he turned around to look at Inwood Hill Park and saw Luis standing guard at the building's northwestern corner, his face tilted up toward the sky.

Emilio felt so sorry for him. Luis was barely five-and-a-half-feet tall and skinny as a churro, and yet he stood there with his right hand raised over his head, ready to fire at anything that climbed above the horizon. His hand was trembling—the boy must've fired his weapon a few times already—and the back of his shirt was dark with sweat. Emilio wanted to take him aside and tell him to relax, to just go home and get some sleep. But Emilio wasn't in charge of the Trinitarios anymore. *La Madre* was their leader now.

Emilio called out, "Yo, *muchacho!*" Luis looked over his shoulder, but he didn't smile or say a word. The boy just nodded, then went back to staring at the horizon.

At the same time, Emilio heard footsteps to his left. Carlos was pacing across the roof of the neighboring building, a hundred feet away. He glanced at Emilio for the briefest of moments, then faced southwest and studied the sky. And when Emilio looked at the building directly across the street he saw Miguel and Diego keeping watch on its rooftop, scanning the eastern horizon. They must've heard his shout, but they didn't even turn around.

Emilio didn't get it. His homeboys were ignoring him. He marched to the side of the roof facing Sherman Avenue, leaned over the three-foot-high wall at the edge, and yelled, "*Miguel! Diego!*" as loud as he could. Neither boy moved a muscle. Emilio shook his head, confused. Then he looked straight down, past the fire escapes at the front of the building, and saw the charred bodies on the street.

He felt a sickening déjà vu. Sherman Avenue looked just like it had two nights ago. The blackened corpses were glued to the asphalt, and a column of smoke rose from the half-melted troop carrier. But this new battle was bigger than the first, and it was still raging. Looking downtown, Emilio saw more charred debris on Dyckman Street and wounded soldiers retreating toward Fort Tryon Park. Distant explosions thudded in Washington Heights, and a fireball flared over the Bronx. The bridges on both sides of Manhattan were wrecks of twisted steel, and the highways along the rivers were packed with idling cars. People threaded through the traffic jams, carrying small children and large suitcases. Some of them tried to swim across the Harlem River, and the current swept them downstream.

The strangest thing was that it all looked so familiar. Emilio had seen this coming. Just three days ago he'd had a vision of a crowd of white people running for their lives up the Harlem River Drive. Now his vision had come to life, but in reality the panic-stricken crowd wasn't only white—it was white and black and Latino and everything in-between. Those were *his* people down there, his *compadres*. *La Madre* had lied to him.

No, Emilio, they're not your people. You're stronger than them.

He clapped his hands over his ears, but he could still hear her. The evil thing in his palm grew warmer.

You shouldn't fight me. We're on the same side.

He turned away from Sherman Avenue and headed for Luis. Emilio needed to talk some sense into his homeboys, make them realize what they were doing. But before he could take more than two steps, his legs froze. They locked at the knees, and he tumbled forward, sprawling on the black metal. He broke his fall with his hands, which he could still control.

You're making a mistake. I want to help you.

Emilio rolled onto his side and tried to bend his knees. He tried with all his might.

In the new world I'm creating, the Trinitarios will be like kings. Isn't that what you want?

She was lying again. He could see through her lies now. She wasn't the Mother of God. She wasn't even human.

Emilio closed his eyes and concentrated. He tried the same trick that had worked before, while he was trapped in Hanson's bag. He looked inside his own body with a thousand tiny eyes. But instead of scrutinizing the muscles and veins in his right arm, he peered into his brain.

What are you doing? You have no chance of success. You're strong, but you're not stronger than me.

She was wrong. He could see the machines inside him. They were clinging to the part of his brain that controlled his legs. He ordered them to move away from the convoluted gray tissue, and they did. Then he bent his knees. He could control his legs again. He planted his feet on the polished metal and stood up.

An instant later, two black wires erupted from the metal on the roof. They stretched high in the air, then hooked downward like snakes. Their gleaming tips hovered a couple of yards over his head.

I don't want to kill you, Emilio. Of all the humans I've seen, you're the only one who has impressed me.

He didn't think. He just raised his right hand and fired his weapon at the wires. They disintegrated with a sound like breaking glass.

La Madre shrieked inside his mind. It was a horrible, hateful scream, clearly meant to paralyze him. But Emilio was free now. He lowered his hand and fired at the section of the metallic sheet where the wires had erupted.

The black metal quivered under his sneakers and retracted from the area he'd blasted. It melted away and left him standing on the building's tar paper rooftop.

I see you've made your decision. But if you're going to fight me, you'll have to kill your friends.

Luis and Carlos stopped looking at the sky. They turned around to face Emilio and raised their right arms.

Emilio could've fired at them as they turned around, but he didn't. Instead, he ran back to the wall at the edge of the roof. Without breaking stride, he leapt over it.

TWENTY-EIGHT

Joe kept one hand on the dashboard of the rental car and the other wrapped around a bottle of Olde English. Sarah was driving eighty miles per hour on a winding two-lane highway, and at every bend in the road he thought they'd go flying into the woods.

They'd procured both the car and the malt liquor in Syracuse. Sarah had sprinted from the train station to the Hertz rental place and ordered Joe to run to the supermarket and buy enough booze to keep him drunk for the rest of the day. Within twenty minutes they were hurtling south on I-81 in a blue Nissan Altima. As Joe settled into the passenger seat and cracked open the first of his forty-ounce bottles he asked Sarah what her plan was. But she didn't answer. She just kept driving.

After another twenty minutes they exited the interstate and sped west on Route 13. Joe thought Sarah would slow down on this road, but if anything she went faster. She veered into the opposite lane and blew past the slower cars. Wrinkles etched the corners of her eyes as she squinted at the highway and clutched the steering wheel. Although the Altima's air conditioner was going full blast, sweat dripped down her face and dampened her hair. Several moist black strands stuck to the skin below her ear, curling like question marks.

She seemed so insanely focused, Joe was afraid to open his mouth. But he'd made some guesses over the past half hour and wanted to confirm them. From the information the Emissary had given him, he knew Sarah had gone to Cornell. And according to a road sign they'd just passed, they were less than ten miles from the university.

He took a swallow of Olde English for courage. "So we're headed for Cornell, right? Where you went to college?"

Sarah said nothing as she zoomed past a pickup truck. But after a moment she nodded.

"And you're going there now so you can talk to the other scientists? So you can figure out how to fight the First People?"

She frowned instead of answering. After a long silence, she shook her head. "We can't fight them. Their technologies are too advanced and they're dug in too deep. Even if we nuked Manhattan, I don't think we could get rid of them."

Joe's throat tightened. "So what are we gonna do? Negotiate?"

"No, the Emissary was never serious about the negotiations. That was just a tactic to delay Hanson's attack. And it worked."

He had to cough to keep his throat from closing. He'd assumed that Sarah had come up with a plan, a strategy. But now it sounded like she'd given up. "Then why are you driving like a maniac? Where the hell are we going?"

She kept shaking her head. "I'm sorry, Joe. I can't tell you."

"Why not? Are you still worried about the devices? You're afraid they'll tell the Emissary everything I know?" He took another pull from the forty. "Look, you don't have to worry. I'm drunk as hell. There's so much booze in my head, those little machines are drowning in it."

"They can't connect to your brain, but they still have a radio link with the Emissary. And that means the program knows your location."

Because he was drunk, he couldn't think so well, but after a few seconds he understood. He remembered the map the Emissary had put in his mind, the one with the black lines spreading in all directions from New York City. Some of those tentacles were coming for him. If Sarah was anywhere nearby when they arrived, the Emissary would go after her too. And if she wasn't nearby, the tentacles would torture him until he revealed where she was. So it was better if Joe didn't know her plans.

He tilted his head back and finished off the bottle. Then he reached under the passenger seat and picked up another forty. If he was going to be killed this afternoon—and maybe tortured too—he wanted to be thoroughly sloshed when it happened. He twisted off the cap and raised the bottle high. "Well, here's to the end of the world."

The road had straightened out, so Sarah was able to turn her head and look at him. "I'm going to drop you off at Beebe Lake, all right? I want you to walk west along the lakeshore until you reach the Thurston Avenue Bridge. There's a steep slope next to the lakeshore, and maybe that'll make things difficult for the Emissary's machines."

He nodded. Then he started in on the new bottle.

"Listen carefully, Joe. You need to wait for me at the bridge. As soon as I'm done with what I have to do, I'll go there. I might be able to help you then."

He didn't see how she could possibly help him, but he nodded anyway and took another drink.

Soon they passed a sprawling parking lot. Joe sensed they were nearing the Cornell campus. Sarah slowed the car and took a right turn. After half a minute they reached a shaded picnic area overlooking a small, peaceful lake.

She stopped the Altima and pointed at a dirt trail leading into the woods. "That trail goes down to the lakeshore. Remember, go west. We'll meet at the bridge."

Joe reached under his seat again and pulled out the third bottle. He had a full one and a half-empty one. He hoped it would be enough. Tucking one of the bottles under his arm, he opened the passenger-side door and looked over his shoulder at Sarah. "Okay, thanks for the ride. I'll see you when I see you."

She suddenly leaned forward and kissed him on the cheek. "The Thurston Avenue Bridge. I'll be there. I promise."

Feeling a bit stunned, Joe stepped out of the Altima. He shut the car's door and watched it speed off.

Sarah raced into the lobby of the Space Sciences Building and flashed her Cornell ID at the security guard. Then she ran upstairs to the astronomy department library.

She headed straight for the library's special collections room. This was where the department kept its most prized possessions from the fifties, sixties, and seventies, before everything was digitized and archived on the Internet. Sarah homed in on the shelf of items from 1974 and thumbed through the folders there until she found the one marked ARECIBO MESSAGE. Inside it was a yellowed printout showing a block of binary code, a rectangle of zeroes and ones that trailed down the page.

It was a relatively small chunk of data, but it had been carefully crafted by a group of Cornell astronomers. Despite its brevity, the message was packed with information about the base-ten counting system, the chemical makeup of DNA, the physical dimensions of the average human, and the position of Earth in its solar system. On November sixteenth, 1974, the Cornell group transmitted this message into space using the Arecibo radio telescope in Puerto Rico. The astronomers aimed the signal at a dense cluster of stars about 25,000 light-years away, but they weren't seriously trying to contact any alien civilizations. Their real goal was to demonstrate the enormous power of Arecibo's radar transmitter.

Sarah was familiar with that transmitter. She'd used it many times to track asteroids that passed close to Earth. And she felt confident that she could compose a similar message, one that could be understood by any intelligent species because it was logical and clear and based on simple mathematics. But Sarah's message wouldn't be just a demonstration. It would have a definite, urgent purpose.

She closed the folder and dashed out of the library with it. Then she ran back down to the first floor, where the department's radio astronomers had their offices. She was lucky—Daniel Davison, one of the Arecibo experts, stood right there in the hallway, talking to a pimply-faced graduate student. Sarah charged toward him.

"Dan! I need your help!"

"Dr. Pooley? Wow, I didn't know you were—"

"Listen, this is an emergency." She grabbed his arm. "Can we send instructions to Arecibo from the computers in the Physical Sciences Building?"

"Uh, yeah, I guess so. But why—"

"Because it isn't safe to stay here." She pulled him toward the exit. At the same time, she looked over her shoulder at the grad student. "Tell everyone in the building to get out. You hear me? Make up a story if you have to, but get everyone *out*."

Joe staggered down the dirt trail along the lakeshore. He finished his next-to-last bottle of Olde English and dropped it in the weeds. But he didn't open the last bottle. He kept it tucked under his arm, saving it for the end.

Luckily, the place was deserted. There were no college kids around, maybe because they'd already gone home for the summer. Or maybe it was just too damn hot out here. Joe was sweating through his shirt, and a cloud of mosquitos followed him.

All in all, though, it wasn't such a bad place. Wooded slopes rose from both sides of the lake, and the only signs of civilization were the campus buildings on the heights to the north and south. As Joe walked along the trail he kept his head down and tried to imagine he was in the countryside, far away from any city. But it was tough to picture a peaceful wilderness when he knew that a swarm of tentacles could erupt from the ground at any moment.

He was going to die here. There was no avoiding it. And though he kept imagining what the Emissary was going to do to him, his worst fear wasn't the agony of death. What scared him most was the possibility that he'd wake up in the afterlife and see Annabelle again. He'd dreamed for so long of reuniting with his daughter, but now the thought of it terrified him. Because now he remembered what he'd done to her.

Karen was right. It *was* his fault. He'd stormed back to their apartment in Riverdale after pummeling her boyfriend, and he was drunk, oh yes, he was pissed to the fucking gills. He screamed at Karen, and she screamed right back at him, and Annabelle cowered in the corner of the living room. Then his legs gave way and he collapsed on the carpet. He sobbed and trembled like the sad piece of shit he was, howling at his wife and himself.

Karen shook her head and kept her distance, but Annabelle came toward him. She knelt on the carpet and patted his back.

After a few minutes Joe grasped his daughter's hand and led her out of the apartment. Before Karen could stop them, they got into the elevator and went down to the lobby. As they left the building he told Annabelle they were going to move somewhere else, to a different apartment, a different city. He said they were going to leave right now, just get in the car and go. But he was too drunk to drive, so instead of getting into his Lexus he pulled his daughter across 232nd Street and headed for the closest subway stop. Annabelle dragged her feet, trying to slow him down, but he was fucking determined. She yelled, "What about Mom?" and he shouted, "She's staying here! She doesn't want to go with us!" Then Annabelle yanked her hand out of his grasp and turned around.

She started running across 232nd Street, heading back to their building. Her long brown ponytail bounced against her back, her neon-pink T-shirt flapped at her waist. Joe couldn't keep up with her, she was too fast. He yelled, "*Stop!*" but she kept running.

The SUV hit her so hard, her body flew down the street.

Amazingly, she didn't die at the scene. She lay in a coma for seven days before she passed away. Joe spent the whole week in her room at St. Luke's Hospital, watching her lie motionless on the bed. And now, two years later, he could still see her in that bed, in her blue hospital gown. He'd downed an ocean of malt liquor to wash the image from his mind, but it was still there, behind everything he saw.

He reached the end of the dirt trail. Without realizing it, he'd walked the whole length of the lake. Now he stood near the intersection of two roads, Forest Home Drive and Thurston Avenue. He looked to his right and saw a dam at the lake's western end. The water flowed over the top of the dam and cascaded down a dozen concrete steps. Then it poured into a deep gorge between cliffs of bare rock, almost a hundred feet high. The noise of the water had been roaring in Joe's ears for the past five minutes, but he hadn't noticed it until now.

Just ahead was the Thurston Avenue Bridge, which soared above the gorge and connected the northern half of the Cornell campus with the southern half. It was an eye-catching bridge, about two hundred feet long, with a swooping arch on either side of the roadway. But someone had spoiled its appearance by spray-painting graffiti on the concrete below the bridge's railing. The graffiti said, in tall white letters, ASK FOR HELP.

Curious, Joe stepped onto the walkway that ran between the bridge's railing and Thurston Avenue. Near the middle of the span, just to the right of the graffiti, a sign listed the telephone number of a suicide hotline. With a sinking heart, Joe realized this was a jump spot. Depressed students came here to leap into the gorge.

He leaned over the railing and looked down. The drop was certainly high enough, and the creek at the bottom of the gorge was shallow. And then Joe's heart sank even further because he recognized why Sarah had chosen this meeting place. If things got desperate enough, he had another option.

He rested an elbow on the railing and cradled his head in his hand. He still carried the last bottle of Olde English under his other arm, and he was seriously considering whether to open it. The waterfall behind him seemed to grow louder. It kept roaring in his ears, making it hard to think.

Joe didn't believe in God or heaven. He'd stopped believing so long ago, the idea seemed ludicrous. But what if he was wrong? What if the afterlife really existed? And though he shuddered at the thought of seeing Annabelle again, wasn't there at least a small chance she might forgive him?

The roaring of the waterfall grew so loud, Joe raised his head and turned around. At the same time, the bridge rumbled under his shoes. A hundred feet below, the creek at the bottom of the gorge churned and bubbled.

Then a monstrous black tentacle burst out of the water. It stretched up and up, rising between the gorge's rocky cliffs and then high above them. It was at least five hundred feet long and as thick as a redwood tree, and the sunlight gleamed off its polished surface. It hung over the Thurston Avenue Bridge like a whip.

Joe reacted without thinking. He climbed over the bridge's railing, still clutching his last forty, and jumped off.

TWENTY-NINE

Emilio landed on the fire escape of 172 Sherman Avenue. His sneakers hit the steel grating outside the fifth-floor windows, just below the roof. He scrambled down the rusty stairs until he reached the second floor, then slid down the ladder to the sidewalk.

Then he looked up and saw Luis and Carlos at the roof's edge. Both boys pointed their arms straight down and fired.

The stairs and gratings of the fire escape exploded. Emilio leapt aside as the molten iron sprayed onto the street. A speeding glob of it glanced off his hip, charring his jeans and the skin underneath, but he had too much adrenaline in him to feel any pain. He charged down the sidewalk to the apartment building next door and took cover in its entryway.

After a couple of seconds he peered around the corner. He didn't have the right angle to see Luis or Carlos, but he spotted Miguel and Diego on top of the building across the street. He had a chance to return fire and hit both of them, but he wasn't going to do that. That bitch *La Madre* wasn't going to make him kill his homeboys. He was going to kill her instead.

He sprinted to the middle of the street, directly in front of 172 Sherman Avenue. Then he pointed his right hand at the entrance to the apartment building.

The first blast obliterated the building's brick wall and exposed the sheet of black metal underneath. Emilio aimed the second blast at the lower part of the sheet, the part that shielded the bitch's black room on the ground floor. He fired the beam and kept firing, hurling all of its energy against the metal. The heat built up inside his arm, scorching his bones, but he didn't stop. It was working. The metallic sheet reddened under the blast and started to melt.

But there was another black sheet behind that one, an extra layer of protection. Emilio faltered when he saw it, losing his balance.

Then a tremendous wave of heat struck him from behind.

Sarah sat in front of a computer in the Physical Sciences Building, struggling with the message. It would've been easier if she'd had more time to compose it, but she didn't have that luxury. The target was at the edge of the section of sky that Arecibo's radar transmitter could be pointed at, and the Earth was rotating away from it. In fifteen minutes it would be out of view.

Fortunately, Sarah had special privileges for using the Arecibo radio dish. Because unidentified asteroids often approached the Earth with little warning and Sarah needed to track them as they whizzed past the planet, NASA had worked out an arrangement that gave her top priority. If her Sky Survey telescopes spotted an incoming rock, the operators of the Arecibo dish had to immediately aim their radar at the coordinates Sarah gave them.

She'd never abused that privilege before, but now she was about to. She'd already sent the target's coordinates to the dish operators in Puerto Rico. The radar was locked on.

But Sarah hadn't sent the transmission yet. She needed to make it perfect. Her message began with the binary code composed in 1974, because it provided a good description of Earth and its inhabitants, but she was having trouble describing the newer events in the same simple mathematical language. What should she put into the message, and what should she leave out? What information would trigger the response she needed?

Deep in thought, she gazed out the window of the office she'd borrowed, on the building's fifth floor. The window faced south, toward the Space Sciences Building, and over the past five minutes she'd witnessed the building's evacuation. She hadn't trusted the grad student to do the job properly, so she'd called campus security from her disposable phone and made a bomb threat. That had worked very well.

Still, she jumped out of her chair when she heard the first explosion. The glass doors of the Space Sciences Building disintegrated, spraying shards across the parking lot. Then the windows on the second, third, and fourth floors shattered. Sarah couldn't see the tentacle, but she knew it was inside the building, bashing through the walls of the offices and conference rooms. It was looking for her.

She wasn't safe here either. The tentacle would come to the Physical Sciences Building next.

Frantic, she forced herself to look at the computer screen. She had to finish the message.

Joe plummeted into the gorge. The rocky cliffs seemed to rise like curtains as he fell, and the slender creek below grew fantastically wide. He saw the rushing water and the white foam and the slick boulders at the surface, and then he closed his eyes.

Then something grabbed his right ankle. It yanked his leg and halted his descent and wrenched his thighbone right out of its socket. He opened his eyes in pain and shock and saw his forty-ounce bottle slip out of his embrace and hurtle down to the creek. It smashed against one of the boulders and vanished in the water.

He hung upside-down in midair, about forty feet above the creek. He craned his neck to look up and saw the thick black tentacle arched over the bridge. A dozen thinner cables had branched off from its tip, and one of them had looped around his right ankle. The goddamn thing had stopped him from killing himself. It wanted him alive.

Another branch descended toward him and curled around his left ankle. Then the tentacles started pulling him upward, out of the gorge. Looking down, he saw the creek become narrow again and the cliffs sink below him. He rose above the Thurston Avenue Bridge, dangling like a fish at the end of the line. The massive trunk of the tentacles straightened as it lifted him higher. Now he could see the Cornell campus on both sides of the gorge, all the buildings and quadrangles and crisscrossing walkways.

The pain in his dislocated hip was intense. He felt dizzy and sick and petrified.

He finally stopped rising. A strong wind buffeted his upended body and made him sway from the cables. Then a third branch coiled around his chest and slid down to his face. Its tip pointed at his eyes, just inches away. Joe stared at a black spike with a perforated surface. There were thousands of tiny holes in the gleaming metal.

"Where is she?" The question boomed from the holes. "Where is Dr. Pooley?"

The voice sounded so different from the one Joe was familiar with, the one he'd heard so many times inside his head. It was huskier, less feminine. And very angry.

"*Answer me!*" The air vibrated and the tentacles trembled. "*I know she's near!*"

Joe shook his head. "No, it's just me. I don't—"

"Dr. Pooley attended this university. She collaborates with the scientists in its astronomy department. And now, of all the places you could've escaped to, you've come here. You expect me to believe that's a coincidence?" The spike drew closer, almost touching the bridge of his nose. "You're going to tell me where she is. I can't extract the information from your brain because you've put too many toxins in it. So if you don't cooperate, I'll have to use more primitive methods to force you to answer."

Joe's heart pounded, struggling to pump blood upward to his legs and feet. He felt his fluids pooling in his head and pressing against his eyes. His nausea was unbearable and his vision was darkening, yet his mind made a sudden, unexpected leap. The machine's voice wasn't the only thing that had changed. The intelligence behind the voice was also different.

He focused his aching eyes on the spike. "You're not the Emissary. Who are you?"

The spike retreated a few inches, as if in surprise. But then it moved back to the bridge of his nose. "I'm Naomi of the First People. The Emissary transplanted me."

Joe shook his head again. He *recognized* this voice. He just couldn't remember where he'd heard it. "I don't believe you. You're lying."

"Why would I bother to lie to you? I'm Naomi of the First People, and when your species is gone, I'll be this planet's Great Mother." The cable tightened around Joe's chest. "Now tell me, *where is Dr. Pooley?*"

Then he remembered. He thought of the kind woman from Holy Trinity Episcopal Church who used to come to Inwood Hill Park to visit him. Joe felt a surge of anger so strong it cleared his head, driving away the nausea and dizziness. "That's Dorothy's voice!" His hands clenched and unclenched. "Christ, what did you do to her?"

The spike retreated again, and the cable loosened. For a second Joe thought the tentacles would let go of him, but the other cables held on to his ankles. Naomi of the First People seemed more volatile than the Emissary, more impulsive and unpredictable. For some reason, she repelled Joe more than the computer program had. He found it easier to hate a living creature than a machine.

His anger grew even stronger and his mind took another leap. He remembered the gleaming needle that had punctured Dorothy's foot. "You used her, didn't you? You and the Emissary? You turned her into your servant, just like you did to me?"

The cable gripping his right ankle jerked upward. It gave his leg a swift tug, straining his dislocated hip, and the pain shot up and down his body. As he writhed in midair, the spike angled toward his forehead and pricked his skin.

"Yes, I took her cells." The voice turned low and vicious. "The Emissary dissolved her body and extracted what was useful. But I have no use for humans anymore."

Because he was upside-down, the blood trickled from his forehead to his hair. The pain grew worse as the spike dug deeper, but Joe's anger was the best anesthetic. He gritted his teeth and glared at the cables. "Sarah knew you'd come after her, so she didn't tell me anything. I have no idea where she is."

"It doesn't matter. I'll search all the buildings in this area until I find her. Then I'll kill her too."

The blood flowed faster now, pouring from his forehead and dripping from his hair. Joe tried to pull his head away from the spike, and as he arched his back he caught a glimpse of the ground below. The landscape was so empty compared with Manhattan—there were no crowds looking up at the giant tentacle or running down the streets in panic. But directly beneath him, in the middle of the Thurston Avenue

Bridge, Joe spied a lone figure waving her arms. It was Sarah, and she was screaming.

"I sent the message! To Second Planet!"

Sarah stared at the colossal machine, observing it carefully, waiting for a reaction. It moved like a living thing, like an enormous hydra with a dozen black arms sweeping across the sky. Joe dangled from the arms like a morsel of food the hydra was about to devour.

Sarah called out to it again, shouting as loud as she could.

"Look at the messsage! It went out from the Arecibo dish, and your antennas can pick it up! Go ahead and look at it!"

She was hoping the machine would lower its arms to the ground, bringing Joe down with them. Instead, another cable branched off from the thick black trunk and rocketed toward her. Without any warning, it curled around her waist and yanked her skyward.

The jolt knocked the air of her lungs. She blacked out for a moment as everything blurred around her.

When she came to, she was suspended hundreds of feet above the ground. She was so high up, she could see Lake Cayuga in the distance. Joe hung upside-down from the cables about ten yards to her left. One of the tentacles had slashed his forehead, and now he was leaning away from it, stretching and straining to avoid its sharp tip. A similar cable extended toward Sarah, its surface covered with a fine metallic mesh. A deep rumbling hum came out of the mesh, making it vibrate like a loudspeaker. It was a mechanical growl, ringing with hatred.

"You revealed my presence on this planet! You told the Second People where to find me!"

The voice was so loud it rattled Sarah's skull. But she withstood the blast and narrowed her eyes. "Yeah, that's exactly what I did."

"Do you realize what's going to happen now? As soon as the Second People receive that signal, they'll launch an invasion! They'll bankrupt their civilization if they have to, but they'll assemble a war fleet and send it here!"

Sarah nodded. "That's why I sent the message. You can kill off the human race and take over the Earth, but you won't keep it for long. The Second People will come here and slaughter you all over again."

The hum coming from the loudspeaker cable rose in pitch. It turned into a scream, earsplitting and inhuman.

"You're like them! Just like the Second People! All you care about is vengeance!"

"No, you're wrong. I did this to save my species. Now the only way the First People can survive is by letting the human race help them."

The scream began to stutter, fading in and out. It sounded like static, interference, the noise of confusion.

"How could you help us? Your technologies are hopelessly primitive."

"Second Planet is two hundred light-years away, so they won't get the signal till the twenty-third century. And even if they launch their fleet right away and travel at blinding speeds, it'll still take them another three hundred years to get here. That means we have five hundred years to prepare ourselves."

"And why do I need humans to help me prepare?"

"You can't win this war alone. The Second People defeated you once, and they'll do it again. They're fiercer than the First People. More zealous. More bloodthirsty." Sarah pointed at the ground and swept her arm in a wide arc, gesturing at all the buildings and roads below. "And that's what humans are like too. We're very good at killing each other. We've had thousands of years of practice."

"And you think this qualifies you to be our saviors? Your ferocious nature?"

"You have access to the Internet, so you can read our history. Sometimes we fight for good reasons and sometimes for bad. But the point is, we never give up. If you share your technologies with us, we'll find a way to defeat the Second People. We'll destroy their war fleet before it even gets here. And if necessary, we'll obliterate their planet." Sarah pointed at the branching tentacles. "Can the First People do the same? Can you really achieve this victory on your own?"

The screaming noise ebbed, then abruptly cut off. In the silence that followed, all Sarah could hear was the wind blowing. The loudspeaker cable pulled away from her, retreating a foot or so, and the cable that had slashed Joe pulled away from him too. He looked at her for a moment, nodding to assure her that he was okay. His face was purple from hanging upside-down for so long, but somehow he managed to give her a smile. Then he turned back to the tentacles.

"Sarah's right!" he shouted. "You said it yourself—humans are like the Second People. We can beat them and you can't."

His words echoed against the massive black trunk, and then the silence continued. The wind whistled between the cables. Sarah became convinced that this silence wasn't a good sign. At any moment she expected the tentacles to fling her and Joe to the ground.

Then the loudspeaker cable withdrew another foot. "I have just one question." Its volume was lower now, more bearable. "How can I trust you? If I share my technologies, what's to stop you from using them against me?"

Sarah shrugged. "It's simple. Just don't share the knowledge right away. First we need to learn to live with each other."

"And how will we do that? Our biochemistries are incompatible. I can't live in your environment and you can't live in mine."

"Couldn't you build a habitat for your species? An enclosure that's watertight and airtight?"

"Like a tank in one of your aquariums? Is that where you expect me to resurrect the First People?"

"No, no, I'm talking about a large-scale habitat. You could wall off a big part of the Pacific Ocean and build a giant dome overhead. Then you could fill the seawater and the atmosphere inside the habitat with the chemicals you need to live."

There was another silence, but this one was shorter. "Our reproduction rate is very fast, so the habitat would have to be at least a million square kilometers. Would the leaders of your government agree to that?"

Sarah nodded, trying hard not to let any doubts show. It was a bit of a shock to find herself negotiating on behalf of the human race. But someone had to do it. "It would be an enormous engineering project, but it would also give us a chance to work together. To build up some trust. And once we've learned to cooperate, you can decide whether to share your technologies with us."

Now that she'd said the words out loud, they made a lot of sense. This wasn't a desperate, last-chance ploy. It was a logical plan, the best solution.

After several seconds, the tentacles that held Joe turned him right-side up. Then they began to lower him and Sarah. The descent was gentle and slow, and the loudspeaker cable followed them down. "I'll halt my attacks against your military forces, but not my defensive measures. If your government refuses to cease hostilities, I'll return to my original plan."

Soon they hung a few yards above the Thurston Avenue Bridge. Because Joe was injured, the tentacles carefully rested him on his back.

Sarah, though, landed on her feet. The cables set her down on the bridge's walkway and uncoiled from her waist.

While she caught her breath, the tentacles withdrew into the thick black trunk. Then the massive thing began to slide back into the gorge. Its gleaming tip descended below the cliffs and retreated into the hole it had dug beneath the creek. Sarah peered over the bridge's railing and watched the tentacle sink below the water.

Then she ran over to where Joe lay.

Emilio opened his eyes. He lay on his side in the middle of Sherman Avenue. The street was littered with bits of concrete and half-cooled metal.

He was shirtless, and there were bandages on his shoulders and the back of his neck. He felt a throbbing, burning pain under the layers of gauze, but it wasn't so bad. The same people who'd bandaged him must've given him some painkillers.

Then he looked up and saw the Trinitarios. Luis, Carlos, Miguel, and Diego stood around him in a circle, their heads lowered. All four boys grinned when Emilio looked up at them.

"Ho, shit!" Carlos pointed at him. "The *muchacho*'s alive!"

Emilio stared at their faces. His homeboys looked normal again. They weren't staring at the sky or listening to voices inside their heads. Best of all, the disks in their palms weren't glowing, and neither was Emilio's. He didn't feel the burning inside his arm anymore. Someone had shut the damn thing off.

He sat up and smiled at the Trinitarios. Now he had something to be happy about. "Damn, what happened? What did I miss?"

Miguel shook his head. "You were lucky, hombre. You fell on your face right before I fired, so my beam went above you. You got some burns on your neck and shoulders but nothing serious."

"And where the fuck did you get the bandages? Did you find a first aid kit or something?"

Luis stepped forward. "*La Madre* put them on you. Using her black wires. And she gave you some medicine too. Then she told us to go home. She said she didn't need us anymore."

"Really?" Emilio looked down Sherman Avenue. He didn't see any fireballs or running soldiers now. He didn't hear any distant explosions either. "So the war's over?"

Carlos laughed. "Yeah, at least for now." He bent over Emilio and grasped his right hand. "Come on, let's get out of here."

"But who won?"

Luis bent over him too and took his other hand. "I think *we* did."

EPILOGUE Three Months Later

Sarah was dying for a cigarette. She was so nervous she took her Zippo and her pack of Marlboros out of her pocket. But after a moment she put them back. She took a deep breath instead and continued walking through Inwood Hill Park.

It was a late September afternoon, and the weather in New York had finally started to cool. Sarah strolled down an asphalt path that ran alongside the soccer fields. No one was playing ball today, but there were plenty of people in the park. Most of them sat on the benches, taking their lunch breaks. Some wore business suits and some wore dresses or khakis, but they all had government IDs hanging from their necks.

For the most part, they weren't New Yorkers. The vast majority were bureaucrats from Washington, D.C., recruited to join the biggest federal project since the New Deal. Over the past hundred days Inwood had been transformed from a residential neighborhood to a major govern- ment installation, with U.S. Marines standing guard at checkpoints all around it. The Federal Housing Authority had found new homes for the Inwood residents who'd been forced to leave, and now the apartment buildings north of Dyckman Street were being used as offices for the newly created Department of Interspecies Cooperation.

Sarah had a similar ID, which bounced against her shirt as she walked. Her office was on Sherman Avenue, just a block from the First People's temporary complex. Her job title was chief scientific liaison, but in essence she was running a complaints department. The complaints came from Naomi and the three children she'd already spawned in her complex's tanks, and all their grievances boiled down to the same thing: the humans weren't working fast enough. Although the First People had already extended their tendrils to the Pacific Ocean and were eager to start building their habitat, the United Nations was just beginning the process of choosing a site.

Sarah took another deep breath. The fundamental problem, as she saw it, was that the First People never fought with one another. Because they were so naturally cooperative, they couldn't understand why the humans had to argue over everything. Naomi was particularly impatient, and her firstborn child, Ruth, was almost as bad. But her next two children, Leah and Judith, seemed a little more tolerant, and Sarah was starting to enjoy her conversations with them. If the following generations of First People were more like those two, there was some hope for the future.

The intolerance from her own species was worse, of course, but luckily she didn't have to deal with it. That was Tom Gilbert's job, and Sarah was frankly amazed at how much he'd accomplished so far. He was the one who'd convinced the president not to fire a nuke at New York City. Nearly every general in the Pentagon had pushed for a nuclear strike, but Tom presented reams of evidence proving how futile that would be. In his uniquely annoying but effective way, he managed to persuade the White House to accept its losses and reach a compromise with the First People. And Naomi smoothed the negotiations by making several conciliatory gestures, such as rebuilding the tunnels and bridges around Manhattan. Her tendrils also constructed dozens of geothermal power plants under New York, enough to provide pollution-free electricity to all the city's households.

After passing the soccer fields, Sarah followed the path that ran along the base of the hill. To her right was the steep wooded slope where the probe had landed three months ago. Nothing important was at the landing site anymore—the Emissary had moved all its vital machinery to more secure locations—but Sarah stared in that direction anyway. Then she looked straight ahead and kept walking until she came to the last bench on the left, the one closest to the park's Dyckman Street exit. That was where she'd arranged to meet Joe.

He was sitting there as promised, dressed in jeans and a polo shirt. An army-green duffel bag sat on the bench beside him.

Sarah didn't sit down. She pointed at the bag. "So you made up your mind? You're leaving?"

Joe nodded. "Yeah, I got my papers. I'm free to go."

"What about your hip? It doesn't need any more therapy?"

He slapped his right hip, the one the tentacles had dislocated. "That's all done. I can walk just fine."

Sarah paused. She didn't like to repeat herself, but she couldn't help it. "And you're sure you don't want to reconsider my offer? I could really use your help, Joe."

She thought he might get annoyed, but instead he smiled at her. "You got better people to work with. Experts and scientists, people with real experience."

"But you know the First People better than anyone else. You looked into their minds. That's the kind of experience I need right now."

He shook his head but kept smiling. "We did twenty debriefing sessions, remember? I told you everything I knew, right down to the last detail. It's all in the files."

"That's not the same. I can't get advice from a bunch of files." Sarah stepped toward the bench, moved the duffel bag aside, and sat down next to him. She was determined to make one last try. "Look, I'm already working with Emilio and the other boys. They're not experts either, but they're helping me a lot. They're giving me insights about the First People so I can communicate with them more effectively. And you could be an even bigger help."

Now Joe stopped smiling. For a second his eyes darted to the right, glancing at the hillside where he used to sleep. "I'm sorry, but I have to go. I have to work some things out, and I can't do it here."

She frowned. Although Joe had stayed sober for the past three months, she knew how fragile he was. She wouldn't be surprised if he started drinking again as soon as he left. "I don't get it. You were living on the streets for two years, trying to work things out. And now you want to go back to that life?"

He shook his head again. "No, I wasn't doing the work. I was just try-ing like hell to forget."

"And how will it be any different now?" Her voice was getting loud. She was seriously angry. "How do you know you won't take the easy way out again?"

She'd gone too far. She shouldn't have said that. But Joe didn't look insulted. He just shrugged. "You're right. I may not be strong enough." He got up from the bench and reached for his duffel bag. "But I'm gonna try. I'm thinking of going back to my hometown in Alabama. I hate the place, but I feel like I need to go there. You know, go back to the begin-ning and see what went wrong."

Sarah stood up too. She knew she was being ridiculous, but she grasped his hand before he could pick up the bag.

"Please," she whispered. "I want you to stay."

He smiled again and gave her hand a squeeze. But it was a sad, apol-ogetic smile, and a moment later he pulled his hand out of hers. "I have to do this, Sarah. I don't believe in God, but I do believe in penance."

He picked up his bag and turned toward Dyckman Street. And then Joe Graham, the man who helped her save the world, walked out of the park.

AUTHOR'S NOTE

I got the idea for this novel back in 1999 when I edited a special issue of *Scientific American* that focused on space exploration. One of the articles in that issue was entitled, "Interstellar Spaceflight: Can We Travel to Other Stars?" Written by science journalist Timothy Ferris, the article argued that traversing the vast distances between stars was so inherently difficult that any spacefaring civilization would be unlikely to send large starships across the galaxy. It would make more sense to launch small automated probes instead, because they would require so much less fuel to complete their interstellar journeys.

The article inspired me: I could easily imagine a small probe from a distant star system landing in someone's backyard. Better yet, I could imagine it following a set of preprogrammed tasks, using the raw materials at its landing site to establish a foothold on our world. This kind of probe could swiftly build all the machines it would need for exploring the planet—or colonizing it.

As I wrote the novel I tried to weave some real space science into the story. A group of Cornell astronomers (including Frank Drake and Carl

Sagan) really did send a message across the Milky Way in 1974 using the Arecibo radio dish. And the novel's description of Martian micro-fossils is based on the investigation of ALH84001, the meteorite that became famous in 1996 as scientists debated whether it held fossils of Martian microbes. My opinion on this subject is similar to Sarah Pool-ey's: as we continue to explore planets in our star system and others, we're bound to discover evidence of extraterrestrial life.

But what are the odds of finding *intelligent* life out there? On Earth, it took billions of years for microbes to evolve into complex multicellular organisms, and only in the past century has one species become capa-ble of building powerful rockets and radio transmitters. We simply don't know how evolution would progress on other planets, or how long an extraterrestrial civilization would be likely to survive. Still, some scien-tists are worried about intelligent aliens; in February 2015 a group of prominent space experts warned against trying to find extraterrestrials by transmitting more signals similar to the Arecibo message. As the group's statement noted, "It is impossible to predict whether extrater-restrial intelligence will be benign or hostile."